GREAT ILLUSTRATED CLASSICS

Joseph Conrad in 1923, the year before his death. Photograph by Craig Annam.

TYPHOON
AND OTHER TALES
OF THE SEA

BY JOSEPH CONRAD

*With photographs of the author and his
environment as well as illustrations
from early editions, together
with an introduction by
Edouard A. Stackpole*

NEW YORK · DODD, MEAD & COMPANY

TYPHOON AND OTHER TALES OF THE SEA
Introduction Copyright © 1963 by Dodd, Mead & Company, Inc.

LIBRARY OF CONGRESS CATALOG CARD NUMBER: 63-9543
PRINTED IN THE UNITED STATES OF AMERICA

Introduction

IT HAS been often noted that seamen are for the most part men of action who are not given to writing of their experiences or their thoughts. Joseph Conrad was an exception. He was not only an experienced mariner but was able to express himself by the written word in a manner which made literary history. What is more unusual is that he was a Polish native who wrote in English—a language which he adopted as a medium for his stories of the sea.

Born in Southern Poland in 1857, the boy who was to become Joseph Conrad was christened Teodor Josef Konrad Korzeniowski. His father, a man of literary accomplishments and of aristocratic descent, was an outstanding Polish patriot; his mother a gentle woman of deep sensitivity. As a boy, Conrad lived in the shadow of revolutionary activities against Russian domination. He even shared his parents' exile when his father was forced to leave his beloved Poland for organizing patriotic resistance groups. The death of his mother at this period had a marked effect on the sensitive boy. As an escape from reality he became a prodigious reader in his father's fine library. He read everything from Shakespeare to Marryat, enjoying especially the sea tales of James Fenimore Cooper and Victor Hugo. The death of his father a few years after that of his mother placed him under the guardianship of his uncle, to whom he soon grew devoted, particularly so since the uncle engaged the services of a young University of Cracow student as a tutor for him.

When he was fifteen, Conrad expressed a desire to go to sea. Finding he was not being taken seriously, he ran away to the port of Trieste, on the Adriatic. The pleas of his pursuing tutor brought him back to Cracow and a reunion with his understanding uncle. Although Conrad passed his examinations with marked credit, his desire for the sea was still apparent. In 1874, at the age of sixteen, he was allowed to journey to Marseilles in France, where he first met the sea and sailors. Here the friendship of the Provençal fishermen and pilots was a vital factor in his introduction to this new maritime world. A year later he was outward bound on his first ocean voyage, sailing for the West Indies as a fo'c's'le hand aboard the ship *Mont Blanc*. A second voyage to Martinique was made on the *Saint Antoine*. With this taste of the sea as a background he indulged in a romantic adventure with three friends, purchasing a small two-masted coastal craft called the *Tremolino* and smuggling arms to revolutionists in Spain.

Soon after this adventure, Conrad shipped aboard the English ship *Mavis* on a voyage to the Azov Sea for a load of grain. This was to be a voyage of destiny as it brought Conrad to England, where he was to find a new language and a new home. Upon his arrival at Lowestoft (on the east coast), he found employment for several months on various colliers. Applying himself with characteristic energy, he took up a study of English. A local boat builder was his tutor and his text mainly newspapers. The new language interested him, and he learned rapidly. Desiring to continue his sea career, he made his way to London, where he shipped out before the mast on the ship *Duke of Sutherland*, bound for Australia. Upon his return, Conrad passed his examination as a second mate and signed on in this capacity on the wool clipper *Loch-Etire* for Sydney. Next came a voyage on the *Palestine*, which was carrying coal from England to Bangkok—a memorable voyage as the ship foundered in the Malacca Straits and the crew had to make their way to Singapore in open boats.

Over the next decade, Conrad was constantly at sea, serving on both sailing craft and steamers, advancing to first mate. In 1886, he assumed his first command: the square-rigged barque *Otago*, voyaging between Australia and the Malay Archipelago. It was during this time that Captain Conrad made a passage through the Torres Straits, deriving much satisfaction from following in the wake of the old navigators who had been pioneers in those seas.

When Joseph Conrad left the sea for a vacation in England in 1889, he took up lodgings in London, where he began work on a story titled *Almayer's Folly*. A trip to Poland to visit his uncle (for the first time since leaving home) was succeeded by experiences on the Congo as a river steamer skipper. From this venture he was invalided home because of tropical fever. He went to Switzerland to recover his strength at a Geneva hospital and here he completed the eighth chapter of his story.

Almayer's Folly was not actually completed until after Conrad made a voyage on the ship *Torrens,* and another visit to the Ukraine. The story was at last submitted to a London publisher, and in 1895, it made its appearance at six shillings a copy. Despite its lack of success commercially critics recognized in it a superior writer, and Conrad was encouraged to continue his literary career.

Once he had found himself immersed in this art of letters, he forsook the more vigorous and active life of the mariner for that of a writer. *The Outcast of the Islands* and *The Lagoon,* founded on his experiences in the Malay seas, were next to appear in print. In 1896, Conrad married an Englishwoman, Miss Jessie George. After a honeymoon in Brittany, the couple returned to England to live in Essex and then in Kent. England now became Conrad's home.

The mariner who had thus come ashore to launch a new career worked at his craft with a zeal and devotedness which was to mark his whole life. In his creative spirit he labored and drove on toward his goal, much as a strong ship, ably handled, worked her way around Cape Horn during a stormy winter passage. Using his dearly won new language, applying himself in his adopted England, Conrad produced a series of novels, ranging from *The End of the Tether* and *Typhoon* to *Nostromo* and *The Rescue.* While on a visit to Poland in 1914, he was nearly trapped there by the outbreak of World War I. Returning to England, he threw himself into the war effort in England's behalf, and saw his eldest son join the British army.

Conrad visited the United States in 1923. He was welcomed by the literary world as no other writer in English since Dickens. His was a quiet visit, with no tours or banquets or testimonials, although he was besieged by requests. But he did visit New England and several of her seaports. Returning to his beloved England, he wrote one more novel, *The Rover*, and was engaged upon another when in 1924 death came suddenly to him in his sixty-seventh year.

As one of the greatest of sea-writers, Conrad has a special niche of his own making. The sea had called him from his native land, to take him through a series of adventures which were to become vital parts of his stories and essays. It was with the very mystery of life that Conrad was concerned, and he recognized fully that at sea one can become more sharply aware than elsewhere of the elemental forces of nature and of the immortality of man. In Conrad's careful prose, the beauty and mystery of maritime life are portrayed. His sympathy and understanding are revealed not through sentimentality but through romantic realism. We get the flavor of life but also some of the grim character of the rawness of human endeavor.

Within the stories contained in this volume we may read Conrad at his best. In *Youth* we have him expressing the exuberance of his young manhood in a narrative based on his own experience as second officer aboard the ship *Palestine* in 1881. The old ship was in sad condition; she leaked, and her cargo of coal was to prove her doom. But, as Conrad describes the voyage, the reader feels the spirit of adventure, the thirst for new horizons which youth must always bring. And the story does not disappoint—it carries the reader through the adventures of the young men who are making their first voyage to the mysterious Far East.

Thus, in each of his novels, Conrad was able to present different characters against the background of his own maritime experience. In *Typhoon* he tells of an obstinate Captain Mac-

Whirr. This was undoubtedly the skipper under whom he served while mate of the thousand-ton sailing craft *Highland Forest*. However, due to an accident, Conrad had to leave the ship and go to a hospital at Singapore. Later, as a matter of necessity, with officers' berths at a premium, he signed on as first mate of the steamer *Vidar* (his second experience in steam) and entered upon a period which was to be most important in his life as a writer. The *Vidar*, under the Dutch flag, was a trader, visiting ports among the islands of the Malay seas and along the coast of Borneo. In *Typhoon* we find reflected some of that telling experience, especially the memorable scene in the engine-room of the *Nan-Shan* when the engineers and stokers were trying to keep the fires under her boilers going. The vivid picture, the dramatic vitality of the telling are Conrad at his best. ". . . the glow under each fire-door was like a pool of flaming blood, radiating quietly in the velvety darkness." The old steamer becomes a test for the unquenchable spirit of youth, "an endeavor, a trial of life," as he termed it.

The Nigger of the "Narcissus" is considered by many as Conrad's masterpiece. Unquestionably it stands as one of the finest stories of men and the sea ever written, both from the authenticity of its background and the motives of the men involved. Here again Conrad dipped deeply into his vast store of personal experience. Late in the year 1883, he found himself ashore at Madras, India, having left the ship on which he was second officer following a disagreement with the captain. Making his way to Bombay he was not able to decide as to shipping out again when, one evening, he saw the beautiful sailing ship *Narcissus* coming into the harbor. Two days later he signed on as second mate and made the voyage to Dunkirk. In *The Nigger of the "Narcissus,"* with this voyage as a background, Conrad's imagination soared to new heights. There is a sense of poetry to his prose, but most important of all, there is retained that fine quality of realism which places the story in a class by itself. Never has a narrative of man's relentless struggle with environment

and circumstances, spiritually and physically, been better portrayed.

In the fourth selection, *Heart of Darkness,* Conrad gives us
another kind of tale, and again his rich imagination draws upon
his unique practical experiences. In 1890, he followed a latent
urge to go to Africa by accepting a post as mate on a Belgian
steamer S.S. *Roi des Belges* plying the Congo River. There is
little doubt that Marlow, the narrator in *Heart of Darkness,* is
actually Conrad and is close to being autobiographical. Because
of the illness of the regular captain, Conrad assumed command
of the nondescript river craft. Here he met the jungle river he
described so completely in the story, and found himself immersed in the mysterious tropical world of the Congo— ". . . this
stillness of life did not in the least resemble a peace. It was the
stillness of an implacable force brooding over an implacable
intention. It looked at you with a vengeful aspect." The hero
of the tale is not a happy hero, but he has the undeniable character of true life. Conrad is concerned with remorse in this story,
a powerful emotional motivation which he wove throughout
the magic of his famous *Lord Jim.*

It is probable that the illness which overcame Conrad during
his Congo adventure, while bringing on a depression of spirit
as well as of health, gave Conrad time to develop his first work,
Almayer's Folly, the manuscript of which he had not touched
for a year. Offered a berth as chief mate on the handsome
square-rigged ship *Torrens,* Conrad sailed from Plymouth to
Adelaide, Australia, where he arrived in February, 1892. The
homeward passage was uneventful, with stops at Cape Town
and St. Helena. His last sea experience was on this same ship,
and it was during the voyage to Australia that he allowed a
passenger—a young university student named Jacques—to read
his unfinished manuscript of *Almayer's Folly.* It was the first
time he had ever allowed anyone to read his literary efforts. On
the homeward passage, two other passengers became friendly
with the *Torrens'* first mate and enjoyed his company. One of
them was John Galsworthy, later to become the famous Eng-

lish novelist. Although Conrad struck up a strong friendship with this young man, he did not show him his manuscript.

Fate now took a hand. Conrad abandoned the sea as a profession, and with the death of his beloved uncle, his long-held illusion of returning to Poland and his original home was abandoned. With a burst of energy he finished *Almayer's Folly*. The rest is literary history.

It is in his preface to *The Nigger of the "Narcissus"* that Conrad presents his creed as a writer. He carefully states that there must be an appeal to "the sense of mystery surrounding our lives . . . to the latent feeling of fellowship with all creation . . . that knits together the loneliness of innumerable hearts . . . by the power of the written word to make you hear, to make you feel . . . to make you see."

This is the accomplishment of Joseph Conrad. In the English language he chose as his medium this native of Poland wrote prose masterpieces which belong to world literature. His contemplative style enabled him to present narratives that appeal to the mind as well as to the spirit and reward the reader who wants to learn of the soul of the men of the sea as well as of their outward actions.

EDOUARD A. STACKPOLE

A SELECTED LIST OF WORKS BY JOSEPH CONRAD
AND THEIR DATES

Almayer's Folly—1895
An Outcast of the Islands—1896
The Nigger of the Narcissus—1897
Lord Jim—1900
Youth (short stories)—1902
Typhoon (short stories)—1903
Nostromo—1904
The Mirror of the Sea (reminiscences)—1906
The Secret Agent—1907 (dramatized 1922)
Under Western Eyes—1911
Chance—1913
Victory—1915 (dramatized 1919)
The Shadow-Line—1917
The Arrow of Gold—1919
The Rescue—1920
The Rover—1922
Tales of Hearsay (short stories)—1925

Contents

Illustrations

I

CAPTAIN MacWHIRR of the steamer *Nan-Shan* had a physi-
ognomy that, in the order of material appearances, was the exact
counterpart of his mind; it presented no marked characteristics
of firmness or stupidity; it had no pronounced characteristics
whatever: it was simply ordinary, irresponsive, and unruffled.

The only thing his aspect might have been said to suggest, at
times, was bashfulness; because he would sit, in business offices
ashore, sunburnt and smiling faintly, with downcast eyes. When
he raised them they were perceived to be direct in their glance
and of blue colour. His hair was fair and extremely fine,
clasping from temple to temple the bald dome of his skull in a
clamp as of fluffy silk. The hair of his face, on the contrary, car-
roty and flaming, resembled a growth of copper wire clipped
short to the line of the lip; while, no matter how close he shaved,
fiery metallic gleams passed, when he moved his head, over the
surface of his cheeks. He was rather below the medium height,
a bit round-shouldered, and so sturdy of limb that his clothes
always looked a shade too tight for his arms and legs. As if unable to grasp what is due to the difference of latitudes, he wore
a brown bowler hat, a complete suit of a brownish hue, and
clumsy black boots. These harbour togs gave to his thick figure
an air of stiff and uncouth smartness. A thin silver watch-chain
looped his waistcoat, and he never left his ship for the shore
without clutching in his powerful hairy fist an elegant umbrella
of the very best quality, but generally unrolled. Young Jukes,
the chief mate, attending his commander to the gangway, would
sometimes venture to say with the greatest gentleness: "Allow
me, sir"—and, possessing himself of the umbrella deferentially,

3

would elevate the ferrule, shake the folds, twirl a neat furl in a jiffy, and hand it back; going through the performance with a face of such portentous gravity that Mr. Solomon Rout, the chief-engineer, smoking his morning cigar over the skylight, would turn away his head in order to hide a smile. "Oh! Aye! The blessed gamp. . . . Thank 'ee, Jukes, thank 'ee," would mutter Captain MacWhirr heartily, without looking up.

Having just enough imagination to carry him through each successive day, and no more, he was tranquilly sure of himself, and from the very same cause he was not in the least conceited. It is your imaginative superior who is touchy, overbearing, and difficult to please; but every ship Captain MacWhirr commanded was the floating abode of harmony and peace. It was, in truth, as impossible for him to take a flight of fancy as it would be for a watch-maker to put together a chronometer with nothing except a two-pound hammer and a whip-saw in the way of tools. Yet the uninteresting lives of men so entirely given to the actuality of the bare existence have their mysterious side. It was impossible in Captain MacWhirr's case, for instance, to understand what under heaven could have induced that perfectly satisfactory son of a petty grocer in Belfast to run away to sea. And yet he had done that very thing at the age of fifteen. It was enough, when you thought it over, to give you the idea of an immense, potent, and invisible hand thrust into the ant-heap of the earth, laying hold of shoulders, knocking heads together, and setting the unconscious faces of the multitude towards inconceivable goals and in undreamt-of directions.

His father never really forgave him for this undutiful stupidity. "We could have got on without him," he used to say, later on; "but there's the business. And he an only son, too!" His mother wept very much after his disappearance. As it had never occurred to him to leave word behind, he was mourned over for dead till, after eight months, his first letter arrived from Taleahuano. It was short and contained the statement, "We had very fine weather on our passage out." But evidently, in the writer's mind, the only important intelligence was to the effect that his Captain had, on the very day of writing, entered him regularly on the ship's articles as Ordinary Seaman. "Because I can do the work," he explained. The mother again wept copiously, while the remark, "Tom's an ass," expressed the emotions of the father. He was a corpulent man, with a gift for sly chaffing, which to the end of his life he exercised in his intercourse with his son, a little pityingly, as if upon a half-witted person.

MacWhirr's visits to his home were necessarily rare, and in the course of years he despatched other letters to his parents, informing them of his successive promotions and of his movements upon the vast earth. In these missives could be found sentences like this: "The heat here is very great"; or, "On Xmas day at 4 P.M. we fell in with some icebergs." The old people became ultimately acquainted with a good many names of ships and with the names of the skippers who commanded them, with the names of Scotch and English shipowners, with the names of seas, oceans, straits, promontories; with outlandish names of lumber-ports, of rice-ports, of cotton-ports; with the names of islands; with the name of their son's young woman. She was called Lucy. It did not suggest itself to him to mention whether he thought the name pretty. And then they died.

The great day of MacWhirr's marriage came in due course, following shortly upon the great day when he got his first command. All these events had taken place many years before the morning when, in the chart-room of the steamer *Nan-Shan,* he stood confronted by the fall of a barometer he had no reason to distrust. The fall—taking into account the excellence of the instrument, the time of the year, and the ship's position on the terrestrial globe—was of a nature ominously prophetic, but the red face of the man betrayed no sort of inward disturbance. Omens were as nothing to him, and he was unable to discover the message of a prophecy till the fulfilment had brought it home to his very door. "That's a fall and no mistake," he thought. "There must be some uncommonly dirty weather knocking about."

II

THE *Nan-Shan* was on her way from the southward to the treaty
port of Fu-chau with some cargo in her lower holds and two
hundred Chinese coolies returning to their village homes in the
province of Fo-Kien, after a few years of work in various tropical
colonies. The morning was fine, the oily sea heaved without a
sparkle, and there was a queer white, misty patch in the sky
like a halo of the sun. The fore-deck, packed with Chinamen,
was full of sombre clothing, yellow faces, and pigtails, and
sprinkled over with a good many naked shoulders, for there was
no wind, and the heat was close. The coolies lounged, talked,
smoked, or stared over the rail; some, drawing water over the
side, sluiced each other; a few slept on hatches, while several
small parties of six sat on their heels, surrounding iron trays with
plates of rice and tiny teacups; and every single Celestial of them
was carrying with him all he had in the world—a wooden chest
with a ringing lock and brass on the corners, containing the
savings of his labour: some clothes of ceremony, sticks of incense,
a little opium maybe, bits of nameless rubbish of conventional
value, and a small hoard of silver dollars, toiled for in coal-
lighters, won in gambling-houses or in petty trading, grubbed
out of earth, sweated out in mines, on railway lines, in deadly
jungle, under heavy burdens—amassed patiently, guarded with
care, cherished fiercely.

A cross swell had set in from the direction of Formosa channel
about ten o'clock without disturbing these passengers much, because the *Nan-Shan*, with her flat bottom, rolling chocks on
bilges, and great breadth of beam, had a reputation of an exceptionally steady ship in a seaway. Mr. Jukes, in moments of ex-
pansion on shore, would proclaim loudly that the "old girl was
as good as she was pretty." It would never have occurred to Captain MacWhirr to express his favourable opinion so loud or in
terms so fanciful.

She was a good ship, undoubtedly, and not old, either. She had been built in Dumbarton less than three years before to the order of a firm of merchants in Siam—Messrs. Sigg & Son. When she lay afloat, finished in every detail and ready to take up the work of her life, the builders contemplated her with pride. "Sigg has asked us for a reliable skipper to take her out," remarked one of the partners; and the other, after reflecting for a while, said: "I think MacWhirr is ashore just at present."

"Is he? Then wire him at once. He's the very man," declared the senior, without a moment's hesitation.

Next morning, MacWhirr stood before them unperturbed, having travelled from London by the midnight express, after a sudden but undemonstrative parting with his wife. She was the daughter of a superior couple who had seen better days.

"We had better be going together over the ship, Captain," said the senior partner; and the three men started to explore the perfections of the *Nan-Shan* from stem to stern and from keelson to the trucks of her two stumpy pole-masts. Captain Mac-Whirr had begun by taking off his coat, which he hung on the end of a steam-windlass embodying all the latest improvements.

"My uncle wrote of you favourably by yesterday's mail to our good friends, Messrs. Sigg, you know; and doubtless they'll continue you out there in command," said the junior. "You'll be able to boast of being in charge of the handiest boat of her size on the coast of China, Captain," he added.

"Have you? Thank 'ee," mumbled vaguely MacWhirr, to whom the view of a distant eventuality could appeal no more than the beauty of a wide landscape to a purblind tourist; and his eyes happening at the moment to be at rest upon the lock of the cabin door, he walked up to it, full of purpose, and began to rattle the handle vigorously, while he observed in his low earnest voice: "You can't trust the workmen nowadays. A brand new lock, and it won't act at all. Stuck fast. See? See?"

As soon as they found themselves alone in their office across the yard: "You praised that fellow up to Sigg. What is it you see in him?" asked the nephew, with faint contempt.

"I admit he has nothing of your fancy skipper about him, if that's what you mean," said the elder man, curtly. "Is the foreman of the joiners on the *Nan-Shan* outside?—Come in, Bates. How is it that you let Tait's people put us off with a defective lock on the cabin door? The Captain could see directly he set eye on it. Have it replaced at once. The little straws, Bates; the little straws." The lock was replaced accordingly, and a few days afterwards the *Nan-Shan* steamed out to the East without MacWhirr having offered any further remark as to her fittings, or having been heard to utter a single word hinting at pride in his ship, gratitude for his appointment, or satisfaction at his prospects.

With a temperament neither loquacious nor taciturn, he found very little occasion to talk. There were matters of duty, of course,—directions, orders, and so on, but the past being to his mind done with, and the future not there yet, the more general actualities of the day required no comment, because facts can speak for themselves with overwhelming precision.

Old Mr. Sigg liked a man of few words, and one that "you could be sure would not try to improve upon his instructions." MacWhirr, satisfying these requirements, was continued in command of the *Nan-Shan,* and applied himself to the careful navigation of his ship in the China seas. She had come out on a British register, but, after some time, Messrs. Sigg judged it expedient to transfer her to the Siamese flag.

At the news of the contemplated transfer, Jukes grew restless, as if under a sense of personal affront. He went about grumbling to himself and uttering short, scornful laughs. "Fancy having a ridiculous Noah's-ark elephant in the ensign of one's ship," he said once at the engine-room door. "Dash me if I can stand it. I'll throw up the billet. Don't it make *you* sick, Mr. Rout?" The chief-engineer only cleared his throat with the air of a man who knows the value of a good billet.

The first morning the new flag floated over the stern of the *Nan-Shan,* Jukes stood looking at it bitterly from the bridge. He struggled with his feelings for a while, and then remarked: "Queer flag for a man to sail under, sir."

"What's the matter with the flag?" inquired Captain Mac-Whirr. "Seems all right to me." And he walked across to the end of the bridge to have a good look.

"Well, it is queer to me," burst out Jukes, greatly exasperated, and flung off the bridge.

Captain MacWhirr was amazed at these manners. After a while he stepped quietly into the chart-room and opened his *International Signal Code-Book* at the place where the flags of all the nations are correctly figured in gaudy rows. He ran his fingers over them, and when he came to Siam he contemplated with great attention the red field and the white elephant. Nothing could be more simple; but to make sure he brought the book out on the bridge for the purpose of comparing the coloured drawing with the real thing at the flagstaff astern. When next Jukes, who was carrying on the duty that day with a sort of suppressed fierceness, happened on the bridge his commander observed:

"There's nothing amiss with that flag."

"Isn't there?" mumbled Jukes, falling on his knees before a deck-locker and jerking therefrom viciously a spare lead-line.

"No. I looked up the book. Length twice the breadth and the elephant exactly in the middle. I thought the people ashore would know how to make the local flag. Stands to reason. You were wrong, Jukes."

"Well, sir," began Jukes, getting up excitedly, "all I can say—" He fumbled for the end of the coil of line with trembling hands.

"That's all right." Captain MacWhirr soothed him, sitting heavily on a little canvas folding stool he greatly affected. "All you have to do is to take care they don't hoist the elephant up-side down before they get quite used to it."

Jukes flung the new lead-line over on the fore-deck with a loud "Here you are, bo's'n. Don't forget to wet it thoroughly," and turned with immense resolution towards his commander, but Captain MacWhirr spread his elbows on the bridge-rail comfortably.

"Because it would be, I suppose, understood as a signal of

distress," he went on. "What do you think? That elephant there, I take it, stands for something in the nature of the Union-Jack in the flag."

"Does it?" yelled Jukes so that every head on the *Nan-Shan's* decks looked towards the bridge. Then he sighed, and with sudden resignation, "It would certainly be a damn distressful sight," he said meekly.

Later in the day he accosted the chief engineer with a confidential "Here! Let me tell you the old man's latest."

Mr. Solomon Rout (frequently alluded to as Long Sol, Old Sol, or Father Rout), from finding himself almost invariably the tallest man on board every ship he joined, had acquired the habit of a stooping, leisurely condescension. His hair was scant and sandy, his flat cheeks were pale, his bony wrists and long scholarly hands were pale, too, as though he had lived all his life in the shade.

He smiled from on high at Jukes and went on smoking and glancing about quietly, in the manner of a kind uncle lending an ear to the tale of an excited schoolboy. Then, greatly amused but impassive, he asked:

"And did you throw up the billet?"

"No," cried Jukes, in a weary, discouraged voice, above the harsh buzz of the *Nan-Shan's* friction winches. All of them were hard at work, snatching slings of cargo, high up, to the end of long derricks, only, as it seemed, to let them rip down recklessly by the run. The cargo chains groaned in the gins, clinked on coamings, rattled over the side; and the whole ship quivered, with her long grey flanks smoking in wreaths of steam. "No," cried Jukes; "I didn't. What's the good? I might just as well fling my resignation at this bulkhead. I don't believe you can make a man like that understand anything. He simply knocks me over."

At that moment, Captain MacWhirr, back from the shore, crossed the deck, umbrella in hand, escorted by a mournful, self-possessed Chinaman, walking behind in paper-soled silk shoes, who also carried an umbrella.

The master of the *Nan-Shan,* speaking just audibly and gazing at his boots as his manner was, remarked that it would be necessary to call at Fu-chau this trip, and desired Mr. Rout to have steam up tomorrow afternoon at one o'clock, sharp. He pushed back his hat to wipe his forehead, observing at the same time that he hated going ashore, anyhow; while overtopping him, Mr. Rout, without deigning a word, smoked austerely, nursing his right elbow in the palm of his left hand. Then Jukes was directed in the same subdued voice to keep the forward 'tween-deck clear of cargo. Two hundred coolies were going to be put down there. The Bun Hin Company were sending that lot home. Twenty-five bags of rice would be coming off in a sampan directly for stores. All seven-years' men they were, said Captain MacWhirr, with a chest to every man. The carpenter should be set to work nailing three-inch battens along the deck below, fore and aft, to keep these boxes from shifting in a seaway. Jukes had better look to it at once. "D' ye hear, Jukes?" This Chinaman here was coming with the ship as far as Fu-chau—a sort of interpreter he would be. Bun Hin's clerk he was, and wanted to have a look at the space. Jukes had better take him forward. "D' ye hear, Jukes?"

Jukes took good care to punctuate these instructions in proper places with the obligatory "Yes, sir," ejaculated without enthusiasm. His brusque "Come along, John. Make look see," set the Chinaman in motion at his heels.

"Wanchee look see, all same look see can do," said Jukes, who, having no talent for foreign languages, mangled the very pigeon English cruelly. He pointed at the open hatch. "Catchee number one piecie place to sleep in. Eh?"

He was gruff, as became his racial superiority, but not unfriendly. The Chinaman, gazing sad and speechless into the darkness of the hatchway, seemed to stand at the head of a yawning grave.

"No catchee rain down there—savee?" pointed out Jukes. "Suppose allee same fine weather, one piecie coolie-man come topside," he pursued, warming up imaginatively. "Make so— phooooo!" He expanded his chest and blew out his cheeks.

"Savee, John? Breathe—fresh air. Good. Eh? Washee him piecie pants, chow-chow topside see, John?"

With his mouth and hands he made exuberant motions of eating rice and washing clothes, and the Chinaman, who concealed his distrust of this pantomime under a collected demeanour, tinged by a gentle and refined melancholy, glanced out of his almond eyes from Jukes to the hatch and back again. "Velly good," he murmured, in a disconsolate undertone, and, hastening smoothly along the decks, dodging obstacles in his course, he disappeared, ducking low under a sling of ten dirty gunnybags full of some costly merchandise and exhaling a repulsive smell.

III

CAPTAIN MacWHIRR meantime had gone on the bridge and into the chart-room, where a letter, commenced two days before, awaited termination. These long letters began with the words, "My darling wife," and the steward, between the scrubbing of the floors and the dusting of chronometer-boxes, snatched at every opportunity to read them. They interested him much more than they possibly could the woman for whose eye they were intended; and for this reason, that they related in minute detail each successive trip of the *Nan-Shan*.

Her master, faithful to facts, which alone his consciousness reflected, would set them down with painstaking care upon many pages. The house, in a Northern suburb, to which these pages were addressed, had a bit of garden before the bow-windows, a deep porch of good appearance, coloured glass with imitation lead frame in the front door. He paid five-and-forty pounds a year for it, and did not think the rent too high, because Mrs. MacWhirr, a pretentious person with a scraggy neck and a disdainful manner, was admittedly ladylike, and in the neighbourhood considered as "quite superior." The only secret of her life was her abject terror of the time when her husband would come home to stay for good. Under the same roof there dwelt also a daughter called Lydia, and a son, Tom. These two were but slightly acquainted with their father. Mainly, they knew him as a rare but privileged visitor, who of an evening smoked his pipe in the dining-room and slept in the house. The lanky girl, upon the whole, was rather ashamed of him; the boy was frankly and utterly indifferent, in a straightforward, delightful, unaffected way manly boys have.

And Captain MacWhirr wrote home from the coast of China twelve times every year, desiring queerly to be "remembered to the children," and subscribing himself "Your loving husband" as calmly as if the words so long used by so many men were, apart from their shape, worn out things of a faded meaning.

The China seas, North and South, are narrow seas. They are seas full of every-day, eloquent facts, such as islands, sand-banks, reefs, swift and changeable currents—tangled facts that nevertheless speak to a seaman in clear and definite language. Their speech appealed to Captain MacWhirr's sense of realities so forcibly that he had given up his stateroom below and practically lived all his days on the bridge of his ship, often having his meals sent up, and sleeping at night in the chart-room. And he indited there his home letters. Each of them without exception, contained the phrase, "The weather has been very fine this trip," or some other form of a statement to that effect. And this statement, too, in its wonderful persistence, was of the same perfect accuracy as all the others they contained.

Mr. Rout likewise wrote letters, only no one on board knew how chatty he could be, pen in hand, because the chief-engineer had enough imagination to keep his desk locked. His wife relished his style greatly. They were a childless couple, and Mrs. Rout—a big, high-bosomed, jolly woman of forty—shared with Mr. Rout's toothless and venerable mother a little cottage near Teddington. She would run over her correspondence at breakfast with lively eyes, and scream out interesting passages in a joyous voice at the deaf old lady, prefacing each extract by the warning shout, "Solomon says!" She had the trick of firing off

Solomon's utterances also upon strangers, astonishing them easily by the unfamiliar text and the unexpectedly jocular vein of these quotations. On the day the new curate called for the first time at the cottage, she found occasion to remark, "As Solomon says, the engineers that go down to the sea in ships behold the wonders of sailor nature"; when a change in the visitor's countenance made her stop and stare.

"Solomon! Oh!—Mrs. Rout!" stuttered the young man, startled, shocked, and red in the face. "I must say—I don't——"

"He's my husband," she announced in a great shout, throwing herself back in the chair. Perceiving the joke, she laughed immoderately with a handkerchief to her eyes, while he sat wearing a forced smile and, from his inexperience of jolly women, was persuaded that she must be deplorably insane. They were excellent friends afterwards; for, absolving her from irreverent intention, he came to think she was a very worthy person indeed; and he learned in time to receive without flinching other scraps of Solomon's wisdom.

"For my part," Solomon was reported by his wife to have said once, "give me the dullest ass for a skipper before a rogue. There is a way to take a fool, but a rogue is smart and slippery." This was an airy generalisation drawn from the particular case of Captain MacWhirr's honesty, which, in itself, had the heavy obviousness of a lump of clay. On the other hand, Mr. Jukes, unable to generalise, unmarried, and unengaged, was in the habit of opening his heart after another fashion to an old chum and former shipmate, actually serving as second officer on board an Atlantic liner.

First of all, he would insist upon the advantages of the Eastern trade, hinting at its superiority to the Western ocean service. He extolled the sky, the seas, the ships, and the easy life of the Far East. The *Nan-Shan*, he affirmed, was second to none as a seaboat. "We have no brass-bound uniforms, but then we are like brothers here," he wrote. "We all mess together and live like fighting cocks. . . . All the chaps of the black-squad are as decent

as they make that kind, and old Sol, the chief, is a dry stick. We
are good friends. As to our old man, you could not find a quieter
skipper. Sometimes you would think he hadn't sense enough to
see anything wrong. And yet it isn't that. Can't be. He has been
in command for a good few years now. He doesn't do anything
actually foolish, and gets his ship along all right without worrying anybody. I believe he hasn't brains enough to enjoy kicking
up a row. I don't take advantage of him. I would scorn it. Outside the routine of duty he doesn't seem to understand more than
half of what you tell him. We get a laugh out of this at times,
but it is dull, too, to be with a man like this—in the long run.
Old Sol says he hasn't much conversation. Conversation! Oh,
Lord! He never talks. The other day I had been yarning under
the bridge with one of the engineers and he must have heard us.
When I came up to take my watch he steps out of the chart-
room and has a good look all round, peeps over at the sidelights,
glances at the compass, squints upwards at the stars. That's his
regular performance. By-and-bye he says: 'Was that you talking
just now in the port alley-way?'—'Yes, sir.'—'With the third engineer?'—'Yes, sir.' He walks off to starboard and sits under the
dodger on a little campstool of his and for half an hour, perhaps,
he makes no sound except that I heard him sneeze once. Then
after a while I hear him getting up over there and he strolls
across to port where I was. 'I can't understand what you can
find to talk about,' says he. 'Two solid hours. I am not blaming
you. I see people ashore at it all day long, and then in the evening they sit down and keep at it over the drinks. Must be saying
the same things over and over again. I can't understand.' Did
you ever hear anything like that? And he was so patient about
it! It made me quite sorry for him. But he is exasperating, too,
sometimes. Of course, one would not do anything to vex him
even if it were worth while. But it isn't. He's so jolly dense that
if you were to put your thumb to your nose and wave your
fingers at him, he would only wonder gravely to himself what
got into you. He told me once quite simply that he found it

very difficult to make out what made people always act so queerly. He's too dense to trouble about and that's the truth."

Thus wrote Mr. Jukes to his chum in the Western ocean trade, out of the fulness of his heart and the liveliness of his fancy.

He had expressed his honest opinion. It was not worth while trying to impress a man like that. If the world had been full of such men life would have probably appeared to Jukes an unentertaining and unprofitable business. He was not alone in his opinion. The sea itself, as if sharing Mr. Jukes's good-natured forbearance, had never put itself out to startle the silent man who seldom looked up and wandered innocently over the waters with the only visible purpose of getting food, raiment, and house-room for three people ashore. Dirty weather he had known, of course. He had been made wet, uncomfortable, tired in the usual way,—felt at the time and presently forgotten. So that upon the whole he had been justified in reporting fine weather at home. But he had never been given a glimpse of immeasurable strength and of immoderate wrath, the wrath that passes exhausted but never appeased—the wrath and fury of the passionate sea. He knew it existed, as we know that crime and abominations exist; he had heard of it as a peaceable citizen in a town hears of battles, famines, and floods, and yet knows nothing of what these things mean, though, indeed, he may have been mixed up in a street row, have gone without his dinner once, or been soaked to the skin in a shower. He sailed over the surface of the oceans as some men go skimming over the years of existence and sink at last into a placid grave, ignorant of life to the last, without ever having been made to see all it contains of perfidy, violence, and terror. There are on sea and land such men, thus fortunate, or thus disdained by destiny or by the sea.

IV

OBSERVING the steady fall of the barometer, Captain Mac-Whirr thought, "There's some dirty weather knocking about." This is precisely what he thought. He had had an experience of moderately dirty weather, the term dirty, as applied to the weather in itself, implying only moderate discomfort to the seaman. Had he been informed by an indisputable authority that the end of the world was to be finally accomplished by a catastrophic disturbance of the atmosphere, he would have assimilated the information under the simple idea of dirty weather, and no other, because he had no experience of cataclysms and belief does not necessarily imply comprehension. The wisdom of his country had pronounced by means of an Act of Parliament that before he could be considered as fit to take charge of a ship he should be able to answer certain simple questions on the subject of circular storms, such as hurricanes, cyclones, typhoons,—and apparently he had answered them, since he was now in command of the *Nan-Shan* in the China seas during the season of typhoons. But if he had answered, he remembered nothing of it. He was, however, conscious of being made uncomfortable by the clammy heat. He came out on the bridge and found no relief to this oppression. The air seemed thick. He gasped like a fish and began to believe himself greatly out of sorts.

The *Nan-Shan* was ploughing a vanishing furrow upon the circle of the sea that had a surface like a piece of grey satin; and under this surface slow undulations passed, unbroken and smooth, swinging the ship bodily up and down at regular intervals. The white patch of mist declined down the sky together with the sun which, pale and without rays, poured a leaden heat in a strangely indecisive light, and the Chinamen were lying prostrate about the decks. Their bloodless, pinched yellow faces were like the faces of bilious invalids. Captain MacWhirr no-

ticed two of them especially, stretched out on their backs below
the bridge. As soon as they had closed their eyes they seemed
dead. Three others, however, were quarrelling barbarously away
forward, and one big fellow, half naked, with herculean shoulders, was hanging limply over a winch; while another, sitting
on the deck, his knees up and his head drooping sideways in a
girlish attitude, was plaiting his tail with infinite languor
depicted in his whole person and in the very movement of his
fingers. The smoke struggled with difficulty out of the funnel,
and instead of streaming away spread out like an infernal sort
of cloud, smelling of sulphur and raining soot on the decks.

"What the devil are you doing there, Mr. Jukes?" asked Captain MacWhirr.

This unusual form of address, though mumbled rather than
spoken, caused the body of Mr. Jukes to start as though it had
been prodded under the fifth rib. He had had a low bench
brought on the bridge, and, sitting on it with a length of rope
curled about his feet and a piece of canvas stretched over his
knees, was pushing a sail-needle vigorously. He looked up, and
his surprise gave to his eyes an expression of innocence and
candour.

"I am only roping some of that new set of bags we made last
trip for whipping up coals," he remonstrated gently. "We shall
want them for the next coaling, sir."

"What became of the others?"

"Why! Worn out, of course, sir."

Captain MacWhirr, after glaring down irresolutely at his
chief mate, disclosed the gloomy and cynical conviction that
more than half of them had been lost overboard, "if only the
truth was known," and retired to the other end of the bridge.
Jukes, exasperated by this unprovoked attack, broke the needle
at the second stitch, and, dropping his work, got up and cursed
the heat in a violent undertone.

The propeller thumped, the three Chinamen forward had
given up squabbling very suddenly, and the one who had been
plaiting his tail clasped his legs and stared dejectedly over his

"All you have to do is to take care they don't hoist the elephant upside-down." Illustration by Maurice Greiffenhagen for an early edition of *Typhoon*. (*p. 9*)

knees. The lurid sunshine cast faint and sickly shadows. The swell ran higher and swifter every moment, and the ship lurched heavily in the smooth, deep hollows of the sea.

"I wonder where that beastly swell comes from," said Jukes aloud, recovering himself after a stagger.

"Northeast," grunted the literal MacWhirr, from his side of the bridge. "There's some dirty weather knocking about. Go and look at the glass."

When Jukes came out of the chart-room the cast of his countenance had changed to thoughtfulness and concern. He caught hold of the bridge-rail and stared ahead.

The temperature in the engine-room had gone up to 110 degrees. Irritated voices were ascending through the skylight and through the fiddle of the stoke-hole. They made a harsh and resonant uproar, mingled with angry clangs and scrapes of metal, as if men with limbs of iron and throats of bronze had been quarrelling down there. The second engineer was falling foul of the stokers for letting the steam go down. He was a man with arms like a blacksmith and generally feared, but that afternoon the stokers were answering him back recklessly and slammed the furnace doors with the fury of despair. Then the noise ceased suddenly and the second engineer appeared, emerging out of the stoke-hole, streaked with grime and soaking wet, like a chimney-sweep coming out of a well. As soon as his head was clear of the fiddle he began upbraiding Jukes for not trimming properly the stoke-hole ventilators, and in answer Jukes made with his hands deprecatory, soothing signs, meaning: no wind—can't be helped—you can see for yourself. But the other wouldn't hear reason. His teeth flashed angrily in his dirty face, and he cursed like a madman. He didn't mind, he said, the trouble of punching their blanked heads down there, blank his soul, but did the condemned sailors think you could keep steam up in the God-forsaken boilers simply by knocking the blanked stokers about? No, by George! You had to get some draught, too—may he be everlastingly blanked for a swab-headed deckhand, if you didn't! And the chief, too, rampaging before the steam-gauge and carrying on like a lunatic all over the engine-room ever since noon. What did Jukes think he was stuck up there for, if he couldn't get one of his decayed, good-for-nothing, deck-cripples to turn the ventilators to the wind?

The relations of the "engine-room" and the "deck" of the *Nan-Shan* were, as is known, of a brotherly nature; therefore Jukes leaned over and begged the other in a restrained tone not to make a disgusting ass of himself—the skipper was on the other side of the bridge. But the second declared mutinously that he didn't care who was on the other side of the bridge, and Jukes, passing in a flash from lofty disapproval into a state of exaltation, invited him in unflattering terms to come up and twist the beastly things to please himself, and to catch such wind as a donkey of his sort could find. The second rushed up to the fray. He flung himself at the port ventilator as though he meant to tear it out bodily and toss it overboard. All he did was to move round the cowl a few inches, with an enormous expenditure of force, and seemed spent in the effort. He leaned against the back of the wheel-house, and Jukes walked up to him.

"Oh, heavens!" ejaculated the engineer in a feeble voice. He lifted his eyes to the sky and then let the glassy stare descend to meet the horizon that, tilting up to an angle of forty degrees, seemed to hang on a slant for awhile and settle down slowly. "Heavens! Phew! What's up, anyhow?"

Jukes, straddling his long legs like a pair of compasses, put on an air of superiority. "We're going to catch it this time," he said. "The barometer is tumbling down like anything, Harry. And you trying to kick up that silly row."

It seemed as though the word "barometer" had revived the second engineer's mad animosity. Collecting afresh all his energies he directed Jukes in a low and brutal tone to shove the unmentionable instrument down his gory throat. Who cared for his crimson barometer? It was the steam—the steam—that was going down; and what between the firemen going faint and the chief going silly, it was worse than a dog's life for him; and he didn't care a tinker's curse how soon the whole show was blown out of the water. He semed on the point of having a cry, but, after regaining his breath, he muttered darkly, "I'll faint them," and dashed off. He stopped upon the fiddle long enough to shake his fist at the unnatural daylight and dropped into the dark hole with a whoop.

V

WHEN Jukes turned round, his eyes fell upon the rounded back and the big red ears of Captain MacWhirr, who had come across. He did not look at his chief officer, but said at once:

"That's a very violent man, that second engineer."

"Jolly good second, anyhow," grunted Jukes. "They can't keep up steam," he added rapidly, and made a grab at the rail against the coming lurch.

Captain MacWhirr, unprepared, took a run and brought himself up with a jerk by an awning stanchion.

"A profane man," he said obstinately. "If this goes on I'll have to get rid of him the first chance."

"It's the heat," said Jukes. "The weather's awful. It would make a saint swear. Even up here I feel exactly as if I had my head tied up in a woollen blanket."

Captain MacWhirr looked up.

"D'ye mean to say, Mr. Jukes, you ever had your head tied up in a blanket? What was that for?"

"It's a manner of speaking, sir," said Jukes, stolidly.

"Some of you fellows do go on! What's that about saints swearing? I wish you wouldn't talk so wild. What sort of saint would that be that would swear? No more saint than yourself, I expect. And what's a blanket got to do with it—or the weather either? The heat does not make me swear—does it? It's filthy bad temper. That's what it is. And what's the good of you talking like this? . . ."

Thus Captain MacWhirr expostulated against the use of images in speech, and at the end electrified Jukes by a con-

temptuous snort followed by words of passion and resentment.
"Damme! I'll fire him out of the ship if he don't look out."

And Jukes, incorrigible, thought:

"Goodness me! Somebody's put a new inside to my old man.
Here's temper, if you like. Of course it's the weather; what else?
It would make an angel quarrelsome—let alone a saint."

All the Chinamen on deck appeared at their last gasp.

At its setting the sun had a diminished diameter and an ex-
piring brown, rayless glow, as if millions of centuries elapsing
since the morning had brought it near its end. A dense bank of
cloud became visible to the northward: it had a sinister dark
olive tint, and lay low and motionless upon the sea, resembling
a solid obstacle in the path of the ship. She went floundering
towards it like an exhausted creature driven to its death. The
coppery twilight retired slowly, and the darkness brought out
overhead a swarm of unsteady big stars that, as if blown upon,
flickered exceedingly and seemed to hang very near the earth.
At eight o'clock Jukes went into the chart-room to write up the
ship's log.

He copied neatly out of the rough-book the number of miles,
the course of the ship, and in the column for "Wind" he
scrawled the word "Calm" from top to bottom of the eight hours
since noon. He was exasperated by the continuous, monotonous
rolling of the ship. The heavy inkstand would slide away in a
manner that suggested perverse intelligence in dodging the pen.
Having written in the large space under the head of "Remarks,"
"Heat very oppressive," he stuck the end of the penholder in his
teeth, pipe-fashion, and mopped his face carefully.

"Ship rolling heavily in a high cross-swell," he began again,
and commented to himself, " 'Heavily' is no word for it." Then
he wrote: "Sunset threatening, with a low bank of clouds to N.
and E. Sky clear overhead."

Sprawling over the table with arrested pen he glanced out of
the door, and in that frame of his vision he saw all the stars
flying upwards between the teakwood jambs on a black sky. The
whole lot took flight together and disappeared, leaving only a

blackness flecked with white flashes, for the sea was as black as the sky and speckled with foam afar. The stars had flown to the roll and came back on the return swing of the ship, rushing downwards in a swarming glitter not of fiery points but enlarged to tiny discs, brilliant with a clear, wet sheen.

He watched the flying big stars for a moment, and then wrote: "8 P.M. Swell increasing. Ship labouring and taking water on her decks. Battened down the coolies for the night. Barometer still falling." He paused and thought to himself, "Perhaps nothing whatever'll come of it." And then he closed resolutely his entries: "Every appearance of a typhoon coming on."

On going out he had to stand aside, and Captain MacWhirr strode over the doorstep without saying a word or making a sign.

"Shut the door, Mr. Jukes, will you?" he cried from within.

Jukes turned back to do so, muttering ironically, "Afraid to catch cold, I suppose." It was his watch below, but he yearned for communion with his kind; and he remarked cheerily to the second mate: "Doesn't look so bad, after all, does it?"

The second mate was marching to and fro on the bridge, tripping down with small steps one moment, and the next climbing with difficulty the shifting slope of the deck. At the sound of Jukes's voice he stood still, facing forward, but made no answer.

"Hallo! That's a heavy one," said Jukes, swaying to meet the long roll till his lowered hand touched the planks. This time the second mate made in his throat a noise of an unfriendly nature.

He was an oldish, shabby little fellow, with bad teeth and no hair on his face. He had been shipped in a hurry in Shanghai that trip when the second officer brought from home had delayed the ship three hours in port by contriving (in some manner Captain MacWhirr could never understand) to fall overboard into an empty coal-lighter alongside; and had to be sent ashore to the hospital with concussion of the brain and a broken limb or two.

VI

JUKES was not discouraged by the unsympathetic sound. "The Chinamen must be having a lovely time of it down there," he said. "It's lucky for them the old girl has the easiest roll of any ship I've ever been in. There, now. This one wasn't so bad."

"You wait," snarled the second mate. With his sharp nose, red at the tip, and his thin, pinched lips, he always looked as though he were raging inwardly, and he was concise in his speech to the point of rudeness. All his time off duty he spent in his cabin with the door shut, and keeping so still in there that he was supposed to fall asleep as soon as he had disappeared; but the man who came in to wake him for his watch on deck would invariably find him with his eyes wide open, flat on his back in the bunk, and glaring irritably from a soiled pillow. He never wrote any letters, did not seem to hope for news from any-where, and though he had been heard once to mention West Hartlepool, it was with extreme bitterness and only in connec-tion with the charges in a boarding-house. He was one of those men who are picked up by ships in the ports of the world. They are competent enough, appear hopelessly hard up, show no evidence of any sort of vice, and carry about them all the signs of manifest failure. They come aboard on an emergency, care for no ship afloat, live in their own atmosphere of casual con-nection amongst their shipmates, who know nothing of them, and make up their minds to leave at inconvenient times. They clear out, with no words of leave-taking, in some God-forsaken port that other men would fear to be stranded in, and go ashore in company with a shabby sea-chest corded like a treasure-box, and with an air of shaking the ship's dust off their feet.

"You wait," he repeated, balancing in great swings with his back to Jukes, motionless and implacable.

"Do you mean to say we are going to catch it hot?" asked Jukes, with boyish interest.

"Say? I say nothing. You don't catch me!" snapped the little second mate with a mixture of pride, scorn, and cunning, as if Jukes's question had been a trap cleverly detected. "Oh, no! None of you here shall make a fool of me if I know it," he mumbled to himself.

Jukes reflected rapidly that this second mate was a mean little beast, and in his heart he wished poor Jack Allen had never smashed himself up in the coal-lighter. The far-off blackness ahead of the ship was like another night seen through the starry night of the earth—a blackness without stars—the night of the immensities beyond the created universe revealed in its appalling stillness through a low fissure in the glittering sphere of which the earth is the kernel.

"Whatever there might be about," said Jukes, "we are steaming straight into it."

"*You've* said it," caught up the second mate, always with his back to Jukes. "You've said it—mind. Not I."

"Oh, go to Jericho!" said Jukes, frankly; and the other emitted a triumphant little chuckle. "You've said it," he repeated.

"And what of that?"

"I've known some real good men get into trouble with their skippers for saying a dam' sight less," answered the second mate feverishly. "Oh, no! You don't catch me."

"You seem deucedly anxious not to give yourself away," said Jukes, completely soured by such absurdity. "I wouldn't be afraid to say what I think."

"Aye, to me! That's no great trick. I am nobody, and well I know it."

The ship, after a pause of comparative steadiness, started upon a series of rolls, one worse than the other, and for a time Jukes, preserving his equilibrium, was too busy to open his mouth. As soon as the violent swinging had quieted down somewhat he said:

"This is a bit too much of a good thing. Whether anything

is coming or not, I think she ought to be put head-on to that swell. The old man is just gone in to lie down. Hang me if I don't speak to him!"

But when he opened the door of the chart-room he saw his Captain reading a book. Captain MacWhirr was not lying down: he was standing up, with one hand grasping the edge of the bookshelf and the other holding open before his face a thick volume. The lamp wriggled in the gimbals, the loosened books toppled from side to side on the shelf, the long barometer swung in jerky circles, the table altered its slant every moment. In the midst of all this stir and movement Captain MacWhirr, very steady on his feet and holding on, was reading in a book.

VII

WHEN Jukes opened the door the Captain showed his eyes above the upper edge, and asked:

"What's the matter?"

"Swell getting worse, sir."

"Noticed that in here," muttered Captain MacWhirr. "Anything wrong?"

Jukes, inwardly disconcerted by the seriousness of the eyes looking at him over the top of the book, produced an embarrassed grin.

"Rolling like old boots," he said sheepishly.

"Aye! Very heavy. Very heavy. What do you want?"

At this Jukes lost his footing and began to flounder.

"I was thinking of our passengers," he said, in the manner of a man clutching at a straw.

"Passengers?" wondered the Captain, gravely. "What passengers?"

"Why! The Chinamen, sir!" explained Jukes, very sick of this conversation.

"The Chinamen! Why don't you speak plainly? Couldn't tell

what you meant. Never heard a lot of coolies spoken of as passengers before. Passengers, indeed! What's come to you?"

Captain MacWhirr, closing the book on his forefinger, lowered his arm and looked completely mystified. "Why are you thinking of the Chinamen, Mr. Jukes?" he inquired.

Jukes took a plunge like a man driven to it.

"She's rolling her decks full of water, sir. Thought you might put her head-on perhaps—for a while. Till this goes down a bit —very soon. Head to the eastward. I never knew a ship roll like this."

He held on in the doorway, and Captain MacWhirr, feeling his grip on the shelf inadequate, made up his mind to let go in a hurry and fell heavily on the couch.

"Head to the eastward," he said, struggling to sit up. "That's more than four points off her course."

"Yes, sir. Fifty degress . . . would just bring her head far enough round to meet this. . . ."

Captain MacWhirr was now sitting up. He had not dropped the book and he had not lost his place.

"To the eastward," he repeated, with dawning astonishment. "To the . . . Where do you think we are bound to? You want me to haul a full-powered steamship four points off her course to make the Chinamen comfortable! Now I've heard more than enough of mad things done in the world—but this. . . . If I didn't know you, Jukes, I would think you were in liquor. Steer four points off . . . and what afterwards? Steer four points over the other way, I suppose, to make the course good. What put it into your head that I would start to tack a steamer as if she were a sailing ship?"

"Jolly good thing she isn't," threw in Jukes, with bitter readiness. "She would have rolled every blessed stick out of her this afternoon."

"Aye! And you just would have had to stand and see them go," said Captain MacWhirr, showing a certain animation. "It's a dead calm, isn't it?"

"It is, sir. But there's something out of the common coming
for sure."

"Maybe. I suppose you have a notion I should be getting out
of the way of that dirt," said Captain MacWhirr, speaking with
the utmost simplicity of manner and tone, and fixing the oil-
cloth on the floor with a heavy stare. Thus he noticed neither
Jukes's discomfiture nor the mixture of vexation and astonished
respect on his face.

"Now here's this book," he continued with deliberation,
slapping his thigh with the closed volume. "I've been reading
the chapter on the winds there."

This was true. He had been reading the chapter on the winds.
When he had entered the chart-room it was with no intention
of taking the book down. Some influence in the air—the same
influence, probably, that caused the steward to bring without
orders the Captain's sea-boots and oilskin coat up to the chart-
room—had, as it were, guided his hand to the shelf. And without
condescending to sit down he had waded with a conscious effort
into the terminology of the subject. He lost himself amongst
advancing semicircles, left- and right-hand quadrants, the curves
of the tracks, the probable bearing of the centre, the shifts of
winds, and the readings of barometer. He tried to bring all these
things into a definite relation to himself, and ended by becoming contemptuously angry with such a lot of words and with
so much advice that seemed to him all sheer headwork and sup-
position without a glimmer of certitude.

"It's the confoundest thing, Jukes," he said. "If a fellow was
to believe all that's in there he would be running most of his
time all over the sea trying to get behind the weather."

Again he slapped his leg with the book, and Jukes opened his
mouth, but said nothing.

"Running to get behind the weather! Do you understand that,
Mr. Jukes? It's the maddest thing," ejaculated Captain Mac-
Whirr, with pauses, gazing at the floor profoundly. "You would
think an old woman had been writing this. It passes me. If that
thing means anything useful, then it means that I should at once

"The sun, pale and without rays, poured down a leaden heat, and the Chinamen were lying prostrate about the decks." Illustration for *Typhoon* by Maurice Greiffenhagen (*p. 17*)

alter the course away—away to the devil somewhere, and come booming down on Fu-chau from the northward at the tail of this dirty weather that's supposed to be knocking about in our way. From the north! Do you understand, Mr. Jukes? Three hundred extra miles to the distance, and a pretty coal bill to show. I couldn't bring myself to do that if every word in there was gospel truth, Mr. Jukes. Don't you expect me. . . ."

And Jukes, silent, marvelled at this display of feeling and loquacity.

"But the truth is that you don't know if the fellow is right, anyhow. How can you tell what a gale is made of till you get it? He isn't aboard here, is he? Very well. Here he says that the centre of them things bears eight points off the wind. But we haven't got any wind, for all the barometer falling. Where's his centre now?"

"We shall get the wind presently," mumbled Jukes.

"Let it come, then," said Captain MacWhirr, with dignified indignation. "It's only to let you see, Mr. Jukes, that you don't find everything in books. All these rules for dodging breezes and circumventing the winds of heaven, Mr. Jukes, seem to me the maddest thing, when you come to look at it sensibly."

He looked up, saw Jukes gazing at him dubiously, and tried to illustrate his meaning.

"About as queer as your extraordinary notion of dodging the ship head to sea, for I don't know how long, to make the Chinamen comfortable; while all we've got to do is to take them to Fu-chau, being expected to get there before noon on Friday. If the weather delays me—very well. There's your log-book to talk straight about the weather. But suppose I went swinging off three hundred miles out of my course and came in two days late, and they asked me: 'Where have you been all that time, Captain?' What could I say to that? 'Went around to dodge the bad weather,' I would say. 'It must've been dam' bad,' they would say. 'Don't know,' I would have to say; 'I've dodged clear of it.' See that, Jukes? I have been thinking it all out this afternoon."

He looked up again in his unseeing, unimaginative way. No one had ever heard him say so much at one time. Jukes, with his arms open, in the doorway, was like a man invited to confront a miracle. Unbounded wonder was the intellectual meaning of his eye, while hard incredulity was seated in his whole countenance.

"A gale is a gale, Mr. Jukes," resumed the Captain, "and a full-powered steamship has got to face it. There's just so much dirty weather knocking about the world, and the proper thing is to go through it with none of what old Captain Wilson of the *Melita* calls storm-strategy. The other day ashore I heard him hold forth about it to a lot of shipmasters who came in and sat at a table next to mine. It seemed to me the greatest nonsense. He was telling them how he—outmanoeuvred, I think he said— a terrific gale, so that it never came nearer than fifty miles to him. A neat piece of headwork, he called it. How he knew there was a gale fifty miles off beats me altogether. It was like listening to a crazy man. I would have thought Captain Wilson was old enough to know better."

Captain MacWhirr ceased for a moment, then said: "It's your watch below, Mr. Jukes?" Jukes came to himself with a start.

"Yes, sir."

"Leave orders to call me at the slightest change," said the Captain. He reached up to put the book away and tucked his legs upon the couch. "Shut the door so that it don't fly open— will you? I can't stand a door banging. They've put a lot of rubbishy locks in this ship—I must say."

VIII

CAPTAIN MacWHIRR closed his eyes. He did so to rest himself. He was tired, and he experienced that state of mental vacuity which comes upon one at the end of an exhaustive discussion that had liberated some belief matured in the course of meditative years. He had indeed been making his confession of faith, had he only known it. And its effect was to make Jukes on the other side of the door stand scratching his head for a good while.

Captain MacWhirr opened his eyes.

He thought he must have been asleep. What was that loud noise? Wind? Why had he not been called? The lamp wriggled in its gimbals, the barometer swung in circles, the table altered its slant every moment: a pair of limp sea-boots with collapsed long tops went sliding past the couch. He put out his hand instantly and captured one.

Jukes's face appeared in a crack of the door,—only his face, very red, with staring eyes. The flame of the lamp leaped; a piece of paper flew up; a rush of air struck and enveloped Captain MacWhirr. Beginning to draw on the boot he directed an expectant gaze at Jukes's swollen, excited features.

"Came on like this," shouted Jukes. "Five minutes ago . . . all of a sudden."

The head disappeared with a bang, and a heavy splash and patter of drops swept past the closed door as if a pailful of melted lead had been flung against the house. A whistling could be heard now upon the deep, vibrating noise outside.

The stuffy chart-room seemed as full of draughts as a shed. Captain MacWhirr collared the other sea-boot on its violent passage along the floor. He was not flustered, but he could not find at once the opening for inserting his foot. The shoes he had flung off were scurrying from end to end of the cabin, gambolling playfully over each other like puppies. As soon as he stood up he kicked at them viciously, but without effect.

He threw himself into the attitude of a lounging fencer to reach after his oilskin coat; and afterwards he staggered all over the confined space while he jerked himself into it. Very grave, straddling his legs far apart, and stretching his neck, he started to tie deliberately the strings of his sou'wester under his chin, with thick fingers that trembled slightly. He went through all the movements of a woman putting on her bonnet before a glass, with a mien of strained, listening attention, as though he expected every moment to hear the shout of his name, shouted in the confused clamour that had suddenly beset his ship. Its increase filled his ears while he was getting ready to go out and confront whatever it might mean. It was tumultuous and very loud, too, made up of the rush of the wind, the crashes of the sea, with that prolonged, deep vibration of the air, like the roll of an immense and remote drum beating the charge of the gale.

He stood for a moment in the light of the lamp—thick, clumsy, shapeless, in his panoply of combat, vigilant and red-faced.

"There's a lot of weight in this," he muttered.

As soon as he attempted to open the door the wind caught it and he was absolutely dragged out over the doorstep; clinging to the handle, he was flung around, and at once found himself engaged with the wind in a sort of personal scuffle whose object was the shutting of that door. At the last moment a tongue of air scurried in and licked out the flame of the lamp.

Ahead of the ship he perceived a great darkness lying upon a multitude of white flashes; on the starboard beam a few amazing stars drooped, dim and fitful, above an immense waste of broken seas as if seen through a mad drift of smoke.

On the bridge a knot of men, indistinct and toiling, were making great efforts in the light of the wheel-house windows that shone mistily on their heads and backs. Suddenly, darkness closed upon one pane, then on another. The voices of the lost group reached him after the manner of men's voices in a gale, in shreds and fragments of forlorn shouting snatched past the ear. All at once Jukes appeared at his side, yelling, with his head down:

"Watch—put in—wheel-house shutters—glass—afraid—blow in."

Jukes heard his commander upbraiding.

"This—come—anything—warning—call me."

He tried to explain with the uproar pressing on his lips:

"Light air—remained—bridge—sudden—northeast—could turn
—thought—you—sure—hear."

They had gained the shelter of the weather-cloth and could
converse with raised voices as people quarrel.

"I got the hands to cover up all the ventilators. Good job I
had remained on deck. I didn't think you would be asleep, and
so . . . What did you say, sir? What?"

"Nothing," cried Captain MacWhirr. "I said—all right."

"By all the powers! We've got it this time," observed Jukes
in a howl.

"You haven't altered her course?" inquired Captain Mac-
Whirr, straining his voice.

"No, sir. Certainly not. Wind came out right ahead. And here
comes the head sea."

A plunge of the ship ended in a shock as if she had landed
her forefoot upon something solid. After a moment of stillness a
lofty flight of sprays drove hard with the wind upon their faces.

"Keep her at it as long as we can," shouted Captain Mac-
Whirr.

Before Jukes had squeezed the salt water out of his eyes all the
stars had disappeared.

IX

JUKES was as ready a man as any half-dozen young mates that
may be caught by casting a net upon the waters, and though he
had been somewhat taken aback by the startling viciousness of
the first squall he had pulled himself together on the instant,
had called out the hands, and had rushed then to secure such
openings about the deck as had not been already battened down
earlier in the evening. Shouting in his fresh, stentorian voice,
"Jump, boys, and bear a hand!" he led in the work, telling himself the while that he had "just expected this."

But at the same time he was growing aware that this was

rather more than he had expected. From the first stir of the air on his cheek the gale seemed to take upon itself the accumulated impetus of an avalanche. Heavy sprays enveloped the *Nan-Shan* from stem to stern, and instantly, in the midst of her regular rolling, she began to jerk and plunge as though she had gone mad with fright.

Jukes thought: "This is no joke." While he was exchanging explanatory yells with his Captain a sudden lowering of the darkness came upon the night, falling before their vision like something palpable. It was as if the masked lights of the world had been turned down. Jukes was uncritically glad to have his Captain at hand. It relieved him, as though that man had, by simply coming on deck, taken at once most of the gale's weight upon his shoulders. Such is the prestige, the privilege, and the burden of command.

Captain MacWhirr could expect no comfort of that sort from any one on earth. Such is the loneliness of command. He was trying to see, with that watchful manner of a seaman who stares into the wind's eye as if into the eye of an adversary, to penetrate the hidden intention and guess the aim and force of the thrust. The strong wind swept at him out of a vast obscurity; he felt under his feet the uneasiness of his ship, and he could not even discern a shadow of her shape. He wished it were not so; and very still he waited, feeling stricken by a blind man's helplessness.

To be silent was natural to him, dark or shine. Jukes at his elbow made himself heard, yelling cheerily in the gusts: "We must have got the worst of it at once, sir." A faint burst of lightning quivered all round as if flashed into a cavern—into a black and secret chamber of the sea, with a floor of foaming crests.

It unveiled for a sinister, fluttering moment a ragged mass of clouds hanging low, the lurch of the long outlines of the ship, the black figures of men caught on the bridge, heads forward, as if petrified in the act of butting. The darkness palpitated down upon all this, and then the real thing came at last.

X

IT was something formidable and swift, like the sudden smashing of a Vial of Wrath. It seemed to explode all round the ship with an overpowering concussion and a rush of great waters, as if an immense dam had been blown up to windward. It destroyed at once the organised life of the ship by its scattering effect. In an instant the men lost touch of each other. This is the disintegrating power of a great wind. It isolates one from one's kind. An earthquake, a landslip, an avalanche, overtake a man incidentally, as it were—without passion. A furious gale attacks him like a personal enemy, tries to grasp his limbs, fastens upon his mind, seeks to rout his very spirit out of him.

Jukes was driven away from his commander. He fancied himself whirled a great distance through the air. Everything disappeared, even for a moment his power of thinking, but his hand had found within six feet of him one of the rail-stanchions. This he embraced with the ardour of love that will not be thwarted. It saved his body and steadied his soul so far that it became conscious of an intolerable distress. It was by no means alleviated by an inclination to disbelieve the reality of this experience. Though young, he had seen some bad weather and had never doubted his ability to imagine the worst; but this was so much beyond his powers of fancy that it appeared incompatible with the existence of any ship whatever. He would have been incredulous about himself in the same way, perhaps, had he not been so greatly harassed by the necessity of exerting a continuous wrestling effort against a force trying to tear him away from his hold. Moreover, the conviction of not being utterly destroyed returned to him through the sensations of being half drowned, bestially shaken, and partly choked. He thought: "Heavens! What's this?"

It seemed to him he remained there precariously alone with

the stanchion for a long, long time. The rain poured on him,
flowed, drove in sheets. He was plunged in rushing water like a
diver holding on to a stake planted in the bed of a swollen river.
He breathed in gasps, and sometimes the water he swallowed
was fresh, and sometimes it was salt. For the most part he kept
his eyes shut tight, as if suspecting his sight might be destroyed
in the immense flurry of the elements. When he ventured to
blink hastily, he derived some moral support from the green
gleam of the starboard light shining feebly upon the flight of
rain and sprays. He was actually looking at it when its ray fell
upon the uprearing head of the sea which put it out. He saw the
head of the wave topple over, adding the mite of its crash to the
tremendous uproar raging around him, and almost at the same
instant the stanchion was wrenched from his grasp. After a
crushing thump on his back he found himself suddenly afloat
and borne away. His first irresistible notion was that the whole
China Sea had climbed on the bridge. Then, more sanely, he
concluded himself gone overboard. All the time he was being
tossed, flung, and rolled in great volumes of water, he kept on
repeating mentally, with the utmost precipitation, the words:
"My God! My God! My God! My God!"

All at once, in a revolt of misery and despair, he formed the
crazy resolution to get out of that. And he began to thresh about
with his arms and legs. But as soon as he commenced his
wretched struggles he discovered himself to have become somehow mixed up with a face, an oilskin coat, somebody's boots.
He clawed ferociously all these things in turn, lost them, found
them again, lost them once more, and was caught in the firm
clasp of a pair of stout arms. He returned the embrace closely
round a thick, soft body. He had found his Captain.

They tumbled over and over each other, tightening their
hug. Suddenly the water let them down with a brutal bang,
and, stranded against the side of the wheel-house, out of breath
and bruised, they were left to stagger up in the wind and hold on
where they could.

Jukes came out of it rather horrified, as though he had just escaped some unparallelled outrage directed at his feelings. It had weakened his faith in himself. He started, shouting aimlessly to the man he could feel near him in that fiendish blackness, "Is it you, sir? Is it you, sir?" till his temples seemed ready to burst. And he heard in answer a voice, as if crying far away, as if screaming to him fretfully from a very great distance the one word, "Yes!" It was this tinge of irritation which silenced him rather than the difficulty of making himself heard. Other seas swept again over the bridge. He received them defencelessly right over his bare head, with both his hands engaged in holding.

The motion of the ship was extravagant. Her lurches had an appalling helplessness; she pitched, as if taking a header into a void and seemed to find a wall to hit every time. When she rolled she fell on her side headlong as if she were beginning to tumble, turning down a slope, and she would be righted by such a demolishing blow that Jukes felt her reeling as a clubbed man reels before he collapses. In the darkness round her the gale howled and scuffled about gigantically, as though the entire world were a black gully. At certain moments the air would stream against the ship as if sucked through a tunnel with a concentrated, solid force of impact that seemed to lift her clean out of the water, and to keep her up for an instant with only a quiver running through her from end to end. And then she would begin her tumbling again as if dropped back into a boiling caldron. Jukes tried hard to compose his mind and judge things coolly.

Both ends of the *Nan-Shan* were under water, as though she had no more freeboard than a raft. The sea, flattened down in the heavier gusts, would uprise and overwhelm them in snowy rushes of foam expanding wide, beyond both rails, into the night. And on this dazzling sheet, spread under the blackness of the clouds and emitting a bluish glow, Captain MacWhirr could catch a desolate glimpse of a few tiny specks black as ebony, the tops of the hatches, the battened companions, the heads of the covered winches, the foot of a mast. This was all he could see of his ship. Her middle structure—covered by the bridge which bore him, his mate, the dark wheel-house where a man was steering, shut up with the fear of being swept overboard together with the whole thing in one great crash—her middle structure was like a half-tide rock awash upon a coast. It was like an outlying rock in the night, with the water boiling up, streaming over, pouring off, beating round—like a rock in the surf to which shipwrecked people cling before they let go —only it rose, it sank, it rolled continuously, without respite and rest, like a rock that had miraculously struck adrift from a coast and gone wallowing upon the sea.

She was being looted with a senseless, destructive fury; trysails torn out from the extra gaskets, double-lashed awnings blown away, bridge swept clean, weathercloths burst, rails twisted, light-screens smashed—and two of the boats had gone already. They had gone unheard and unseen, melting, as it were, in the shock and smother of the wave. It was only later, when, upon the white flash of another high sea hurling itself amidships, Jukes had a rapid vision of two pairs of davits leaping black and empty out of the solid blackness, with one overhauled fall flying and an iron-bound block threshing in the wind, that he became aware of what had happened within about three yards of his back.

He poked his head forward, groping for the ear of his commander. His lips touched it—big, fleshy, very wet. He cried in an agitated tone:

"The boats are going now, sir."

And again he heard that voice, distinct and faint, forced and ringing feebly, but with a penetrating effect of quietness in the enormous discord of noises, as if sent out from some remote spot of peace beyond the black wastes of the gale; again he heard a man's voice,—the frail and indomitable sound that can be made to carry an infinity of thought, resolution, and purpose, that shall be pronouncing confident words on the last day, when heavens fall and justice is done,—and it was crying to him as if from very, very far:—"All right."

Jukes thought he had not managed to make himself understood.

"Our boats—I say boats—the boats, sir! Two gone!"

The same voice, within a foot of him, and yet so remote, yelled sensibly:

"Can't be helped."

Captain MacWhirr had never turned his face, but Jukes caught some more words on the wind.

"What can—expect—Hammering through—Such—Bound to leave—something behind—Stands to reason."

Watchfully Jukes listened for more. No more came. This was all Captain MacWhirr had to say; and Jukes could picture to himself rather than see the broad squat back before him. An impenetrable obscurity pressing down upon the ghostly glimmers of the sea harboured the mysterious madness of all this rush, deluge, and uproar. Suddenly Jukes imagined himself completely indifferent to it all. It was too much. A sort of dull conviction seized upon him that there was nothing to be done.

If the steering-gear did not give way, if the sea did not burst the deck in or smash one of the hatches, if the engines did not give up, if way could be kept on her against this terrific wind, and she did not bury herself in one of these awful seas, of whose white crests alone, topping high above her bows, he could now and then get a sickening glimpse,—then there was a chance of her coming out of it. Something within him seemed to turn over, bringing uppermost the feeling that the ship was lost.

"She's done for," he said to himself with a surprising mental agitation, as though he had discovered an unexpected meaning in this thought. One of these things was bound to happen. Nothing could be prevented now and nothing could be remedied. The men on board did not count, and the ship could not last. This weather was too impossible.

It was like the maddest of dreams: a dream in which you inhabit a world ready to fly to pieces and are jostled rudely against a man you cannot see. Jukes felt an arm thrown heavily over his shoulders. And to this overture he responded with great intelligence by catching hold of his Captain round the waist.

They stood clasped thus in the blind night, bracing each other against the wind, cheek to cheek and lip to ear, in the manner of two battered hulks lashed stem-to-stern together.

XI

JUKES heard the voice of his commander hardly any louder than before, but nearer, as though, starting to march athwart the prodigious rush of the hurricane, it had approached him, bearing that strange effect of quietness like the serene glow of a halo.

"D'ye know where the hands got to?" it asked, vigorous and evanescent at the same time, overcoming the strength of the wind, and swept away from Jukes instantly.

Jukes didn't know. They were all on the bridge when the real force of the hurricane struck the ship. He had no idea where they had crawled to. Under the circumstances they were nowhere, for all the use that could be made of them. Somehow the Captain's wish to know distressed Jukes.

"Want the hands, sir?" he cried, apprehensively.

"Ought to know," asserted Captain MacWhirr. "Hold hard."

They held hard. An outburst of unchained fury, a vicious rush of the wind, absolutely steadied the ship. Her disordered motion was checked and she only rolled short and swift; she rocked quick and light like a child's cradle for a terrific moment of suspense, while the whole atmosphere, as it seemed, streamed furiously past her, roaring away from the tenebrous earth.

It suffocated them, and with eyes shut they tightened their grasp. What, from the magnitude of the shock, might have been a column of water, running upright in the dark, butted against the ship, broke short, and fell on her bridge, crushingly from on high, with a dead, burying weight.

A flying fragment of that collapse, a mere splash, enveloped them in one swirl from their feet over their heads, violently, filling their ears, mouths, and nostrils with salt water. It knocked out their legs, wrenched hastily at their arms, seethed away swiftly under their chins, and opening their eyes they saw the piled-up masses of foam dashing to and fro amongst what looked like the fragments of a ship. She had given way as if driven straight in. They had felt her give under them, and in their panting breasts their hearts yielded, too, before the tremendous blow; and all at once she sprang up to her desperate plunging as if trying to scramble out from under the ruins.

The seas in the dark seemed to rush from all sides to keep her back where she might perish. There was hate in the way she was handled, and a ferocity in the blows that fell. She was like a living creature thrown to the rage of a mob: hustled terribly, struck at, borne up, flung down, leaped upon. Captain Mac-Whirr and Jukes kept hold of each other, deafened by the noise, gagged by the wind; and the great physical tumult beating about their bodies brought, like an unbridled display of passion, a profound trouble to their souls. One of those wild and appalling shrieks that are heard at times passing mysteriously overhead in the steady roar of a hurricane, like a long scream of pain from something living, immense and tormented, swooped, as if borne on wings, upon the ship, and Jukes tried to outscream it.

"Will she live?"

The cry was wrenched out of his breast. It was as unintentional as the birth of a thought in the head, and he heard nothing of it himself. It all became extinct at once—thought, intention, effort; and of his cry the inaudible vibration added to the tempest-waves of the air.

He expected nothing from it—nothing at all. For, indeed, what answer could be made? But after a while he heard with amazement the frail and resisting voice in his ear,—the dwarf sound, unconquered in the giant tumult,—

"She may!"

It was a dull yell, more difficult to seize than a whisper,—the unsubstantial and passing shadow of a yell. Jukes accepted it with bitterness. And presently the voice returned again, half submerged in the vast crashes, like a ship battling against the waves of an ocean.

"Let's hope so!" it cried, small, lonely, and unmoved, a stranger to the visions of hope or fear, and it flickered into disconnected words: "Ship—This—Never—Anyhow—For the best." Jukes gave it up contemptuously.

And then, as if it had come suddenly upon the one thing fit to withstand the power of a storm, it seemed to gain force and firmness for the last broken shouts:

"Keep on hammering—builders—Good men—And chance it— Rout—Engines—Good man."

XII

CAPTAIN MacWHIRR removed his arm from Jukes's shoulders and thereby ceased to exist for his mate, so dark it was. Jukes experienced a great deception, as though of undeniable right he had expected to obtain an utterance of precise effect. After a tense stiffening of every muscle he would let himself go limp all over. The gnawing of profound discomfort existed side by side with an incredible disposition to somnolence, as though he had been buffeted and worried into drowsiness. The wind would get hold of his head and try to shake it off his shoulders; his clothes, full of water, were as heavy as lead, stiff like sheet-iron, cold and dripping like an armour of melting ice: he shivered. It lasted a long time; and, with his hands contracted by cramp closed hard on his hold, he was letting himself sink slowly into the depths of bodily misery. There was no suggestion of end to it, as there is no end to the horror of a nightmare. Jukes's mind became concentrated upon himself in an aimless, idle way, and when something pushed lightly at the back of his knees he nearly, as the saying is, jumped out of his skin.

In the start forward he bumped the back of Captain Mac-

Whirr, who didn't move, and then a hand gripped his thigh. A lull had come, a menacing lull of the wind, the holding of a stormy breath—and he felt himself pawed all over. It was the boatswain. He had recognised the hands, so thick and enormous that they seemed to belong to some new species of man.

The boatswain had arrived on the bridge, crawling on all fours against the wind, and had found the chief mate's legs with the top of his head. Immediately he crouched and began to explore Jukes's person upwards, with clumsy, prudent, apologetic touches, as became an inferior.

He was an ill-favoured, undersized, gruff sailor of fifty, coarsely hairy, short-legged, long-armed, resembling an elderly ape. His strength was immense; and in his great lumpy paws, bulging like brown boxing-gloves on the end of his furry forearms, the heaviest objects were handled like playthings. Apart from the grizzled pelt on his chest, the menacing demeanour, and the hoarse voice, he had none of the classical attributes of his rating. His good nature amounted almost to imbecility; the men did what they liked with him, and he had not an ounce of initiative in his character, which was easy-going and talkative. For these reasons Jukes naturally disliked him; but Captain MacWhirr, to Jukes's scornful disgust, seemed to regard him as a first rate petty officer.

He pulled himself up by Jukes's coat, taking that liberty with the greatest moderation, and only so far as it was forced upon him by the hurricane. "What is it, bo's'n, what is it?" yelled Jukes, impatient with the foreboding of some odious trouble. What could that fraud of a bo's'n want on the bridge? The typhoon had got on Jukes's nerves. The husky bellowings of the other, though unintelligible, seemed to suggest a state of lively satisfaction. There could be no mistake. The old fool was pleased with something.

The boatswain's other hand had found some other body, for in a changed tone he began to inquire: "Is it you, sir? Is it you, sir?" The wind strangled his howls.

"Yes!" cried Captain MacWhirr.

XIII

ALL that the boatswain, out of a superabundance of yells, could make clear to Captain MacWhirr was the bizarre intelligence that "All them Chinamen in the fore 'tween-deck had fetched away, sir." Jukes, to leeward, could hear these two shouting within six inches of his face, as you may hear on a still night half a mile away two men conversing across a field. He heard Captain MacWhirr's exasperated "What?—What?" and the strained pitch of the other's hoarseness. "In a lump . . . seen . . . myself. Awful sight, sir . . . thought . . . tell you."

Jukes remained indifferent in the overpowering force of the hurricane, which made the very thought of action utterly vain. Besides, being very young, he had found the occupation of keeping his heart completely steeled against the worst so full of excitement that he had come to feel an impatient dislike towards any other form of activity whatever. The immediate peril had an atrocious side—the violence, the darkness, the uproar—which made the business of enduring it all surprisingly engrossing. He wasn't in the least scared; he knew that very well; and the proof of it was that, firmly believing he would never see another sunrise, he could be now sitting down, in a manner of speaking, as calm as possible under that belief.

These are the moments of do-nothing heroics to which even good men surrender at times. Many officers of ships can no doubt recall a case in their experience when just such a trance of confounded stoicism would come all at once over a whole ship's company. The mere recollection of such a passage is enough to bring back all the original dismay. It is difficult to allude to it without flinging swear-words backwards into the past; not precisely at the men themselves, which would be like throwing stones, but upon the unhonoured memory at large.

Jukes, however, had no wide experience of men or storms. He conceived himself to be calm—inexorably calm; calm as the very

"The little brass wheel in his hands had the appearance of a bright and fragile toy." Illustration for *Typhoon* by Maurice Greiffenhagen. *(p. 55)*

statue of calmness in the night and terror of a storm. It suited him to be left alone thus, and it seemed also as though really nothing more could be required of him. But as a matter of fact he was cowed; not abjectly, but only so far as a decent man may, without becoming loathsome to himself.

It was rather like a forced-on numbness of spirit. The long, long stress of a gale does it; the suspense of the interminably culminating catastrophe; the trial of sustained violence going on endlessly, as though time itself were hurled upon one; the formidable hint of annihilation in the sweep and roar of the wind. And there is a bodily fatigue in the mere holding on to existence within the excessive tumult; a searching and insidious fatigue that penetrates deep into a man's breast to cast down and sadden his heart, which is incorrigible, and of all the gifts of the earth—even before life itself—aspires to peace.

Jukes was benumbed much more than he supposed. He stood very wet, very cold, stiff in every limb, and in a momentary hallucination of swift visions (it is said a drowning man thus reviews all his life) he was run up against by memories altogether unconnected with his present situation. He remembered his father, for instance; a worthy but fanciful business man, who, at an unfortunate crisis in his affairs, went quietly to bed and died forthwith in a state of resignation. Jukes did not recall these circumstances, of course; but, remaining otherwise unconcerned, he remembered distinctly the poor man's face, a certain game of nap played when quite a boy in Table Bay, on board a ship since lost with all hands, the thick eyebrows of his first skipper; and, without any emotion, as he might years ago have walked listlessly into her room and seen her sitting there with a book, he remembered his mother,—dead, too, now,—the resolute woman left badly off, who had been very firm in his bringing up.

It could not have lasted more than a second, perhaps not so much. A heavy arm had fallen about his shoulders; Captain MacWhirr's voice was speaking his name into his ear. "Jukes! Jukes!"

He detected the tone of deep concern. The wind had thrown its weight on the ship, trying to pin her down amongst the seas. They made a clean breach over her as over a deep-swimming log; and the gathered weight of crashes menaced monstrously from afar. They flung out of the night with a ghostly light on their crests, the light of sea-foam that in an expanding, boiling up, pale flash showed upon the slender body of the ship the toppling rush, the downfall, and the seething, mad scurry of each wave. Never for a moment could she shake herself clear of the water. Jukes, rigid, perceived in her motion the ominous sign of haphazard floundering. She was no longer struggling intelligently. It was like the beginning of the end; and the note of busy concern in Captain MacWhirr's voice sickened him like an exhibition of blind and pernicious folly.

The spell of the storm had fallen upon Jukes. He was penetrated by it, absorbed by it; he was rooted in it with a rigour of dumb attention. Captain MacWhirr persisted in his cries, but the wind got between them like a solid wedge. He hung round Juke's neck as heavy as a stone, and suddenly the sides of their heads knocked together. "Jukes. Mr. Jukes—I say."

He had to answer that voice that would not be silenced. He answered in the customary manner: "Yes, sir."

And directly his heart, corrupted by the storm that breeds a craving for peace, rebelled desperately against the tyranny of training and command.

XIV

CAPTAIN MacWHIRR continued his efforts. He had his mate's head fixed firm in the crook of his elbow and pressed it to his yelling lips mysteriously. Sometimes Jukes would break in, admonishing hastily, "Look out, sir"; or Captain MacWhirr would bawl an earnest exhortation to "Hold hard, there," and the whole black universe seemed to reel together with the ship.

They paused. She floated yet. And Captain MacWhirr would resume his shouts. ". . . Says—whole lot—fetched away . . . ought to see . . . what's the matter?"

At the beginning of the gale all hands had taken refuge in the port alleyway. It had a door aft, which they shut; it was very dark, cold, and dismal there. At a heavy fling of the ship they would groan all together in the dark, and there were uneasy mutters when an exceptionally heavy sea boarded the ship and tons of water could be heard scuttling about as if trying to get at them. The boatswain was keeping up a gruff talk, but a more unreasonable lot of men, he said afterwards, he had never been with. They were snug enough there out of harm's way, and not wanted to do anything either, and yet they did nothing but grumble and complain peevishly like so many sick kids. Finally one of them said that if there had been at least some light to see each other's noses by it would not be so bad. It was making him crazy, he declared, to lie there in the dark waiting for the blamed hooker to sink. "Why don't you go outside, then, and be done with it?" the boatswain turned on him.

This called up general execration. The boatswain found himself overwhelmed with reproaches of all sorts. They seemed to take it ill that a lamp was not instantly created for them out of nothing. They would whine after a light to get drowned by— anyhow! And though the unreason of their revilings was patent, since no one could hope to reach the lamp-room, which was forward, he became greatly distressed. He did not think it was decent of them to nag at him like this. He said so and was met by a general contumely. He sought refuge, therefore, in an embittered silence. Their grumbling and sighing and muttering worried him greatly, but by-and-by it occurred to him that there were six globe lamps hung in the 'tween-deck and that there could be no harm in depriving the coolies of one of them.

The *Nan-Shan* had an athwartship bunker which, being frequently used as cargo space, communicated by an iron door with the fore 'tween-deck. Its manhole was the foremost one in the alleyway. The boatswain could get in, therefore, without coming out on deck at all; but, to his great surprise, he found he could induce no one to help him in taking off the manhole cover. He groped for it all the same, but one of the crew lying in his way refused to budge. "Why! I only want to get you that blamed light you are crying for," he expostulated, almost pitifully. Somebody told him to go and put his head in a bag. He regretted he could not recognise the voice and that it was too dark to see, otherwise, as he said, he would have put a head on *that* son of a sea-cook, anyway, sink or swim. Nevertheless, he had made up his mind to show them he could get light, if he were to die for it. Through the violence of the ship's rolling, every movement was dangerous. To be lying down seemed labour enough. He nearly broke his neck dropping into the bunker. He said he fell down, and was kept shooting from side to side in the dangerous company of a heavy iron bar—a coal-trimmer's slice probably—left down there by somebody. This thing made him as nervous as though it had been a wild beast. He could not see it, the inside of the bunker coated with coal dust being perfectly and impenetrably black, but he heard it sliding and clattering and striking, here and there, always in the neighbourhood of his head. It seemed to make an extraordinary noise, too, to give heavy thumps as though it had been as big as a bridge girder. This was remarkable enough for him to notice while he was flung from port to starboard and back again, and clawing desperately the smooth sides of the bunker in the endeavour to stop himself. The door into the 'tween-deck not fitting quite true, he saw a thread of dim light at the bottom.

Being a sailor and a still active man, he did not want much of a chance to regain his feet; and, as luck would have it, in scrambling up he put his hand on the iron slice, picking it up as he rose. Otherwise he would have been afraid of the thing breaking his legs or at least knocking him down again. At first he stood still. He felt unsafe in this darkness that seemed to make the ship's motion unfamiliar, unforeseen, and difficult to counteract. He felt so much shaken for a moment that he dared

not move for fear of "taking charge again." He had no mind
to get battered to pieces in that bunker.

He had hit his head twice; he was dazed a little. He seemed to
hear yet so plainly the clatter and bangs of the iron slice flying
about his ears that he tightened his grip to prove to himself he
had it there safe in his hand. He was vaguely amazed at the
plainness with which down there he could hear the gale raging.
Its howls and shrieks seemed to take on in the emptiness of the
bunker something of the human character, of human rage and
pain—being not vast, but infinitely poignant. And there were,
with every roll, thumps, too,—profound, ponderous thumps, as
if a bulky object of five-ton weight or so had got play in the hold.
But there was no such thing in the cargo. Something on deck?
Impossible. Or alongside? Couldn't be.

XV

HE thought all this quickly, clearly, competently, like a seaman,
and in the end was puzzled. It occurred to him, too, that the
hands in the alleyway had started scrambling and howling since
he had left them, in a sort of confused, uproarious way. But as
the manhole had remained open he ought to have heard them
more distinctly, much nearer, as it were. This noise, though,
came deadened, from outside, together with the washing and
pouring of water on deck above his head. Wind? Must be. It
made down there a row like the shouting of a big lot of crazed
men. And he discovered in himself a desire for a light, too, if
only to get drowned by, and a nervous anxiety to get out of that
bunker as quick as possible.

He pulled back the bolt; the heavy iron plate turned on its
hinges; and it was as though he had opened the door to sounds
of the tempest. A gust of hoarse yelling met him; the air was
still; and the rushing of water overhead was covered by a tumult
of strangled, throaty shrieks that produced the effect of desperate

confusion. He straddled his legs the whole width of the doorway and stretched his neck. And at first he perceived only what he had come to seek—four small, yellow flames swinging violently on the great body of the dusk.

It was like the gallery of a mine, with a row of stanchions in the middle and cross-beams overhead, penetrating into the gloom ahead—infinitely. And to port there loomed like the caving in of one of the sides a bulky mass with a slanting outline. The whole place, with the shadows and the shapes, moved all the time—irresistibly. The boatswain glared; the ship lurched to starboard and a great howl came from that mass that had the slant of fallen earth.

Pieces of wood whizzed past. Planks, he thought, inexpressibly startled and flinging back his head. At his feet a man went sliding over, open-eyed, on his back, straining with uplifted arms for nothing; and another came bounding like a detached stone with his head between his legs and his hands clenched. His pigtail whipped in the air, he made a grab at the boatswain's legs, and from his opened hand a bright white disc rolled against the boatswain's foot. He recognised a silver dollar, as one would recognise a familiar object in the improbabilities of a nightmare.

He yelled at it with astonishment. With a precipitated sound of trampling and shuffling of bare feet and with guttural cries, the vague mound piled up to port, detached itself from the ship's side, and shifted to starboard, sliding, inert and struggling, to a dull, brutal thump. The cries ceased. The boatswain heard a long moan, the roar and whistling of the wind; he saw an inextricable confusion of heads and shoulders, naked soles kicking upwards, fists raised, tumbling backs, legs, pigtails, faces. "Good Lord!" he cried, horrified, and banged to the iron door upon this vision.

This was what he had come on the bridge to tell. He could not keep it to himself, and on board ship there is only one man to whom it is worth while to unburden yourself. On his passage back the hands in the alleyway swore at him for a fool. Why didn't he bring that lamp? What the devil did coolies matter to anybody? And when he came out the extremity of the ship made what went on inside of her appear indeed of little moment.

At first he thought he had left the alleyway in the very moment of her sinking. The bridge ladders had been washed away, but an enormous sea filling the after-deck floated him up. After that he had to lie on his stomach for some time, holding to a ring-bolt, getting his breath now and then, and swallowing salt water. He struggled farther on his hands and knees, too frightened and distracted to turn back. In this way he reached the after part of the wheel-house. In that comparatively sheltered spot he found the second mate. He was pleasantly surprised, his impression being that everybody on deck must have been washed away a long time ago. He asked eagerly where the Captain was.

The second mate was lying low, like a malignant little animal under a hedge. "Captain? Gone overboard after getting us into this mess." The mate, too, for all he knew or cared. Another fool. They wouldn't have a chance to kill any more good men. Didn't matter. Everybody was going by-and-by.

The boatswain crawled out again into the strength of the wind; not because he much expected to find anybody, he said, but just to get away from "that man." He crawled out as outcasts go to face an inclement world. Hence his great joy at finding Jukes and the Captain. But what was going on in the 'tween-deck was to him a minor matter by that time, like a distant and still memory made more faint by the exigencies of a turbulent existence. Besides, it was difficult to make yourself heard. But he managed to convey the idea that the Chinamen had broken adrift and that he had come up on purpose to report this. As to the hands, they were all right. Then, almost appeased, he subsided on the deck in a sitting posture, hugging with his arms and legs the stand of the engine-room telegraph—an iron casting as thick as a post. When that went—why, he expected he would go too. He gave no more thought to the coolies.

Captain MacWhirr made Jukes understand he wanted him to go down below—to see.

"What could I do, sir?" and the trembling of his whole wet body caused his voice to sound like bleating.

"See! Bo's'n—says—adrift."

"That bo's'n is a confounded fool," howled Jukes shakily.

What was the good of going to see? He didn't want to see. What could one do single-handed with two hundred Chinamen? It was impossible to make that man understand the most obvious things. The absurdity of the demand made upon him revolted Jukes. He was as unwilling to go as if the moment he had left the deck the ship were sure to sink.

"I must know—can't leave——"

"They'll settle, sir."

"Fight—bo's'n says fight—Why? Can't have—fighting—board ship. . . . Rather keep you here—case—I should—washed overboard myself. . . . Stop it—some way—You see and tell me—through engine-room tube. . . . Don't want you—come up here—too often. . . . Dangerous—moving about—deck."

Jukes, held with his head in chancery, had to listen to what seemed horrible suggestions.

"Don't want—you get lost—so long—ship don't. . . . Rout—Good man—Ship—through this—all right yet."

All at once Jukes understood he would have to go.

"Do you think she will?" he screamed.

But the wind, as if made angry by Captain MacWhirr, seemed to throw itself at them with redoubled force and devoured the reply out of which Jukes heard only the one word pronounced with great energy.

". . . Always. . . ."

Captain MacWhirr released Jukes and, bending over the boatswain, yelled, "Get back with the mate." Jukes only knew that the arm was gone off his shoulders. He was dismissed with his orders—to do what? He was exasperated into letting go his hold carelessly and on the instant was blown away. It seemed to him he would be blown right over the stern. He flung himself down and the boatswain, who was following, fell on him.

"Don't you get up yet, sir," cried the boatswain. "No hurry!"

"He and Jukes looked at each other." Illustration for *Typhoon* by Maurice Greiffenhagen. *(p. 65)*

A sea swept over. Jukes understood the boatswain to say that the bridge ladders were gone. "I'll lower you down, sir, by your hands," he screamed. He shouted also something about the smokestack being as likely to go overboard as not. Jukes thought it very possible and imagined the fires out, the ship helpless—and he down there. The boatswain by his side kept on yelling. Was it a warning? "What? What is it?" Jukes cried ·distressfully, and the other repeated, "What would my old woman say if she saw me now?"

XVI

IN the alleyway, where a lot of water splashed in the dark, the men were still as death, till Jukes stumbled against one of them and cursed him savagely for being in the way. Two or three voices then asked, eager and weak, "Any chance for us, sir?"

"What's the matter with you fools?" he said brutally. He felt as though he could throw himself down amongst them and never move any more. But they seemed cheered, and, in the midst of warnings, "Look out!"—"Mind the manhole lid, sir," they lowered him into the bunker. The boatswain tumbled down after him, and as soon as he had picked himself up he remarked:

"She would say, 'Serve you right, you old fool, for going to sea.' "

The boatswain had some means, and made a point of alluding to them frequently. His wife—a fat woman—and two grown-up daughters kept a green-grocer's shop.

In the dark, Jukes, unsteady on his legs, listened to a faint thunderous patter. A deadened screaming went on steadily at his elbow as it were; and from above the louder tumult of the storm descended upon these near sounds. His head swam. To him, too, in that bunker, the motion of the ship seemed novel and menacing, sapping his resolution as though he had never been afloat before.

He had half a mind to scramble out, but the remembrance of

Captain MacWhirr's voice made this impossible. And yet he felt he could do nothing. He had an inclination to sit down, and the feeling of helplessness in that beastly black hole made him sick of his life. His orders were to go and see. What was the good of it? he wanted to know. Enraged, he told himself he would see—of course. But the boatswain, staggering clumsily, warned him to be careful how he opened that door; there was a blamed fight going on. And Jukes, as if in great bodily pain, desired irritably to know what the devil they were fighting for.

"Dollars. Dollars, sir. All them rotten chests got burst open. Blamed money skipping all over the place and they are tumbling after it head over heels, tearing and biting like anything. A regular little hell in there."

Jukes convulsively opened the door. The short boatswain by his side peered too, like a curious baboon.

One of the lamps had gone out, broken perhaps. Rancorous, guttural cries burst out loudly on their ears, and a strange panting sound,—the working of all these straining breasts. A hard blow hit the side of the ship; water fell above with a stunning shock, and in the forefront of the gloom, where the air was reddish and thick, Jukes saw a head bang the deck violently, two thick calves waving, muscular arms twined round a naked body, a yellow face open-mouthed and with a set, wild stare look up and slide away. An empty chest clattered, turning over, a man fell head first with a jump as if lifted by a kick; and further off, indistinct, a mass of men streamed like rolling stones down a bank, beating the deck with their feet and flourishing their arms wildly. The hatchway ladder was loaded with coolies, swarming on it like bees on a branch. They hung in a crawling, stirring cluster, beating with their fists the underside of the battened hatch, and the headlong rush of water was heard in the intervals of their yelling. The ship heeled over more and they began to drop off; first one, then two, then all the rest together, falling straight with a great cry. Jukes was confounded. The boatswain, with gruff anxiety, begged him, "Don't you go in there, sir."

The whole place seemed to twist upon itself, jumping incessantly the while, and when the ship rose to a sea Jukes fancied that all these men would be shot upon him in a body. He swung the door to, and with trembling hands pushed at the bolt.

As soon as his mate had gone, Captain MacWhirr sidled and staggered as far as the wheel-house. Its door being hinged forward, he had to fight the gale for admittance, and when at last he managed to enter, it was as if he had been fired through the wood. He stood within, holding the handle.

The steering gear leaked steam and in the confined space the glass of the binnacle made a shiny oval in a thin white fog. The wind howled, hummed, whistled, with sudden booming gusts that rattled the doors and the shutters in the vicious patter of sprays. Two coils of lead-line and a small canvas bag hung on a long lanyard swung wide off and came back, clinging to the bulkheads. The gratings under foot were nearly afloat, with every sweeping blow of a sea water squirted violently through the cracks all round the door, and the man at the helm had flung down his cap, his coat, and stood propped against the gear-casing in a striped cotton shirt open on his breast. The little brass wheel in his hands seemed a bright and fragile toy. The cords of his neck stood hard and lean, a dark patch lay in the hollow of his throat, and his face was still and sunken as in death.

Captain MacWhirr wiped his eyes. The sea that had nearly taken him overboard had to his great annoyance washed his sou'wester hat off his bald head. The fluffy, fair hair, soaked and darkened, resembled a mean skein of cotton threads festooned round his bare skull. He breathed heavily and his face, glistening with sea water, was a hot crimson with the wind, with the sting of sprays. He looked as though he had come off sweating from before a furnace.

"You here?" he muttered heavily.

The second mate had also found his way into the wheel-house. He had fixed himself in a corner with his knees up, a fist pressed against each temple, and this attitude suggested rage, sorrow,

resignation, surrender, with a sort of concentrated unforgive-
ness. He said mournfully and defiantly:

"My watch below now. Ain't it?"

The steam-gear clattered, stopped, clattered again; and the
helmsman's eyeballs seemed to project out of a hungry face, as
if the compass card behind the binnacle glass had been meat.
God knows how long he had been there steering, as if forgotten
by all his shipmates. The bells had not been struck, there had
been no reliefs, the ship's routine had gone down wind, but he
was trying to keep her head north-northeast. The rudder might
have been gone for all he knew, the fires out, the engines broken
down, the ship ready to roll over like a corpse. He was anxious
not to get muddled and lose control of her head, because the
compass card swung far both ways, wriggling on the pivot, and
sometimes seemed to whirl right around. It was hard to make
out the course she was making. He suffered from mental stress.
He was horribly afraid also of the wheel-house going. Mountains
of water kept on falling on it. When the ship took one of her
desperate dives the corners of his lips twitched.

Captain MacWhirr looked up at the wheel-house clock.
Screwed to the bulkhead, it had a white face, on which the
black hands appeared to stand quite still. It was half-past one
in the morning.

"Another day," he muttered to himself. The second mate
heard him and, lifting his head as one grieving amongst ruins:

"You won't see it break," he exclaimed. His wrists and his
knees could be seen to shake violently. "No, by God, you
won't! . . ." He took his head again between his fists.

The body of the helmsman had moved slightly, but his head
didn't budge on his neck,—like a stone head fixed to look one
way from a column. During a roll that all but took his booted
legs from under him, and in the very stagger to save himself,
Captain MacWhirr said austerely:

"Don't you pay any attention to that man."

And then, with an indefinable change of tone, very grave,
he added:

"He isn't on duty."

The sailor said nothing. The hurricane boomed, shaking the little place, which seemed air-tight; and the light of the binnacle flickered all the time.

"You haven't been relieved," Captain MacWhirr went on, looking down. "I want you to stick on, though, as long as you can. You've got the hang of her. Another man coming here might make a mess of it. Wouldn't do. No child's play. And the hands are probably busy with a job down below. . . . Think you can?"

The steering-gear leaped into an abrupt short clatter, stopped smouldering like an ember, and the still man, with a motionless gaze, burst out as if all the passion in him had gone into his lips:

"By heavens, sir, I can steer for ever if you don't talk to me."

"Oh! Aye! All right. . . ." The Captain lifted his eyes for the first time to the man. . . . "Hackett."

And he seemed to dismiss this matter from his mind. He stooped to the engine-room speaking-tube, blew in, and bent his head. Mr. Rout, below, answered, and at once Captain Mac-Whirr put his lips to the mouthpiece.

XVII

WITH the uproar of the gale around him he applied alternately his lips and his ear, and the engineer's voice mounted to him, harsh and as if out of the heat of an engagement. One of the stokers was disabled, the others had given up, the second engineer and the donkey-man were firing up. The third was standing by the steam valve. The engines were being tended by hand. How was it above?

"Bad enough. It rests with you," said Captain MacWhirr. Was the mate down there yet? No? He would be presently. Would Mr. Rout let him talk through the speaking-tube. Through the deck speaking-tube. Because he—the Captain—was

going out again on the bridge directly. There was some trouble
with the Chinamen. They were fighting amongst themselves.
Couldn't allow fighting, anyhow.

Mr. Rout had gone away, and Captain MacWhirr could feel
against his ear the pulsation of the engines like the beat of the
ship's heart. Mr. Rout's voice down there cried something, dis-
tantly. The ship pitched headlong, the pulsation leaped with
a hissing tumult and stopped dead. Captain MacWhirr's face
was impassive and his eyes were fixed aimlessly at the crouching
shape of the second mate. Again Mr. Rout's voice cried out in
the depths, and the pulsating beat recommenced, with slow
strokes—growing swift.

Mr. Rout came back to the tube.

"It don't matter much what they do," he said hastily; and
then, with irritation, "She takes these dives as if she never meant
to come up again."

"Awful sea," said the Captain's voice from above.

"Don't let me drive her under," barked Solomon Rout up
the pipe.

"Dark and rain. Can't see what's coming," uttered the voice.
"Must—keep—her—moving—enough to steer—and chance it," it
went on to state distinctly.

"I am doing as much as I dare."

"We are—getting—smashed up—a good deal up here," proceeded the voice mildly. "Doing—fairly well—though. Of course,
if the wheel-house should go——"

Mr. Rout, bending an attentive ear, muttered peevishly something under his breath.

But the deliberate voice up there became animated to ask:

"Jukes turned up yet?" Then, after a short wait: "I wish he
would bear a hand. I want him to be done and come up here
in case of anything—look after the ship. I am all alone. The
second mate lost . . ."

"What?" shouted Mr. Rout into the engine-room, taking his
head away. Then up the tube he cried, "Gone overboard?" and
clapped his ear to.

"Lost his nerve," the voice from above was proceeding in a matter-of-fact tone. "Damn awkward, this."

Mr. Rout, listening with bowed neck, opened his eyes wide. However, he heard something like the sounds of a scuffle and broken exclamations coming down to him. He strained his hearing, and all the time Beale, the third engineer, with his arms upraised, held between the palms of his hands the rim of a little black wheel projecting at the side of a big copper pipe. He seemed to be poising it above his head, as though it were a correct attitude in some sort of game.

To steady himself he pressed his shoulder against the white bulkhead, with one knee bent and a sweat-rag tucked in the belt hung upon his hip. His smooth cheek was begrimed and flushed, and the coal-dust on his eyelids, like the black pencilling of a make-up, enhanced the liquid brilliance of the whites, giving to his youthful face something of a feminine, exotic, and fascinating aspect. When the ship pitched he would with hasty movements of his hands screw hard at the little wheel.

"Gone crazy," began the Captain's voice suddenly. "Rushed at me—just now. Had to knock him down—this minute. You heard, Mr. Rout?"

"The devil!" muttered Mr. Rout. "Look out, Beale."

His voice rang out like the blast of a warning trumpet between the iron walls of the engine-room. Painted white, they rose high into the dusk of the skylight, sloping like a roof; and the whole lofty space resembled a chamber in a monument, divided by floors of iron grating, with lights flickering at different levels, and the still gloom within the columnar stir of machinery under the motionless swelling of the cylinders. A loud and wild resonance, made up of all the noises of the hurricane, dwelt in the still warmth of the air. There was in it the smell of hot metal, of oil, and a slight mist of steam. The blows of the sea seemed to traverse it, in an unringing, stunning shock, from side to side.

Gleams, like pale, long flames, trembled upon the polish of metal, from the flooring below the enormous crank-heads emerged in their turns with a flash of brass and steel—going over; while the connecting rods, big-jointed, like skeleton limbs, seemed to thrust them down and pull them up again with an irresistible precision. And deep in the half-light other rods dodged to and fro, crossheads nodded quickly, disks of metal rubbed against each other, swift and gentle in a commingling of shadows and gleams.

XVIII

SOMETIMES all those movements would slow down simultaneously, as if they had been the functions of a living organism —powerful, silent, patient, and unerring, but stricken suddenly by the blight of languor; and Mr. Rout's eyes would blaze darker in his long, pale face. He was fighting this fight in a pair of carpet slippers. A short, shiny jacket barely covered his loins, and his pale wrists protruded far out of the tight sleeves as though the emergency had added to his stature, lengthened his limbs, augmented his pallor, hollowed his eyes.

He moved, climbing high up, disappeared low down, with a restless, purposeful industry, and when he stood still, holding the guard-rail in front of the starting-gear, he would keep glancing to the right at the steam-gauge, at the water-gauge, upon the white wall in the light of a swaying lamp. The mouths of two speaking-tubes gaped stupidly at his elbow, and the dial of the engine-room telegraph resembled a clock of large diameter, bearing on its face curt words instead of figures. They stood out heavily black, around the black pivot-head of the solitary hand, emphatically symbolic of loud exclamations: Ahead—Astern— Slow—Half—Stand by . . . and the fat black hand pointed down to the word Full—which, thus singled out, captured the eye as a sharp cry secures attention.

The wood-encased bulk of the low-pressure cylinder, frowning portly from above, emitted a faint wheeze at every thrust, and, except for that low hiss, the engines worked their steel limbs headlong or slow with a silent, determined smoothness. And all this—the white walls, the moving steel, the floor plates under Solomon Rout's feet, the floors of iron grating above his head, the dusk and the gleams—uprose and sank continuously, with one accord, upon the harsh wash of the waves against the ship's side. The whole loftiness of the place, booming hollow to the great voice of the wind, swayed at the top like a tree, would lay over bodily, as if borne down this way and that by tremendous blasts.

"You've got to hurry up," shouted Mr. Rout, as soon as he saw Jukes.

Jukes's glance was wandering and tipsy, his red face was puffy, as though he had overslept himself. He burst into the engine-room like a man who had been racing over hills and dales for his life. He had had an arduous road and had travelled over it with immense vivacity, the agitation of his mind corresponding to the scrambling exertions of his body. He had rushed up out of the bunker—stumbling in the alleyway amongst a lot of bewildered men who, trod upon, asked "What's up, sir?" in awed mutters all round him in the dark—down into the stoke-hole, missing many iron rungs in his hurry, into a place deep as a well, black as Tophet, narrow like a corridor, tipping over back and forth like a seesaw. Lumps of coal skipped to and fro from end to end, rattling like an avalanche of pebbles on a slope of iron.

Somebody in there moaned with pain, and somebody else crouched over what seemed the body of a man; a lusty voice blasphemed, and the glow under each fire-grate was like a pool of flaming blood radiating quietly in a velvety blackness.

A gust of wind struck upon the nape of Jukes's neck, and next moment he felt it streaming about his wet ankles. The stoke-hole ventilators hummed; and in front of the six fire-doors two men, stripped to the waist, staggered and stopped, apparently wrestling with two shovels.

"Hallo! Plenty of draught now," yelled the second at once, as though he had been all the time looking out for Jukes. The donkey-man, a dapper little chap with a dazzling fair skin and a tiny, gingery mustache, worked in a sort of mute transport. They were keeping a full head of steam, and a profound rumbling sound, as of an empty furniture van trotting over a bridge, made a sustained bass to all the other noises of the place.

"Blowing off all the time," went on yelling the second. With a sound as of a hundred scoured saucepans the orifice of a ventilator spat upon his shoulder a sudden gush of salt water, and he volleyed a stream of curses upon all things on earth, including his own soul; ripping and raving, and all the time attending to his business. With a sharp clash of metal, the ardent pale glare of the fire opened upon his bullet head, showing his spluttering lips, his insolent eyes, and with a clash closed like the white-hot wink of an iron eye.

"Where's the blooming ship? Can you tell me—blast my eyes! Under water—or what? Are the condemned cowls gone to Hades, hey? Don't you know anything—you jolly sailor-man, you?"

Jukes, after a bewildered moment, had been helped by a roll to dart through, and as soon as his eyes took in the comparative vastness, peace, and brilliance of the engine-room, the ship, settling her stern heavily in the water, sent him charging head down upon Mr. Rout.

The chief's arm, long like a tentacle and straightening as if worked by a spring, went out to meet him and deflected his rush into a spin towards the speaking-tubes. At the same time Mr. Rout repeated earnestly:

"You've got to hurry up—whatever it is."

Jukes yelled, "Are you there, sir?" and listened. Nothing. Suddenly the roar of the wind fell straight into his ear, but presently a small voice shoved aside the shouting hurricane quietly:

"You, Jukes?—Well?"

Jukes was ready to talk; it was only time that seemed to be wanting. And, somehow, he mistrusted the ability of the other man to understand. It was easy enough to account for everything. He could perfectly imagine the coolies battened down in the reeking 'tween-deck, lying sick and scared between the rows of chests. Then one of these chests, or perhaps several at once breaking loose in a roll, knocking out others, sides splitting, lids flying open, and all these clumsy Chinamen staggering up in a body to save their property. Afterwards, every fling of the ship would hurl that tramping, yelling mob here and there, from side to side, in a whirl of smashed wood, torn clothing, rolling dollars. And a struggle once started, they would be unable to stop themselves. Nothing could stop them now except main force. It was a disaster. He had seen it, and that was all he could say. Some of them must be dead, he believed. The rest would go on fighting. . . .

He sent up his words tripping over each other, crowding the narrow tube. They mounted as if into a silence of an enlightened comprehension dwelling alone up there with a storm. There was no circumventing this development. And he wanted to be dismissed from the face of that odious trouble intruding on the great need of the ship.

XIX

HE listened. Before his eyes the engines turned with slow labour that in the moment of going off into a mad fling would stop dead at Mr. Rout's shout, "Look out, Beale!" They seemed to wait in an intelligent immobility stilled in midstroke, a heavy crank arrested on the cant, as if conscious of time itself being on their side. Then, with a "Now, then!" from the chief and the sound of a breath expelled through clenched teeth, they would accomplish the interrupted revolution and begin another.

There was the prudent sagacity of enormous strength in their movements. This was their work—this coaxing of a ship over the fury of waves and into the fierce eye of the wind. Mr. Rout's chin had sunk on his breast, and at times he watched them from under his forehead like a man plunged deep in thought.

The voice that kept the hurricane out of Jukes's ear began: "Take the hands . . ." and left off unexpectedly.

"What could I do with the hands, sir?"

A harsh, abrupt, imperious clang exploded suddenly. The three pairs of eyes flew up to the telegraph dial to see the hand dart upwards from "Full" to "Stop" as if snatched by a devil. And then these three men in the engine-room had the intimate sensation of a check upon the ship, of a strange shrinking, as if she had gathered herself for a leap.

"Stop her!" bellowed Mr. Rout.

Nobody,—not even Captain MacWhirr, who caught sight of a white line of foam coming on at such a height that he couldn't believe his eyes,—nobody knew the deepness of that sea and the awful depth of the hollow the hurricane had scooped behind that running wall of water.

It raced to meet the ship, and, with a pause, as of girding the loins, she lifted her bows and leaped. The flames in all the lamps sank, darkening the engine-room. One went out. She had not leaped quite high enough, for with a tearing crash and a swirling, raving tumult, tons of water fell upon her deck as though she had darted under the very foot of a cataract.

Down there they looked at each other, stunned.

"Swept from end to end, by God!" bawled Jukes.

She pitched into the hollow straight down as if tumbling from a cliff. The engine-room toppled forward menacingly, like the inside of a tower nodding in an earthquake. An awful racket of iron things falling came from the stoke-hole.

Instead of recovering herself she hung head down while the souls of men on board cried aloud to her to rise. She hung long enough for Beale to drop on his hands and knees as if he meant to fly on all fours out of the engine-room, and for Mr. Rout to turn his head slowly, rigid, cavernous, with the lower jaw dropping. Jukes had shut his eyes, and his face in a moment became hopelessly blank, like the face of a blind man.

But she rose slowly, staggering as if she had to lift a mountain with her bows.

Mr. Rout shut his mouth, Jukes blinked, and little Beale stood up hastily.

"Another one like this and that's the last of her!" cried the chief.

He and Jukes looked at each other, and the same thought came into their heads—the Captain! Everything must have been swept away. Steering-gear gone—men gone—ship like a log. All over directly.

"Rush!" ejaculated Mr. Rout thickly, glaring with enlarged, doubtful eyes at Jukes, who answered him by an irresolute glance.

The clang of the telegraph gong soothed them instantly. The black hand dropped in a flash from "Stop" to "Full."

"Now then, Beale!" cried Mr. Rout.

The steam hissed low. The piston-rods slid in and out. Jukes put his ear to the tube. The voice was ready for him. It said:

"Pick up all the money. Bear a hand now. I'll want you up here." And that was all.

"Sir?" called up Jukes. There was no answer. It struck him that if he had got an answer he wouldn't have known what to say. Nothing could be said.

He staggered away as a defeated man staggers way from the field of battle. He had got in some way or other a cut above his eyebrow, a cut to the bone. He was not aware of it in the least: quantities of the China Sea, large enough to break his neck for him, had gone over his head, had cleaned, washed, and salted that wound. It did not bleed, but only gaped red; and this gash over the eye, his dishevelled hair, the disorder of his streaming clothes, gave him the aspect of a man worsted in a fight with fists.

"Got to pick up the dollars," he appealed to Mr. Rout, smiling pitifully, at random.

"What's that? Pick up . . . ? I don't care . . ." Then quivering in every muscle, but with an exaggeration of paternal tone, "Go away now, for God's sake. You deck people'll drive me silly. There's that second mate been going for the old man. Don't you know? You fellows are going wrong for want of something to do . . ."

At these words Jukes discovered in himself the beginnings of anger. He turned to go the way he had come, full of hot scorn for the chief. In the stoke-hole the plump donkey-man manœuvred his shovel mutely, as if his tongue had been cut out; but the second was carrying on like a sort of noisy, undaunted maniac, who, nevertheless, had preserved his skill in the art of stoking under a marine boiler.

"Hallo, you wandering officer! Hey! Can't you get some of your slush-slingers to wind up a few of them ashes? I am getting choked with them here. Curse it! Hallo! Hey! Remember the articles!—'sailors and firemen to assist each other.' Hey! D' ye hear?"

Jukes was climbing out frantically, and the other, lifting up his face after him, howled:

"Can't you speak? What are you poking about here for? What's your game, anyhow?"

A frenzy possessed Jukes. By the time he was back amongst the men in the darkness of the alleyway he felt ready to wring all their necks at the slightest sign of hanging back. The very thought of it exasperated him. *He* couldn't hang back. They shouldn't!

XX

THE impetuosity with which he came amongst them carried them along. They had already been excited and startled at all his comings and goings. By the fierceness and rapidity of his movements, more felt than seen in his rushes, he appeared formidable—busied with matters of life and death that brooked no delay. At his first word he heard them drop into the bunker one after another obediently, with heavy thumps.

They were not clear as to what would have to be done. "What is it? What is it?" they were asking each other. The boatswain tried to explain; the sounds of a great scuffle surprised them; and the mighty shocks reverberating awfully in the black bunker made them think fearfully of the gale. When the boat-swain threw open the door it seemed to them that an eddy of the hurricane stealing through the iron sides of the ship had set all the coolies whirling like dust: there came to them a con-fused uproar, a tempestuous tumult, a fierce mutter, gusts of screams dying away, and the tramping of feet mingling with the blows of the sea.

For a moment they glared, blocking the doorway. Jukes pushed through them brutally. He said nothing and simply darted in. The Chinamen on the ladder, struggling suicidally to break through the battened hatch to a swamped deck, fell off, and he disappeared under them like a man overtaken by an ava-lanche. The boatswain yelled excitedly:

"Come along! Get the mate! He'll be trampled to death. Come on!"

They rushed in, stamping on breasts, on fingers, on faces, catching their feet in heaps of clothing, kicking broken wood; but before they could get hold of him Jukes emerged, waist-deep amongst clawing hands. In the instant he had been lost to view all the buttons of his jacket had gone, its back got split up to the collar, his waistcoat had been torn open. The central, struggling mass went over to the roll, dark, indistinct, helpless, with a wild gleam of eyes in the dim light that swayed after it and jerked when it thumped the ship's side.

"Leave me alone—damn you!" screeched Jukes. "Drive them forward! Watch your chance when she pitches. Forward with them! Drive them against the bulkhead! Jam 'em up!"

The rushing of these eleven men into the seething 'tween-deck was like a splash of cold water into a boiling caldron. The commotion as it were sank for a moment.

The bulk of Chinamen were locked in such a compact scrimmage that, linking their arms and aided by an appalling dive of the ship, the seamen sent it forward in one great shove, like a solid block. Behind their backs small clusters and loose bodies tumbled from side to side.

The boatswain performed prodigious feats of strength. With his long arms open and each great paw clutching at a stanchion, he stopped the rush of seven entwined Chinamen rolling like a boulder. His joints cracked; he said, "Ha!" and they flew apart. But the carpenter showed the greater intelligence. He went back into the alleyway, where he found several coils of cargo gear, chain, and rope. With these, life-lines were rigged.

There was really no resistance. The struggle, however it began, had turned into a scramble of blind panic. If they had started after their dollars, they were by that time fighting only for their footing. They would take each other by the throat merely to save themselves from being hurled about. Whoever got a hold anywhere would kick at the others who caught at his legs and hung on, till a roll sent them flying together across the deck.

The coming of the white devils was a terror. Had they come to kill? Those torn out of the ruck became very limp in the seamen's hands; some, dragged aside by the heels, were passive —like dead bodies, with open, fixed eyes; here and there one would fall on his knees as if begging for mercy; several whom the excess of fear made unruly were hit with hard fists between the eyes and cowed, while those who were hurt submitted to rough handling, blinking rapidly without a plaint. Faces streamed with blood; there were raw places on the shaven heads, scratches, bruises, gashes. The broken porcelain out of the chests was mostly responsible for the latter. Here and there a China-man with his pig-tail unplaited nursed a bleeding sole.

They had been ranged closely after having been shaken into submission, cuffed a little to allay excitement, addressed in gruff words of encouragement that sounded like promises of evil. They sat on the deck in ghastly, drooping rows; and, at the end, the carpenter, with two hands to help him, moved from place to place, setting taut and hitching the lines. The boat-swain, with one leg and one arm embracing a stanchion, was busy with a lamp pressed to his breast, trying to get a light, and growling all the time like an industrious gorilla. The figures of seamen stooped repeatedly, with the movements of gleaners, and everything was being flung into the bunker—clothing, smashed wood, broken china, and the dollars too, gathered up in men's jackets. Now and then one of them would stagger towards the doorway with his arms full of rubbish, and rows of dolorous, slanting eyes followed his movements.

With every roll of the ship the long rows of Celestials would sway forward brokenly, and her headlong dives knocked together the line of shaven polls from end to end. When the wash of tons of water rolling on the deck, within reach of his hand, died away for a moment, it seemed to Jukes, yet quivering from his exertions, that in his mad struggle down there he had overcome the wind somehow; that a silence had fallen upon the ship, a silence in which the sea knocked thunderously at her sides.

Everything had been cleared out of the 'tween-deck; all the wreckage, as the men said. They stood erect and tottering, out of a multitude of heads and drooping shoulders. Here and there a coolie sobbed for his breath; where the high light fell Jukes could see the salient ribs of one, the yellow, wishful face of another; bowed necks; or would meet a dull stare directed at his face. He was amazed that there had been no corpses, but the lot of them seemed at their last gasp, and they appeared to him more pitiful than if they had all been dead.

Suddenly one of the coolies began to speak. The light came and went on his lean, straining face; he threw his head up like a baying hound. From the bunker came the sounds of knocking and the tinkle of some dollars rolling loose: he stretched out his arm, his mouth yawned black, and the incomprehensible guttural words that did not seem to belong to a human language—the hooting, babbling utterance of the man—startled Jukes as if a brute had tried to be eloquent.

Grunts began to be heard about the 'tween-deck. Two more started mouthing what seemed to Jukes fierce denunciations.

He ordered the hands out hurriedly. He went last himself, backing through the door, while the grunts rose to a loud murmur and hands were extended after him as after a malefactor. The boatswain shot the bolt and remarked uneasily:

"Seems as if the wind had dropped, sir."

The men were glad to get back into the alleyway. Secretly each of them thought that at the last moment he could rush out on deck, and that was a comfort. There is something horribly repugnant in the idea of being drowned under a deck. Now they had done with the Chinamen, they again became conscious of the ship's position.

Jukes, on coming out, found himself up to the neck in the noisy water. He gained the bridge and discovered he could see shapes as if his sight had become preternaturally penetrating. He saw faint outlines. They recalled not the familiar aspect of the *Nan-Shan*, but something remembered—an old dismantled steamer he had seen years ago rotting on a mudbank. She recalled that wreck.

There was no wind, not a breath, except the faint currents created by the lurches of the ship. The smoke tossed out of the funnel was settling down upon her deck. He breathed it as he passed forward. He felt the deliberate throb of the engines and heard small sounds that seemed to have survived the great uproar: the knocking of broken fittings, the rapid tumbling of some piece of wreckage on the bridge. He traced the squat shape of his Captain holding on to a twisted bridge-rail, motionless, and swaying as if rooted to the planks. The unexpected stillness of the air oppressed him like an overpowering wind.

"We have done it, sir," he gasped.

"Thought you would," said Captain MacWhirr.

"Did you?" murmured Jukes to himself, bitterly.

"Wind fell all at once," went on the Captain. Jukes burst out:

"If you think it was an easy job . . ."

But his Captain, clinging to the rail, paid no attention.

"According to the books the worst is not over yet."

"If most of them hadn't been half dead with seasickness and fright not one of us would have come out alive," said Jukes.

"Had to do what's fair by them," mumbled MacWhirr, stolidly. "You don't find everything in books."

"Why, I believe they would have risen on us if I hadn't ordered the hands out of that, pretty quick," continued Jukes with warmth.

XXI

AFTER the whisper of their shouts their ordinary tones, so distinct, seemed to them very loud in the amazing stillness of the air. It seemed to them they were talking in a dark and echoing vault.

Through a jagged aperture in the dome of clouds the light of a few stars fell upon the black sea, rising and falling confusedly with heavy splashes, all about the ship. Sometimes the head of a watery cone would fall on board and mingle with the rolling flurry of foam on the swamped deck; and the *Nan-Shan* wallowed heavily within a cistern of circular form in the depth of the clouds resting on the sea. This ring of dense vapours gyrating madly around the calm of the centre encompassed the ship like a motionless and unbroken wall of a blackness inconceivably sinister. Within, the sea, as if agitated by an internal commotion, leaped in peaked mounds that jostled each other, slapping heavily against the ship, and a low moaning sound—the infinite plaint of the storm's fury—came from beyond the limits of the menacing calm. Captain MacWhirr remained silent and Jukes's ready ear caught suddenly the faint, long-drawn roar of some immense wave rushing under that thick blackness which made the appalling boundary of his vision.

"Of course," he started, "they thought we had caught at the chance to plunder them. Of course! You said—pick up the money. Easier said than done. They couldn't tell what was in our heads. We came in, smash!—right into the middle of them. Had to do it by a rush. . . ."

"As long as it's done," mumbled the Captain, without attempting to look at Jukes. "Had to do what's fair."

"We shall find yet there's the devil to pay when this is over," said Jukes, feeling very sore. "Let them only recover a bit and you'll see. They will fly at our throats, sir. Don't forget, sir, she isn't a British ship now. These brutes know it well, too. The damn'd Siamese flag!"

"We are on board all the same," remarked Captain Mac-Whirr.

"The trouble's not over yet," insisted Jukes, prophetically, reeling and catching on. "She's a wreck," he added faintly.

"The trouble's not over yet," assented Captain MacWhirr, half aloud. "Look out for her a minute."

"Are you going off the deck, sir?" asked Jukes, hurriedly, as if the storm was sure to pounce upon him as soon as he had been left alone with the ship.

He saw her, battered and solitary, labouring heavily in a wild scene of mountainous black waters lit by the gleams of distant worlds. She moved slowly, breathing into the still core of the hurricane the excess of her strength in a white cloud of steam; and the deep-toned vibration of the escape was like the defiant trumpeting of a living creature of the sea impatient for the renewal of the contest. It ceased suddenly. A moan in the stillness of the air swooped upon Jukes's head.

It was so plain that he looked up. He saw the stars shining into the pit of black vapours marking the circle of rushing winds and headlong seas. The ship was cut off from the peace of the earth. The wall rose high, with smoky drifts issuing from the inky edge that frowned upon the ship under the patch of glittering sky. The stars, too, seemed to look at her intently, as if for the last time, and the cluster of their splendour sat like a diadem on a lowering brow.

Captain MacWhirr had gone into the chart-room. There was no light there, but he could feel the disorder of that place where

he used to live tidily. His arm-chair was upset. The books had
tumbled out on the floor; he scrunched a piece of glass under his
boot. He felt for the matches and found a box on a shelf with a
deep ledge. He struck one and, puckering the corners of his
eyes, he held out the little flame towards the barometer, whose
glittering top of glass and metal nodded at him continuously.

It stood very low—incredibly low—so low that Captain Mac-
Whirr grunted. The match went out, and hurriedly he extracted
another with thick, stiff fingers.

Again a little flame burst before the nodding glass and metal
of the top. His eyes looked at it, out of the puckers, with attention, as if expecting a whisper. With his grave face he was like a
hooded and misshapen pagan burning incense before the oracle
of a joss. There was no mistake. It was low.

Captain MacWhirr emitted a low whistle. He forgot himself
till the flame diminished to a blue spark, burnt his fingers, and
vanished. Perhaps something had gone wrong with the thing?

There was an aneroid glass screwed above the couch. He
turned that way, struck another match, and discovered the white
face of the instrument looking at him from the bulkhead mean-
ingly, not to be gainsaid, as though the wisdom of men were
made unerring by the indifference of matter. There was no
room for doubt now. Captain MacWhirr pshawed at it and
threw the match down.

The worst was to come, then, and if the books were right this
worst would be very bad. The experience of the last six hours
had enlarged his conception of what heavy weather could be
like. "It'll be terrific," he pronounced mentally. He had not
consciously looked at anything by the light of the matches but
the barometer, and yet somehow he had seen that the water-
bottle and glass had been flung out of their stand. It seemed to
give him a more intimate knowledge of the tossing the ship had
gone through. "I wouldn't have believed it," he thought. And
his table had been cleared too; his rulers, his pencils, the inkstand,—all the things that had their safe, appointed places,—
they were gone from them as if a mischievous hand had plucked

them out and flung them on the wet floor. The hurricane had broken in upon the orderly arrangements of his privacy. This had never happened before and the dismay reached the very seat of his composure. And the worst was coming yet! He was glad the trouble in the 'tween-deck had been discovered in time. If she had to go after all, then at least she wouldn't be going with a lot of people in her fighting tooth and claw. That would have been odious. And in that feeling there was a humane intention and a vague sense of the fitness of things.

These instantaneous thoughts were yet in their essence heavy and slow, partaking of the nature of the man. He extended his hand to put back the match-box in its corner of the shelf. There were always matches there—by order. The steward had his instructions impressed upon him. "A box—just there, see? Not so very full—where I can put my hand on it, steward. Might want a light in a hurry. Can't tell on board ship *what* you might want in a hurry. Mind now."

And, of course, on his side he would be careful to put it back scrupulously. He did so now, but before he removed his hand it occurred to him that perhaps he would never have occasion to use that box again. The vividness of the notion checked him, and for an infinitesimal fraction of a second his fingers closed again on the small object. This man, disturbed by a storm, hung on to a matchbox absurdly, as though it had been a symbol of all those habits that make manifest the reality of life. He released it at last, and, letting himself fall on the settee, listened for the first sounds of returning wind.

Not yet. He heard only the wash of water, the heavy splashes and the dull shocks of the confused seas boarding his ship from all sides. She would never have a chance to clear her decks.

XXII

THIS quietude of the air was startlingly tense and unsafe, like a slender hair holding a sword suspended over his head. By this awful pause the storm penetrated the defences of the man and unsealed his lips. He spoke out in the solitude and the pitch-darkness of the cabin, as if addressing another being awakened into a stir of life within his breast.

"I shouldn't like to lose her," he said, half aloud.

He sat unseen, apart from the sea, from his ship, isolated, as if withdrawn from the very current of his own existence, where such freaks as talking to himself surely had no place. His palms reposed on his knees, he bowed his bull-neck and breathed heavily, surrendering to a strange sensation of weariness, but was not enlightened enough to recognize in it the fatigue of mental stress.

From where he sat he could reach the door of a wash-stand locker. There should have been a towel there. There was. Good! He wiped his face, then went on rubbing his wet head. He towelled himself with energy in the dark, and then sat still with the towel on his knees. A moment passed in which one could not have known there was a man sitting in that cabin. Then a murmur arose.

"She may come out of it yet."

When Captain MacWhirr came out on deck, which he did brusquely, as though he had suddenly become conscious of having stayed away too long, the calm had lasted already more than fifteen minutes—long enough to make itself intolerable even to his imagination. Jukes, motionless on the forepart of the bridge, began to speak at once. His voice, blank and forced, as though he were talking through hard-set teeth, seemed to spread out on all sides into the darkness, deepening again upon the confused unrest of the sea.

"I had the wheel relieved. Hackett began to call he was done. He's lying in there alongside the steering-gear with a face like death. At first I couldn't get anybody to crawl out. That bo's'n's worse than no good, I always said. Thought I would have had to go myself and haul out one of them by the neck."

"Ah, well!" muttered the Captain. He stood watchful by Jukes's side.

"The second mate's in there, too, holding his head. Is he hurt, sir?"

"No, crazy," said Captain MacWhirr, with decision.

"Looks as if he had had a tumble, though."

"I had to give him a push," explained the Captain.

Jukes gave an impatient sigh.

"It will come very sudden," said Captain MacWhirr, "and from over there, I fancy. God only knows, though. These books are only good to muddle your head and make you jumpy. It will be bad, and there's an end. If we only can steam her round in time to meet it! . . ."

A minute passed. Some of the stars winked rapidly and went out.

"You left them pretty safe?" began the Captain abruptly, as though the silence were unbearable.

"Are you thinking of the coolies, sir? I rigged life-lines all ways across that 'tween-deck."

"Did you? Good idea, Mr. Jukes."

"I didn't—think you cared to—know," said Jukes,—the lurching of the ship cut his speech as though somebody had been jerking him around while he talked,—"how I got on with—that infernal job. We did it. And it may not matter in the end."

"Had to do what's fair, for all—they are only Chinamen. Give them the same chance with ourselves—hang it all! She isn't lost yet. Bad enough to be shut up—below in a gale——"

"That's what I thought when you gave me the job, sir," interjected Jukes, moodily.

"—without being battered to pieces," pursued Captain Mac-Whirr, with rising vehemence. "Couldn't let that go on in my ship if I knew she hadn't five minutes to live. Couldn't bear it, Mr. Jukes."

A hollow, rolling noise, like that of a shout echoing in a rocky chasm, approached the ship and went away again. The last star, blurred, enlarged, as if turning into the fiery mist of its beginning, struggled with the colossal depth of blackness hanging over the ship—and went out.

"Now for it!" muttered Captain MacWhirr. "Mr. Jukes."

"Here, sir."

The two men were growing indistinct to each other. The gathering darkness embraced, absorbed their erect figures into the opaque gloom.

"We must trust her to go through and come out on the other side. That's plain and straight. There's no room for Captain Wilson's storm-strategy here."

"No, sir."

"She will be smothered and swept again for hours," mumbled the Captain. "There's not much left above deck for the sea to take away—unless you or me."

"Both, sir?" whispered Jukes, breathlessly.

"You are always meeting trouble halfway, Jukes," Captain MacWhirr remonstrated, quaintly. "Though it's a fact that the second mate is no good. D'ye hear, Mr. Jukes? You would be left alone if——"

Captain MacWhirr interrupted himself, and Jukes, glancing on all sides, remained silent.

"Don't you be put out by anything," the Captain continued, mumbling rather fast. "Keep her facing it. They may say what they like, but the heaviest seas run with the wind. Facing it—always facing it—that's the way to get through. You are a young sailor. Face it. That's enough work for any man. Keep a cool head."

"Yes, sir," said Jukes, with a flutter of the heart. In the next few seconds the Captain spoke to the engine-room and got an answer. For some reason Jukes experienced an access of confidence, a thing that came from outside like a warm breath and made him feel equal to every demand. The distant muttering of the darkness stole into his ears. He noted it unmoved, out of that sudden belief in himself, as a man in a shirt of mail would watch a point.

The ship laboured without intermission amongst the black hills of water, paying with this hard tumbling the price of her life. She rumbled in her depths, shaking a white plummet of steam into the night, and Jukes's thought darted like a skimming bird through the engine-room where Mr. Rout—good man —was ready. When the rumbling ceased it seemed to him that there was a pause of every sound, a dead pause, in which Captain MacWhirr's voice rang out startlingly.

"What's that? A puff?" It spoke much louder than Jukes had ever heard it before. "On the bow? That's right. She may come out of it yet."

The mutter of the winds drew near apace. In the forefront could be distinguished a drowsy, waking plaint passing on—and far off the growth of a multiple clamour, marching and expanding. There was the throb as of many drums in it, a vicious, rushing note, and like the chant of a tramping multitude.

Jukes could no longer see his Captain distinctly. The darkness was absolutely piling itself up upon the ship. At most he made out movements, a hint of elbows spread out, of a head thrown up. Captain MacWhirr was trying to do up the top button of his coat with unwonted haste. The hurricane that has the power to madden the seas, to sink ships, to uproot, trees, to overturn strong walls, and dash the very birds of the air to the ground had found this taciturn man in its path and, doing its utmost, had managed to make him loquacious. Before the renewed wrath of the winds swooped on the ship, Captain MacWhirr found time to declare, in a tone of vexation as it were: "I wouldn't like to lose her."

He was spared that annoyance.

XXIII

WHEN the *Nan-Shan* came to an anchor the sunshine was bright, the breeze fresh. She came in from a green, hard sea, green like a furrowed slab of jade, streaked and splashed with frosted silver. Even before her story got about, her arrival was noticed on shore and the seamen in harbour said: "Look! Look at that steamer. What's that? Siamese—isn't she? Just look at her."

She seemed indeed to have served as a target for the secondary batteries of a whole fleet. A hail of shells could not have given her upper works a more broken, torn, and devastated aspect; and she had about her the worn, weary air of ships coming from the far ends of the world—and, indeed, with truth, for in her short passage she had been very far, sighting, verily, even the coast of the Great Beyond, whence no ship ever returns to give up her crew to the dust of the earth. She was incrusted and grey with salt to the trucks of her masts and to the top of her funnel; as though, as some facetious seaman said, "the crowd on board had fished her out somewhere from the bottom of the sea and brought her in here for salvage." And further, excited by the felicity of his own wit, he offered to give five pounds for her— "as she stands."

Before she had been quite an hour at rest a meagre little man, with a red-tipped nose and a face cast in an angry mould, landed from a sampan on the quay of the Foreign Concession and incontinently turned to shake his fist at her. A tall individual with legs much too thin for a rotund stomach, and with watery eyes, strolled up and remarked:

"Just left her—eh? Quick work."

He wore a soiled suit of blue flannel, with a pair of dirty cricketing shoes; a dingy grey moustache drooped from his lip, and daylight could be seen in two places between the rim and the crown of his hat.

"Hallo! What are you doing here?" asked the ex-second mate of the *Nan-Shan,* shaking hands hurriedly.

"Standing by—chance worth taking—got a quiet hint," explained the man with the broken hat, in hollow, apathetic wheezes.

The second shook his fist again at the ship.

"There's a fellow there that ain't fit to have charge of a scow," he declared, quivering with passion, while the other looked about listlessly.

"Is there?"

But he caught sight on the quay of a heavy seaman's chest, painted brown under a fringed sailcloth cover, and lashed with new manila line. He eyed it with pensive interest.

"I would talk and raise trouble if it wasn't for that damned Siamese flag. Nobody to go to—or I would make it hot for him, the fraud! Told his chief—that's another fraud for you—I had lost my nerve. The greatest lot of ignorant fools that ever sailed the seas! No! You can't think . . ."

"Got your money all right?" inquired his seedy acquaintance, suddenly.

"Yes. Paid me off on board," raged the second mate. " 'Get your breakfast on shore,' says he."

"Mean skunk!" commented the tall man, vaguely, and passed his tongue on his lips. "What about having a drink of some sort?"

"He struck me," hissed the second mate.

"No! You don't say!" The man in blue began to bustle about exceedingly. "Can't possibly talk here. I want to know all about it. Struck—eh? Let's get a fellow for your chest. I know a quiet place."

Mr. Jukes, who had been scanning the shore through a pair of glasses, informed the chief engineer afterwards that "our late second mate hasn't been long in finding a friend. A chap looking uncommonly like a bummer. I saw them walk away together from the quay."

The hammering and banging of the needful repairs did not disturb Captain MacWhirr. The steward found, in the letter he wrote in a tidy chart-room, passages of such absorbing interest that twice he was nearly caught in the act; but Mrs. MacWhirr, in the drawing-room of the forty-pound house, stifled a yawn—perhaps out of self-respect. For she was alone.

She reclined in a plush-bottomed and gilt hammock-chair, near a tiled fireplace, with Japanese fans on the mantel and a glow of coals in the grate. Lifting her hands from time to time she glanced wearily here and there into the many pages. It was not her fault they were so prosy, so completely uninteresting— from "My darling wife" at the beginning to "Your loving husband" at the end. She couldn't be really expected to understand all these ship affairs. She was glad, of course, to hear from him, but she had never asked herself why, precisely. ". . . They are called typhoons . . . not in books. . . . The mate did not seem to like it . . . couldn't think of letting it go on. . . ."

She rustled the pages. ". . . A calm that lasted over twenty minutes," she read perfunctorily, and the next words her thoughtless eyes caught on the top of another page were, ". . . see you and the children again. . . ." He was always thinking of coming home. He had never had such a good salary.

It did not occur to her to turn back over the leaf to look. She would have found it recorded there that between 4 and 6 A.M., on the 25th of December, Captain MacWhirr did actually think that his ship could not possibly live in such a sea, and that he would never see his wife and children again. Nobody was to know this (his letters got mislaid and lost so often)—nobody but the steward, who had been greatly impressed by that disclosure; so much so, that he risked trying to give the cook some idea of the "narrow squeak we all had" by saying solemnly, "The old man himself had a damn poor opinion of our chance." "How do you know?" contemptuously asked the cook—an old soldier. "He hasn't told you, maybe?" "Well, he did drop something," the steward stammered. "Get along with you! He will be coming to tell me next," jeered the old cook over his shoulder.

Mrs. MacWhirr glanced farther, on the alert. ". . . do what's fair . . . miserable objects. . . . Only three, with a broken leg each, and one. . . . Thought had better keep the matter quiet . . . hope to have done the fair thing. . . ."

She let her hands fall. No. There was nothing about coming home. Must have been expressing merely a pious wish. Mrs. MacWhirr's mind was at ease, and a black marble clock, priced by the local jeweller at £3 18s. 6d., had a discreet, stealthy tick.

The door flew open and a girl in the long-legged, short-frocked period of existence flung into the room. A lot of colourless, rather lanky hair was scattered over her shoulders. Seeing her mother, she stood still and directed her pale, prying eyes upon the letter.

"From father," murmured Mrs. MacWhirr. "What have you done with your ribbon?"

The girl put her hands up and pouted. "He's well," continued Mrs. MacWhirr, languidly. "At least, I think so. He never says." She had a little laugh. The girl's face expressed a blank, wandering indifference, and Mrs. MacWhirr surveyed her with fond pride.

"Go and get your hat," she said after a while. "I am going out to do some shopping. There is a sale at Linom's."

"Oh, how jolly!" uttered the child, impressively, in unexpectedly grave vibrating tones, and bounded out.

XXIV

THE afternoon was fine; the sidewalks were dry. Outside the draper's, Mrs. MacWhirr smiled upon a woman in a black mantle of generous proportions, armoured in jet, ornate with flowers blooming falsely above a bilious matronly countenance. They broke into a swift little babble of greetings and exclamations both together, very hurried, as if the street were ready to yawn open and swallow all that pleasure before it could be adequately voiced.

Behind them the high glass doors were kept on the swing, people couldn't pass, men stood aside waiting patiently, and Lydia was absorbed in poking the end of her parasol between the stone flags. Mrs. MacWhirr talked rapidly.

"Thank you so much! This very day. He's not coming home yet. Of course, it's very sad to have him away, but it's such a comfort to know he keeps so well!" Mrs. MacWhirr drew breath: "The climate there agrees with him," she added, beamingly, as if poor MacWhirr had been away touring in China for the sake of his health.

Neither was the chief engineer coming home yet. Mr. Rout knew too well the value of a good billet.

"Solomon says wonders will never cease," cried Mrs. Rout, joyously, at the old lady in her arm-chair by the fire. Mr. Rout's mother moved slightly her withered hands lying in black half-mittens on her lap.

The engineer's wife's eyes fairly danced on the paper.

"That Captain of the ship he is in—a rather simple man—you remember, mother?—has done something rather clever, Solomon says."

"Yes, my dear," said the old woman meekly, sitting with bowed silvery head, and that air of still, far-away meditation only very old people have, as if absorbed in nursing the last flickers of life, "I think I remember."

Solomon, Old Sol, Father Sol, The Chief, "Rout, good man —" Mr. Rout, the austere and paternal friend of youth, had been the baby of her many children—all dead now. And she remembered him best as a boy of ten—before he went away to serve his time in some great engineering works in the North. She had seen so little of him since; she had gone through so many years that she had now to retrace her steps to meet him again in the mist of time. Sometimes it seemed as if her daughter-in-law were talking of some strange man.

Mrs. Rout, junior, was disappointed. "H'm, h'm." She turned the page. "How provoking! He doesn't say what it is. Says I couldn't understand how much there was in it. Fancy! What could it be, so very clever? What a wretched man not to tell us!"

She read on without further remark, soberly, and at last sat looking silently into the fire. The Chief wrote just a word or two about the typhoon, but something had moved him to express his growing desire for the companionship of the jolly woman. "If it hadn't been that mother must be looked after, I would send you your passage money today. You could set up a small house out here. I could see you sometimes then. We are not growing younger. . . ."

"He's well, mother," sighed Mrs. Rout, rousing herself.

"He always was a strong, healthy boy," said the old woman, placidly.

But it was Mr. Jukes's account that was really animated and interesting. His friend in the Western ocean trade imparted it freely to the other officers. "A chap I know writes to me about an extraordinary affair that happened on board his ship in that typhoon—you know—that was in the papers two months ago. It's the funniest thing. Just see for yourself what he says. I'll show you his letter."

There were phrases in it calculated to give the impression of light-hearted indomitable resolution. Jukes had written them in good faith, for he felt thus when he wrote. He described with lurid effect the scenes in the 'tween-deck. ". . . It struck me in a flash that those confounded Chinamen couldn't tell we weren't a desperate kind of robbers. 'Tisn't good to part the Chinaman from his money if he is the stronger party. We need have been desperate indeed to go thieving in such weather, but what could these beggars know of us? So, without thinking of it twice, I got the hands away in a jiffy. Our work was done—that the old man had set his heart about. We cleared out without staying to inquire how they felt. I am convinced that if they had not been

Joseph Conrad photographed in Marienbad, 1883, aged twenty-six, while pursuing a life on the sea and two years after his experience aboard the ship *Palestine* upon which his story *Youth* was based

so unmercifully shaken, and afraid—each individual one of them—to stand up, we would have been torn to pieces. Oh! it was pretty complete, I can tell you; and you may run to and fro across the pond to the end of time before you find yourself with such a job on your hands."

After this he alluded professionally to the damage done to the ship and went on thus:

"It was when the weather quieted down that the situation became confoundedly delicate. It wasn't made any better by us having been lately transferred to the Siamese flag; though the skipper can't see that it makes any difference—'as long as *we* are on board,' he says. There are feelings that this man simply hasn't got—and there's an end of it. You might just as well try to make a bedpost understand. But apart from this, it is an infernally lonely state for a ship to be going about in the China seas with no proper Consuls, not even a gunboat of her own anywhere—not a body to go to in case of any trouble.

"My notion was to keep them under hatches another fifteen hours or so; we weren't much farther than that from Fu-chau. We would find there most likely some sort of man-of-war, and once under her guns we were safe enough, for surely any skipper of a man-of-war, English, French, or Dutch, would see white men through as far as a row on board goes. We could get rid of them and their money by delivering them to their Mandarins or Two-tail, or whatever they call these chaps in goggles you see being carried in sedan chairs about their stinking streets.

"The old man wouldn't see it, somehow. He wanted to keep the matter quiet. He got that notion into his head and a steam windlass couldn't drag it out of him. He wanted as little fuss made as possible, 'for the sake of the ship's name and the owners, for the sake of all concerned,' says he, looking at me very hard. It made me angry, hot. Of course you couldn't keep a thing like that quiet, but the chests had been secured in the usual manner, and were safe enough for any earthly gale, but this had been an altogether fiendish business I couldn't give you even an idea of.

"Meantime I could hardly keep on my feet. None of us had had a spell of any sort for nearly thirty hours, and there he sat rubbing his chin, rubbing the top of his head, and so bothered he didn't even think of taking his long boots off.

" 'I hope, sir,' says I, 'you won't be letting them out on deck before we make ready for them in some shape or other.' Not, mind you, that I felt very sanguine about controlling if they took charge. Trouble with a cargo of Chinamen is no child's play; I was dam' tired, too. 'I wish,' said I, 'we could throw the whole lot of these dollars down to them and let them fight it out amongst themselves, while we get a rest.'

" 'Now you talk wild, Jukes,' says he, looking up in his slow way, that makes you ache all over, somehow. 'We must plan out something that would be fair to all parties.'

XXV

"I HAD no end of work on hand, and by-and-by I set the hands going, and then I thought I would turn in a bit. I hadn't been in my bunk ten minutes when in rushes the steward and begins to pull at my leg.

" 'For God's sake, Mr. Jukes, come out! Come on deck, quick, sir! Oh, do come out!'

"The fellow scared all the sense out of me. I didn't know what had happened—another hurricane, or what. Could hear no wind.

" 'The Captain's letting them out. Oh, he is letting them out! Jump on deck, sir, and save us. The chief engineer has just run below for his revolver.'

"That's what the fool made me understand. However, Father Rout swears he went in there to get a clean pocket-handkerchief. Anyhow, I made one jump into my trousers and flew on deck aft. There was certainly a good deal of noise going on where I couldn't see forward of the bridge. Four of the hands with the bo's'n were at work abaft. I passed up to them through the skylight some of the rifles all the ships on the China coast carry in the cabin and led them on the bridge. On the way I ran against Old Sol, looking startled and sucking at an unlighted cigar. 'Come along!' I shouted to him.

"We charged, seven of us, up to the chart-room. All was over. There was the old man, with his sea-boots still drawn up to the hips and in shirt-sleeves—got warm thinking it out, I suppose. Bun Lim's dandy clerk stood at his elbow, as dirty as a sweep and still green in the face. I could see directly I was in for something.

" 'What the devil are these monkey tricks, Mr. Jukes?' asks the old man, as angry as ever he could be. I tell you frankly it made me lose my tongue.

" 'For God's sake, Mr. Jukes,' says he, 'do take away these rifles from the men. Somebody's sure to get shot before long if you don't. Damme, if this ship isn't worse than Bedlam! Look sharp, now! I want you up here to help me and Bun Lim's Chinaman to count that money. You wouldn't mind lending a hand, too, Mr. Rout, now you are here? The more of us the better.'

"He had settled it all while I was having a snooze. Had we been an English ship, or only going to land our cargo of coolies in an English port like Hong-Kong, for instance, there would have been no end of inquiries and bother, claims for damages, and so on. But these Chinamen know their officials better than we do.

"The old man had the hatches taken off, and they were all on deck after a night and a day down below. It made you feel queer to see so many gaunt, wild faces together. The beggars were staring at the sky, at the sea, at the ship, as though they had expected the whole thing to have been blown to pieces. And no wonder. They had had a doing that would have shaken the soul out of a white man. But then they say a Chinaman has no soul.

He has, though, something about him that is deuced tough. There was a fellow (amongst others of the badly hurt) who had had his eye all but knocked out. It stood out of his head awful swollen, like half a hen's egg. This would have laid a white man on his back; and there was that chap elbowing here and there and talking to the others as if nothing was the matter. They made a great hubbub amongst themselves, and whenever the old man showed his bald head on the foreside of the bridge, they would all leave off and look at him.

"After he had done his thinking he made that Bun Lim's fellow go down and explain to them how they could get their money. He told me afterwards that all the coolies having worked in the same place and for the same length of time, he reckoned he would be doing the fair thing by them as near as possible if he distributed all we had picked up equally among the lot. You couldn't tell one man's dollars from another's, and if you asked each man he was afraid they would lie and he would find himself a long way short. I think he was right there. As to giving up the cash into the hands of any Chinese official he could scare up in Fu-chau, he said he might just as well put the money in his pocket at once for all the good it would be to them. I suppose they thought so too.

"We finished the distribution before dark. It was rather a sight: the sea running high, the ship a wreck to look at, these Chinamen staggering on the bridge one by one for their share; and the old man, still booted and in his shirt-sleeves, solemnly busy paying out, perspiring like anything, and now and then coming down sharp on myself or Father Rout about one thing or another not quite to his mind. He himself took the share of those who were disabled to them on the No. 2 hatch. There were three dollars left over, and these went to the three most damaged coolies—one to each. We turned to afterwards and shovelled out on deck heaps of wet rags, all sorts of fragments of things without shape, and that you couldn't give a name to, and let them settle the ownership themselves.

"This certainly is coming as near as can be to keeping the

thing quiet for the benefit of all concerned. What's your opinion, you pampered Mail-boat swell? The old Chief says that this
was plainly the only thing that could be done. The skipper remarked to me the other day, 'These are things you find nothing
about in books.' I think that he had not done badly for such a
stupid man. . . ."

The Nigger of the
"Narcissus"

PREFACE

A WORK that aspires, however humbly, to the condition of art should carry its justification in every line. And art itself may be defined as a single-minded attempt to render the highest kind of justice to the visible universe, by bringing to light the truth, manifold and one, underlying its every aspect. It is an attempt to find in its forms, in its colours, in its light, in its shadows, in the aspects of matter and in the facts of life what of each is fundamental, what is enduring and essential—their one illuminating and convincing quality—the very truth of their existence. The artist, then, like the thinker or the scientist, seeks the truth and makes his appeal. Impressed by the aspect of the world the thinker plunges into ideas, the scientist into facts—whence, presently, emerging they make their appeal to those qualities of our being that fit us best for the hazardous enterprise of living. They speak authoritatively to our common-sense, to our intelligence, to our desire of peace or to our desire of unrest; not seldom to our prejudices, sometimes to our fears, often to our egoism—but always to our credulity. And their words are heard with reverence, for their concern is with weighty matters: with the cultivation of our minds and the proper care of our bodies, with the attainment of our ambitions, with the perfection of the means and the glorification of our precious aims.

It is otherwise with the artist.

Confronted by the same enigmatical spectacle the artist descends within himself, and in that lonely region of stress and

93

strife, if he be deserving and fortunate, he finds the terms of his appeal. His appeal is made to our less obvious capacities: to that part of our nature which, because of the warlike conditions of existence, is necessarily kept out of sight within the more resisting and hard qualities—like the vulnerable body within a steel armour. His appeal is less loud, more profound, less distinct, more stirring—and sooner forgotten. Yet its effect endures forever. The changing wisdom of successive generations discards ideas, questions facts, demolishes theories. But the artist appeals to that part of our being which is not dependent on wisdom; to that in us which is a gift and not an acquisition—and, therefore, more permanently enduring. He speaks to our capacity for delight and wonder, to the sense of mystery surrounding our lives; to our sense of pity, and beauty, and pain; to the latent feeling of fellowship with all creation—and to the subtle but invincible conviction of solidarity that knits together the loneliness of innumerable hearts, to the solidarity in dreams, in joy, in sorrow, in aspirations, in illusions, in hope, in fear, which binds men to each other, which binds together all humanity— the dead to the living and the living to the unborn.

It is only some such train of thought, or rather of feeling, that can in a measure explain the aim of the attempt, made in the tale which follows, to present an unrestful episode in the obscure lives of a few individuals out of all the disregarded multitude of the bewildered, the simple and the voiceless. For, if any part of truth dwells in the belief confessed above, it becomes evident that there is not a place of splendour or a dark corner of the earth that does not deserve, if only a passing glance of wonder and pity. The motive then, may be held to justify the matter of the work; but this preface, which is simply an avowal of endeavour, cannot end here—for the avowal is not yet complete.

Fiction—if it at all aspires to be art—appeals to temperament. And in truth it must be, like painting, like music, like all art, the appeal of one temperament to all the other innumerable temperaments whose subtle and resistless power endows passing events with their true meaning, and creates the moral, the emotional atmosphere of the place and time. Such an appeal to be effective must be an impression conveyed through the senses; and, in fact, it cannot be made in any other way, because temperament, whether individual or collective, is not amenable to persuasion. All art, therefore, appeals primarily to the senses, and the artistic aim when expressing itself in written words must also make its appeal through the senses, if its high desire is to reach the secret spring of responsive emotions. It must strenuously aspire to the plasticity of sculpture, to the colour of painting, and to the magic suggestiveness of music—which is the art of arts. And it is only through complete, unswerving devotion to the perfect blending of form and substance; it is only through an unremitting never-discouraged care for the shape and ring of sentences that an approach can be made to plasticity, to colour, and that the light of magic suggestiveness may be brought to play for an evanescent instant over the commonplace surface of words: of the old, old words, worn thin, defaced by ages of careless usage.

The sincere endeavour to accomplish that creative task, to go as far on that road as his strength will carry him, to go undeterred by faltering, weariness or reproach, is the only valid justification for the worker in prose. And if his conscience is clear, his answer to those who in the fulness of a wisdom which looks for immediate profit, demand specifically to be edified, consoled, amused; who demand to be promptly improved, or encouraged, or frightened, or shocked, or charmed, must run thus:—My task which I am trying to achieve is, by the power of the written word to make you hear, to make you feel—it is, before all, to make you *see*. That—and no more, and it is everything. If I succeed, you shall find there according to your deserts: encouragement, consolation, fear, charm—all you demand—and, perhaps, also that glimpse of truth for which you have forgotten to ask.

To snatch in a moment of courage, from the remorseless rush of time, a passing phase of life, is only the beginning of the task.

The task approached in tenderness and faith is to hold up unquestioningly, without choice and without fear, the rescued fragment before all eyes in the light of a sincere mood. It is to show its vibration, its colour, its form; and through its movement, its form, and its colour, reveal the substance of its truth—disclose its inspiring secret: the stress and passion within the core of each convincing moment. In a single-minded attempt of that kind, if one be deserving and fortunate, one may perchance attain to such clearness of sincerity that at last the presented vision of regret or pity, of terror or mirth, shall awaken in the hearts of the beholders that feeling of unavoidable solidarity; of the solidarity in mysterious origin, in toil, in joy, in hope, in uncertain fate, which binds men to each other and all mankind to the visible world.

It is evident that he who, rightly or wrongly, holds by the convictions expressed above cannot be faithful to any one of the temporary formulas of his craft. The enduring part of them—the truth which each only imperfectly veils—should abide with him as the most precious of his possessions, but they all: Realism, Romanticism, Naturalism, even the unofficial sentimentalism (which like the poor, is exceedingly difficult to get rid of,) all these gods must, after a short period of fellowship, abandon him—even on the very threshold of the temple—to the stammerings of his conscience and to the outspoken consciousness of the difficulties of his work. In that uneasy solitude the supreme cry of Art for Art itself, loses the exciting ring of its apparent immorality. It sounds far off. It has ceased to be a cry, and is heard only as a whisper, often incomprehensible, but at times and faintly encouraging.

Sometimes, stretched at ease in the shade of a roadside tree, we watch the motions of a labourer in a distant field, and after a time, begin to wonder languidly as to what the fellow may be at. We watch the movements of his body, the waving of his arms, we see him bend down, stand up, hesitate, begin again. It may add to the charm of an idle hour to be told the purpose of his exertions. If we know he is trying to lift a stone, to dig a ditch, to uproot a stump, we look with a more real interest at his efforts; we are disposed to condone the jar of his agitation upon the restfulness of the landscape; and even, if in a brotherly frame of mind, we may bring ourselves to forgive his failure. We understood his object, and, after all, the fellow has tried, and perhaps he had not the strength—and perhaps he had not the knowledge. We forgive, go on our way—and forget.

And so it is with the workman of art. Art is long and life is short, and success is very far off. And thus, doubtful of strength to travel so far, we talk a little about the aim—the aim of art, which, like itself, is inspiring, difficult—obscured by mists. It is not in the clear logic of a triumphant conclusion; it is not in the unveiling of one of those heartless secrets which are called the Laws of Nature. It is not less great, but only more difficult.

To arrest, for the space of a breath, the hands busy about the work of the earth, and compel men entranced by the sight of distant goals to glance for a moment at the surrounding vision of form and colour, of sunshine and shadows; to make them pause for a look, for a sigh, for a smile—such is the aim, difficult and evanescent, and reserved only for a very few to achieve. But sometimes, by the deserving and the fortunate, even that task is accomplished. And when it is accomplished—behold!— all the truth of life is there: a moment of vision, a sigh, a smile— and the return to an eternal rest.

1897.   J. C.

I

MR. BAKER, chief mate of the ship *Narcissus,* stepped in one stride out of his lighted cabin into the darkness of the quarter-deck. Above his head, on the break of the poop, the night-watchman rang a double stroke. It was nine o'clock. Mr. Baker, speaking up to the man above him, asked:—"Are all the hands aboard, Knowles?"

The man limped down the ladder, then said reflectively:—

"I think so, sir. All our old chaps are there, and a lot of new men has come. . . . They must be all there."

"Tell the boatswain to send all hands aft," went on Mr. Baker; "and tell one of the youngsters to bring a good lamp here. I want to muster our crowd."

The main deck was dark aft, but halfway from forward, through the open doors of the forecastle, two streaks of brilliant light cut the shadow of the quiet night that lay upon the ship. A hum of voices was heard there, while port and starboard, in the illuminated doorways, silhouettes of moving men appeared for a moment, very black, without relief, like figures cut out of sheet tin. The ship was ready for sea. The carpenter had driven in the last wedge of the main hatch battens, and, throwing down his maul, had wiped his face with great deliberation, just on the stroke of five. The decks had been swept, the windlass oiled and made ready to heave up the anchor; the big tow-rope lay in long bights along one side of the main deck, with one end carried up and hung over the bows, in readiness for the tug that would come paddling and hissing noisily, hot and smoky, in the limpid, cool quietness of the early morning. The captain was ashore, where he had been engaging some new hands to make up his full crew; and, the work of the day over, the ship's officers had kept out of the way, glad of a little breathing-time. Soon after dark the few liberty-men and the new hands began to arrive in shore-boats rowed by white-clad Asiatics, who clamoured fiercely for payment before coming alongside the gangway-ladder. The feverish and shrill babble of Eastern language struggled against the masterful tones of tipsy seamen, who argued against brazen claims and dishonest hopes by profane shouts. The resplendent and bestarred peace of the East was torn into squalid tatters by howls of rage and shrieks of lament raised over sums ranging from five annas to half a rupee; and every soul afloat in Bombay Harbour became aware that the new hands were joining the *Narcissus*.

Gradually the distracting noise had subsided. The boats came no longer in splashing clusters of three or four together, but dropped alongside singly, in a subdued buzz of expostulation cut short by a "Not a pice more! You go to the devil!" from some man staggering up the accommodation-ladder—a dark figure, with a long bag poised on the shoulder. In the forecastle the newcomers, upright and swaying amongst corded boxes and bundles of bedding, made friends with the old hands, who sat one above another in the two tiers of bunks, gazing at their future shipmates with glances critical but friendly. The two forecastle lamps were turned up high, and shed an intense hard glare; shore-going round hats were pushed far on the backs of heads, or rolled about on the deck amongst the chain-cables; white collars, undone, stuck out on each side of red faces; big arms in white sleeves gesticulated; the growling voices hummed steady amongst bursts of laughter and hoarse calls. "Here, sonny, take that bunk! . . . Don't you do it! . . . What's your last ship? . . . I know her. . . . Three years ago, in Puget Sound. . . . This here berth leaks, I tell you! . . . Come on; give us a chance to swing that chest! . . . Did you bring a bottle, any of you shore toffs? . . . Give us a bit of 'baccy. . . . I know her; her skipper drank himself to death. . . . He was a dandy boy! . . . Liked his lotion inside, he did! . . . No! . . . Hold your row, you chaps!

. . . I tell you, you came on board a hooker, where they get their money's worth out of poor Jack, by——! . . ."

A little fellow, called Craik and nicknamed Belfast, abused the ship violently, romancing on principle, just to give the new hands something to think over. Archie, sitting aslant on his sea-chest, kept his knees out of the way, and pushed the needle steadily through a white patch in a pair of blue trousers. Men in black jackets and stand-up collars, mixed with men bare-footed, bare-armed, with coloured shirts open on hairy chests, pushed against one another in the middle of the forecastle. The group swayed, reeled, turning upon itself with the motion of a scrimmage, in a haze of tobacco smoke. All were speaking to-gether, swearing at every second word. A Russian Finn, wearing a yellow shirt with pink stripes, stared upwards, dreamy-eyed, from under a mop of tumbled hair. Two young giants with smooth, baby faces—two Scandinavians—helped each other to spread their bedding, silent, and smiling placidly at the tempest of good-humoured and meaningless curses. Old Singleton, the oldest able seaman in the ship, sat apart on the deck right under the lamps, stripped to the waist, tattooed like a cannibal chief all over his powerful chest and enormous biceps. Between the blue and red patterns his white skin gleamed like satin; his bare back was propped against the heel of the bow-sprit, and he held a book at arm's length before his big, sunburnt face. With his spectacles and a venerable white beard, he resembled a learned and savage patriarch, the incarnation of barbarian wisdom serene in the blasphemous turmoil of the world. He was intensely absorbed, and as he turned the pages an expression of grave surprise would pass over his rugged features. He was reading "Pelham." The popularity of Bulwer Lytton in the forecastles of Southern-going ships is a wonderful and bizarre phenomenon. What ideas do his polished and so curiously in-sincere sentences awaken in the simple minds of the big children who people those dark and wandering places of the earth? What meaning can their rough, inexperienced souls find in the elegant verbiage of his pages? What excitement?—what forgetfulness?

—what appeasement? Mystery! Is it the fascination of the incomprehensible?—is it the charm of the impossible? Or are those beings who exist beyond the pale of life stirred by his tales as by an enigmatical disclosure of a resplendent world that exists within the frontier of infamy and filth, within that border of dirt and hunger, of misery and dissipation, that comes down on all sides to the water's edge of the incorruptible ocean, and is the only thing they know of life, the only thing they see of surrounding land—those life-long prisoners of the sea? Mystery!

Singleton, who had sailed to the southward since the age of twelve, who in the last forty-five years had lived (as we had calculated from his papers) no more than forty months ashore—old Singleton, who boasted, with the mild composure of long years well spent, that generally from the day he was paid off from one ship till the day he shipped in another he seldom was in a condition to distinguish daylight—old Singleton sat unmoved in the clash of voices and cries, spelling through "Pelham" with slow labour, and lost in an absorption profound enough to resemble a trance. He breathed regularly. Every time he turned the book in his enormous and blackened hands the muscles of his big white arms rolled slightly under the smooth skin. Hidden by the white moustache, his lips, stained with tobacco-juice that trickled down the long beard, moved in inward whisper. His bleared eyes gazed fixedly from behind the glitter of black-rimmed glasses. Opposite to him, and on a level with his face, the ship's cat sat on the barrel of the windlass in the pose of a crouching chimera, blinking its green eyes at its old friend. It seemed to meditate a leap on to the old man's lap over the bent back of the ordinary seaman who sat at Singleton's feet. Young Charley was lean and long-necked. The ridge of his backbone made a chain of small hills under the old shirt. His face of a street-boy—a face precocious, sagacious, and ironic, with deep downward folds on each side of the thin, wide mouth—hung low over his bony knees. He was learning to make a lanyard knot with a bit of an old rope. Small drops of perspiration stood out on his bulging forehead; he sniffed strongly from time to time, glancing out of the corners of his restless eyes at the old seaman, who took no notice of the puzzled youngster muttering at his work.

The noise increased. Little Belfast seemed, in the heavy heat of the forecastle, to boil with facetious fury. His eyes danced; in the crimson of his face, comical as a mask, the mouth yawned black, with strange grimaces. Facing him, a half-undressed man held his sides, and, throwing his head back, laughed with wet eyelashes. Others stared with amazed eyes. Men sitting doubled up in the upper bunks smoked short pipes, swinging bare brown feet above the heads of those who, sprawling below on sea-chests, listened, smiling stupidly or scornfully. Over the white rims of berths stuck out heads with blinking eyes; but the bodies were lost in the gloom of those places, that resembled narrow niches for coffins in a whitewashed and lighted mortuary. Voices buzzed louder. Archie, with compressed lips, drew himself in, seemed to shrink into a smaller space, and sewed steadily, industrious and dumb. Belfast shrieked like an inspired Dervish:— ". . . So I seez to him, boys, seez I, 'Beggin' yer pardon, sorr," seez I to that second mate of that steamer—'beggin' your-r-r pardon, sorr, the Board of Trade must 'ave been drunk when they granted you your certificate!' 'What do you say, you——!' seez he, comin' at me like a mad bull . . . all in his white clothes; and I up with my tar-pot and capsizes it all over his blamed lovely face and his lovely jacket. . . . 'Take that!' seez I. 'I am a sailor, anyhow, you nosing, skipper-licking, useless, sooperfloos bridge-stanchion, you! That's the kind of man I am!' shouts I. . . . You should have seed him skip, boys! Drowned, blind with tar, he was! So . . ."

"Don't 'ee believe him! He never upset no tar; I was there!" shouted somebody. The two Norwegians sat on a chest side by side, alike and placid, resembling a pair of love-birds on a perch, and with round eyes stared innocently; but the Russian Finn, in the racket of explosive shouts and rolling laughter, remained motionless, limp and dull, like a deaf man without a backbone. Near him Archie smiled at his needle. A broad-chested, slow-eyed newcomer spoke deliberately to Belfast during an ex-hausted lull in the noise:—"I wonder any of the mates here are alive yet with such a chap as you on board! I concloode they ain't that bad now, if you had the taming of them, sonny."

"Not bad! Not bad!" screamed Belfast. "If it wasn't for us sticking together. . . . Not bad! They ain't never bad when they ain't got a chawnce, blast their black 'arts. . . ." He foamed, whirling his arms, then suddenly grinned and, taking a tablet of black tobacco out of his pocket, bit a piece off with a funny show of ferocity. Another new hand—a man with shifty eyes and a yellow hatchet face, who had been listening open-mouthed in the shadow of the midship locker—observed in a squeaky voice: —"Well, it's a 'omeward trip, anyhow. Bad or good, I can do it on my 'ed—s'long as I get 'ome. And I can look after my rights! I will show 'em!" All the heads turned towards him. Only the ordinary seaman and the cat took no notice. He stood with arms akimbo, a little fellow with white eyelashes. He looked as if he had known all the degradations and all the furies. He looked as if he had been cuffed, kicked, rolled in the mud; he looked as if he had been scratched, spat upon, pelted with unmentionable filth . . . and he smiled with a sense of security at the faces around. His ears were bending down under the weight of his battered felt hat. The torn tails of his black coat flapped in fringes about the calves of his legs. He unbuttoned the only two buttons that remained and every one saw that he had no shirt under it. It was his deserved misfortune that those rags which nobody could possibly be supposed to own looked on him as if they had been stolen. His neck was long and thin; his eyelids were red; rare hairs hung about his jaws; his shoulders were peaked and drooped like the broken wings of a bird; all his left side was caked with mud which showed that he had lately slept in a wet ditch. He had saved his inefficient carcass from violent destruction by running away from an American ship where, in a moment of forgetful folly, he had dared to engage himself; and he had knocked about for a fortnight ashore in the native quarter, cadging for drinks, starving, sleeping on rubbish-heaps, wandering in sunshine: a startling visitor from a world of night-mares. He stood repulsive and smiling in the sudden silence. This clean white forecastle was his refuge; the place where he could be lazy; where he could wallow, and lie and eat—and curse the food he ate; where he could display his talents for shirking work, for cheating, for cadging; where he could find surely some one to wheedle and some one to bully—and where he would be paid for doing all this. They all knew him. Is there a spot on earth where such a man is unknown, an ominous survival testifying to the eternal fitness of lies and impudence? A taciturn long-armed shellback, with hooked fingers, who had been lying on his back smoking, turned in his bed to examine him dispas-sionately, then, over his head, sent a long jet of clear saliva to-wards the door. They all knew him! He was the man that cannot steer, that cannot splice, that dodges the work on dark nights; that, aloft, holds on frantically with both arms and legs, and swears at the wind, the sleet, the darkness; the man who curses the sea while others work. The man who is the last out and the first in when all hands are called. The man who can't do most things and won't do the rest. The pet of philanthropists and self-seeking landlubbers. The sympathetic and deserving crea-ture that knows all about his rights, but knows nothing of courage, of endurance, and of the unexpressed faith, of the unspoken loyalty that knits together a ship's company. The in-dependent offspring of the ignoble freedom of the slums full of disdain and hate for the austere servitude of the sea.

Some one cried at him: "What's your name?"—"Donkin," he said, looking round with cheerful effrontery.—"What are you?" asked another voice.—"Why, a sailor like you, old man," he replied, in a tone that meant to be hearty but was impudent. —"Blamme if you don't look a blamed sight worse than a broken-down fireman," was the comment in a convinced mutter. Charley lifted his head and piped in a cheeky voice: "He is a man and a sailor"—then wiping his nose with the back of his hand bent down industriously over his bit of rope. A few laughed. Others stared doubtfully. The ragged newcomer was indignant—"That's a fine way to welcome a chap into a fo'c'sle," he snarled. "Are you men or a lot of 'artless cannybals?"—"Don't take your shirt off for a word, shipmate," called out Belfast, jumping up in front, fiery, menacing, and friendly at the same time.—"Is that 'ere bloke blind?" asked the indomitable scarecrow, looking right and left with affected surprise. "Can't 'ee see I 'aven't got no shirt?"

He held both his arms out crosswise and shook the rags that hung over his bones with dramatic effect.

" 'Cos why?" he continued very loud. "The bloody Yankees been tryin' to jump my guts out 'cos I stood up for my rights like a good 'un. I am an Englishman, I am. They set upon me an' I 'ad to run. That's why. A'n't yer never seed a man 'ard up? Yah! What kind of blamed ship is this? I'm dead broke. I 'aven't got nothink. No bag, no bed, no blanket, no shirt—not a bloomin' rag but what I stand in. But I 'ad the 'art to stand up agin' them Yankees. 'As any of you 'art enough to spare a pair of old pants for a chum?"

He knew how to conquer the naïve instincts of that crowd. In a moment they gave him their compassion, jocularly, contemptuously, or surlily; and at first it took the shape of a blanket thrown at him as he stood there with the white skin of his limbs showing his human kinship through the black fantasy of his rags. Then a pair of old shoes fell at his muddy feet. With a cry:—"From under," a rolled-up pair of canvas trousers, heavy with tar stains, struck him on the shoulder. The gust of their benevolence sent a wave of sentimental pity through their doubting hearts. They were touched by their own readiness to alleviate a shipmate's misery. Voices cried:—"We will fit you out, old man." Murmurs: "Never seed seech a hard case. . . . Poor beggar. . . . I've got an old singlet. . . . Will that be of any use to you? . . . Take it, matey. . . ." Those friendly murmurs filled the forecastle. He pawed around with his naked foot, gathering the things in a heap and looked about for more. Unemotional Archie perfunctorily contributed to the pile an old cloth cap with the peak torn off. Old Singleton, lost in the serene regions of fiction, read on unheeding. Charley, pitiless with the wisdom of youth, squeaked:—"If you want brass buttons for your new unyforms I've got two for you." The filthy object of universal charity shook his fist at the youngster.—"I'll make you keep this 'ere fo'c'sle clean, young feller," he snarled viciously. "Never you fear. I will learn you to be civil to an able seaman, you ignerant ass." He glared harmfully, but saw Singleton shut his book, and his little beady eyes began to roam from berth to berth.—"Take that bunk by the door there—it's pretty fair," suggested Belfast. So advised, he gathered the gifts at his feet, pressed them in a bundle against his breast, then looked cautiously at the Russian Finn, who stood on one side with an unconscious gaze, contemplating, perhaps, one of those weird visions that haunt the men of his race.—"Get out of my road, Dutchy," said the victim of Yankee brutality. The Finn did not move—did not hear. "Get out, blast ye," shouted the other, shoving him aside with his elbow. "Get out, you blanked deaf and dumb fool. Get out." The man staggered, recovered himself, and gazed at the speaker in silence.—"Those damned furriners should be kept under," opined the amiable Donkin to the forecastle. "If you don't teach 'em their place they put on you like anythink." He flung all his worldly possessions into the empty bed-place, gauged with another shrewd look the risks of the proceeding, then leaped up to the Finn, who stood pensive and dull.—"I'll teach you to swell around," he yelled. "I'll plug your eyes for you, you blooming square-head." Most of the men were now in their bunks and the two had the forecastle clear to themselves. The development of the destitute Donkin aroused interest. He danced all in tatters before the amazed Finn, squaring from a distance at the heavy, unmoved face. One or two men cried encouragingly: "Go it, Whitechapel!" settling themselves luxuriously in their beds to survey the fight. Others shouted: "Shut yer row! . . . Go an' put yer 'ed in a bag! . . ." The hubbub was recommencing. Suddenly many heavy blows struck with a handspike on the deck above boomed like discharges of small cannon through the forecastle. Then the boatswain's voice rose outside the door with an authoritative note in its drawl:—"D'ye hear, below there? Lay aft! Lay aft to muster all hands!"

There was a moment of surprised stillness. Then the forecastle floor disappeared under men whose bare feet flopped on the planks as they sprang clear out of their berths. Caps were rooted for amongst tumbled blankets. Some, yawning, buttoned waistbands. Half-smoked pipes were knocked hurriedly against woodwork and stuffed under pillows. Voices growled:—"What's up? . . . Is there no rest for us?" Donkin yelped: "If that's the way of this ship, we'll 'ave to change all that. . . . You leave me alone. . . . I will soon. . . . None of the crowd noticed him. They were lurching in twos and threes through the doors, after the manner of merchant Jacks who cannot go out of a door fairly, like mere landsmen. The votary of change followed them. Singleton, struggling into his jacket, came last, tall and fatherly, bearing high his head of a weather-beaten sage on the body of an old athlete. Only Charley remained alone in the white glare of the empty place, sitting between the two rows of iron links that stretched into the narrow gloom forward. He pulled hard at the strands in a hurried endeavour to finish his knot. Suddenly he started up, flung the rope at the cat, and skipped after the black tom which went off leaping sedately over chain compressors, with its tail carried stiff and upright, like a small flag pole.

Outside the glare of the steaming forecastle the serene purity of the night enveloped the seamen with its soothing breath, with its tepid breath flowing under the stars that hung countless above the mastheads in a thin cloud of luminous dust. On the town side the blackness of the water was streaked with trails of light which undulated gently on slight ripples, similar to filaments that float rooted to the shore. Rows of other lights stood away in straight lines as if drawn up on parade between towering buildings; but on the other side of the harbour sombre hills arched high their black spines, on which, here and there, the point of a star resembled a spark fallen from the sky. Far off, Byculla way, the electric lamps at the dock gates shone on the end of lofty standards with a glow blinding and frigid like cap-

tive ghosts of some evil moons. Scattered all over the dark polish
of the roadstead, the ships at anchor floated in perfect stillness
under the feeble gleam of their riding-lights, looming up,
opaque and bulky, like strange and monumental structures
abandoned by men to an everlasting repose.

Before the cabin door Mr. Baker was mustering the crew.
As they stumbled and lurched along past the mainmast, they
could see aft his round, broad face with a white paper before it,
and beside his shoulder the sleepy head, with dropped eyelids,
of the boy, who held, suspended at the end of his raised arm, the
luminous globe of a lamp. Even before the shuffle of naked
soles had ceased along the decks, the mate began to call over the
names. He called distinctly in a serious tone befitting this roll-
call to unquiet loneliness, to inglorious and obscure struggle, or
to the more trying endurance of small privations and wearisome
duties. As the chief mate read out a name, one of the men would
answer: "Yes, sir!" or "Here!" and, detaching himself from the
shadowy mob of heads visible above the blackness of starboard
bulwarks, would step bare-footed into the circle of light, and in
two noiseless strides pass into the shadows on the port side of the
quarter-deck. They answered in divers tones: in thick mutters,
in clear, ringing voices; and some, as if the whole thing had been
an outrage on their feelings, used an injured intonation: for discipline is not ceremonious in merchant ships, where the sense
of hierarchy is weak, and where all feel themselves equal before
the unconcerned immensity of the sea and the exacting appeal
of the work.

Mr. Baker read on steadily:—"Hansen—Campbell—Smith—
Wamibo. Now, then, Wamibo. Why don't you answer? Always
got to call your name twice." The Finn emitted at last an uncouth grunt, and, stepping out, passed through the patch of
light, weird and gaudy, with the face of a man marching through
a dream. The mate went on faster:—"Craik—Singleton—Donkin.
. . . O Lord!" he involuntarily ejaculated as the incredibly dilap-
idated figure appeared in the light. It stopped; it uncovered pale
gums and long, upper teeth in a malevolent grin.—"Is there any-

think wrong with me, Mister Mate?" it asked, with a flavour of insolence in the forced simplicity of its tone. On both sides of the deck subdued titters were heard.—"That'll do. Go over," growled Mr. Baker, fixing the new hand with steady blue eyes. And Donkin vanished suddenly out of the light into the dark group of mustered men, to be slapped on the back and to hear flattering whispers:—"He ain't afeard, he'll give sport to 'em, see if he don't. . . . Reg'lar Punch and Judy show. . . . Did ye see the mate start at him? . . . Well! Damme, if I ever! . . ."

The last man had gone over, and there was a moment of silence while the mate peered at his list.—"Sixteen, seventeen," he muttered. "I am one hand short, bo'sen," he said aloud. The big west-countryman at his elbow, swarthy and bearded like a gigantic Spaniard, said in a rumbling bass:—"There's no one left forward, sir. I had a look round. He ain't aboard, but he may turn up before daylight."—"Ay. He may or he may not," commented the mate, "can't make out that last name. It's all a smudge. . . . That will do, men. Go below."

The distinct and motionless group stirred, broke up, began to move forward.

"Wait!" cried a deep, ringing voice.

All stood still. Mr. Baker, who had turned away yawning, spun round open-mouthed. At last, furious, he blurted out:— "What's this? Who said 'Wait'? What . . ."

But he saw a tall figure standing on the rail. It came down and pushed through the crowd, marching with a heavy tread towards the light on the quarter-deck. Then again the sonorous voice said with insistence:—"Wait!" The lamplight lit up the man's body. He was tall. His head was away up in the shadows of lifeboats that stood on skids above the deck. The whites of his eyes and his teeth gleamed distinctly, but the face was indistinguishable. His hands were big and seemed gloved.

Mr. Baker advanced intrepidly. "Who are you? How dare you . . ." he began.

The boy, amazed like the rest, raised the light to the man's face. It was black. A surprised hum—a faint hum that sounded

like the suppressed mutter of the word "Nigger"—ran along
the deck and escaped out into the night. The nigger seemed not
to hear. He balanced himself where he stood in a swagger that
marked time. After a moment he said calmly:—"My name is
Wait—James Wait."

"Oh!" said Mr. Baker. Then, after a few seconds of smouldering silence, his temper blazed out. "Ah! Your name is Wait.
What of that? What do you want? What do you mean, coming
shouting here?"

The nigger was calm, cool, towering, superb. The men had
approached and stood behind him in a body. He overtopped
the tallest by half a head. He said: "I belong to the ship." He
enunciated distinctly, with soft precision. The deep, rolling
tones of his voice filled the deck without effort. He was naturally
scornful, unaffectedly condescending, as if from his height of six
foot three he had surveyed all the vastness of human folly and
had made up his mind not to be too hard on it. He went
on:—"The captain shipped me this morning. I couldn't get
aboard sooner. I saw you all aft as I came up the ladder, and
could see directly you were mustering the crew. Naturally I
called out my name. I thought you had it on your list, and would
understand. You misapprehended." He stopped short. The folly
around him was confounded. He was right as ever, and as ever
ready to forgive. The disdainful tones had ceased, and, breathing heavily, he stood still, surrounded by all these white men.
He held his head up in the glare of the lamp—a head vigorously
modelled into deep shadows and shining lights—a head powerful and misshapen with a tormented and flattened face—a face
pathetic and brutal: the tragic, the mysterious, the repulsive
mask of a nigger's soul.

Mr. Baker, recovering his composure, looked at the paper
close. "Oh, yes; that's so. All right, Wait. Take your gear forward," he said.

Suddenly the nigger's eyes rolled wildly, became all whites.
He put his hand to his side an coughed twice, a cough metallic,
hollow, and tremendously loud; it resounded like two explosions

in a vault; the dome of the sky rang to it, and the iron plates of the ship's bulwarks seemed to vibrate in unison, then he marched off forward with the others. The officers lingering by the cabin door could hear him say: "Won't some of you chaps lend a hand with my dunnage? I've got a chest and a bag." The words, spoken sonorously, with an even intonation, were heard all over the ship, and the question was put in a manner that made refusal impossible. The short, quick shuffle of men carrying something heavy went away forward, but the tall figure of the nigger lingered by the main hatch in a knot of smaller shapes. Again he was heard asking: "Is your cook a coloured gentleman?" Then a disappointed and disapproving "Ah! h'm!" was his comment upon the information that the cook happened to be a mere white man. Yet, as they went all together towards the forecastle, he condescended to put his head through the galley door and boom out inside a magnificent "Good evening, doctor!" that made all the saucepans ring. In the dim light the cook dozed on the coal locker in front of the captain's supper. He jumped up as if he had been cut with a whip, and dashed wildly on deck to see the backs of several men going away laughing. Afterwards, when talking about that voyage, he used to say:—"The poor fellow had scared me. I thought I had seen the devil." The cook had been seven years in the ship with the same captain. He was a serious-minded man with a wife and three children, whose society he enjoyed on an average one month out of twelve. When on shore he took his family to church twice every Sunday. At sea he went to sleep every evening with his lamp turned up full, a pipe in his mouth, and an open Bible in his hand. Some one had always to go during the night to put out the light, take the book from his hand, and the pipe from between his teeth. "For"—Belfast used to say, irritated and complaining—"some night, you stupid cookie, you'll swallow your ould clay, and we will have no cook."—"Ah! sonny, I am ready for my Maker's call . . . wish you all were," the other would answer with a benign serenity that was altogether imbecile and touching. Belfast outside the galley door danced with vexation.

"You holy fool! I don't want you to die," he howled, looking up with furious, quivering face and tender eyes. "What's the hurry? You blessed wooden-headed ould heretic, the divvle will have you soon enough. Think of Us . . . of Us . . . of Us!" And he would go away, stamping, spitting aside, disgusted and worried; while the other, stepping out, saucepan in hand, hot, begrimed and placid, watched with a superior, cock-sure smile the back of his "queer little man" reeling in a rage. They were great friends.

Mr. Baker, lounging over the after-hatch, sniffed the humid night in the company of the second mate.—"Those West India niggers run fine and large—some of them . . . Ough! . . . Don't they? A fine, big man that, Mr. Creighton. Feel him on a rope. Hey? Ough! I will take him into my watch, I think." The second mate, a fair, gentlemanly young fellow, with a resolute face and a splendid physique, observed quietly that it was just about what he expected. There could be felt in his tone some slight bitterness which Mr. Baker very kindly set himself to argue away. "Come, come, young man," he said, grunting between the words. "Come! Don't be too greedy. You had that big Finn in your watch all the voyage. I will do what's fair. You may have those two young Scandinavians and I . . . Ough! . . . I get the nigger, and will take that . . . Ough! that cheeky coster-monger chap in a black frock-coat. I'll make him . . . Ough! . . . make him toe the mark, or my . . . Ough! . . . name isn't Baker. Ough! Ough! Ough!"

He grunted thrice—ferociously. He had that trick of grunting so between his words and at the end of sentences. It was a fine, effective grunt that went well with his menacing utterance, with his heavy, bullnecked frame, his jerky, rolling gait; with his big, seamed face, his steady eyes, and sardonic mouth. But its effect had been long ago discounted by the men. They liked him; Belfast—who was a favorite, and knew it—mimicked him, not quite behind his back. Charley—but with greater caution—imitated his rolling gait. Some of his sayings became established, daily quotations in the forecastle. Popularity can go no farther! Besides, all hands were ready to admit that on a fitting occasion the mate could "jump down a fellow's throat in a reg'lar Western Ocean style."

Now he was giving his last orders. "Ough! . . . You, Knowles! Call all hands at four. I want . . . Ough! . . . to heave short before the tug comes. Look out for the captain. I am going to lie down in my clothes. . . . Ough! . . . Call me when you see the boat coming. Ough! Ough! . . . The old man is sure to have something to say when he gets aboard," he remarked to Creighton. "Well, good-night. . . . Ough! A long day before us to-morrow. . . . Ough! . . . Better turn in now. Ough! Ough!"

Upon the dark deck a band of light flashed, then a door slammed, and Mr. Baker was gone into his neat cabin. Young Creighton stood leaning over the rail, and looked dreamily into the night of the East. And he saw in it a long country lane, a lane of waving leaves and dancing sunshine. He saw stirring boughs of old trees outspread, and framing in their arch the tender, the caressing blueness of an English sky. And through the arch a girl in a light dress, smiling under a sunshade, seemed to be stepping out of the tender sky.

At the other end of the ship the forecastle, with only one lamp burning now, was going to sleep in a dim emptiness traversed by loud breathings, by sudden short sighs. The double row of berths yawned black, like graves tenanted by uneasy corpses. Here and there a curtain of gaudy chintz, half drawn, marked the resting-place of a sybarite. A leg hung over the edge very white and lifeless. An arm stuck straight out with a dark palm turned up, and thick fingers half closed. Two light snores, that did not synchronise, quarrelled in funny dialogue. Singleton stripped again—the old man suffered much from prickly heat— stood cooling his back in the doorway, with his arms crossed on his bare and adorned chest. His head touched the beam of the deck above. The nigger, half undressed, was busy casting adrift the lashing of his box, and spreading his bedding in an upper berth. He moved about in his socks, tall and noiseless, with a pair of braces beating about his calves. Amongst the shadows of stanchions and bowsprit, Donkin munched a piece of hard ship's bread, sitting on the deck with upturned feet and restless eyes; he held the biscuit up before his mouth in the whole fist and snapped his jaws at it with a raging face. Crumbs fell between his outspread legs. Then he got up.

"Where's our water-cask?" he asked in a contained voice.

Singleton, without a word, pointed with a big hand that held a short smouldering pipe. Donkin bent over the cask, drank out of the tin, splashing the water, turned round and noticed the nigger looking at him over the shoulder with calm loftiness. He moved up sideways.

"There's a blooming supper for a man," he whispered bitterly. "My dorg at 'ome wouldn't 'ave it. It's fit enouf for you an' me. 'Ere's a big ship's fo'c'sle! . . . Not a blooming scrap of meat in the kids. I've looked in all the lockers. . . ."

The nigger stared like a man addressed unexpectedly in a foreign language. Donkin changed his tone:—"Giv' us a bit of 'baccy, mate," he breathed out confidentially, "I 'aven't 'ad smoke or chew for the last month. I am rampin' mad for it. Come on, old man!"

"Don't be familiar," said the nigger. Donkin started and sat down on a chest near by, out of sheer surprise. "We haven't kept pigs together," continued James Wait in a deep undertone. "Here's your tobacco." Then, after a pause, he inquired:— "What ship?"—"*Golden State,*" muttered Donkin indistinctly, biting the tobacco. The nigger whistled low.—"Ran?" he said curtly. Donkin nodded: one of his cheeks bulged out. "In course I ran," he mumbled. "They booted the life hout of one Dago chap on the passage 'ere, then started on me. I cleared hout 'ere. —"Left your dunnage behind?"—"Yes, dunnage and money," answered Donkin, raising his voice a little; "I got nothink. No clothes, no bed. A bandy-legged little Hirish chap 'ere 'as give me a blanket. . . . Think I'll go an' sleep in the fore topmast staysail to-night."

He went on deck trailing behind his back a corner of the blanket. Singleton, without a glance, moved slightly aside to let him pass. The nigger put away his shore togs and sat in clean working clothes on his box, one arm stretched over his knees. After staring at Singleton for some time he asked without emphasis:—"What kind of ship is this? Pretty fair? Eh?"

Singleton didn't stir. A long while after he said, with unmoved face:—"Ship! . . . Ships are all right. It is the men in them!"

He went on smoking in the profound silence. The wisdom of half a century spent in listening to the thunder of the waves had spoken unconsciously through his old lips. The cat purred on the windlass. Then James Wait had a fit of roaring, rattling cough, that shook him, tossed him like a hurricane, and flung him panting with staring eyes headlong on his sea-chest. Several men woke up. One said sleepily out of his bunk: "'Struth! what a blamed row!"—"I have a cold on my chest," gasped Wait.— "Cold! you call it," grumbled the man; "should think 'twas something more. . . ."—"Oh! you think so," said the nigger upright and loftily scornful again. He climbed into his berth and began coughing persistently while he put his head out to glare all round the forecastle. There was no further protest. He fell back on the pillow, and could be heard there wheezing regularly like a man oppressed in his sleep.

Singleton stood at the door with his face to the light and his back to the darkness. And alone in the dim emptiness of the sleeping forecastle he appeared bigger, colossal, very old; old as Father Time himself, who should have come there into this place as quiet as a sepulchre to contemplate with patient eyes the short victory of sleep, the consoler. Yet he was only a child of time, a lonely relic of a devoured and forgotten generation. He stood, still strong, as ever unthinking; a ready man with a vast empty past and with no future, with his childlike impulses and his man's passions already dead within his tattooed breast. The men who could understand his silence were gone—those men who knew how to exist beyond the pale of life and within sight of eternity. They had been strong, as those are strong who know neither doubts nor hopes. They had been impatient and enduring, turbulent and devoted, unruly and faithful. Well-

Conrad in 1896, the year he was married to an English woman, Miss Jessie George

meaning people had tried to represent those men as whining over every mouthful of their food; as going about their work in fear of their lives. But in truth they had been men who knew toil, privation, violence, debauchery—but knew not fear, and had no desire of spite in their hearts. Men hard to manage, but easy to inspire; voiceless men—but men enough to scorn in their hearts the sentimental voices that bewailed the hardness of their fate. It was a fate unique and their own; the capacity to bear it appeared to them the privilege of the chosen! Their generation lived inarticulate and indispensable, without knowing the sweetness of affections or the refuge of a home—and died free from the dark menace of a narrow grave. They were the ever-lasting children of the mysterious sea. Their successors are the grown-up children of a discontented earth. They are less naughty, but less innocent; less profane, but perhaps also less believing; and if they have learned how to speak they have also learned how to whine. But the others were strong and mute; they were effaced, bowed and enduring, like stone caryatides that hold up in the night the lighted halls of a resplendent and glorious edifice. They are gone now—and it does not matter. The sea and the earth are unfaithful to their children: a truth, a faith, a generation of men goes—and is forgotten, and it does not matter! Except, perhaps, to the few of those who believed the truth, confessed the faith—or loved the men.

A breeze was coming. The ship that had been lying tide-rode swung to a heavier puff; and suddenly the slack of the chain cable between the windlass and the hawse-pipe clinked, slipped forward an inch, and rose gently off the deck with a startling suggestion as of unsuspected life that had been lurking stealthily in the iron. In the hawse-pipe the grinding links sent through the ship a sound like a low groan of a man sighing under a burden. The strain came on the windlass, the chain tautened like a string, vibrated—and the handle of the screw-brake moved in slight jerks. Singleton stepped forward.

Till then he had been standing meditative and unthinking, reposeful and hopeless, with a face grim and blank—a sixty-year-old child of the mysterious sea. The thoughts of all his lifetime could have been expressed in six words, but the stir of those things that were as much part of his existence as his beating heart called up a gleam of alert understanding upon the sternness of his aged face. The flame of the lamp swayed, and the old man, with knitted and bushy eyebrows, stood over the brake, watchful and motionless in the wild saraband of dancing shadows. Then the ship, obedient to the call of her anchor, forged ahead slightly and eased the strain. The cable relieved, hung down, and after swaying imperceptibly to and fro dropped with a loud tap on the hard wood planks. Singleton seized the high lever, and, by a violent throw forward of his body, wrung out another half-turn from the brake. He recovered himself, breathed largely, and remained for a while glaring down at the powerful and compact engine that squatted on the deck at his feet like some quiet monster—a creature amazing and tame.

"You . . . hold!" he growled at it masterfully, in the incult tangle of his white beard.

II

NEXT morning, at daylight, the *Narcissus* went to sea.

A slight haze blurred the horizon. Outside the harbour the measureless expanse of smooth water lay sparkling like a floor of jewels, and as empty as the sky. The short black tug gave a pluck to windward, in the usual way, then let go the rope, and hovered for a moment on the quarter with her engines stopped; while the slim, long hull of the ship moved ahead slowly under lower topsails. The loose upper canvas blew out in the breeze with soft round contours, resembling small white clouds snared in the maze of ropes. Then the sheets were hauled home, the yards hoisted, and the ship became a high and lonely pyramid, gliding, all shining and white, through the sunlit mist. The tug turned short and round and went away towards the land. Twenty-six pairs of eyes watched her low broad stern crawling languidly over the smooth swell between the two paddle-wheels that turned fast, beating the water with fierce hurry. She resembled an enormous and aquatic black beetle, surprised by the light, overwhelmed by the sunshine, trying to escape with ineffectual effort into the distant gloom of the land. She left a lingering smudge of smoke on the sky, and two vanishing trails of foam on the water. On the place where she had stopped a round black patch of soot remained, undulating on the swell—an unclean mark of the creature's rest.

The *Narcissus* left alone, heading south, seemed to stand resplendent and still upon the restless sea, under the moving sun. Flakes of foam swept past her sides; the water struck her with flashing blows; the land glided away slowly fading; a few birds screamed on motionless wings over the swaying mastheads. But soon the land disappeared, the birds went away; and to the west the pointed sail of an Arab dhow running for Bombay, rose triangular and upright above the sharp edge of the horizon, lingered and vanished like an illusion. Then the ship's wake, long and straight, stretched itself out through a day of immense solitude. The setting sun, burning on the level of the water, flamed crimson below the blackness of heavy rain clouds. The sunset squall, coming up from behind, dissolved itself into the short deluge of a hissing shower. It left the ship glistening from trucks to waterline, and with darkened sails. She ran easily before a fair monsoon, with her decks cleared for the night; and, moving along with her, was heard the sustained and monotonous swishing of the waves, mingled with the low whispers of men mustered aft for the setting of watches; the short plaint of some block aloft; or, now and then, a loud sigh of wind.

Mr. Baker, coming out of his cabin, called out the first name sharply before closing the door behind him. He was going to take charge of the deck. On the homeward trip, according to an old custom of the sea, the chief officer takes the first nightwatch—from eight till midnight. So Mr. Baker, after he had heard the last "Yes, sir!" said moodily, "Relieve the wheel and look-out"; and climbed with heavy feet the poop ladder to windward. Soon after Mr. Creighton came down, whistling softly, and went into the cabin. On the doorstep the steward lounged, in slippers, meditative, and with his shirt-sleeves rolled up to the armpits. On the main deck the cook, locking up the galley doors, had an altercation with young Charley about a pair of socks. He could be heard saying impressively, in the darkness amidships: "You don't deserve a kindness. I've been drying them for you, and now you complain about the holes—and you swear, too! Right in front of me! If I hadn't been a Christian—which you ain't, you young ruffian—I would give you a clout on the head. . . . Go away!" Men in couples or threes stood pensive or moved silently along the bulwarks in the waist. The first busy day of a homeward passage was sinking into the dull peace of resumed routine. Aft, on the high poop, Mr. Baker walked shuffling and grunted to himself in the pauses of his thoughts. Forward, the look-out man, erect between the flukes of the two anchors, hummed an endless tune, keeping his eyes fixed dutifully ahead in a vacant stare. A multitude of stars coming out into the clear night peopled the emptiness of the sky. They glittered, as if alive above the sea; they surrounded the running ship on all sides; more intense than the eyes of a staring crowd, and as inscrutable as the souls of men.

The passage had begun, and the ship, a fragment detached from the earth, went on lonely and swift like a small planet. Round her the abysses of sky and sea met in an unattainable frontier. A great circular solitude moved with her, ever changing and ever the same, always monotonous and always imposing. Now and then another wandering white speck, burdened with life, appeared far off—disappeared; intent on its own destiny. The sun looked upon her all day, and every morning rose with a burning, round stare of undying curiosity. She had her own future; she was alive with the lives of those beings who trod her decks; like that earth which had given her up to the sea, she had an intolerable load of regrets and hopes. On her lived timid truth and audacious lies; and, like the earth, she was unconscious, fair to see—and condemned by men to an ignoble fate. The august loneliness of her path lent dignity to the sordid inspiration of her pilgrimage. She drove foaming to the southward, as if guided by the courage of a high endeavour. The smiling greatness of the sea dwarfed the extent of time. The days raced after one another, brilliant and quick like the flashes of a lighthouse, and the nights, eventful and short, resembled fleeting dreams.

The men had shaken into their places, and the half-hourly voice of the bells ruled their life of unceasing care. Night and day the head and shoulders of a seaman could be seen aft by the wheel, outlined high against sunshine or starlight, very steady above the stir of revolving spokes. The faces changed, passing in rotation. Youthful faces, bearded faces, dark faces: faces serene, or faces moody, but all akin with the brotherhood of the sea; all with the same attentive expression of eyes, carefully watching the compass or the sails. Captain Allistoun, serious, and with an old red muffler round his throat, all day long pervaded the poop. At night, many times he rose out of the darkness of the companion, such as a phantom above a grave, and stood watchful and mute under the stars, his night-shirt fluttering like a flag—then, without a sound, sank down again. He was born on the shores of the Pentland Firth. In his youth he attained the rank of harpooner in Peterhead whalers. When he spoke of that time his restless grey eyes became still and cold, like the loom of ice. Afterwards he went into the East Indian trade for the sake of change. He had commanded the *Narcissus* since she was built. He loved his ship, and drove her unmercifully; for his secret ambition was to make her accomplish some day a brilliantly quick passage which would be mentioned in nautical papers. He pronounced his owner's name with a sardonic smile, spoke but seldom to his officers, and reproved errors in a gentle voice, with words that cut to the quick. His hair was iron-grey, his face hard and of the colour of pump-leather. He shaved every morning of his life—at six—but once (being caught in a fierce hurricane eighty miles southwest of Mauritius) he had missed three consecutive days. He feared nought but an unforgiving God, and wished to end his days in a little house, with a plot of ground attached—far in the country—out of sight of the sea.

He, the ruler of that minute world, seldom descended from the Olympian heights of his poop. Below him—at his feet, so to speak—common mortals led their busy and insignificant lives. Along the main deck, Mr. Baker grunted in a manner bloodthirsty and innocuous; and kept all our noses to the grindstone, being—as he once remarked—paid for doing that very thing. The men working about the deck were healthy and contented— as most seamen are, when once well out to sea. The true peace of God begins at any spot a thousand miles from the nearest land; and when He sends there the messengers of His might it is not in terrible wrath against crime, presumption, and folly, but paternally, to chasten simple hearts—ignorant hearts that know nothing of life, and beat undisturbed by envy or greed.

In the evening the cleared decks had a reposeful aspect, resembling the autumn of the earth. The sun was sinking to rest, wrapped in a mantle of warm clouds. Forward, on the end of the spare spars, the boatswain and the carpenter sat together with crossed arms; two men friendly, powerful, and deep-chested. Beside them the short, dumpy sailmaker—who had been in the Navy—related, between the whiffs of his pipe, impossible stories about Admirals. Couples tramped backwards and forwards, keeping step and balance without effort, in a confined space. Pigs grunted in the big pigstye. Belfast, leaning thoughtfully on his elbow, above the bars, communed with them through the silence of his meditation. Fellows with shirts open wide on sunburnt breasts sat upon the mooring bits, and all up the steps of the forecastle ladders. By the foremast a few discussed in a circle the characteristics of a gentleman. One said:—"It's money as does it." Another maintained:—"No, it's the way they speak." Lame Knowles stumped up with an unwashed face (he had the distinction of being the dirty man of the forecastle), and show-

ing a few yellow fangs in a shrewd smile, explained craftily that
he "had seen some of their pants." The backsides of them—he
had observed—were thinner than paper from constant sitting
down in offices, yet otherwise they looked first-rate and would
last for years. It was all appearance. "It was," he said, "bloomin'
easy to be a gentleman when you had a clean job for life." They
disputed endlessly, obstinate and childish; they repeated in
shouts and with inflamed faces their amazing arguments; while
the soft breeze, eddying down the enormous cavity of the foresail, distended above their bare heads, stirred the tumbled hair
with a touch passing and light like an indulgent caress.

They were forgetting their toil, they were forgetting themselves. The cook approached to hear, and stood by, beaming
with the inward consciousness of his faith, like a conceited
saint unable to forget his glorious reward; Donkin, solitary and
brooding over his wrongs on the forecastle-head, moved closer to
catch the drift of the discussion below him; he turned his sallow
face to the sea, and his thin nostrils moved, sniffing the breeze,
as he lounged negligently by the rail. In the glow of sunset faces
shone with interest, teeth flashed, eyes sparkled. The walking
couples stood still suddenly, with broad grins; a man, bending
over a washtub, sat up, entranced, with the soapsuds flecking
his wet arms. Even the three petty officers listened leaning back,
comfortably propped, and with superior smiles. Belfast left off
scratching the ear of his favourite pig, and, open mouthed, tried
with eager eyes to have his say. He lifted his arms, grimacing
and baffled. From a distance Charley screamed at the ring:—"I
know about gentlemen more'n any of you. I've been intermit
with 'em. . . . I've blacked their boots." The cook, craning his
neck to hear better, was scandalised. "Keep your mouth shut
when your elders speak, you impudent young heathen—you."
"All right, old Hallelujah, I'm done," answered Charley, soothingly. At some opinion of dirty Knowles, delivered with an air
of supernatural cunning, a ripple of laughter ran along, rose
like a wave, burst with a startling roar. They stamped with both
feet; they turned their shouting faces to the sky; many, sputter-

124   THE NIGGER OF THE "NARCISSUS"

ing, slapped their thighs; while one or two, bent double, gasped, hugging themselves with both arms like men in pain. The carpenter and the boatswain, without changing their attitude, shook with laughter where they sat; the sailmaker, charged with an anecdote about a Commodore, looked sulky; the cook was wiping his eyes with a greasy rag; and lame Knowles, astonished at his own success, stood in their midst showing a slow smile.

Suddenly the face of Donkin leaning high-shouldered over the after-rail became grave. Something like a weak rattle was heard through the forecastle door. It became a murmur; it ended in a sighing groan. The washerman plunged both his arms into the tub abruptly; the cook became more crestfallen than an exposed backslider; the boatswain moved his shoulders uneasily; the carpenter got up with a spring and walked away— while the sailmaker seemed mentally to give his story up, and began to puff at his pipe with sombre determination. In the blackness of the doorway a pair of eyes glimmered white, and big, and staring. Then James Wait's head protruding, became visible, as if suspended between the two hands that grasped a doorpost on each side of the face. The tassel of his blue woollen nightcap, cocked foward, danced gaily over his left eyelid. He stepped out in a tottering stride. He looked powerful as ever, but showed a strange and affected unsteadiness in his gait; his face was perhaps a trifle thinner, and his eyes appeared rather startlingly prominent. He seemed to hasten the retreat of departing light by his very presence; the setting sun dipped sharply, as though fleeing before our nigger; a black mist emanated from him; a subtle and dismal influence; a something cold and gloomy that floated out and settled on all the faces like a mourning veil. The circle broke up. The joy of laughter died on stiffened lips. There was not a smile left among all the ship's company. Not a word was spoken. Many turned their backs, trying to look unconcerned; others, with averted heads, sent half-reluctant glances out of the corners of their eyes. They resembled criminals conscious of misdeeds more than honest men distracted by doubt; only two or three stared frankly, but stupidly, with lips slightly open. All expected James Wait to say something, and, at the same time, had the air of knowing beforehand what he would say. He leaned his back against the doorpost, and with heavy eyes swept over them a glance domineering and pained, like a sick tyrant overawing a crowd of abject but untrustworthy slaves.

No one went away. They waited in fascinated dread. He said ironically, with gasps between the words:—

"Thank you . . . chaps. You . . . are nice . . . and . . . quiet . . . you are! Yelling so . . . before . . . the door. . . ."

He made a longer pause, during which he worked his ribs in an exaggerated labour of breathing. It was intolerable. Feet were shuffled. Belfast let out a groan; but Donkin above blinked his red eyelids with invisible eyelashes, and smiled bitterly over the nigger's head.

The nigger went on again with surprising ease. He gasped no more, and his voice rang, hollow and loud, as though he had been talking in an empty cavern. He was contemptuously angry.

"I tried to get a wink of sleep. You know I can't sleep o' nights. And you come jabbering near the door here like a blooming lot of old women. . . . You think yourselves good shipmates. Do you? . . . Much you care for a dying man!"

Belfast spun away from the pigstye. "Jimmy," he cried tremulously, "if you hadn't been sick I would——"

He stopped. The nigger waited awhile, then said, in a gloomy tone:—"You would. . . . What? Go an' fight another such one as yourself. Leave me alone. It won't be for long. I'll soon die. . . . It's coming right enough!"

Men stood around very still and with exasperated eyes. It was just what they had expected, and hated to hear, that idea of stalking death, thrust at them many times a day like a boast and like a menace by this obnoxious nigger. He seemed to take a pride in that death which, so far, had attended only upon the ease of his life; he was overbearing about it, as if no one else in the world had ever been intimate with such a companion; he paraded it unceasingly before us with an affectionate persistence that made its presence indubitable, and at the same time incredible. No man could be suspected of such monstrous friendship! Was he a reality—or was he a sham—this ever-expected visitor of Jimmy's? We hesitated between pity and mistrust, while, on the slightest provocation, he shook before our eyes the bones of his bothersome and infamous skeleton. He was for ever trotting him out. He would talk of that coming death as though it had been already there, as if it had been walking the deck outside, as if it would presently come in to sleep in the only empty bunk; as if it had sat by his side at every meal. It interfered daily with our occupations, with our leisure, with our amusements. We had no songs and no music in the evening, because Jimmy (we all lovingly called him Jimmy, to conceal our hate of his accomplice) had managed, with that prospective decease of his, to disturb even Archie's mental balance. Archie was the owner of the concertina; but after a couple of stinging lectures from Jimmy he refused to play any more. He said:— "Yon's an uncanny joker. I dinna ken what's wrang wi' him, but there's something verra wrang, verra wrang. It's nae manner of use asking me. I won't play." Our singers became mute because Jimmy was a dying man. For the same reason no chap—as Knowles remarked—could "drive in a nail to hang his few poor rags upon," without being made aware of the enormity he committed in disturbing Jimmy's interminable last moments. At night, instead of the cheerful yell, "One bell! Turn out! Do you hear there? Hey! hey! hey! Show leg!" the watches were called man by man, in whispers, so as not to interfere with Jimmy's, possibly, last slumber on earth. True, he was always awake, and managed, as we sneaked out on deck, to plant in our backs some cutting remark that, for the moment, made us feel as if we had been brutes, and afterwards made us suspect ourselves of being fools. We spoke in low tones within that fo'c'sle as though it had been a church. We ate our meals in silence and dread, for Jimmy was capricious with his food, and railed bitterly at the salt meat, at the biscuits, at the tea, as at

articles unfit for human consumption—"let alone for a dying
man!" He would say:—"Can't you find a better slice of meat for
a sick man who's trying to get home to be cured—or buried?
But there! If I had a chance, you fellows would do away with it.
You would poison me. Look at what you have given me!" We
served him in his bed with rage and humility, as though we had
been the base courtiers of a hated prince; and he rewarded us
by his unconciliating criticism. He had found the secret of keeping for ever on the run the fundamental imbecility of mankind;
he had the secret of life, that confounded dying man, and he
made himself master of every moment of our existence. We grew
desperate, and remained submissive. Emotional little Belfast
was for ever on the verge of assault or on the verge of tears. One
evening he confided to Archie:—"For a ha'penny I would
knock his ugly black head off—the skulking dodger!" And the
straightforward Archie pretended to be shocked! Such was the
infernal spell which that casual St. Kitt's nigger had cast upon
our guileless manhood! But the same night Belfast stole from
the galley the officers' Sunday fruit pie, to tempt the fastidious
appetite of Jimmy. He endangered not only his long friendship
with the cook but also—as it appeared—his eternal welfare. The
cook was overwhelmed with grief; he did not know the culprit
but he knew that wickedness flourished; he knew that Satan
was abroad amongst those men, whom he looked upon as in
some way under his spiritual care. Whenever he saw three or
four of us standing together he would leave his stove, to run out
and preach. We fled from him; and only Charley (who knew the
thief) affronted the cook with a candid gaze which irritated the
good man. "It's you, I believe," he groaned, sorrowful and with
a patch of soot on his chin. "It's you. You are a brand for the
burning! No more of YOUR socks in my galley." Soon, unoffi-
cially, the information was spread about that, should there be
another case of stealing, our marmalade (an extra allowance:
half a pound per man) would be stopped. Mr. Baker ceased to
heap jocular abuse upon his favourites, and grunted suspi-
ciously at all. The captain's cold eyes, high up on the poop,

glittered mistrustful, as he surveyed us trooping in a small mob from halyards to braces for the usual evening pull at all the ropes. Such stealing in a merchant ship is difficult to check, and may be taken as a declaration by men of their dislike for their officers. It is a bad symptom. It may end in God knows what trouble. The *Narcissus* was still a peaceful ship, but mutual confidence was shaken. Donkin did not conceal his delight. We were dismayed.

Then illogical Belfast reproached our nigger with great fury. James Wait, with his elbow on the pillow, choked, gasped out:— "Did I ask you to bone the dratted thing? Blow your blamed pie. It has made me worse—you little Irish lunatic, you!" Belfast, with scarlet face and trembling lips, made a dash at him. Every man in the forecastle rose with a shout. There was a moment of wild tumult. Some one shrieked piercingly:—"Easy, Belfast! Easy! . . ." We expected Belfast to strangle Wait without more ado. Dust flew. We heard through it the nigger's cough, metallic and explosive like a gong. Next moment we saw Belfast hanging over him. He was saying plaintively:—"Don't! Don't, Jimmy! Don't be like that. An angel couldn't put up with ye— sick as ye are." He looked round at us from Jimmy's bedside, his comical mouth twitching, and through tearful eyes; then he tried to put straight the disarranged blankets. The unceasing whisper of the sea filled the forecastle. Was James Wait frightened, or touched, or repentant? He lay on his back with a hand to his side, and as motionless as if his expected visitor had come at last. Belfast fumbled about his feet, repeating with emotion:— "Yes. We know. Ye are bad, but. . . . Just say what ye want done, and. . . . We all know ye are bad—very bad. . . ." No! Decidedly James Wait was not touched or repentant. Truth to say, he seemed rather startled. He sat up with incredible suddenness and ease. "Ah! You think I am bad, do you?" he said gloomily, in his clearest baritone voice (to hear him speak sometimes you would never think there was anything wrong with that man). "Do you? . . . Well, act according! Some of you haven't sense enough to put a blanket shipshape over a sick man. There!

Leave it alone! I can die anyhow!" Belfast turned away limply
with a gesture of discouragement. In the silence of the forecastle, full of interested men, Donkin pronounced distinctly:—
'Well, I'm blowed!" and sniggered. Wait looked at him. He
looked at him in a quite friendly manner. Nobody could tell
what would please our incomprehensible invalid: but for us the
scorn of that snigger was hard to bear.

Donkin's position in the forecastle was distinguished but unsafe. He stood on the bad eminence of a general dislike. He was
left alone; and in his isolation he could do nothing but think of
the gales of the Cape of Good Hope and envy us the possession
of warm clothing and waterproofs. Our sea-boots, our oilskin
coats, our well-filled sea-chests, were to him so many causes for
bitter meditation: he had none of those things, and he felt instinctively that no man, when the need arose, would offer to
share them with him. He was impudently cringing to us and
systematically insolent to the officers. He anticipated the best
results, for himself, from such a line of conduct—and was mis-
taken. Such natures forget that under extreme provocation men
will be just—whether they want to be so or not. Donkin's insolence to long-suffering Mr. Baker became at last intolerable to
us, and we rejoiced when the mate, one dark night, tamed him
for good. It was done neatly, with great decency and decorum,
and with little noise. We had been called—just before midnight—to trim the yards, and Donkin—as usual—made insulting
remarks. We stood sleepily in a row with the forebrace in our
hands waiting for the next order, and heard in the darkness a
scuffly trampling of feet, an exclamation of surprise, sounds of
cuffs and slaps, suppressed, hissing whispers:—"Ah! Will you!"
. . . "Don't! . . . Don't!" . . . "Then behave." . . . "Oh! Oh! . . ."
Afterwards there were soft thuds mixed with the rattle of iron
things as if a man's body had been tumbling helplessly amongst
the main-pump rods. Before we could realise the situation, Mr.
Baker's voice was heard very near and a little impatient:—"Haul
away, men! Lay back on that rope!" And we did lay back on the
rope with great alacrity. As if nothing had happened, the chief

mate went on trimming the yards with his usual and exasperating fastidiousness. We didn't at the time see anything of Donkin, and did not care. Had the chief officer thrown him overboard, no man would have said as much as "Hallo! he's gone!" But, in truth, no great harm was done—even if Donkin did lose one of his front teeth. We perceived this in the morning, and preserved a ceremonious silence; the etiquette of the forecastle commanded us to be blind and dumb in such a case, and we cherished the decencies of our life more than ordinary landsmen respect theirs. Charley, with unpardonable want of *savoir vivre*, yelled out:—"'Ave you been to your dentyst? . . . Hurt ye, didn't it?" He got a box on the ear from one of his best friends. The boy was surprised, and remained plunged in grief for at least three hours. We were sorry for him, but youth requires even more discipline than age. Donkin grinned venomously. From that day he became pitiless; told Jimmy that he was a "black fraud"; hinted to us that we were an imbecile lot, daily taken in by a vulgar nigger. And Jimmy seemed to like the fellow!

Singleton lived untouched by human emotions. Taciturn and unsmiling, he breathed amongst us—in that alone resembling the rest of the crowd. We were trying to be decent chaps, and found it jolly difficult; we oscillated between the desire of virtue and the fear of ridicule; we wished to save ourselves from the pain of remorse, but did not want to be made the contemptible dupes of our sentiment. Jimmy's hateful accomplice seemed to have blown with his impure breath undreamt-of subtleties into our hearts. We were disturbed and cowardly. That we knew. Singleton seemed to know nothing, understand nothing. We had thought him till then as wise as he looked, but now we dared, at times, suspect him of being stupid—from old age. One day, however, at dinner, as we sat on our boxes round a tin dish that stood on the deck within the circle of our feet, Jimmy expressed his general disgust with men and things in words that were particularly disgusting. Singleton lifted his head. We became mute. The old man, addressing Jimmy, asked:—"Are you

dying?" Thus interrogated, James Wait appeared horribly startled and confused. We all were startled. Mouths remained open;
hearts thumped, eyes blinked; a dropped tin fork rattled in the
dish; a man rose as if to go out, and stood still. In less than a
minute Jimmy pulled himself together:—"Why? Can't you see
I am?" he answered shakily. Singleton lifted a piece of soaked
biscuit ("his teeth"—he declared—"had no edge on them now") to
his lips.—"Well, get on with your dying," he said with venerable
mildness; "don't raise a blamed fuss with us over that job. We
can't help you." Jimmy fell back in his bunk, and for a long
time lay very still wiping the perspiration off his chin. The din-
ner-tins were put away quickly. On deck we discussed the inci-
dent in whispers. Some showed a chuckling exultation. Many
looked grave. Wamibo, after long periods of staring dreaminess,
attempted abortive smiles; and one of the young Scandinavians,
much tormented by doubt, ventured in the second dog-watch to
approach Singleton (the old man did not encourage us much to
speak to him) and ask sheepishly:—"You think he will die?"
Singleton looked up.—"Why, of course he will die," he said
deliberately. This seemed decisive. It was promptly imparted
to every one by him who had consulted the oracle. Shy and
eager, he would step up and with averted gaze recite his
formula:—"Old Singleton says he will die." It was a relief! At
last we knew that our compassion would not be misplaced, and
we could again smile without misgivings—but we reckoned without Donkin. Donkin "didn't want to 'ave no truck with 'em
dirty furriners." When Nilsen came to him with the news:
"Singleton says he will die," he answered him by a spiteful
"And so will you—you fat-headed Dutchman. Wish you Dutch-
men were all dead—'stead comin' takin' our money inter your
starvin' country." We were appalled. We perceived that after
all Singleton's answer meant nothing. We began to hate him
for making fun of us. All our certitudes were going; we were on
doubtful terms with our officers; the cook had given us up for
lost; we had overheard the boatswain's opinion that "we were a
crowd of softies." We suspected Jimmy, one another, and even

our very selves. We did not know what to do. At every insignificant turn of our humble life we met Jimmy overbearing and
blocking the way, arm-in-arm with his awful and veiled familiar.
It was a weird servitude.

It began a week after leaving Bombay and came on us stealthily like any other great misfortune. Every one had remarked
that Jimmy from the first was very slack at his work; but we
thought it simply the outcome of his philosophy of life. Donkin said:—"You put no more weight on a rope than a bloody
sparrer." He disdained him. Belfast, ready for a fight, exclaimed
provokingly:—"You don't kill yourself, old man!"—"Would
you?" he retorted with extreme scorn—and Belfast retired. One
morning, as we were washing decks, Mr. Baker called to him:—
"Bring your broom over here, Wait." He strolled languidly.
"Move yourself! Ough!" grunted Mr. Baker; "what's the matter
with your hind legs?" He stopped dead short. He gazed slowly
with eyes that bulged out with an expression audacious and sad.
—"It isn't my legs," he said, "it's my lungs." Everybody listened.
—"What's . . . Ough! . . . What's wrong with them?" inquired
Mr. Baker. All the watch stood around on the wet deck, grinning, and with brooms or buckets in their hands. He said mournfully:—"Going—or gone. Can't you see I'm a dying man? I know
it!" Mr. Baker was disgusted.—"Then why the devil did you
ship aboard here?"—"I must live till I die—mustn't I?" he replied. The grins became audible.—"Go off the deck—get out of
my sight," said Mr. Baker. He was nonplussed. It was a unique
experience. James Wait, obedient, dropped his broom, and
walked slowly forward. A burst of laughter followed him. It was
too funny. All hands laughed. . . . They laughed! . . . Alas!

He became the tormentor of all our moments; he was worse
than a nightmare. You couldn't see that there was anything
wrong with him: a nigger does not show. He was not very fat—
certainly—but then he was no leaner than other niggers we had
known. He coughed often, but the most prejudiced person
could perceive that, mostly, he coughed when it suited his purpose. He wouldn't, or couldn't, do his work—and he wouldn't

lie-up. One day he would skip aloft with the best of them, and next time we would be obliged to risk our lives to get his limp body down. He was reported, he was examined; he was remonstrated with, threatened, cajoled, lectured. He was called into the cabin to interview the captain. There were wild rumours. It was said he had cheeked the old man; it was said he had frightened him. Charley maintained that the "skipper, weepin,' 'as giv' 'im 'is blessin' an' a pot of jam." Knowles had it from the steward that the unspeakable Jimmy had been reeling against the cabin furniture; that he had groaned; that he had complained of general brutality and disbelief; and had ended by coughing all over the old man's meteorological journals which were then spread on the table. At any rate, Wait returned forward supported by the steward, who, in a pained and shocked voice, entreated us:—"Here! Catch hold of him, one of you. He is to lie-up." Jimmy drank a tin mugful of coffee, and, after bullying first one and then another, went to bed. He remained there most of the time, but when it suited him would come on deck and appear amongst us. He was scornful and brooding; he looked ahead upon the sea, and no one could tell what was the meaning of that black man sitting apart in a meditative attitude and as motionless as a carving.

He refused steadily all medicine; he threw sago and cornflour overboard till the steward got tired of bringing it to him. He asked for paregoric. They sent him a big bottle; enough to poison a wilderness of babies. He kept it between his mattress and the deal lining of the ship's side; and nobody ever saw him take a dose. Donkin abused him to his face, jeered at him while he gasped; and the same day Wait would lend him a warm jersey. Once Donkin reviled him for half an hour; reproached him with the extra work his malingering gave to the watch; and ended by calling him "a black-faced swine." Under the spell of our accursed perversity we were horror-struck. But Jimmy positively seemed to revel in that abuse. It made him look cheerful—and Donkin had a pair of old sea boots thrown at him. "Here, you East-end trash," boomed Wait, "you may have that."

At last Mr. Baker had to tell the captain that James Wait was disturbing the peace of the ship. "Knock discipline on the head —he will, Ough," grunted Mr. Baker. As a matter of fact, the starboard watch came as near as possible to refusing duty, when ordered one morning by the boatswain to wash out their forecastle. It appears Jimmy objected to a wet floor—and that morning we were in a compassionate mood. We thought the boatswain a brute, and, practically, told him so. Only Mr. Baker's delicate tact prevented an all-fired row: he refused to take us seriously. He came bustling forward, and called us many unpolite names but in such a hearty and seamanlike manner that we began to feel ashamed of ourselves. In truth, we thought him much too good a sailor to annoy him willingly: and after all Jimmy might have been a fraud—probably was! The forecastle got a clean up that morning; but in the afternoon a sick-bay was fitted up in the deck-house. It was a nice little cabin opening on deck, and with two berths. Jimmy's belongings were transported there, and then—notwithstanding his protests—Jimmy himself. He said he couldn't walk. Four men carried him on a blanket. He complained that he would have to die there alone, like a dog. We grieved for him, and were delighted to have him removed from the forecastle. We attended him as before. The galley was next door, and the cook looked in many times a day. Wait became a little more cheerful. Knowles affirmed having heard him laugh to himself in peals one day. Others had seen him walking about on deck at night. His little place, with the door ajar on a long hook, was always full of tobacco smoke. We spoke through the crack cheerfully, sometimes abusively, as we passed by, intent on our work. He fascinated us. He would never let doubt die. He overshadowed the ship. Invulnerable in his promise of speedy corruption he trampled on our self respect, he demonstrated to us daily our want of moral courage; he tainted our lives. Had we been a miserable gang of wretched immortals, unhallowed alike by hope and fear, he could not have lorded it over us with a more pitiless assertion of his sublime privilege.

III

MEANTIME the *Narcissus*, with square yards, ran out of the fair monsoon. She drifted slowly, swinging round and round the compass, through a few days of baffling light airs. Under the patter of short warm showers, grumbling men whirled the heavy yards from side to side; they caught hold of the soaked ropes with groans and sighs, while their officers, sulky and dripping with rain water, unceasingly ordered them about in wearied voices. During the short respites they looked with disgust into the smarting palms of their stiff hands, and asked one another bitterly:—"Who would be a sailor if he could be a farmer?" All the tempers were spoilt, and no man cared what he said. One black night, when the watch, panting in the heat and half-drowned with rain, had been through four mortal hours hunted from brace to brace, Belfast declared that he would "chuck the sea for ever and go in a steamer." This was excessive, no doubt. Captain Allistoun, with great self-control, would mutter sadly to Mr. Baker:—"It is not so bad—not so bad," when he had managed to shove, and dodge, and manœuvre his smart ship through sixty miles in twenty-four hours. From the doorstep of the little cabin, Jimmy, chin in hand, watched our distasteful labours with insolent and melancholy eyes. We spoke to him gently—and out of his sight exchanged our smiles.

Then, again, with a fair wind and under a clear sky, the ship went on piling up the South Latitude. She passed outside Madagascar and Mauritius without a glimpse of the land. Extra lashings were put on the spare spars. Hatches were looked to. The steward in his leisure moments and with a worried air tried to fit washboards to the cabin doors. Stout canvas was bent with care. Anxious eyes looked to the westward, towards the cape of storms. The ship began to dip into a southwest swell, and the softly luminous sky of low latitudes took on a harder

sheen from day to day above our heads: it arched high above
the ship vibrating and pale, like an immense dome of steel, resonant with the deep voice of freshening gales. The sunshine
gleamed cold on the white curls of black waves. Before the strong
breath of westerly squalls the ship, with reduced sail, lay slowly
over, obstinate and yielding. She drove to and fro in the unceasing endeavour to fight her way through the invisible violence
of the winds: she pitched headlong into dark smooth hollows;
she struggled upwards over the snowy ridges of great running
seas; she rolled, restless, from side to side, like a thing in pain.
Enduring and valiant, she answered to the call of men; and her
slim spars waving for ever in abrupt semicircle, seemed to
beckon in vain for help towards the stormy sky.

It was a bad winter off the Cape that year. The relieved helms-
men came off flapping their arms, or ran stamping hard and
blowing into swollen, red fingers. The watch on deck dodged
the sting of cold sprays or, crouching in sheltered corners,
watched dismally the high and merciless seas boarding the ship
time after time in unappeasable fury. Water tumbled in cata-
racts over the forecastle doors. You had to dash through a water-
fall to get into your damp bed. The men turned in wet and
turned out stiff to face the redeeming and ruthless exactions of
their glorious and obscure fate. Far aft, and peering watchfully
to windward, the officers could be seen through the mist of
squalls. They stood by the weather-rail, holding on grimly,
straight and glistening in their long coats; and in the disordered
plunges of the hard-driven ship, they appeared high up, attentive, tossing violently above the grey line of a clouded horizon
in motionless attitudes.

They watched the weather and the ship as men on shore
watch the momentous chances of fortune. Captain Allistoun
never left the deck, as though he had been part of the ship's
fittings. Now and then the steward, shivering, but always in
shirt sleeves, would struggle towards him with some hot coffee,
half of which the gale blew out of the cup before it reached the
master's lips. He drank what was left gravely in one long gulp,

while heavy sprays pattered loudly on his oilskin coat, the seas swishing broke about his high boots; and he never took his eyes off the ship. He kept his gaze riveted upon her as a loving man watches the unselfish toil of a delicate woman upon the slender thread of whose existence is hung the whole meaning and joy of the world. We all watched her. She was beautiful and had a weakness. We loved her no less for that. We admired her qual· ities aloud, we boasted of them to one another, as though they had been our own, and the consciousness of her only fault we kept buried in the silence of our profound affection. She was born in the thundering peal of hammers beating upon iron, in black eddies of smoke, under a grey sky, on the banks of the Clyde. The clamorous and sombre stream gives birth to things of beauty that float away into the sunshine of the world to be loved by men. The *Narcissus* was one of that perfect brood. Less perfect than many perhaps, but she was ours, and, consequently, incomparable. We were proud of her. In Bombay, ignorant landlubbers alluded to her as that "pretty grey ship." Pretty! A scurvy meed of commendation! We knew she was the most magnificent sea-boat ever launched. We tried to forget that, like many good sea-boats, she was at times rather cranky. She was ex- acting. She wanted care in loading and handling, and no one knew exactly how much care would be enough. Such are the imperfections of mere men! The ship knew, and sometimes would correct the presumptuous human ignorance by the whole- some discipline of fear. We had heard ominous stories about past voyages. The cook (technically a seaman, but in reality no sailor)—the cook, when unstrung by some misfortune, such as the rolling over of a saucepan, would mutter gloomily while he wiped the floor:—"There! Look at what she has done! Some voy'ge she will drown all hands! You'll see if she won't." To which the steward, snatching in the galley a moment to draw breath in the hurry of his worried life, would remark philosoph- ically:—"Those that see won't tell, anyhow. I don't want to see it." We derided those fears. Our hearts went out to the old man when he pressed her hard so as to make her hold her own, hold to every inch gained to windward; when he made her, under reefed sails, leap obliquely at enormous waves. The men, knitted together aft into a ready group by the first sharp order of an officer coming to take charge of the deck in bad weather:—"Keep handy the watch," stood admiring her valiance. Their eyes blinked in the wind; their dark faces were wet with drops of water more salt and bitter than human tears; beards and moustaches, soaked, hung straight and dripping like fine seaweed. They were fantastically misshapen; in high boots, in hats like helmets, and swaying clumsily, stiff and bulky in glistening oilskins, they resembled men strangely equipped for some fabulous adventure. Whenever she rose easily to a towering green sea, elbows dug ribs, faces brightened, lips murmured:—"Didn't she do it cleverly," and all the heads turning like one watched with sardonic grins the foiled wave go roaring to leeward, white with the foam of a monstrous rage. But when she had not been quick enough and, struck heavily, lay over trembling under the blow, we clutched at ropes, and looking up at the narrow bands of drenched and strained sails waving desperately aloft, we thought in our hearts:—"No wonder. Poor thing!"

The thirty-second day out of Bombay began inauspiciously. In the morning a sea smashed one of the galley doors. We dashed in through lots of steam and found the cook very wet and indignant with the ship:—"She's getting worse every day. She's trying to drown me in front of my own stove!" He was very angry. We pacified him, and the carpenter, though washed away twice from there, managed to repair the door. Through that accident our dinner was not ready till late, but it didn't matter in the end because Knowles, who went to fetch it, got knocked down by a sea and the dinner went over the side. Captain Allistoun, looking more hard and thin-lipped than ever, hung on to full topsails and foresail, and would not notice that the ship, asked to do too much, appeared to lose heart altogether for the first time since we knew her. She refused to rise, and bored her way sullenly through the seas. Twice running, as though she had been blind or weary of life, she put her nose deliberately

into a big wave and swept the decks from end to end. As the
boatswain observed with marked annoyance, while we were
splashing about in a body to try and save a worthless wash-tub:
—"Every blooming thing in the ship is going overboard this
afternoon." Venerable Singleton broke his habitual silence and
said with a glance aloft:—"The old man's in a temper with the
weather, but it's no good bein' angry with the winds of heaven."
Jimmy had shut his door, of course. We knew he was dry and
comfortable within his little cabin, and in our absurd way were
pleased one moment, exasperated the next, by that certitude.
Donkin skulked shamelessly, uneasy and miserable. He grumbled:—"I'm perishin' with cold outside in bloomin' wet rags,
an' that 'ere black sojer sits dry on a blamed chest full of
bloomin' clothes; blank his black soul!" We took no notice of
him; we hardly gave a thought to Jimmy and his bosom friend.
There was no leisure for idle probing of hearts. Sails blew adrift.
Things broke loose. Cold and wet, we were washed about the
deck while trying to repair damages. The ship tossed about,
shaken furiously, like a toy in the hand of a lunatic. Just at sunset there was a rush to shorten sail before the menace of a
sombre hail cloud. The hard gust of wind came brutal like the
blow of a fist. The ship relieved of her canvas in time received it
pluckily: she yielded reluctantly to the violent onset; then,
coming up with a stately and irresistible motion, brought her
spars to windward in the teeth of the screeching squall. Out of
the abysmal darkness of the black cloud overhead white hail
streamed on her, rattled on the rigging, leaped in handfuls off
the yards, rebounded on the deck—round and gleaming in the
murky turmoil like a shower of pearls. It passed away. For a
moment a livid sun shot horizontally the last rays of sinister light
between the hills of steep, rolling waves. Then a wild night
rushed in—stamped out in a great howl that dismal remnant of
a stormy day.

There was no sleep on board that night. Most seamen remember in their life one or two such nights of a culminating
gale. Nothing seems left of the whole universe but darkness,

clamour, fury—and the ship. And like the last vestige of a shattered creation she drifts, bearing an anguished remnant of sinful mankind, through the distress, tumult, and pain of an avenging terror. No one slept in the forecastle. The tin oil-lamp suspended on a long string, smoking, described wide circles; wet clothing made dark heaps on the glistening floor; a thin layer of water rushed to and fro. In the bed-places men lay booted, resting on elbows and with open eyes. Hung-up suits of oilskin swung out and in, lively and disquieting like reckless ghosts of decapitated seamen dancing in a tempest. No one spoke and all listened. Outside the night moaned and sobbed to the accompaniment of a continuous loud tremor as of innumerable drums beating far off. Shrieks passed through the air. Tremendous dull blows made the ship tremble while she rolled under the weight of the seas toppling on her deck. At times she soared up swiftly as if to leave this earth for ever, then during interminable moments fell through a void with all the hearts on board of her standing still, till a frightful shock, expected and sudden, started them off again with a big thump. After every dislocating jerk of the ship, Wamibo, stretched full length, his face on the pillow, groaned slightly with the pain of his tormented universe. Now and then, for the fraction of an intolerable second, the ship, in the fiercer burst of a terrible uproar, remained on her side, vibrating and still, with a stillness more appalling than the wildest motion. Then upon all those prone bodies a stir would pass, a shiver of suspense. A man would protrude his anxious head and a pair of eyes glistened in the sway of light glaring wildly. Some moved their legs a little as if making ready to jump out. But several, motionless on their backs and with one hand gripping hard the edge of the bunk, smoked nervously with quick puffs, staring upwards; immobilised in a great craving for peace.

At midnight, orders were given to furl the fore and mizen topsails. With immense efforts men crawled aloft through a merciless buffeting, saved the canvas and crawled down almost exhausted, to bear in panting silence the cruel battering of the seas. Perhaps for the first time in the history of the merchant service the watch, told to go below, did not leave the deck, as if compelled to remain there by the fascination of a venomous violence. At every heavy gust men, huddled together, whispered to one another:—"It can blow no harder"—and presently the gale would give them the lie with a piercing shriek, and drive their breath back into their throats. A fierce squall seemed to burst asunder the thick mass of sooty vapours; and above the wrack of torn clouds glimpses could be caught of the high moon rushing backwards with frightful speed over the sky, right into the wind's eye. Many hung their heads, muttering that it "turned their inwards out" to look at it. Soon the clouds closed up and the world again became a raging, blind darkness that howled, flinging at the lonely ship salt sprays and sleet.

About half-past seven the pitchy obscurity round us turned a ghastly grey, and we knew that the sun had risen. This unnatural and threatening daylight, in which we could see one another's wild eyes and drawn faces, was only an added tax on our endurance. The horizon seemed to have come on all sides within arm's length of the ship. Into that narrowed circle furious seas leaped in, struck, and leaped out. A rain of salt, heavy drops flew aslant like mist. The main-topsail had to be goose-winged, and with stolid resignation every one prepared to go aloft once more; but the officers yelled, pushed back, and at last we understood that no more men would be allowed to go on the yard than were absolutely necessary for the work. As at any moment the masts were likely to be jumped out or blown overboard, we concluded that the captain didn't want to see all his crowd go over the side at once. That was reasonable. The watch then on duty, led by Mr. Creighton, began to struggle up the rigging The wind flattened them against the ratlines; then, easing a little, would let them ascend a couple of steps; and again, with a sudden gust, pin all up the shrouds the whole crawling line in attitudes of crucifixion. The other watch plunged down on the main deck to haul up the sail. Men's heads bobbed up as the water flung them irresistibly from side to side. Mr. Baker

grunted encouragingly in our midst, spluttering and blowing
amongst the tangled ropes like an energetic porpoise. Favoured
by an ominous and untrustworthy lull, the work was done without any one being lost either off the deck or from the yard. For
the moment the gale seemed to take off, and the ship, as if grateful for our efforts, plucked up heart and made better weather
of it.

At eight the men off duty, watching their chance, ran forward
over the flooded deck to get some rest. The other half of the
crew remained aft for their turn of "seeing her through her
trouble," as they expressed it. The two mates urged the master
to go below. Mr. Baker grunted in his ear:—"Ough! surely
now . . . Ough! . . . confidence in us . . . nothing more to
do . . . she must lay it out or go. Ough! Ough!" Tall young Mr.
Creighton smiled down at him cheerfully:—". . . She's as right
as a trivet! Take a spell, sir." He looked at them stonily with
bloodshot, sleepless eyes. The rims of his eyelids were scarlet,
and he moved his jaws unceasingly with a slow effort, as though
he had been masticating a lump of india-rubber. He shook his
head. He repeated:—"Never mind me. I must see it out—I must
see it out," but he consented to sit down for a moment on the
skylight, with his hard face turned unflinchingly to windward.
The sea spat at it—and stoical, it streamed with water as though
he had been weeping. On the weather side of the poop the watch,
hanging on to the mizen rigging and to one another, tried to
exchange encouraging words. Singleton, at the wheel, yelled
out:—"Look out for yourselves!" His voice reached them in a
warning whisper. They were startled.

A big, foaming sea came out of the mist; it made for the ship,
roaring wildly, and in its rush it looked as mischievous and dis-
composing as a madman with an axe. One or two, shouting,
scrambled up the rigging; most, with a convulsive catch of the
breath, held on where they stood. Singleton dug his knees under
the wheel-box, and carefully eased the helm to the headlong
pitch of the ship, but without taking his eyes off the coming
wave. It towered close-to and high, like a wall of green glass

topped with snow. The ship rose to it as though she had soared on wings, and for a moment rested poised upon the foaming crest as if she had been a great sea-bird. Before we could draw breath a heavy gust struck her, another roller took her unfairly under the weather bow, she gave a toppling lurch, and filled her decks. Captain Allistoun leaped up, and fell; Archie rolled over him, screaming:—"She will rise!" She gave another lurch to leeward; the lower deadeyes dipped heavily; the men's feet flew from under them, and they hung kicking above the slanting poop. They could see the ship putting her side in the water, and shouted all together:—"She's going!" Forward the forecastle doors flew open, and the watch below were seen leaping out one after another, throwing their arms up; and, falling on hands and knees, scrambled aft on all fours along the high side of the deck, sloping more than the roof of a house. From leeward the seas rose, pursuing them; they looked wretched in a hopeless struggle, like vermin fleeing before a flood; they fought up the weather ladder of the poop one after another, half naked and staring wildly; and as soon as they got up they shot to leeward in clusters, with closed eyes, till they brought up heavily with their ribs against the iron stanchions of the rail; then, groaning, they rolled in a confused mass. The immense volume of water thrown forward by the last scend of the ship had burst the lee door of the forecastle. They could see their chests, pillows, blankets, clothing, come out floating upon the sea. While they struggled back to windward they looked in dismay. The straw beds swam high, the blankets, spread out, undulated; while the chests, waterlogged and with a heavy list, pitched heavily like dismasted hulks, before they sank; Archie's big coat passed with outspread arms, resembling a drowned seaman floating with his head under water. Men were slipping down while try-ing to dig their fingers into the planks; others, jammed in corners, rolled enormous eyes. They all yelled unceasingly:— "The masts! Cut! Cut! . . ." A black squall howled low over the ship, that lay on her side with the weather yard-arms pointing to the clouds; while the tall masts, inclined nearly to the horizon, seemed to be of an immeasurable length. The carpenter let go his hold, rolled against the skylight, and began to crawl to the cabin entrance, where a big axe was kept ready for just such an emergency. At that moment the topsail sheet parted, the end of the heavy chain racketed aloft, and sparks of red fire streamed down through the flying sprays. The sail flapped once with a jerk that seemed to tear our hearts out through our teeth, and instantly changed into a bunch of fluttering narrow ribbons that tied themselves into knots and became quiet along the yard. Captain Allistoun struggled, managed to stand up with his face near the deck, upon which men swung on the ends of ropes, like nest robbers upon a cliff. One of his feet was on somebody's chest; his face was purple; his lips moved. He yelled also; he yelled, bending down:—"No! No!" Mr. Baker, one leg over the binnacle-stand, roared out:—"Did you say no? Not cut?" He shook his head madly. "No! No!" Between his legs the crawling carpenter heard, collapsed at once, and lay full length in the angle of the skylight. Voices took up the shout—"No! No!" Then all became still. They waited for the ship to turn over altogether, and shake them out into the sea; and upon the terrific noise of wind and sea not a murmur of remonstrance came out from those men, who each would have given ever so many years of life to see "them damned sticks go overboard!" They all believed it their only chance; but a little hard-faced man shook his grey head and shouted "No!" without giving them as much as a glance. They were silent, and gasped. They gripped rails, they had wound ropes'-ends under their arms; they clutched ringbolts, they crawled in heaps where there was foothold; they held on with both arms, hooked themselves to anything to windward with elbows, with chins, almost with their teeth: and some, unable to crawl away from where they had been flung, felt the sea leap up, striking against their backs as they struggled upwards. Singleton had stuck to the wheel. His hair flew out in the wind; the gale seemed to take its life-long adversary by the beard and shake his old head. He wouldn't let go, and, with his knees forced between the spokes, flew up and down like a man on a bough.

As Death appeared unready. they began to look about. Donkin, caught by one foot in a loop of some rope, hung, head down, below us, and yelled, with his face to the deck:—"Cut! Cut!" Two men lowered themselves cautiously to him; others hauled on the rope. They caught him up, shoved him into a safer place, held him. He shouted curses at the master, shook his fist at him with horrible blasphemies, called upon us in filthy words to "Cut! Don't mind that murdering fool! Cut, some of you!" One of his rescuers struck him a back-handed blow over the mouth; his head banged on the deck, and he became suddenly very quiet, with a white face, breathing hard, and with a few drops of blood trickling from his cut lip. On the lee side another man could be seen stretched out as if stunned; only the washboard prevented him from going over the side. It was the steward. We had to sling him up like a bale, for he was paralysed with fright. He had rushed up out of the pantry when he felt the ship go over, and had rolled down helplessly, clutching a china mug. It was not broken. With difficulty we tore it away from him, and when he saw it in our hands he was amazed. "Where did you get that thing?" he kept on asking us in a trembling voice. His shirt was blown to shreds; the ripped sleeves flapped like wings. Two men made him fast, and, doubled over the rope that held him, he resembled a bundle of wet rags. Mr. Baker crawled along the line of men, asking:—"Are you all there?" and looking them over. Some blinked vacantly, others shook convulsively; Wamibo's head hung over his breast; and in painful attitudes, cut by lashings, exhausted with clutching, screwed up in corners, they breathed heavily. Their lips twitched, and at every sickening heave of the overturned ship they opened them wide as if to shout. The cook, embracing a wooden stanchion, unconsciously repeated a prayer. In every short interval of the fiendish noises around he could be heard there, without cap or slippers, imploring in that storm the Master of our lives not to lead him into temptation. Soon he also became silent. In all that crowd of cold and hungry men, waiting wearily for a violent death, not a voice was heard; they were mute, and in sombre thoughtfulness listened to the horrible imprecations of the gale.

Hours passed. They were sheltered by the heavy inclination of the ship from the wind that rushed in one long unbroken moan above their heads, but cold rain showers fell at times into the uneasy calm of their refuge. Under the torment of that new infliction a pair of shoulders would writhe a little. Teeth chattered. The sky was clearing, and bright sunshine gleamed over the ship. After every burst of battering seas, vivid and fleeting rainbows arched over the drifting hull in the flick of sprays. The gale was ending in a clear blow, which gleamed and cut like a knife. Between two bearded shellbacks Charley, fastened with somebody's long muffler to a deck ring-bolt, wept quietly, with rare tears wrung out by bewilderment, cold, hunger, and general misery. One of his neighbours punched him in the ribs asking roughly:—"What's the matter with your cheek? In fine weather there's no holding you, youngster." Turning about with prudence he worked himself out of his coat and threw it over the boy. The other man closed up, muttering:—" 'Twill make a bloomin' man of you, sonny." They flung their arms over and pressed against him. Charley drew his feet up and his eyelids dropped. Sighs were heard, as men, perceiving that they were not to be "drowned in a hurry," tried easier positions. Mr. Creighton, who had hurt his leg, lay amongst us with compressed lips. Some fellows belonging to his watch set about securing him better. Without a word or a glance he lifted his arms one after another to facilitate the operation, and not a muscle moved in his stern, young face. They asked him with solicitude:—"Easier now, sir?" He answered with a curt:—"That'll do." He was a hard young officer, but many of his watch used to say they liked him well enough because he had "such a gentlemanly way of damning us up and down the deck." Others unable to discern such fine shades of refinement, respected him for his smartness. For the first time since the ship had gone on her beam ends Captain Allistoun gave a short glance down at his men. He was almost upright—one foot against the side of the skylight, one

knee on the deck; and with the end of the vang round his waist
swung back and forth with his gaze fixed ahead, watchful, like
a man looking out for a sign. Before his eyes the ship, with half
her deck below water, rose and fell on heavy seas that rushed
from under her flashing in the cold sunshine. We began to
think she was wonderfully buoyant—considering. Confident
voices were heard shouting:—"She'll do, boys!" Belfast exclaimed
with fervour:—"I would giv' a month's pay for a draw at a pipe!"
One or two, passing dry tongues on their salt lips, muttered
something about a "drink of water." The cook, as if inspired,
scrambled up with his breast against the poop water-cask and
looked in. There was a little at the bottom. He yelled, waving his
arms, and two men began to crawl backwards and forwards with
the mug. We had a good mouthful all round. The master shook
his head impatiently, refusing. When it came to Charley one
of his neighbours shouted:—"That bloomin' boy's asleep." He
slept as though he had been dosed with narcotics. They let him
be. Singleton held to the wheel with one hand while he drank,
bending down to shelter his lips from the wind. Wamibo
had to be poked and yelled at before he saw the mug held before
his eyes. Knowles said sagaciously:—"It's better'n a tot o' rum."
Mr. Baker grunted:—"Thank ye." Mr. Creighton drank and
nodded. Donkin gulped greedily, glaring over the rim. Belfast
made us laugh when with grimacing mouth he shouted:—"Pass
it this way. We're all taytottlers here." The master, presented
with the mug again by a crouching man, who screamed up at
him:—"We all had a drink, captain," groped for it without
ceasing to look ahead, and handed it back stiffly as though he
could not spare half a glance away from the ship. Faces
brightened. We shouted to the cook:—"Well done, doctor!" He
sat to leeward, propped by the water-cask and yelled back abundantly, but the seas were breaking in thunder just then, and we
only caught snatches that sounded like: "Providence" and "born
again." He was at his old game of preaching. We made friendly
but derisive gestures at him, and from below he lifted one arm,
holding on with the other, moved his lips; he beamed up to us,

straining his voice—earnest, and ducking his head before the sprays.

Suddenly some one cried:—"Where's Jimmy?" and we were appalled once more. On the end of the row the boatswain shouted hoarsely:—"Has any one seed him come out?" Voices exclaimed dismally:—"Drowned—is he? . . . No! In his cabin! . . . Good Lord! . . . Caught like a bloomin' rat in a trap. . . . Couldn't open his door . . . Aye! She went over too quick and the water jammed it . . . Poor beggar! . . . No help for 'im. . . . Let's go and see . . ." "Damn him, who could go?" screamed Donkin.—"Nobody expects you to," growled the man next to him: "you're only a thing."—"Is there half a chance to get at 'im?" inquired two or three men together. Belfast untied himself with blind impetuosity, and all at once shot down to leeward quicker than a flash of lightning. We shouted all together with dismay; but with his legs overboard he held and yelled for a rope. In our extremity nothing could be terrible; so we judged him funny kicking there, and with his scared face. Some one began to laugh, and, as if hysterically infected with screaming merriment, all those haggard men went off laughing, wild-eyed, like a lot of maniacs tied up on a wall. Mr. Baker swung off the binnacle-stand and tendered him one leg. He scrambled up rather scared, and consigning us with abominable words to the "divvle." "You are. . . . Ough! You're a foul-mouthed beggar, Craik," grunted Mr. Baker. He answered, stuttering with indignation:—"Look at 'em, sorr. The bloomin' dirty images! laughing at a chum going overboard. Call themselves men, too." But from the break of the poop the boatswain called out:—"Come along," and Belfast crawled away in a hurry to join him. The five men, poised and gazing over the edge of the poop, looked for the best way to get forward. They seemed to hesitate. The others, twisting in their lashings, turning painfully, stared with open lips. Captain Allistoun saw nothing; he seemed with his eyes to hold the ship up in a superhuman concentration of effort. The wind screamed loud in sunshine; columns of spray rose straight up; and in the glitter of rainbows

Ivy Walls, Stanford-le-Hope, Essex, the Conrads' first home after their marriage

bursting over the trembling hull the men went over cautiously, disappearing from sight with deliberate movements.

They went swinging from belaying pin to cleat above the seas that beat the half-submerged deck. Their toes scraped the planks. Lumps of green cold water toppled over the bulwark and on their heads. They hung for a moment on strained arms, with the breath knocked out of them, and with closed eyes—then, letting go with one hand, balanced with lolling heads, trying to grab some rope or stanchion further forward. The long-armed and athletic boatswain swung quickly, gripping things with a fist hard as iron, and remembering suddenly snatches of the last letter from his "old woman." Little Belfast scrambled in a rage spluttering "cursed nigger." Wamibo's tongue hung out with excitement; and Archie, intrepid and calm, watched his chance to move with intelligent coolness.

When above the side of the house, they let go one after another, and falling heavily, sprawled, pressing their palms to the smooth teak wood. Round them the backwash of waves seethed white and hissing. All the doors had become trap-doors, of course. The first was the galley door. The galley extended from side to side, and they could hear the sea splashing with hollow noises in there. The next door was that of the carpenter's shop. They lifted it, and looked down. The room seemed to have been devastated by an earthquake. Everything in it had tumbled on the bulkhead facing the door, and on the other side of that bulkhead there was Jimmy dead or alive. The bench, a half-finished meat-safe, saws, chisels, wire rods, axes, crowbars, lay in a heap besprinkled with loose nails. A sharp adze stuck up with a shining edge that gleamed dangerously down there like a wicked smile. The men clung to one another, peering. A sickening, sly lurch of the ship nearly sent them overboard in a body. Belfast howled "Here goes!" and leaped down. Archie followed cannily, catching at shelves that gave way with him, and eased himself in a great crash of ripped wood. There was hardly room for three men to move. And in the sunshiny blue square of the door, the boatswain's face, bearded and dark, Wamibo's face, wild and pale, hung over—watching.

Together they shouted: "Jimmy! Jim!" From above the boatswain contributed a deep growl: "You . . . Wait!" In a pause, Belfast entreated: "Jimmy, darlin', are ye aloive?" The boatswain said: "Again! All together, boys!" All yelled excitedly. Wamibo made noises resembling loud barks. Belfast drummed on the side of the bulkhead with a piece of iron. All ceased suddenly. The sound of screaming and hammering went on thin and distinct—like a solo after a chorus. He was alive. He was screaming and knocking below us with the hurry of a man prematurely shut up in a coffin. We went to work. We attacked with desperation the abominable heap of things heavy, of things sharp, of things clumsy to handle. The boatswain crawled away to find somewhere a flying end of a rope; and Wamibo, held back by shouts:—"Don't jump! . . . Don't come in here, muddle-head!"—remained glaring above us—all shining eyes, gleaming fangs, tumbled hair; resembling an amazed and half-witted fiend gloating over the extraordinary agitation of the damned. The boatswain adjured us to "bear a hand," and a rope descended. We made things fast to it and they went up spinning, never to be seen by man again. A rage to fling things overboard possessed us. We worked fiercely, cutting our hands and speaking brutally to one another. Jimmy kept up a distracting row; he screamed piercingly, without drawing breath, like a tortured woman; he banged with hands and feet. The agony of his fear wrung our hearts so terribly that we longed to abandon him, to get out of that place deep as a well and swaying like a tree, to get out of his hearing, back on the poop where we could wait passively for death in incomparable repose. We shouted to him to "shut up, for God's sake." He redoubled his cries. He must have fancied we could not hear him. Probably he heard his own clamour but faintly. We could picture him crouching on the edge of the upper berth, letting out with both fists at the wood, in the dark, and with his mouth wide open for that unceasing cry. Those were loathsome moments. A cloud driving across the sun would darken the doorway menacingly. Every movement of the ship was pain. We scrambled about with no room to breathe, and felt frightfully sick. The boatswain yelled down at us:—"Bear a hand! Bear a hand! We two will be washed away from here directly if you ain't quick!" Three times a sea leaped over the high side and flung bucketfuls of water on our heads. Then Jimmy, startled by the shock, would stop his noise for a moment—waiting for the ship to sink, perhaps—and began again, distressingly loud, as if invigorated by the gust of fear. At the bottom the nails lay in a layer several inches thick. It was ghastly. Every nail in the world, not driven in firmly somewhere, seemed to have found its way into that carpenter's shop. There they were, of all kinds, the remnants of stores from seven voyages. Tin-tacks, copper tacks (sharp as needles); pump nails with big heads, like tiny iron mushrooms; nails without any heads (horrible); French nails polished and slim. They lay in a solid mass more inabordable than a hedgehog. We hesitated, yearning for a shovel, while Jimmy below us yelled as though he had been flayed. Groaning, we dug our fingers in, and very much hurt, shook our hands, scattering nails and drops of blood. We passed up our hats full of assorted nails to the boatswain, who, as if performing a mysterious and appeasing rite, cast them wide upon a raging sea.

We got to the bulkhead at last. Those were stout planks. She was a ship, well finished in every detail—the *Narcissus* was. They were the stoutest planks ever put into a ship's bulkhead—we thought—and then we perceived that, in our hurry, we had sent all the tools overboard. Absurd little Belfast wanted to break it down with his own weight, and with both feet leaped straight up like a springbok, cursing the Clyde shipwrights for not scamping their work. Incidentally he reviled all North Britain, the rest of the earth, the sea—and all his companions. He swore, as he alighted heavily on his heels, that he would never, never any more associate with any fool that "hadn't savee enough to know his knee from his elbow." He managed by his thumping to scare the last remnant of wits out of Jimmy. We could hear the object of our exasperated solicitude darting to and fro under the planks. He had cracked his voice at last, and could only squeak miserably. His back or else his head rubbed the planks, now here, now there, in a puzzling manner. He squeaked as he dodged the invisible blows. It was more heartrending even than his yells. Suddenly Archie produced a crowbar. He had kept it back; also a small hatchet. We howled with satisfaction. He struck a mighty blow and small chips flew at our eyes. The boatswain above shouted:—"Look out! Look out there. Don't kill the man. Easy does it!" Wamibo, maddened with excitement, hung head down and insanely urged us:—"Hoo! Strook 'im! Hoo! Hoo!" We were afraid he would fall in and kill one of us and, hurriedly, we entreated the boatswain to "shove the blamed Finn overboard." Then, all together, we yelled down at the planks:—"Stand from under! Get forward," and listened. We only heard the deep hum and moan of the wind above us, the mingled roar and hiss of the seas. The ship, as if overcome with despair, wallowed lifelessly, and our heads swam with that unnatural motion. Belfast clamoured:—"For the love of God, Jimmy, where are ye? . . . Knock! Jimmy darlint! . . . Knock! You bloody black beast! Knock!" He was as quiet as a dead man inside a grave; and, like men standing above a grave, we were on the verge of tears—but with vexation, the strain, the fatigue; with the great longing to be done with it, to get away, and lie down to rest somewhere where we could see our danger and breathe. Archie shouted:—"Gi'e me room!" We crouched behind him, guarding our heads, and he struck time after time in the joint of planks. They cracked. Suddenly the crowbar went halfway in through a splintered oblong hole. It must have missed Jimmy's head by less than an inch. Archie withdrew it quickly, and that infamous nigger rushed at the hole, put his lips to it, and whispered "Help" in an almost extinct voice; he pressed his head to it, trying madly to get out through that opening one inch wide and three inches long. In our disturbed state we were absolutely paralysed by his incredible action. It seemed impossible to drive him away. Even Archie at last lost his composure. "If ye don't clear oot I'll drive the crowbar thro' your head," he shouted in a determined voice. He meant what he said, and his earnestness seemed to make an impression on Jimmy. He disappeared suddenly, and we set to prising and tearing at the planks with the eagerness of men trying to get at a mortal enemy, and spurred by the desire to tear him limb from limb. The wood split, cracked, gave way. Belfast plunged in head and shoulders and groped viciously. "I've got 'im! Got 'im," he shouted. "Oh! There! . . . He's gone; I've got 'im! . . . Pull at my legs! . . . Pull!" Wamibo hooted unceasingly. The boatswain shouted directions:—"Catch hold of his hair, Belfast; pull straight up, you two! . . . Pull fair!" We pulled fair. We pulled Belfast out with a jerk, and dropped him with disgust. In a sitting posture, purple-faced, he sobbed despairingly:—"How can I hold on to 'is blooming short wool?" Suddenly Jimmy's head and shoulders appeared. He stuck halfway, and with rolling eyes foamed at our feet. We flew at him with brutal impatience, we tore the shirt off his back, we tugged at his ears, we panted over him; and all at once he came away in our hands as though somebody had let go his legs. With the same movement, without a pause, we swung him up. His breath whistled, he kicked our upturned faces, he grasped two pairs of arms above his head, and he squirmed up with such precipitation that he seemed positively to escape from our hands like a bladder full of gas. Streaming with perspiration, we swarmed up the rope, and, coming into the blast of cold wind, gasped like men plunged into icy water. With burning faces we shivered to the very marrow of our bones. Never before had the gale seemed to us more furious, the sea more mad, the sunshine more merciless and mocking, and the position of the ship more hopeless and appalling. Every movement of her was ominous of the end of her agony and of the beginning of ours. We staggered away from the door, and, alarmed by a sudden roll, fell down in a bunch. It appeared to us that the side of the house was more smooth than glass and more slippery than ice. There was nothing to hang on to but a long brass hook used sometimes to keep back an open door. Wamibo held on to it and we held on to Wamibo, clutching our Jimmy. He had completely collapsed now. He did not seem to have the strength to close his hand. We stuck to him blindly in our fear. We were not afraid of Wamibo letting go (we remembered that the brute was stronger than any three men in the ship), but we were afraid of the hook giving way, and we also believed that the ship had made up her mind to turn over at last. But she didn't. A sea swept over us. The boatswain spluttered:— "Up and away. There's a lull. Away aft with you, or we will all go to the devil here." We stood up surrounding Jimmy. We begged him to hold up, to hold on, at least. He glared with his bulging eyes, mute as a fish, and with all the stiffening knocked out of him. He wouldn't stand; he wouldn't even as much as clutch at our necks; he was only a cold black skin loosely stuffed with soft cotton wool; his arms and legs swung jointless and pliable; his head rolled about; the lower lip hung down, enormous and heavy. We pressed round him, bothered and dismayed; sheltering him we swung here and there in a body; and on the very brink of eternity we tottered all together with concealing and absurd gestures, like a lot of drunken men embarrassed with a stolen corpse.

Something had to be done. We had to get him aft. A rope was tied slack under his armpits, and, reaching up at the risk of our lives, we hung him on the foresheet cleet. He emitted no sound; he looked as ridiculously lamentable as a doll that had lost half its sawdust, and we started on our perilous journey over the main deck, dragging along with care that pitiful, that limp, that hateful burden. He was not very heavy, but had he weighed a ton he could not have been more awkward to handle. We literally passed him from hand to hand. Now and then we had to hang him up on a handy belaying-pin, to draw a breath and reform the line. Had the pin broken he would have irretrievably gone into the Southern Ocean, but he had to take his chance of that; and after a little while, becoming apparently aware of it, he groaned slightly, and with a great effort whispered a few words. We listened eagerly. He was reproaching us with our carelessness in letting him run such risks: "Now, after I got myself out from there," he breathed out weakly. "There" was his cabin. And he got himself out. We had nothing to do with it apparently! . . . No matter. . . . We went on and let him take his chances, simply because we could not help it; for though at that time we hated him more than ever—more than anything under heaven—we did not want to lose him. We had so far saved him; and it had become a personal matter between us and the sea. We meant to stick to him. Had we (by an incredible hypothesis) undergone similar toil and trouble for an empty cask, that cask would have become as precious to us as Jimmy was. More precious, in fact, because we would have had no reason to hate the cask. And we hated James Wait. We could not get rid of the monstrous suspicion that this astounding black-man was shamming sick, had been malingering heartlessly in the face of our toil, of our scorn, of our patience—and now was malingering in the face of our devotion—in the face of death. Our vague and imperfect morality rose with disgust at his unmanly lie. But he stuck to it manfully—amazingly. No! It couldn't be. He was at all extremity. His cantankerous temper was only the result of the provoking invincibleness of that death he felt by his side. Any man may be angry with such a masterful chum. But, then, what kind of men were we—with our thoughts! Indignation and doubt grappled within us in a scuffle that trampled upon the finest of our feelings. And we hated him because of the suspicion; we detested him because of the doubt. We could not scorn him safely—neither could we pity him without risk to our dignity. So we hated him, and passed him carefully from hand to hand. We cried, "Got him?"—"Yes. All right. Let go." And he swung from one enemy to another, showing about as much life as an old bolster would do. His eyes made two narrow white slits in the black face. The air escaped through his lips with a noise like the sound of bellows. We reached the poop ladder at last, and it being a comparatively safe place, we lay for a moment in an exhausted heap to rest a little. He began to mutter. We were always incurably anxious to hear what he had to say. This time he mumbled peevishly, "It took you some time to come. I began to think the whole smart lot of you had been washed overboard. What kept you back? Hey? Funk?" We said nothing. With sighs we started again to drag him up. The secret and ardent desire of our hearts was the desire to beat him viciously with our fists about the head; and we handled him as tenderly as though he had been made of glass. . . .

The return on the poop was like the return of wanderers after many years amongst people marked by the desolation of time. Eyes were turned slowly in their sockets, glancing at us. Faint murmurs were heard, "Have you got 'im after all?" The well-known faces looked strange and familiar; they seemed faded and grimy; they had a mingled expression of fatigue and eagerness. They seemed to have become much thinner during our absence, as if all these men had been starving for a long time in their abandoned attitudes. The captain, with a round turn of a rope on his wrist, and kneeling on one knee, swung with a face cold and stiff; but with living eyes he was still holding the ship up, heeding no one, as if lost in the unearthly effort of that endeavour. We fastened up James Wait in a safe place. Mr. Baker scrambled along to lend a hand. Mr. Creighton, on his back, and very pale, muttered, "Well done," and gave us, Jimmy and the sky, a scornful glance, then closed his eyes slowly. Here and there a man stirred a little, but most of them remained apathetic, in cramped positions, muttering between shivers. The sun was setting. A sun enormous, unclouded and red, declining low as if bending down to look into their faces. The wind whistled across long sunbeams that, resplendent and cold, struck full on the dilated pupils of staring eyes without making them wink. The wisps of hair and the tangled beards were grey with the salt of the sea. The faces were earthy, and the dark patches under the eyes extended to the ears, smudged into the hollows of sunken cheeks. The lips were livid and thin, and when they moved it was with difficulty, as though they had been glued to the teeth. Some grinned sadly in the sunlight, shaking

Portrait of Conrad in 1898, aged forty-one, by Miss E. M. Heath

with cold. Others were sad and still. Charley, subdued by the
sudden disclosure of the insignificance of his youth, darted fearful glances. The two smooth-faced Norwegians resembled de-
crepit children, staring stupidly. To leeward, on the edge of the
horizon, black seas leaped up towards the glowing sun. It sank
slowly, round and blazing, and the crests of waves splashed on
the edge of the luminous circle. One of the Norwegians appeared to catch sight of it, and, after giving a violent start, began to speak. His voice, startling the others, made them stir.
They moved their heads stiffly, or turning with difficulty, looked
at him with surprise, with fear, or in grave silence. He chattered
at the setting sun, nodding his head, while the big seas began to
roll across the crimson disc; and over miles of turbulent waters
the shadows of high waves swept with a running darkness the
faces of men. A crested roller broke with a loud hissing roar,
and the sun, as if put out, disappeared. The chattering voice
faltered, went out together with the light. There were sighs. In
the sudden lull that follows the crash of a broken sea a man said
wearily, "Here's that blooming Dutchman gone off his chump."
A seaman, lashed by the middle, tapped the deck with his open
hand with unceasing quick flaps. In the gathering greyness of
twilight a bulky form was seen rising aft, and began marching
on all fours with the movements of some big cautious beast. It
was Mr. Baker passing along the line of men. He grunted encouragingly over every one, felt their fastenings. Some, with
half-open eyes, puffed like men oppressed by heat; others mechanically and in dreamy voices answered him, "Aye! aye! sir!"
He went from one to another grunting, "Ough! . . . See her
through it yet;" and unexpectedly, with loud angry outbursts,
blew up Knowles for cutting off a long piece from the fall of
the relieving tackle. "Ough!——Ashamed of yourself——Relieving tackle——Don't you know better!——Ough!—Able seaman!
Ough!" The lame man was crushed. He muttered, "Get
som'think for a lashing for myself, sir."—"Ough! Lashing——
yourself. Are you a tinker or a sailor——What? Ough!——May
want that tackle directly——Ough!——More use to the ship than

your lame carcass. Ough!——Keep it!——Keep it, now you've done it." He crawled away slowly, muttering to himself about some men being "worse than children." It had been a comforting row. Low exclamations were heard: "Hallo . . . Hallo." . . . Those who had been painfully dozing asked with convulsive starts, "What's up? . . . What is it?" The answer came with unexpected cheerfulness: "The mate is going bald-headed for lame Jack about something or other." "No!" . . . . "What 'as he done?" Some one even chuckled. It was like a whiff of hope, like a reminder of safe days. Donkin, who had been stupefied with fear, revived suddenly and began to shout:—" 'Ear 'im; that's the way they tawlk to us. Vy donch 'ee 'it 'im—one ov yer? 'It 'im. 'It 'im! Comin' the mate over us. We are as good men as 'ee! We're all goin' to 'ell now. We 'ave been starved in this rotten ship, an' now we're goin' to be drowned for them black 'earted bullies! 'It 'im!" He shrieked in the deepening gloom, he blubbered and sobbed, screaming:——" 'It 'im! 'It 'im!" The rage and fear of his disregarded right to live tried the steadfastness of hearts more than the menacing shadows of the night that advanced through the unceasing clamour of the gale. From aft Mr. Baker was heard:—"Is one of you men going to stop him—must I come along?" "Shut up!" . . . "Keep quiet!" cried various voices, exasperated, trembling with cold.—"You'll get one across the mug from me directly," said an invisible seaman, in a weary tone, "I won't let the mate have the trouble." He ceased and lay still with the silence of despair. On the black sky the stars, coming out, gleamed over an inky sea that, speckled with foam, flashed back at them the evanescent and pale light of a dazzling whiteness born from the black turmoil of the waves. Remote in the eternal calm they glittered hard and cold above the uproar of the earth; they surrounded the vanquished and tormented ship on all sides: more pitiless than the eyes of a triumphant mob, and as unapproachable as the hearts of men.

The icy south wind howled exultingly under the sombre splendour of the sky. The cold shook the men with a resistless violence as though it had tried to shake them to pieces. Short moans were swept unheard off the stiff lips. Some complained in mutters of "not feeling themselves below the waist;" while those who had closed their eyes, imagined they had a block of ice on their chests. Others, alarmed at not feeling any pain in their fingers, beat the deck feebly with their hands—obstinate and exhausted. Wamibo stared vacant and dreamy. The Scandinavians kept on a meaningless mutter through chattering teeth. The spare Scotchmen, with determined efforts, kept their lower jaws still. The West-country men lay big and stolid in an invulnerable surliness. A man yawned and swore in turns. Another breathed with a rattle in his throat. Two elderly hard-weather shellbacks, fast side by side, whispered dismally to one another about the landlady of a boarding-house in Sunderland, whom they both knew. They extolled her motherliness and her liberality; they tried to talk about the joint of beef and the big fire in the downstairs kitchen. The words dying faintly on their lips, ended in light sighs. A sudden voice cried into the cold night, "O Lord!" No one changed his position or took any notice of the cry. One or two passed, with a repeated and vague gesture, their hand over their faces, but most of them kept very still. In the benumbed immobility of their bodies they were excessively wearied by their thoughts, which rushed with the rapidity and vividness of dreams. Now and then, by an abrupt and startling exclamation, they answered the weird hail of some illusion; then, again, in silence contemplated the vision of known faces and familiar things. They recalled the aspect of forgotten shipmates and heard the voice of dead and gone skippers. They remembered the noise of gaslit streets, the steamy heat of tap-rooms or the scorching sunshine of calm days at sea.

Mr. Baker left his insecure place, and crawled, with stoppages, along the poop. In the dark and on all fours he resembled some carnivorous animal prowling amongst corpses. At the break, propped to windward of a stanchion, he looked down on the main deck. It seemed to him that the ship had a tendency to stand up a little more. The wind had eased a little, he thought, but the sea ran as high as ever. The waves foamed viciously, and

the lee side of the deck disappeared under a hissing whiteness
as of boiling milk, while the rigging sang steadily with a deep
vibrating note, and, at every upward swing of the ship, the wind
rushed with a long-drawn clamour amongst the spars. Mr.
Baker watched very still. A man near him began to make a blab-
bing noise with his lips, all at once and very loud, as though the
cold had broken brutally through him. He went on:—"Ba—ba—
ba—brrr—brr—ba—ba."—"Stop that!" cried Mr. Baker, groping
in the dark. "Stop it!" He went on shaking the leg he found
under his hand.—"What is it, sir?" called out Belfast, in the
tone of a man awakened suddenly; "we are looking after that
'ere Jimmy."—"Are you? Ough! Don't make that row then.
Who's that near you?"—"It's me—the boatswain, sir," growled
the West-country man; "we are trying to keep life in that poor
devil."—"Aye, aye!" said Mr. Baker. "Do it quietly, can't you?"
—"He wants us to hold him up above the rail," went on the boatswain, with irritation, "says he can't breathe here under our
jackets."—"If we lift 'im, we drop 'im overboard," said another
voice, "we can't feel our hands with cold."—"I don't care. I am
choking!" exclaimed James Wait in a clear tone.—"Oh, no, my
son," said the boatswain, desperately, "you don't go till we all go
on this fine night."—"You will see yet many a worse," said Mr.
Baker, cheerfully.—"It's no child's play, sir!" answered the boatswain. "Some of us further aft, here, are in a pretty bad way."—
"If the blamed sticks had been cut out of her she would be running along on her bottom now like any decent ship, an' giv' us
all a chance," said some one, with a sigh.—"The old man
wouldn't have it . . . much he cares for us," whispered another.—
"Care for you!" exclaimed Mr. Baker, angrily. "Why should he
care for you? Are you a lot of women passengers to be taken care
of? We are here to take care of the ship—and some of you ain't
up to that. Ough! . . . What have you done so very smart to be
taken care of? Ough! . . . Some of you can't stand a bit of a
breeze without crying over it."—"Come, sorr. We ain't so bad,"
protested Belfast, in a voice shaken by shivers; "we ain't . . .
brrr . . . "—"Again," shouted the mate, grabbing at the shad-

owy form; "again! . . . Why, you're in your shirt! What have
you done?"—"I've put my oilskin and jacket over that half-dead
nayggur—and he says he chokes," said Belfast, complainingly.—
"You wouldn't call me nigger if I wasn't half dead, you Irish
beggar!" boomed James Wait, vigorously.—"You . . . brrr . . .
You wouldn't be white if you were ever so well . . . I will fight
you . . . brrrr . . . in fine weather . . . brrr . . . with one hand
tied behind my back . . . brrrrrr . . ."—"I don't want your rags—I
want air," gasped out the other faintly, as if suddenly exhausted.

The sprays swept over whistling and pattering. Men disturbed in their peaceful torpor by the pain of quarrelsome
shouts, moaned, muttering curses. Mr. Baker crawled off a little
way to leeward where a watercask loomed up big, with something white against it. "Is it you, Podmore?" asked Mr. Baker.
He had to repeat the question twice before the cook turned,
coughing feebly.—"Yes, sir. I've been praying in my mind for
a quick deliverance; for I am prepared for any call. . . . I——"—
"Look here, cook," interrupted Mr. Baker, "the men are perishing with cold."—"Cold!" said the cook, mournfully; "they will
be warm enough before long."—"What?" asked Mr. Baker, looking along the deck into the faint sheen of frothing water.—
"They are a wicked lot," continued the cook solemnly, but in
an unsteady voice, "about as wicked as any ship's company in
this sinful world! Now, I"—he trembled so that he could hardly
speak; his was an exposed place, and in a cotton shirt, a thin
pair of trousers, and with his knees under his nose, he received,
quaking, the flicks of stinging, salt drops; his voice sounded exhausted—"now. I—any time . . . My eldest youngster, Mr. Baker
. . . a clever boy . . . last Sunday on shore before this voyage he
wouldn't go to church, sir. Says I, 'You go and clean yourself,
or I'll know the reason why!' What does he do? . . . Pond, Mr.
Baker—fell into the pond in his best rig, sir! . . . Accident? . . .
'Nothing will save you, fine scholar though you are!' says I. . . .
Accident! . . . I whopped him, sir, till I couldn't lift my arm.
. . . " His voice faltered. "I whopped 'im!" he repeated, rattling
his teeth; then, after a while, let out a mournful sound that was

half a groan, half a snore. Mr. Baker shook him by the shoulders. "Hey! Cook! Hold up, Podmore! Tell me—is there any fresh water in the galley tank? The ship is lying along less, I think; I would try to get forward. A little water would do them good. Hallo! Look out! Look out!" The cook struggled.—"Not you, sir—not you!" He began to scramble to windward. "Galley! . . . my business!" he shouted.—"Cook's gone crazy now," said several voices. He yelled:—"Crazy, am I? I am more ready to die than any of you, officers incloosive—there! As long as she swims I will cook! I will get you coffee."—"Cook, ye are a gentleman!" cried Belfast. But the cook was already going over the weather-ladder. He stopped for a moment to shout back on the poop:— "As long as she swims I will cook!" and disappeared as though he had gone overboard. The men who had heard sent after him a cheer that sounded like a wail of sick children. An hour or more afterwards some one said distinctly: "He's gone for good." —"Very likely," assented the boatswain; "even in fine weather he was as smart about the deck as a milch-cow on her first voyage. We ought to go and see." Nobody moved. As the hours dragged slowly through the darkness Mr. Baker crawled back and forth along the poop several times. Some men fancied they had heard him exchange murmurs with the master, but at that time the memories were incomparably more vivid than anything actual, and they were not certain whether the murmurs were heard now or many years ago. They did not try to find out. A mutter more or less did not matter. It was too cold for curiosity, and almost for hope. They could not spare a moment or a thought from the great mental occupation of wishing to live. And the desire of life kept them alive, apathetic and enduring, under the cruel persistence of wind and cold; while the bestarred black dome of the sky revolved slowly above the ship, that drifted, bearing their patience and their suffering, through the stormy solitude of the sea.

Huddled close to one another, they fancied themselves utterly alone. They heard sustained loud noises, and again bore the pain of existence through long hours of profound silence. In the

night they saw sunshine, felt warmth, and suddenly, with a
start, thought that the sun would never rise upon a freezing
world. Some heard laughter, listened to songs; others, near the
end of the poop, could hear loud human shrieks, and opening
their eyes, were surprised to hear them still, though very faint,
and far away. The boatswain said:—"Why, it's the cook, hailing
from forward, I think." He hardly believed his own words or
recognised his own voice. It was a long time before the man next
to him gave a sign of life. He punched hard his other neighbour
and said:—"The cook's shouting!" Many did not understand,
others did not care; the majority further aft did not believe. But
the boatswain and another man had the pluck to crawl away forward to see. They seemed to have been gone for hours, and were
very soon forgotten. Then suddenly men who had been plunged
in a hopeless resignation became as if possessed with a desire to
hurt. They belaboured one another with fists. In the darkness
they struck persistently anything soft they could feel near, and,
with a greater effort than for a shout, whispered excitedly:—
"They've got some hot coffee. . . . Boss'en got it. . . ." "No! . . .
Where?" . . . . "It's coming! Cook made it." James Wait moaned.
Donkin scrambled viciously, caring not where he kicked, and
anxious that the officers should have none of it. It came in a
pot, and they drank in turns. It was hot, and while it blistered
the greedy palates, it seemed incredible. The men sighed out
parting with the mug:——"How 'as he done it?" Some cried
weakly:—"Bully for you, doctor!"

He had done it somehow. Afterwards Archie declared that
the thing was "meeraculous." For many days we wondered, and
it was the one ever-interesting subject of conversation to the
end of the voyage. We asked the cook, in fine weather, how he
felt when he saw his stove "reared up on end." We inquired, in
the north-east trade and on serene evenings, whether he had to
stand on his head to put things right somewhat. We suggested
he had used his bread-board for a raft, and from there comfortably had stoked his grate; and we did our best to conceal our
admiration under the wit of fine irony. He affirmed not to know

anything about it, rebuked our levity, declared himself, with solemn animation, to have been the object of a special mercy for the saving of our unholy lives. Fundamentally he was right, no doubt; but he need not have been so offensively positive about it—he need not have hinted so often that it would have gone hard with us had he not been there, meritorious and pure, to receive the inspiration and the strength for the work of grace. Had we been saved by his recklessness or his agility, we could have at length become reconciled to the fact; but to admit our obligation to anybody's virtue and holiness alone was as difficult for us as for any other handful of mankind. Like many bene- factors of humanity, the cook took himself too seriously, and reaped the reward of irreverence. We were not ungrateful, how- ever. He remained heroic. His saying—*the* saying of his life—be- came proverbial in the mouth of men as are the sayings of conquerors or sages. Later, whenever one of us was puzzled by a task and advised to relinquish it, he would express his deter- mination to persevere and to succeed by the words:—"As long as she swims I will cook!"

The hot drink helped us through the bleak hours that pre- cede the dawn. The sky low by the horizon took on the delicate tints of pink and yellow like the inside of a rare shell. And higher, where it glowed with a pearly sheen, a small black cloud appeared, like a forgotten fragment of the night set in a border of dazzling gold. The beams of light skipped on the crests of waves. The eyes of men turned to the eastward. The sunlight flooded their weary faces. They were giving themselves up to fatigue as though they had done for ever with their work. On Singleton's black oilskin coat the dried salt glistened like hoar frost. He hung on by the wheel, with open and lifeless eyes. Captain Allistoun, unblinking, faced the rising sun. His lips stirred, opened for the first time in twenty-four hours, and with a fresh firm voice he cried, "Wear ship!"

The commanding sharp tones made all these torpid men start like a sudden flick of a whip. Then again, motionless where they lay, the force of habit made some of them repeat the order in

hardly audible murmurs. Captain Allistoun glanced down at
his crew, and several, with fumbling fingers and hopeless movements, tried to cast themselves adrift. He repeated impatiently,
"Wear ship. Now then, Mr. Baker, get the men along. What's
the matter with them?"—"Wear ship. Do you hear there?—Wear
ship!" thundered out the boatswain suddenly. His voice seemed
to break through a deadly spell. Men began to stir and crawl.—
"I want the fore-top-mast staysail run up smartly," said the
master, very loudly; "if you can't manage it standing up you
must do it lying down—that's all. Bear a hand!"—"Come along!
Let's give the old girl a chance," urged the boatswain.—"Aye!
aye! Wear ship!" exclaimed quavering voices. The forecastle
men, with reluctant faces, prepared to go forward. Mr. Baker
pushed ahead, grunting, on all fours to show the way, and they
followed him over the break. The others lay still with a vile
hope in their hearts of not being required to move till they got
saved or drowned in peace.

After some time they could be seen forward appearing on the
forecastle head, one by one in unsafe attitudes; hanging on to
the rails, clambering over the anchors; embracing the cross-head
of the windlass or hugging the fore-capstan. They were restless
with strange exertions, waved their arms, knelt, lay flat down,
staggered up, seemed to strive their hardest to go overboard.
Suddenly a small white piece of canvas fluttered amongst them,
grew larger, beating. Its narrow head rose in jerks—and at last
it stood distended and triangular in the sunshine.—"They have
done it!" cried the voices aft. Captain Allistoun let go the rope
he had round his wrist and rolled to leeward headlong. He could
be seen casting the lee main braces off the pins while the backwash of waves splashed over him.—"Square the main yard!" he
shouted up to us—who stared at him in wonder. We hesitated to
stir. "The main brace, men. Haul! haul anyhow! Lay on your
back and haul!" he screeched, half drowned down there. We did
not believe we could move the main yard, but the strongest and
the less discouraged tried to execute the order. Others assisted
half-heartedly. Singleton's eyes blazed suddenly as he took a

fresh grip of the spokes. Captain Allistoun fought his way up to windward.—"Haul, men! Try to move it! Haul, and help the ship." His hard face worked suffused and furious. "Is she going off, Singleton?" he cried.—"Not a move yet, sir," croaked the old seaman in a horribly hoarse voice.—"Watch the helm, Singleton," spluttered the master. "Haul, men! Have you no more strength than rats? Haul, and earn your salt." Mr. Creighton, on his back, with a swollen leg and a face as white as a piece of paper, blinked his eyes; his bluish lips twitched. In the wild scramble men grabbed at him, crawled over his hurt leg, knelt on his chest. He kept perfectly still, setting his teeth without a moan, without a sigh. The master's ardour, the cries of that silent man inspired us. We hauled and hung in bunches on the rope. We heard him say with violence to Donkin, who sprawled abjectly on his stomach,—"I will brain you with this belaying pin if you don't catch hold of the brace," and that victim of men's injustice, cowardly and cheeky, whimpered:—"Are you goin' to murder us now?" while with sudden desperation he gripped the rope. Men sighed, shouted, hissed meaningless words, groaned. The yards moved, came slowly square against the wind, that hummed loudly on the yard-arms.—"Going off, sir," shouted Singleton, "she's just started."—"Catch a turn with that brace. Catch a turn!" clamoured the master. Mr. Creighton, nearly suffocated and unable to move, made a mighty effort, and with his left hand managed to nip the rope.—"All fast!" cried some one. He closed his eyes as if going off into a swoon, while huddled together about the brace we watched with scared looks what the ship would do now.

She went off slowly as though she had been weary and disheartened like the men she carried. She paid off very gradually, making us hold our breath till we choked, and as soon as she had brought the wind abaft the beam she started to move, and fluttered our hearts. It was awful to see her, nearly overturned, begin to gather way and drag her submerged side through the water. The dead-eyes of the rigging churned the breaking seas. The lower half of the deck was full of mad whirlpools and eddies; and the long line of the lee rail could be seen showing black now and then in the swirls of a field of foam as dazzling and white as a field of snow. The wind sang shrilly amongst the spars; and at every slight lurch we expected her to slip to the bottom sideways from under our backs. When dead before it she made the first distinct attempt to stand up, and we encouraged her with a feeble and discordant howl. A great sea came running up aft and hung a moment over us with a curling top; then crashed down under the counter and spread out on both sides into a great sheet of bursting froth. Above its fierce hiss we heard Singleton's croak:—"She is steering!" He had both his feet now planted firmly on the grating, and the wheel spun fast as he eased the helm.—"Bring the wind on the port quarter and steady her!" called out the master, staggering to his feet, the first man up from amongst our prostrate heap. One or two screamed with excitement:—"She rises!" Far away forward, Mr. Baker and three others were seen erect and black on the clear sky, lifting their arms, and with open mouths as though they had been shouting all together. The ship trembled, trying to lift her side, lurched back, seemed to give up with a nerveless dip, and suddenly with an unexpected jerk swung violently to windward, as though she had torn herself out from a deadly grasp. The whole immense volume of water, lifted by her deck, was thrown bodily across to starboard. Loud cracks were heard. Iron ports breaking open thundered with ringing blows. The water topped over the starboard rail with the rush of a river falling over a dam. The sea on deck, and the seas on every side of her, mingled together in a deafening roar. She rolled violently. We got up and were helplessly run or flung about from side to side. Men, rolling over and over, yelled,—"The house will go!"—"She clears herself!" Lifted by a towering sea she ran along with it for a moment, spouting thick streams of water through every opening of her wounded sides. The lee braces having been carried away or washed off the pins, all the ponderous yards on the fore swung from side to side and with appalling rapidity at every roll. The men forward were seen crouching here and there with fearful glances upwards at the enormous spars that whirled about over their heads. The torn canvas and the ends of broken gear streamed in the wind like wisps of hair. Through the clear sunshine, over the flashing turmoil and uproar of the seas, the ship ran blindly, dishevelled and headlong, as if fleeing for her life; and on the poop we spun, we tottered about, distracted and noisy. We all spoke at once in a thin babble; we had the aspect of invalids and the gestures of maniacs. Eyes shone, large and haggard, in smiling, meagre faces that seemed to have been dusted over with powdered chalk. We stamped, clapped our hands, feeling ready to jump and do anything; but in reality hardly able to keep on our feet. Captain Allistoun, hard and slim, gesticulated madly from the poop at Mr. Baker: "Steady these fore-yards! Steady them the best you can!" On the main deck, men excited by his cries, splashed, dashing aimlessly here and there with the foam swirling up to their waists. Apart, far aft, and alone by the helm, old Singleton had deliberately tucked his white beard under the top button of his glistening coat. Swaying upon the din and tumult of the seas, with the whole battered length of the ship launched forward in a rolling rush before his steady old eyes, he stood rigidly still, forgotten by all, and with an attentive face. In front of his erect figure only the two arms moved crosswise with a swift and sudden readiness, to check or urge again the rapid stir of circling spokes. He steered with care.

IV

ON MEN reprieved by its disdainful mercy, the immortal sea confers in its justice the full privilege of desired unrest. Through the perfect wisdom of its grace they are not permitted to meditate at ease upon the complicated and acrid savour of existence. They must without pause justify their life to the eternal pity that commands toil to be hard and unceasing, from sunrise to sunset, from sunset to sunrise; till the weary succession of nights and days tainted by the obstinate clamour of sages, demanding bliss and an empty heaven, is redeemed at last by the vast silence of pain and labour, by the dumb fear and the dumb courage of men obscure, forgetful, and enduring.

The master and Mr. Baker coming face to face stared for a moment, with the intense and amazed looks of men meeting unexpectedly after years of trouble. Their voices were gone, and they whispered desperately at one another.—"Any one missing?" asked Captain Allistoun.—"No. All there."—"Anybody hurt?" —"Only the second mate."—"I will look after him directly. We're lucky."—"Very," articulated Mr. Baker, faintly. He gripped the rail and rolled bloodshot eyes. The little grey man made an effort to raise his voice above a dull mutter, and fixed his chief mate with a cold gaze, piercing like a dart.—"Get sail on the ship," he said, speaking authoritatively and with an inflexible snap of his thin lips. "Get sail on her as soon as you can. This is a fair wind. At once, sir—Don't give the men time to feel themselves. They will get done up and stiff, and we will never . . . We must get her along now" . . . He reeled to a long heavy roll; the rail dipped into the glancing, hissing water. He caught a shroud, swung helplessly against the mate . . . "now we have a fair wind at last——Make——sail." His head rolled from shoulder to shoulder. His eyelids began to beat rapidly. "And the pumps——pumps, Mr. Baker." He peered as though the face within a foot of his eyes had been half a mile off. "Keep the men on the move to——to get her along," he mumbled in a drowsy tone, like a man going off into a doze. He pulled himself together suddenly. "Mustn't stand. Won't do," he said with a painful attempt at a smile. He let go his hold, and, propelled by the dip of the ship, ran aft unwillingly, with small steps, till he brought up against the binnacle stand. Hanging on there he looked up in an aimless manner at Singleton, who, unheeding him, watched anxiously the end of the jib-boom—"Steering gear works all right?" he asked. There was a noise in the old seaman's throat, as though the words had been rattling together before they could come out.—"Steers . . . like a little boat," he said, at last, with hoarse tenderness, without giving the master as much as half a glance—then, watchfully, spun the wheel down, steadied, flung it back again. Captain Allistoun tore himself away from the delight of leaning against the binnacle, and began to walk the poop, swaying and reeling to preserve his balance. . . .

The pump-rods, clanking, stamped in short jumps while the fly-wheels turned smoothly, with great speed, at the foot of the mainmast, flinging back and forth with a regular impetuosity two limp clusters of men clinging to the handles. They abandoned themselves, swaying from the hip with twitching faces and stony eyes. The carpenter, sounding from time to time, exclaimed mechanically: "Shake her up! Keep her going!" Mr. Baker could not speak, but found his voice to shout; and under the goad of his objurgations, men looked to the lashings, dragged out new sails; and thinking themselves unable to move, carried heavy blocks aloft—overhauled the gear. They went up the rigging with faltering and desperate efforts. Their heads swam as they shifted their hold, stepped blindly on the yards like men in the dark; or trusted themselves to the first rope at hand with the negligence of exhausted strength. The narrow escapes from falls did not disturb the languid beat of their hearts; the roar of the seas seething far below them sounded continuous and faint like an indistinct noise from another world: the wind filled their eyes with tears, and with heavy gusts tried to push them off from where they swayed in insecure positions. With streaming faces and blowing hair they flew up and down between sky and water, bestriding the ends of yard-arms, crouching on footropes, embracing lifts to have their hands free, or standing up against chain ties. Their thoughts floated vaguely between the desire of rest and the desire of life, while their stiffened fingers cast off head-earrings, fumbled for knives, or held with tenacious grip against the violent shocks of beating canvas. They glared savagely at one another, made frantic signs with one hand while they held their life in the other, looked

down on the narrow strip of flooded deck, shouted along to leeward: "Light-to!" . . . "Haul out!" . . . "Make fast!" Their lips
moved, their eyes started, furious and eager with the desire to
be understood, but the wind tossed their words unheard upon
the disturbed sea. In an unendurable and unending strain they
worked like men driven by a merciless dream to toil in an atmosphere of ice or flame. They burnt and shivered in turns. Their
eyeballs smarted as if in the smoke of a conflagration; their
heads were ready to burst with every shout. Hard fingers
seemed to grip their throats. At every roll they thought: Now I
must let go. It will shake us all off—and thrown about aloft they
cried wildly: "Look out there—catch the end." . . . "Reeve clear"
. . . "Turn this block. . . . " They nodded desperately; shook infuriated faces, "No! No! From down up." They seemed to hate
one another with a deadly hate. The longing to be done with it all
gnawed their breasts, and the wish to do things well was a burning pain. They cursed their fate, contemned their life, and
wasted their breath in deadly imprecations upon one another.
The sailmaker, with his bald head bared, worked feverishly,
forgetting his intimacy with so many admirals. The boatswain,
climbing up with marlinspikes and bunches of spunyarn rov-
ings, or kneeling on the yard and ready to take a turn with the
midship-stop, had acute and fleeting visions of his old woman
and the youngsters in a moorland village. Mr. Baker, feeling
very weak, tottered here and there, grunting and inflexible, like
a man of iron. He waylaid those who, coming from aloft, stood
gasping for breath. He ordered, encouraged, scolded. "Now then
—to the main topsail now! Tally on to that gantline. Don't stand
about there!"—"Is there no rest for us?" muttered voices. He
spun round fiercely, with a sinking heart.—"No! No rest till the
work is done. Work till you drop. That's what you're here for."
A bowed seaman at his elbow gave a short laugh.—"Do or die,"
he croaked bitterly, then spat into his broad palms, swung up his
long arms, and grasping the rope high above his head sent out
a mournful, wailing cry for a pull all together. A sea boarded
the quarter-deck and sent the whole lot sprawling to leeward.

Caps, handspikes floated. Clenched hands, kicking legs, with here and there a spluttering face, stuck out of the white hiss of foaming water. Mr. Baker, knocked down with the rest, screamed—"Don't let go that rope! Hold on to it! Hold!" And sorely bruised by the brutal fling, they held on to it, as though it had been the fortune of their life. The ship ran, rolling heavily, and the topping crests glanced past port and starboard flashing their white heads. Pumps were freed. Braces were rove. The three topsails and foresail were set. She spurted faster over the water, outpacing the swift rush of waves. The menacing thunder of distanced seas rose behind her—filled the air with the tremendous vibrations of its voice. And devastated, battered, and wounded she drove foaming to the northward, as though inspired by the courage of a high endeavour. . . .

The forecastle was a place of damp desolation. They looked at their dwelling with dismay. It was slimy, dripping; it hummed hollow with the wind, and was strewn with shapeless wreckage like a half-tide cavern in a rocky and exposed coast. Many had lost all they had in the world, but most of the starboard watch had preserved their chests; thin streams of water trickled out of them, however. The beds were soaked; the blankets spread out and saved by some nail squashed under foot. They dragged wet rags from evil-smelling corners, and wringing the water out, recognised their property. Some smiled stiffly. Others looked round blank and mute. There were cries of joy over old waistcoats, and groans of sorrow over shapeless things found among the splinters of smashed bed boards. One lamp was discovered jammed under the bowsprit. Charley whimpered a little. Knowles stumped here and there, sniffing, examining dark places for salvage. He poured dirty water out of a boot, and was concerned to find the owner. Those who, overwhelmed by their losses, sat on the forepeak hatch, remained elbows on knees, and, with a fist against each cheek, disdained to look up. He pushed it under their noses. "Here's a good boot. Yours?" They snarled, "No—get out." One snapped at him, "Take it to hell out of this." He seemed surprised. "Why? It's a good boot,"

Pent Farm, Stanford, near Hythe, Kent, where Conrad wrote *Tales of Unrest, Lord Jim, Youth, Typhoon* and *Nostromo*

but remembering suddenly that he had lost every stitch of his clothing, he dropped his find and began to swear. In the dim light cursing voices clashed. A man came in and, dropping his arms, stood still, repeating from the doorstep, "Here's a bloomin' old go! Here's a bloomin' old go!" A few rooted anxiously in flooded chests for tobacco. They breathed hard, clamoured with heads down. "Look at that Jack!" . . . "Here! Sam! Here's my shore-going rig spoilt for ever." One blasphemed tearfully, holding up a pair of dripping trousers. No one looked at him. The cat came out from somewhere. He had an ovation. They snatched him from hand to hand, caressed him in a murmur of pet names. They wondered where he had "weathered it out"; disputed about it. A squabbling argument began. Two men brought in a bucket of fresh water, and all crowded round it; but Tom, lean and mewing, came up with every hair astir and had the first drink. A couple of hands went aft for oil and biscuits.

Then in the yellow light and in the intervals of mopping the deck they crunched hard bread, arranging to "worry through somehow." Men chummed as to beds. Turns were settled for wearing boots and having the use of oilskin coats. They called one another "old man" and "sonny" in cheery voices. Friendly slaps resounded. Jokes were shouted. One or two stretched on the wet deck, with heads pillowed on their bent arms, and several, sitting on the hatch, smoked. Their weary faces appeared through a thin blue haze, pacified and with sparkling eyes. The boatswain put his head through the door. "Relieve the wheel, one of you"—he shouted inside—"it's six. Blamme if that old Singleton hasn't been there more'n thirty hours. You are a fine lot." He slammed the door again. "Mate's watch on deck," said some one. "Hey, Donkin, it's your relief!" shouted three or four together. He had crawled into an empty bunk and on wet planks lay still. "Donkin, your wheel." He made no sound. "Donkin's dead," guffawed some one. "Sell 'is bloomin' clothes," shouted another. "Donkin, if ye don't go to the bloomin' wheel they will sell your clothes—d'ye hear?" jeered a third. He groaned from his dark hole. He complained about pains in all his bones, he whimpered pitifully. "He won't go," exclaimed a contemptuous voice, "your turn, Davis." The young seaman rose painfully, squaring his shoulders. Donkin stuck his head out, and it appeared in the yellow light, fragile and ghastly. "I will giv' yer a pound of tobaccer," he whined in a conciliating voice, "so soon as I draw it from aft. I will—s'elp me . . ." Davis swung his arm backhanded and the head vanished. "I'll go," he said, "but you will pay for it." He walked unsteady but resolute to the door. "So I will," yelped Donkin, popping out behind him. "So I will—s'elp me . . . a pound . . . three bob they chawrge." Davis flung the door open. "You will pay my price . . . in fine weather," he shouted over his shoulder. One of the men unbuttoned his wet coat rapidly, threw it at his head. "Here, Taffy—take that, you thief!" "Thank you!" he cried from the darkness above the swish of rolling water. He could be heard splashing; a sea came on board with a thump. "He's got his bath already," remarked a grim shellback. "Aye, aye!" grunted others. Then, after a long silence, Wamibo made strange noises. "Hallo, what's up with you?" said some one grumpily. "He says he would have gone for Davy," explained Archie, who was the Finn's interpreter generally. "I believe him!" cried voices. . . . "Never mind, Dutchy . . . You'll do, muddle-head. . . . Your turn will come soon enough . . . You don't know when ye're well off." They ceased, and all together turned their faces to the door. Singleton stepped in, advanced two paces, and stood swaying slightly. The sea hissed, flowed roaring past the bows, and the forecastle trembled, full of deep murmurs; the lamp flared, swinging like a pendulum. He looked with a dreamy and puzzled stare, as though he could not distinguish the still men from their restless shadows. There were awestruck exclamations:—"Hallo, hallo" . . . "How does it look outside now, Singleton?" Those who sat on the hatch lifted their eyes in silence, and the next oldest seaman in the ship (those two understood one another, though they hardly exchanged three words in a day) gazed up at his friend attentively for a moment, then taking a short clay pipe out of his mouth, offered it without a word. Singleton put out his arm towards it, missed, staggered, and suddenly fell forward, crashing down, stiff and headlong like an uprooted tree. There was a swift rush. Men pushed, crying:—"He's done!" . . . "Turn him over!" . . . "Stand clear there!" Under a crowd of startled faces bending over him he lay on his back, staring upwards in a continuous and intolerable manner. In the breathless silence of a general consternation, he said in a grating murmur:—"I am all right," and clutched with his hands. They helped him up. He mumbled despondently:—"I am getting old . . . old."—"Not you," cried Belfast, with ready tact. Supported on all sides, he hung his head.—"Are you better?" they asked. He glared at them from under his eyebrows with large black eyes, spreading over his chest the bushy whiteness of a beard long and thick.—"Old! old!" he repeated sternly. Helped along, he reached his bunk. There was in it a slimy soft heap of something that smelt, as does at dead low water a muddy foreshore. It was his soaked straw bed. With a convulsive effort he pitched himself on it, and in the darkness of the narrow place could be heard growling angrily, like an irritated and savage animal uneasy in its den:— "Bit of breeze . . . small thing . . . can't stand up . . . old!" He slept at last, high-booted, sou'wester on head, and his oilskin clothes rustled, when with a deep sighing groan he turned over. Men conversed aout him in quiet, concerned whispers. "This will break 'im up" . . . "Strong as a horse" . . . "Aye. But he ain't what he used to be." . . . In sad murmurs they gave him up. Yet at midnight he turned out to duty as if nothing had been the matter, and answered to his name with a mournful "Here!" He brooded alone more than ever, in an impenetrable silence and with a saddened face. For many years he had heard himself called "Old Singleton," and had serenely accepted the qualification, taking it as a tribute of respect due to a man who through half a century had measured his strength against the favours and the rages of the sea. He had never given a thought to his mortal self. He lived unscathed, as though he had been indestructible, surrendering to all the temptations, weathering many gales. He had panted in sunshine, shivered in the cold; suffered hunger, thirst, debauch; passed through many trials—known all the furies. Old! It seemed to him he was broken at last. And like a man bound treacherously while he sleeps, he woke up fettered by the long chain of disregarded years. He had to take up at once the burden of all his existence, and found it almost too heavy for his strength. Old! He moved his arms, shook his head, felt his limbs. Getting old . . . and then? He looked upon the immortal sea with the awakened and groping perception of its heartless might; he saw it unchanged, black and foaming under the eternal scrutiny of the stars; he heard its impatient voice calling for him out of a pitiless vastness full of unrest, of turmoil, and of terror. He looked afar upon it, and he saw an immensity tormented and blind, moaning and furious, that claimed all the days of his tenacious life, and, when life was over, would claim the worn-out body of its slave. . . .

This was the last of the breeze. It veered quickly, changed to a black south-easter, and blew itself out, giving the ship a famous shove to the northward into the joyous sunshine of the trade. Rapid and white she ran homewards in a straight path, under a blue sky and upon the plain of a blue sea. She carried Singleton's completed wisdom, Donkin's delicate susceptibilities, and the conceited folly of us all. The hours of ineffective turmoil were forgotten; the fear and anguish of these dark moments were never mentioned in the glowing peace of fine days. Yet from that time our life seemed to start afresh as though we had died and had been resuscitated. All the first part of the voyage, the Indian Ocean on the other side of the Cape, all that was lost in a haze, like an ineradicable suspicion of some previous existence. It had ended—then there were blank hours: a livid blurr—and again we lived! Singleton was possessed of sinister truth; Mr. Creighton of a damaged leg; the cook of fame—and shamefully abused the opportunities of his distinction. Donkin had an added grievance. He went about repeating with insistence:—" 'E said 'e would brain me—did yer 'ear? They are goin' to murder us now for the least little thing." We began at last to think it was rather awful. And we were conceited! We boasted of our pluck, of our capacity for work, of our energy. We remembered honourable episodes: our devotion, our indomitable persever-ance—and were proud of them as though they had been the outcome of our unaided impulses. We remembered our danger, our toil—and conveniently forgot our horrible scare. We decried our officers—who had done nothing—and listened to the fascinat-ing Donkin. His care for our rights, his disinterested concern for our dignity, were not discouraged by the invariable contumely of our words, by the disdain of our looks. Our contempt for him was unbounded—and we could not but listen with interest to that consummate artist. He told us we were good men—a "bloomin' condemned lot of good men." Who thanked us? Who took any notice of our wrongs? Didn't we lead a "dorg's loife for two poun' ten a month?" Did we think that miserable pay enough to compensate us for the risk to our lives and for the loss of our clothes? "We've lost every rag!" he cried. He made us forget that he, at any rate, had lost nothing of his own. The younger men listened, thinking—this 'ere Donkin's a long-headed chap, though no kind of man, anyhow. The Scandina-vians were frightened at his audacities; Wamibo did not understand; and the older seamen thoughtfully nodded their heads making the thin gold earrings glitter in the fleshy lobes of hairy ears. Severe, sunburnt faces were propped meditatively on tattooed forearms. Veined, brown fists held in their knotted grip the dirty white clay of smouldering pipes. They listened, impenetrable, broad-backed, with bent shoulders, and in grim silence. He talked with ardour, despised and irrefutable. His picturesque and filthy loquacity flowed like a troubled stream from a poisoned source. His beady little eyes danced, glancing right and left, ever on the watch for the approach of an officer. Sometimes Mr. Baker going forward to take a look at the head sheets would roll with his uncouth gait through the sudden still-ness of the men; or Mr. Creighton limped along, smooth-faced, youthful, and more stern than ever, piercing our short silence with a keen glance of his clear eyes. Behind his back Donkin would begin again darting stealthy, sidelong looks.—"'Ere's one of 'em. Some of yer 'as made 'im fast that day. Much thanks yer got for it. Ain't 'ee a-drivin' yer wusse'n ever? . . . Let 'im slip overboard. . . . Vy not? It would 'ave been less trouble. Vy not?" He advanced confidentially, backed away with great effect; he whispered, he screamed, waved his miserable arms no thicker than pipe-stems—stretched his lean neck—spluttered—squinted. In the pauses of his impassioned orations the wind sighed quietly aloft, the calm sea unheeded murmured in a warning whisper along the ship's side. We abominated the creature and could not deny the luminous truth of his contentions. It was all so obvious. We were indubitably good men; our deserts were great and our pay small. Through our exertions we had saved the ship and the skipper would get the credit of it. What had he done? we wanted to know. Donkin asked:—"What 'ee could do without hus?" and we could not answer. We were oppressed by the injustice of the world, surprised to perceive how long we had lived under its burden without realising our unfortunate state, annoyed by the uneasy suspicion of our undiscerning stupidity. Donkin assured us it was all our "good 'eartedness," but we would not be consoled by such shallow sophistry. We were men enough to courageously admit to ourselves our intellectual short-comings; though from that time we refrained from kicking him, tweaking his nose, or from accidentally knocking him about, which last, after we had weathered the Cape, had been rather a popular amusement. Davis ceased to talk at him provokingly about black eyes and flattened noses. Charley, much subdued since the gale, did not jeer at him. Knowles deferentially and with a crafty air propounded questions such as:—"Could we all have the same grub as the mates? Could we all stop ashore till we got it? What would be the next thing to try for if we got that?" He answered readily with contemptuous certitude; he strutted with assurance in clothes that were much too big for him as though he had tried to disguise himself. These were Jimmy's clothes mostly—though he would accept anything from anybody; but nobody, except Jimmy, had anything to spare. His devotion to Jimmy was unbounded. He was for ever dodging in the little cabin, ministering to Jimmy's wants, humouring his whims, submitting to his exacting peevishness, often laughing with him. Nothing could keep him away from the pious work of visiting the sick, especially when there was some heavy hauling to be done on deck. Mr. Baker had on two occasions jerked him out from there by the scruff of the neck to our inexpressible scandal. Was a sick chap to be left without attendance? Were we to be ill-used for attending a shipmate?—"What?" growled Mr. Baker, turning menacingly at the mutter, and the whole half-circle like one man stepped back a pace. "Set the topmast stunsail. Away aloft, Donkin, overhaul the gear," ordered the mate inflexibly. "Fetch the sail along; bend the down-haul clear. Bear a hand." Then, the sail set, he would go slowly aft and stand looking at the compass for a long time, careworn, pensive, and breathing hard as if stifled by the taint of unaccountable ill-will that pervaded the ship. "What's up amongst them?" he thought. "Can't make out this hanging back and growling. A good crowd, too, as they go nowadays." On deck the men exchanged bitter words, suggested by a silly exasperation against something unjust and irremediable that would not be denied, and would whisper into their ears long after Donkin had ceased speaking. Our little world went on its curved and unswerving path carrying a discontented and aspiring population. They found comfort of a gloomy kind in an interminable and conscientious analysis of their unappreciated worth; and inspired by Donkin's hopeful doctrines they dreamed enthusiastically of the time when every lonely ship would travel over a serene sea, manned by a wealthy and well-fed crew of satisfied skippers.

It looked as if it would be a long passage. The south-east trades, light and unsteady, were left behind; and then, on the equator and under a low grey sky, the ship, in close heat, floated upon a smooth sea that resembled a sheet of ground glass. Thunder squalls hung on the horizon, circled round the ship, far off and growling angrily, like a troop of wild beasts afraid to charge home. The invisible sun, sweeping above the upright masts, made on the clouds a blurred stain of rayless light, and a similar patch of faded radiance kept pace with it from east to west over the unglittering level of the waters. At night, through the impenetrable darkness of earth and heaven, broad sheets of flame waved noiselessly; and for half a second the becalmed craft stood out with its masts and rigging, with every sail and every rope distinct and black in the centre of a fiery outburst, like a charred ship enclosed in a globe of fire. And, again, for long hours she remained lost in a vast universe of night and silence where gentle sighs wandering here and there like forlorn souls, made the still sails flutter as in sudden fear, and the ripple of a beshrouded ocean whisper its compassion afar—in a voice mournful, immense, and faint. . . .

When the lamp was put out, and through the door thrown wide open, Jimmy, turning on his pillow, could see vanishing beyond the straight line of top-gallant rail, the quick, repeated visions of a fabulous world made up of leaping fire and sleeping water. The lightning gleamed in his big sad eyes that seemed in a red flicker to burn themselves out in his black face, and then he would lie blinded and invisible in the midst of an intense darkness. He could hear on the quiet deck soft footfalls, the breathing of some man lounging on the doorstep; the low creak of swaying masts; or the calm voice of the watch-officer reverberating aloft, hard and loud, amongst the unstirring sails. He listened with avidity, taking a rest in the attentive perception of the slightest sound from the fatiguing wanderings of his sleeplessness. He was cheered by the rattling of blocks, reassured by the stir and murmur of the watch, soothed by the slow yawn of some sleepy and weary seaman settling himself deliberately for a snooze on the planks. Life seemed an indestructible thing. It went on in darkness, in sunshine, in sleep; tireless, it hovered affectionately round the imposture of his ready death. It was bright, like the twisted flare of lightning, and more full of surprises than the dark night. It made him safe, and the calm of its

Conrad and Miss Ellen Glasgow in the garden at Capel House
in 1910

overpowering darkness was as precious as its restless and dangerous light.

But in the evening, in the dog-watches, and even far into the
first night-watch, a knot of men could always be seen congregated
before Jimmy's cabin. They leaned on each side of the door peace-
fully interested and with crossed legs; they stood astride the
doorstep discoursing, or sat in silent couples on his sea-chest;
while against the bulwark along the spare topmast, three or four
in a row stared meditatively; with their simple faces lit up by the
projected glare of Jimmy's lamp. The little place, repainted
white, had, in the night, the brilliance of a silver shrine where
a black idol, reclining stiffly under a blanket, blinked its weary
eyes and received our homage. Donkin officiated. He had the air
of a demonstrator showing a phenomenon, a manifestation
bizarre, simple, and meritorious that, to the beholders, should
be a profound and an everlasting lesson. "Just look at 'im, 'ee
knows what's what—never fear!" he exclaimed now and then,
flourishing a hand hard and fleshless like the claw of a snipe.
Jimmy, on his back, smiled with reserve and without moving a
limb. He affected the languor of extreme weakness, so as to make
it manifest to us that our delay in hauling him out from his
horrible confinement, and then that night spent on the poop
among our selfish neglect of his needs, had "done for him." He
rather liked to talk about it, and of course we were always interested. He spoke spasmodically, in fast rushes with long pauses
between, as a tipsy man walks. . . . "Cook had just given me a
pannikin of hot coffee. . . . Slapped it down there, on my chest—
banged the door to. . . . I felt a heavy roll coming; tried to save
my coffee, burnt my fingers . . . and fell out of my bunk. . . .
She went over so quick. . . . Water came in through the ventilator. . . . I couldn't move the door . . . dark as a grave . . . tried
to scramble up into the upper berth. . . . Rats . . . a rat bit my
finger as I got up. . . . I could hear him swimming below me.
. . . I thought you would never come. . . . I thought you were
all gone overboard . . . of course. . . . Could hear nothing but

the wind. . . . Then you came . . . to look for the corpse, I suppose. A little more and. . . ."

"Man! But ye made a rare lot of noise in here," observed
Archie, thoughtfully.

"You chaps kicked up such a confounded row above. . . .
Enough to scare any one. . . . I didn't know what you were
up to. . . . Bash in the blamed planks . . . my head. . . . Just what
a silly, scary gang of fools would do. . . . Not much good to me
anyhow. . . . Just as well . . . drown. . . . Pah."

He groaned, snapped his big white teeth, and gazed with
scorn. Belfast lifted a pair of dolorous eyes, with a broken-
hearted smile, clenched his fists stealthily; blue-eyed Archie
caressed his red whiskers with a hesitating hand; the boatswain
at the door stared a moment, and brusquely went away with
a loud guffaw. Wamibo dreamed. . . . Donkin felt all over his
sterile chin for the few rare hairs, and said, triumphantly, with
a sidelong glance at Jimmy:—"Look at 'im! Wish I was 'arf has
'ealthy as 'ee is—I do." He jerked a short thumb over his shoulder
towards the after end of the ship. "That's the blooming way
to do 'em!" he yelped, with forced heartiness. Jimmy said:—
"Don't be a dam' fool," in a pleasant voice. Knowles, rubbing
his shoulder against the doorpost, remarked shrewdly:—"We
can't all go an' be took sick—it would be mutiny."—"Mutiny—
gawn!" jeered Donkin, "there's no bloomin' law against bein'
sick."—"There's six weeks' hard for refoosing dooty," argued
Knowles, "I mind I once seed in Cardiff the crew of an overloaded ship—leastways she weren't overloaded, only a fatherly
old gentleman with a white beard and an umbreller came along
the quay and talked to the hands. Said as how it was crool hard
to be drowned in winter just for the sake of a few pounds more
for the owner—he said. Nearly cried over them—he did; and he
had a square mainsail coat, and a gaff-topsail hat too—all proper.
So they chaps they said they wouldn't go to be drowned in
winter—depending upon that 'ere Plimsoll man to see 'em
through the court. They thought to have a bloomin' lark and
two or three days' spree. And the beak giv' 'em six weeks—coss

the ship warn't overloaded. Anyways they made it out in court
that she wasn't. There wasn't one overloaded ship in Penarth
Dock at all. 'Pears that old coon he was only on pay and allowance from some kind people, under orders to look for overloaded ships, and he couldn't see no further than the length of
his umbreller. Some of us in the boarding-house, where I live
when I'm looking for a ship in Cardiff, stood by to duck that
old weeping spunger in the dock. We kept a good look-out, too
—but he topped his boom directly he was outside the court. . . .
Yes. They got six weeks' hard. . . ."

They listened, full of curiosity, nodding in the pauses their
rough pensive faces. Donkin opened his mouth once or twice,
but restrained himself. Jimmy lay still with open eyes and not
at all interested. A seaman emitted the opinion that after a
verdict of atrocious partiality "the bloomin' beaks go an' drink
at the skipper's expense." Others assented. It was clear, of course.
Donkin said:—"Well, six weeks ain't much trouble. You sleep
all night in, reg'lar, in chokey. Do it on my 'ead." "You are
used to it ainch'ee, Donkin?" asked somebody. Jimmy condescended to laugh. It cheered up every one wonderfully.
Knowles, with surprising mental agility, shifted his ground. "If
we all went sick what would become of the ship? eh?" He posed
the problem and grinned all round.—"Let 'er go to 'ell," sneered
Donkin. "Damn 'er. She ain't yourn."—"What? Just let her
drift?" insisted Knowles in a tone of unbelief.—"Aye! Drift, an'
be blowed," affirmed Donkin with fine recklessness. The other
did not see it—meditated.—"The stores would run out," he muttered, "and . . . never get anywhere . . . and what about pay-day?"
he added with greater assurance.—"Jack likes a good pay-day,"
exclaimed a listener on the doorstep. "Aye, because then the
girls put one arm round his neck an' t'other in his pocket,
and call him ducky. Don't they, Jack?"—"Jack, you're a terror
with the gals."—"He takes three of 'em in tow to once, like one
of 'em Watkinses two-funnel tugs waddling away with three
schooners behind."—"Jack, you're a lame scamp."—"Jack, tell
us about that one with a blue eye and a black eye. Do."—"There's

plenty of girls with one black eye along the Highway by. . . ."
—"No, that's a speshul one—come, Jack." Donkin looked severe
and disgusted; Jimmy very bored; a grey-haired sea-dog shook
his head slightly, smiling at the bowl of his pipe, discreetly
amused. Knowles turned about bewildered; stammered first at
one, then at another.—"No! . . . I never! . . . can't talk sensible
sense midst you. . . . Always on the kid." He retired bashfully—
muttering and pleased. They laughed, hooting in the crude
light, around Jimmy's bed, where on a white pillow his hollowed
black face moved to an fro restlessly. A puff of wind came, made
the flame of the lamp leap, and outside, high up, the sails fluttered, while near by the block of the foresheet struck a ringing
blow on the iron bulwark. A voice far off cried, "Helm up!"
another, more faint, answered, "Hard-up, sir!" They became
silent—waited expectantly. The grey-haired seaman knocked his
pipe on the doorstep and stood up. The ship leaned over gently
and the sea seemed to wake up, murmuring drowsily. "Here's
a little wind comin'," said some one very low. Jimmy turned
over slowly to face the breeze. The voice in the night cried loud
and commanding:—"Haul the spanker out." The group before
the door vanished out of the light. They could be heard tramping aft while they repeated with varied intonations:—"Spanker
out!" . . . "Out spanker, sir!" Donkin remained alone with
Jimmy. There was a silence. Jimmy opened and shut his lips
several times as if swallowing draughts of fresher air; Donkin
moved the toes of his bare feet and looked at them thoughtfully.

"Ain't you going to give them a hand with the sail?" asked
Jimmy.

"No. If six ov 'em ain't 'nough beef to set that blamed, rotten
spanker, they ain't fit to live," answered Donkin in a bored, far-
away voice, as though he had been talking from the bottom of
a hole. Jimmy considered the conical, fowl-like profile with a
queer kind of interest; he was leaning out of his bunk with the
calculating, uncertain expression of a man who reflects how best
to lay hold of some strange creature that looks as though it could

sting or bite. But he said only:—"The mate will miss you—and there will be ructions."

Donkin got up to go. "I will do for 'im some dark night; see if I don't," he said over his shoulder.

Jimmy went on quickly:—"You're like a poll-parrot, like a screechin' poll-parrot." Donkin stopped and cocked his head attentively on one side. His big ears stood out, transparent and veined, resembling the thin wings of a bat.

"Yuss?" he said, with his back towards Jimmy.

"Yes! Chatter out all you know—like . . . like a dirty white cockatoo."

Donkin waited. He could hear the other's breathing, long and slow; the breathing of a man with a hundredweight or so on the breastbone. Then he asked calmly:—"What do I know?"

"What? . . . What I tell you . . . not much. What do you want . . . to talk about my health so . . ."

"It's a blooming imposyshun. A bloomin', stinkin', first-class imposyshun—but it don't tyke me in. Not it."

Jimmy kept still. Donkin put his hands in his pockets, and in one slouching stride came up to the bunk.

"I talk—what's the odds. They ain't men 'ere—sheep they are. A driven lot of sheep. I 'old you up . . . Vy not? You're well orf."

"I am . . . I don't say anything about that. . . ."

"Well. Let 'em see it. Let 'em larn what a man can do. I am a man, I know all about yer. . . ." Jimmy threw himself further away on the pillow; the other stretched out his skinny neck, jerked his bird face down at him as though pecking at the eyes. "I am a man. I've seen the inside of every chokey in the Colonies rather'n give up my rights. . . ."

"You are a jail-prop," said Jimmy, weakly.

"I am . . . an' proud of it, too. You! You 'aven't the bloomin' nerve—so you inventyd this 'ere dodge. . . ." He paused; then with marked afterthought accentuated slowly:—"Yer ain't sick— are yer?"

"No," said Jimmy, firmly. "Been out of sorts now and again this year," he mumbled with a sudden drop in his voice.

Donkin closed one eye, amicable and confidential. He whispered:—"Ye 'ave done this afore 'aven'tchee?" Jimmy smiled—then as if unable to hold back he let himself go:—"Last ship—yes. I was out of sorts on the passage. See? It was easy. They paid me off in Calcutta, and the skipper made no bones about it either. . . . I got my money all right. Laid up fifty-eight days! The fools! O Lord! The fools! Paid right off." He laughed spasmodically. Donkin chimed in giggling. Then Jimmy coughed violently. "I am as well as ever," he said, as soon as he could draw breath.

Donkin made a derisive gesture. "In course," he said, profoundly, "any one can see that."—"They don't," said Jimmy, gasping like a fish.—"They would swallow any yarn," affirmed Donkin.—"Don't you let on too much," admonished Jimmy in an exhausted voice.—"Your little gyme? Eh?" commented Donkin, jovially. Then with sudden disgust: "Yer all for yerself, s'long as ye're right. . . ."

So charged with egoism James Wait pulled the blanket up to his chin and lay still for a while. His heavy lips protruded in an everlasting black pout. "Why are you so hot on making trouble?" he asked without much interest.

" 'Cos it's a bloomin' shayme. We are put upon . . . bad food, bad pay . . . I want us to kick up a bloomin' row; a blamed 'owling row that would make 'em remember! Knocking people about . . . brain us . . . indeed! Ain't we men?" His altruistic indignation blazed. Then he said calmly:—"I've been airing yer clothes."—"All right," said Jimmy, languidly, "bring them in." —"Giv' us the key of your chest, I'll put 'em away for yer," said Donkin with a friendly eagerness.—"Bring 'em in, I will put them away myself," answered James Wait with severity. Donkin looked down, muttering. . . . "What d'you say? What d'you say?" inquired Wait anxiously.—"Nothink. The night's dry, let 'em 'ang out till the morning," said Donkin, in a strangely trembling voice, as though restraining laughter or rage. Jimmy seemed satisfied.—"Give me a little water for the night in my mug—there," he said. Donkin took a stride over the doorstep.—"Git it yerself," he replied in a surly tone. "You can do it, unless you *are* sick."—"Of course I can do it," said Wait, "only. . . ."—"Well, then, do it," said Donkin, viciously, "if yer can look after yer clothes, yer can look after yerself." He went on deck without a look back.

Jimmy reached out for the mug. Not a drop. He put it back gently with a faint sigh—and closed his eyes. He thought:—That lunatic Belfast will bring me some water if I ask. Fool. I am very thirsty. . . . It was very hot in the cabin, and it seemed to turn slowly round, detach itself from the ship, and swing out smoothly into a luminous, arid space where a black sun shone, spinning very fast. A place without any water! No water! A policeman with the face of Donkin drank a glass of beer by the side of an empty well, and flew away flapping vigorously. A ship whose mastheads protruded through the sky and could not be seen, was discharging grain, and the wind whirled the dry husks in spirals along the quay of a dock with no water in it. He whirled along with the husks—very tired and light. All his inside was gone. He felt lighter than the husks—and more dry. He expanded his hollow chest. The air streamed in, carrying away in its rush a lot of strange things that resembled houses, trees, people, lamp-posts. . . . No more! There was no more air—and he had not finished drawing his long breath. But he was in jail! They were locking him up. A door slammed. They turned the key twice, flung a bucket of water over him—Phoo! What for?

He opened his eyes, thinking the fall had been very heavy for an empty man—empty—empty. He was in his cabin. Ah! All right! His face was streaming with perspiration, his arms heavier than lead. He saw the cook standing in the doorway, a brass key in one hand and a bright tin hook-pot in the other.

"I have locked up the galley for the night," said the cook, beaming benevolently. "Eight bells just gone. I brought you a pot of cold tea for your night's drinking, Jimmy. I sweetened it with some white cabin sugar, too. Well—it won't break the ship."

He came in, hung the pot on the edge of the bunk, asked perfunctorily, "How goes it?" and sat down on the box.—"H'm," grunted Wait, inhospitably. The cook wiped his face with a dirty cotton rag, which, afterwards, he tied round his neck.— "That's how them firemen do in steamboats," he said, serenely, and much pleased with himself. "My work is as heavy as theirs —I'm thinking—and longer hours. Did you ever see them down the stokehold? Like fiends they look—firing—firing—firing—down there."

He pointed his forefinger at the deck. Some gloomy thought darkened his shining face, fleeting, like the shadow of a travelling cloud over the light of a peaceful sea. The relieved watch tramped noisily forward, passing in a body across the sheen of the doorway. Some one cried, "Good-night!" Belfast stopped for a moment and looked at Jimmy, quivering and speechless with repressed emotion. He gave the cook a glance charged with dismal foreboding, and vanished. The cook cleared his throat. Jimmy stared upwards and kept as still as a man in hiding.

The night was clear, with a gentle breeze. Above the mastheads the resplendent curve of the Milky Way spanned the sky like a triumphal arch of eternal light, thrown over the dark pathway of the earth. On the forecastle head a man whistled with loud precision a lively jig, while another could be heard faintly, shuffling and stamping in time. There came from forward a confused murmur of voices, laughter—snatches of song. The cook shook his head, glanced obliquely at Jimmy, and began to mutter. "Aye. Dance and sing. That's all they think of. I am surprised that Providence don't get tired. . . . They forget the day that's sure to come . . . but you. . . ."

Jimmy drank a gulp of tea, hurriedly, as though he had stolen it, and shrank under his blanket, edging away towards the bulkhead. The cook got up, closed the door, then sat down again and said distinctly:—

"Whenever I poke my galley fire I think of you chaps—swearing, stealing, lying, and worse—as if there was no such thing as another world. . . . Not bad fellows, either, in a way," he conceded, slowly; then, after a pause of regretful musing, he went on in a resigned tone:—"Well, well. They will have a hot time of it. Hot! Did I say? The furnaces of one of them White Star boats ain't nothing to it."

He kept very quiet for a while. There was a great stir in his brain; an addled vision of bright outlines; an exciting row of rousing songs and groans of pain. He suffered, enjoyed, admired, approved. He was delighted, frightened, exalted—as on that evening (the only time in his life—twenty-seven years ago; he loved to recall the number of years) when as a young man he had—through keeping bad company—become intoxicated in an East-end music-hall. A tide of sudden feeling swept him clean out of his body. He soared. He contemplated the secret of the hereafter. It commended itself to him. It was excellent; he loved it, himself, all hands, and Jimmy. His heart overflowed with tenderness, with comprehension, with the desire to meddle, with anxiety for the soul of that black man, with the pride of possessed eternity, with the feeling of might. Snatch him up in his arms and pitch him right into the middle of salvation. . . . The black soul—blacker—body—rot—Devil. No! Talk—strength—Samson. . . . There was a great din as of cymbals in his ears; he flashed through an ecstatic jumble of shining faces, lilies, prayer-books, unearthly joy, white skirts, gold harps, black coats, wings. He saw flowing garments, clean shaved faces, a sea of light—a lake of pitch. There were sweet scents, a smell of sulphur—red tongues of flame licking a white mist. An awesome voice thundered! . . . It lasted three seconds.

"Jimmy!" he cried in an inspired tone. Then he hesitated. A spark of human pity glimmered yet through the infernal fog of his supreme conceit.

"What?" said James Wait, unwillingly. There was a silence. He turned his head just the least bit, and stole a cautious glance. The cook's lips moved without a sound; his face was rapt, his eyes turned up. He seemed to be mentally imploring deck beams, the brass hook of the lamp, two cockroaches.

"Look here," said Wait, "I want to go to sleep. I think I could."

"This is no time for sleep!" exclaimed the cook, very loud. He had prayerfully divested himself of the last vestige of his humanity. He was a voice—a fleshless and sublime thing, as on that memorable night—the night when he went walking over the sea to make coffee for perishing sinners. "This is no time for sleeping," he repeated with exaltation. "*I* can't sleep."

"Don't care damn," said Wait, with factitious energy. "I can. Go an' turn in."

"Swear . . . in the very jaws! . . . In the very jaws! Don't you see the everlasting fire . . . don't you feel it? Blind, chockful of sin! Repent, repent! I can't bear to think of you. I hear the call to save you. Night and day. Jimmy, let me save you!" The words of entreaty and menace broke out of him in a roaring torrent. The cockroaches ran away. Jimmy perspired, wriggling stealthily under his blanket. The cook yelled. . . . "Your days are numbered! . . ."—"Get out of this," boomed Wait, courageously.—"Pray with me! . . ."—"I won't! . . ." The little cabin was as hot as an oven. It contained an immensity of fear and pain; an atmosphere of shrieks and moans; prayers vociferated like blasphemies and whispered curses. Outside, the men called by Charley, who informed them in tones of delight that there was a holy row going on in Jimmy's place, crowded before the closed door, too startled to open it. All hands were there. The watch below had jumped out on deck in their shirts, as after a collision. Men running up, asked:—"What is it?" Others said:—"Listen!" The muffled screaming went on:—"On your knees! On your knees!"—"Shut up!"—"Never! You are delivered into my hands. . . . Your life has been saved. . . . Purpose. . . . Mercy. . . . Repent."—"You are a crazy fool! . . ."—"Account of you . . . you . . . Never sleep in this world, if I . . ."—"Leave off."—"No! . . . stokehold . . . only think! . . ." Then an impassioned screeching babble where words pattered like hail.—"No!" shouted Wait.—"Yes. You are! . . . No help. . . . Everybody says so."—"You lie!"—"I see you dying this minnyt . . . before my eyes . . . as good as dead already."—"Help!" shouted Jimmy, piercingly.—"Not in this valley. . . . look upwards," howled the other.—"Go away! Murder! Help!" clamoured Jimmy. His voice broke. There were moanings, low mutters, a few sobs.

"What's the matter now?" said a seldom-heard voice.—"Fall back, men! Fall back, there!" repeated Mr. Creighton, sternly, pushing through.—"Here's the old man," whispered some.— "The cook's in there, sir," exclaimed several, backing away. The door clattered open; a broad stream of light darted out on wondering faces; a warm whiff of vitiated air passed. The two mates towered head and shoulders above the spare, grey-haired man who stood revealed between them, in shabby clothes, stiff and angular, like a small carved figure, and with a thin, composed face. The cook got up from his knees. Jimmy sat high in the bunk, clasping his drawn-up legs. The tassel of the blue night-cap almost imperceptibly trembled over his knees. They gazed astonished at his long, curved back, while the white corner of one eye gleamed blindly at them. He was afraid to turn his head, he shrank within himself; and there was an aspect astounding and animal-like in the perfection of his expectant immobility. A thing of instinct—the unthinking stillness of a sacred brute.

"What are you doing here?" asked Mr. Baker, sharply.—"My duty," said the cook, with ardour.—"Your . . . what?" began the mate. Captain Allistoun touched his arm lightly.—"I know his caper," he said, in a low voice. "Come out of that, Podmore," he ordered, aloud.

The cook wrung his hands, shook his fists above his head, and his arms dropped as if too heavy. For a moment he stood distracted and speechless.—"Never," he stammered, "I . . . he . . . I." —"What—do—you—say?" pronounced Captain Allistoun. "Come out at once—or . . ."—"I am going," said the cook, with a hasty and sombre resignation. He strode over the doorstep firmly— hesitated—made a few steps. They looked at him in silence.—"I make you responsible!" he cried, desperately, turning half round. "That man is dying. I make you . . ."—"You there yet?" called the master in a threatening tone.—"No, sir," he exclaimed, hurriedly, in a startled voice. The boatswain led him away by the arm; some one laughed; Jimmy lifted his head for a stealthy glance, and in one unexpected leap sprang out of his bunk; Mr. Baker made a clever catch and felt him very limp in his arms; the group at the door grunted with surprise.—"He lies," gasped Wait, "he talked about black devils—he is a devil—a white devil —I am all right." He stiffened himself, and Mr. Baker, experimentally, let him go. He staggered a pace or two; Captain Allistoun watched him with a quiet and penetrating gaze; Belfast ran to his support. He did not appear to be aware of any one near him; he stood silent for a moment, battling single-handed with a legion of nameless terrors, amidst the eager looks of excited men who watched him far off, utterly alone in the impenetrable solitude of his fear. The sea gurgled through the scuppers as the ship heeled over to a short puff of wind.

"Keep him away from me," said James Wait at last in his fine baritone voice, and leaning with all his weight on Belfast's neck. "I've been better this last week . . . I am well . . . I was going back to duty . . . to-morrow—now if you like—Captain." Belfast hitched his shoulders to keep him upright.

"No," said the master, looking at him, fixedly.

Under Jimmy's armpit Belfast's red face moved uneasily. A row of eyes gleaming stared on the edge of light. They pushed one another with elbows, turned their heads, whispered. Wait let his chin fall on his breast and, with lowered eyelids, looked round in a suspicious manner.

"Why not?" cried a voice from the shadows, "the man's all right, sir."

"I am all right," said Wait, with eagerness. "Been sick . . . better . . . turn-to now." He sighed.—"Howly Mother!" exclaimed Belfast with a heave of the shoulders, "stand up, Jimmy."—"Keep away from me then," said Wait, giving Belfast a petulant push, and reeling fetched against the doorpost. His cheekbones glistened as though they had been varnished. He snatched off his night-cap, wiped his perspiring face with it,

flung it on the deck. "I am coming out," he declared without
stirring.

"No. You don't," said the master, curtly. Bare feet shuffled,
disapproving voices murmured all round; he went on as if he
had not heard:—"You have been skulking nearly all the passage
and now you want to come out. You think you are near enough
to the paytable now. Smell the shore, hey?"

"I've been sick . . . now—better," mumbled Wait, glaring in
the light.—"You have been shamming sick," retorted Captain
Allistoun with severity; "Why . . ." he hesitated for less than half
a second. "Why, anybody can see that. There's nothing the matter
with you, but you choose to lie-up to please yourself—and now
you shall lie-up to please me. Mr. Baker, my orders are that this
man is not to be allowed on deck to the end of the passage."

There were exclamations of surprise, triumph, indignation.
The dark group of men swung across the light. "What for?"
"Told you so . . ." "Bloomin' shame . . ."—"We've got to say
somethink about that," screeched Donkin from the rear.—
"Never mind, Jim—we will see you righted," cried several together. An elderly seaman stepped to the front. "D'ye mean
to say, sir," he asked ominously, "that a sick chap ain't allowed
to get well in this 'ere hooker?" Behind him Donkin whispered
excitedly amongst a staring crowd where no one spared him a
glance, but Captain Allistoun shook a forefinger at the angry
bronzed face of the speaker.—"You—you hold your tongue," he
said, warningly.—"This isn't the way," clamoured two or three
younger men.—"Are we bloomin' masheens?" inquired Donkin
in a piercing tone, and dived under the elbows of the front
rank.—"Soon show 'im we ain't boys . . ."—"The man's a man if
he is black."—"We ain't goin' to work this bloomin' ship shorthanded if Snowball's all right . . ."—"He says he is."—"Well then,
strike, boys, strike!"—"That's the bloomin' ticket." Captain Allistoun said sharply to the second mate: "Keep quiet, Mr.
Creighton," and stood composed in the tumult, listening with
profound attention to mixed growls and screeches, to every exclamation and every curse of the sudden outbreak. Somebody

slammed the cabin door to with a kick; the darkness full of menacing mutters leaped with a short clatter over the streak of light, and the men became gesticulating shadows that growled, hissed, laughed excitedly. Mr. Baker whispered:—"Get away from them, sir." The big shape of Mr. Creighton hovered silently about the slight figure of the master.—"We have been hymposed upon all this voyage," said a gruff voice, "but this 'ere fancy takes the cake."—"That man is a shipmate."—"Are we bloomin' kids?"—"The port watch will refuse duty." Charley carried away by his feeling whistled shrilly, then yelped:—"Giv' us our Jimmy!" This seemed to cause a variation in the disturbance. There was a fresh burst of squabbling uproar. A lot of quarrels were set going at once.—"Yes."—"No."—"Never been sick."—"Go for them to once."—"Shut yer mouth, youngster—this is men's work."—"Is it?" muttered Captain Allistoun, bitterly. Mr. Baker grunted: "Ough! They're gone silly. They've been simmering for the last month."—"I did notice," said the master.—"They have started a row amongst themselves now," said Mr. Creighton with disdain, "better get aft, sir. We will soothe them.—"Keep your temper, Creighton," said the master. And the three men began to move slowly towards the cabin door.

In the shadows of the fore rigging a dark mass stamped, eddied, advanced, retreated. There were words of reproach, encouragement, unbelief, execration. The elder seamen, bewildered and angry, growled their determination to go through with something or other; but the younger school of advanced thought exposed their and Jimmy's wrongs with confused shouts, arguing amongst themselves. They clustered round that moribund carcass, the fit emblem of their aspirations, and encouraging one another they swayed, they tramped on one spot, shouting that they would not be "put upon." Inside the cabin, Belfast, helping Jimmy into his bunk, twitched all over in his desire not to miss all the row, and with difficulty restrained the tears of his facile emotion. James Wait, flat on his back under the blanket, gasped complaints.—"We will back you up, never fear," assured Belfast, busy about his feet.—"I'll come out to-

morrow morning——take my chance——you fellows must——"
mumbled Wait, "I come out to-morrow——skipper or no skipper." He lifted one arm with great difficulty, passed the hand
over his face; "Don't you let that cook . . ." he breathed out.
—"No, no," said Belfast, turning his back on the bunk, "I will
put a head on him if he comes near you."—"I will smash his
mug!" exclaimed faintly Wait, enraged and weak; "I don't want
to kill a man, but . . ." He panted fast like a dog after a run in
sunshine. Some one just outside the door shouted, "He's as fit
as any ov us!" Belfast put his hand on the door-handle.—"Here!"
called James Wait, hurriedly, and in such a clear voice that the
other spun round with a start. James Wait, stretched out black
and deathlike in the dazzling light, turned his head on the pillow. His eyes stared at Belfast, appealing and impudent. "I am
rather weak from lying-up so long," he said, distinctly. Belfast
nodded. "Getting quite well now," insisted Wait.—"Yes. I
noticed you getting better this . . . last month," said Belfast,
looking down. "Hallo! What's this?" he shouted and ran out.
    He was flattened directly against the side of the house by two
men who lurched against him. A lot of disputes seemed to be
going on all round. He got clear and saw three indistinct figures
standing alone in the fainter darkness under the arched foot of
the mainsail, that rose above their heads like a convex wall of
a high edifice. Donkin hissed:—"Go for them . . . it's dark!" The
crowd took a short run aft in a body—then there was a check.
Donkin, agile and thin, flitted past with his right arm going like
a windmill—and then stood still suddenly with his arm pointing
rigidly above his head. The hurtling flight of some heavy object
was heard; it passed between the heads of the two mates,
bounded heavily along the deck, struck the after hatch with a
ponderous and deadened blow. The bulky shape of Mr. Baker
grew distinct. "Come to your senses, men!" he cried, advancing
at the arrested crowd. "Come back, Mr. Baker!" called the master's quiet voice. He obeyed unwillingly. There was a minute
of silence, then a deafening hubbub arose. Above it Archie was
heard energetically:—"If ye do oot ageen I wull tell!" There

were shouts. "Don't!" "Drop it!"—"We ain't that kind!" The
black cluster of human forms reeled against the bulwark, back
again towards the house. Ringbolts rang under stumbling feet.—
"Drop it!" "Let me!"—"No!"—"Curse you . . . hah!" Then
sounds as of some one's face being slapped; a piece of iron fell
on the deck; a short scuffle, and some one's shadowy body scuttled
rapidly across the main hatch before the shadow of a kick. A
raging voice sobbed out a torrent of filthy language . . . —"Throwing things—good God!" grunted Mr. Baker in dismay.—"That
was meant for me," said the master, quietly; "I felt the wind of
that thing; what was it—an iron belaying-pin?"—"By Jove!"
muttered Mr. Creighton. The confused voices of men talking
amidships mingled with the wash of the sea, ascended between
the silent and distended sails—seemed to flow away into the
night, further than the horizon, higher than the sky. The stars
burned steadily over the inclined mastheads. Trails of light lay
on the water, broke before the advancing hull, and, after she
had passed, trembled for a long time as if in awe of the murmuring sea.

Meantime the helmsman, anxious to know what the row was
about, had let go the wheel, and, bent double, ran with long,
stealthy footsteps to the break of the poop. The *Narcissus*, left to
herself, came up gently to the wind without any one being aware
of it. She gave a slight roll, and the sleeping sails woke suddenly,
coming all together with a mighty flap against the masts, then
filled again one after another in a quick succession of loud re-
ports that ran down the lofty spars, till the collapsed mainsail
flew out last with a violent jerk. The ship trembled from trucks
to keel; the sails kept on rattling like a discharge of musketry;
the chain sheets and loose shackles jingled aloft in a thin peal;
the gin blocks groaned. It was as if an invisible hand had given
the ship an angry shake to recall the men that peopled her decks
to the sense of reality, vigilance, and duty.—"Helm up!" cried
the master, sharply. "Run aft, Mr. Creighton, and see what that
fool there is up to."—"Flatten in the head sheets. Stand by the
weather fore-braces," growled Mr. Baker. Startled men ran

swiftly repeating the orders. The watch below, abandoned all at once by the watch on deck, drifted towards the forecastle in twos and threes, arguing noisily as they went—"We shall see to-morrow!" cried a loud voice, as if to cover with a menacing hint an inglorious retreat. And then only orders were heard, the falling of heavy coils of rope, the rattling of blocks. Singleton's white head flitted here and there in the night, high above the deck, like the ghost of a bird.—"Going off, sir!" shouted Mr. Creighton from aft.—"Full again."—"All right . . ."—"Ease off the head sheets. That will do the braces. Coil the ropes up," grunted Mr. Baker, bustling about.

Gradually the tramping noises, the confused sound of voices, died out, and the officers, coming together on the poop, discussed the events. Mr. Baker was bewildered and grunted; Mr. Creighton was calmly furious; but Captain Allistoun was composed and thoughtful. He listened to Mr. Baker's growling argumentation, to Creighton's interjected and severe remarks, while looking down on the deck he weighed in his hand the iron belaying-pin—that a moment ago had just missed his head—as if it had been the only tangible fact of the whole transaction. He was one of those commanders who speak little, seem to hear nothing, look at no one—and know everything, hear every whisper, see every fleeting shadow of their ship's life. His two big officers towered above his lean, short figure; they talked over his head; they were dismayed, surprised, and angry, while between them the little quiet man seemed to have found his taciturn serenity in the profound depths of a larger experience. Lights were burning in the forecastle; now and then a loud gust of babbling chatter came from forward, swept over the decks, and became faint, as if the unconscious ship, gliding gently through the great peace of the sea, had left behind and for ever the foolish noise of turbulent mankind. But it was renewed again and again. Gesticulating arms, profiles of heads with open mouths appeared for a moment in the illuminated squares of doorways; black fists darted—withdrew . . . "Yes. It was most damnable to have such an unprovoked row sprung on one," assented the mas-

ter. . . . A tumult of yells rose in the light, abruptly ceased. . . .
He didn't think there would be any further trouble just then.
. . . .A bell was struck aft, another, forward, answered in a deeper
tone, and the clamour of ringing metal spread round the ship in
a circle of wide vibrations that ebbed away into the immeasurable night of an empty sea. . . . Didn't he know them! Didn't
he! In past years. Better men, too. Real men to stand by one in
a tight place. Worse than devils too sometimes—downright,
horned devils. Pah! This—nothing. A miss as good as a mile. . . .
The wheel was being relieved in the usual way.—"Full and by,"
said, very loud, the man going off.—"Full and by," repeated the
other, catching hold of the spokes.—"This head wind is my
trouble," exclaimed the master, stamping his foot in sudden
anger; "head wind! all the rest is nothing." He was calm again
in a moment. "Keep them on the move to-night, gentlemen; just
to let them feel we've got hold all the time—quietly, you know.
Mind you keep your hands off them, Creighton. To-morrow I
will talk to them like a Dutch Uncle. A crazy crowd of tinkers!
Yes, tinkers! I could count the real sailors amongst them on the
fingers of one hand. Nothing will do but a row—if—you—please."
He paused. "Did you think I had gone wrong there, Mr. Baker?"
He tapped his forehead, laughed short. "When I saw him standing there, three parts dead and so scared—black amongst that
gaping lot—no grit to face what's coming to us all—the notion
came to me all at once, before I could think. Sorry for him—like
you would be for a sick brute. If ever creature was in a mortal
funk to die! . . . I thought I would let him go out in his own
way. Kind of impulse. It never came into my head, those fools.
. . . H'm! Stand to it now—of course." He stuck the belaying-pin
in his pocket, seemed ashamed of himself, then sharply:—"If you
see Podmore at his tricks again tell him I will have him put
under the pump. Had to do it once before. The fellow breaks
out like that now and then. Good cook tho'." He walked away
quickly, came back to the companion. The two mates followed
him through the starlight with amazed eyes. He went down
deck:—"I shan't turn in to-night, in case of anything; just call

out if . . . Did you see the eyes of that sick nigger, Mr. Baker? I
fancied he begged me for something. What? Past all help. One
lone black beggar amongst the lot of us, and he seemed to look
through me into the very hell. Fancy, this wretched Podmore!
Well, let him die in peace. I am master here after all. Let him be.
He might have been half a man once . . . Keep a good look-out."
He disappeared down below, leaving his mates facing one another, and more impressed than if they had seen a stone image
shed a miraculous tear of compassion over the incertitudes of
life and death. . . .

In the blue mist spreading from twisted threads that stood
upright in the bowls of pipes, the forecastle appeared as vast as
a hall. Between the beams a heavy cloud stagnated; and the
lamps surrounded by halos burned each at the core of a purple
glow in two lifeless flames without rays. Wreaths drifted in
denser wisps. Men sprawled about on the deck, sat in negligent
poses, or, bending a knee, drooped with one shoulder against a
bulkhead. Lips moved, eyes flashed, waving arms made sudden
eddies in the smoke. The murmur of voices seemed to pile itself
higher and higher as if unable to run out quick enough through
the narrow doors. The watch below in their shirts, and striding
on long white legs, resembled raving somnambulists; while now
and then one of the watch on deck would rush in, looking
strangely over-dressed, listen a moment, fling a rapid sentence
into the noise and run out again; but a few remained near the
door, fascinated, and with one ear turned to the deck. "Stick
together, boys," roared Davis. Belfast tried to make himself
heard. Knowles grinned in a slow, dazed way. A short fellow with
a thick clipped beard kept on yelling periodically:—"Who's
afeard? Who's afeard?" Another one jumped up, excited, with
blazing eyes, sent out a string of unattached curses and sat down
quietly. Two men discussed familiarly, striking one another's
breast in turn, to clinch arguments. Three others, with their
heads in a bunch, spoke all together with a confidential air, and
at the top of their voices. It was a stormy chaos of speech where
intelligible fragments tossing, struck the ear. One could hear:

—"In the last ship"—"Who cares? Try it on any one of us if——."
"Knock under"—"Not a hand's turn"—"He says he is all right"—
"I always thought"—"Never mind. . . ." Donkin, crouching all
in a heap against the bowsprit, hunched his shoulderblades as
high as his ears, and hanging a peaked nose, resembled a sick
vulture with ruffled plumes. Belfast, straddling his legs, had a
face red with yelling, and with arms thrown up, figured a Mal-
tese cross. The two Scandinavians, in a corner, had the dumbfounded and distracted aspect of men gazing at a cataclysm. And,
beyond the light, Singleton stood in the smoke, monumental,
indistinct, with his head touching the beam; like a statue of
heroic size in the gloom of a crypt.

He stepped forward, impassive and big. The noise subsided
like a broken wave: but Belfast cried once more with uplifted
arms:—"The man is dying I tell ye!" then sat down suddenly on
the hatch and took his head between his hands. All looked at
Singleton, gazing upwards from the deck, staring out of dark
corners, or turning their heads with curious glances. They were
expectant and appeased as if that old man, who looked at no one,
had possessed the secret of their uneasy indignations and desires,
a sharper vision, a clearer knowledge. And indeed standing
there amongst them, he had the uninterested appearance of one
who had seen multitudes of ships, had listened many times to
voices such as theirs, had already seen all that could happen on
the wide seas. They heard his voice rumble in his broad chest
as though the words had been rolling towards them out of a
rugged past. "What do you want to do?" he asked. No one answered. Only Knowles muttered—"Aye, aye," and somebody
said low:—"It's a bloomin' shame." He waited, made a contemptuous gesture.—"I have seen rows aboard ship before some of
you were born," he said, slowly, "for something or nothing; but
never for such a thing."—"The man is dying, I tell ye," repeated
Belfast, woefully, sitting at Singleton's feet.—"And a black fellow, too," went on the old seaman. "I have seen them die like
flies." He stopped, thoughtful, as if trying to recollect gruesome
things, details of horrors, hecatombs of niggers. They looked at

him fascinated. He was old enough to remember slavers, bloody mutinies, pirates perhaps; who could tell through what violences and terrors he had lived! What would he say? He said:—"You can't help him; die he must." He made another pause. His moustache and beard stirred. He chewed words, mumbled behind tangled white hairs; incomprehensible and exciting, like an oracle behind a veil. . . .—"Stop ashore——sick.——Instead—— bringing all this head wind. Afraid. The sea will have her own.——Die in sight of land. Always so. They know it——long passage——more days, more dollars.——You keep quiet.——What do you want? Can't help him." He seemed to wake up from a dream. "You can't help yourselves," he said, austerely, "Skipper's no fool. He has something in his mind. Look out—I say! I know 'em!" With eyes fixed in front he turned his head from right to left, from left to right, as if inspecting a long row of astute skippers.—" 'Ee said 'ee would brain me!" cried Donkin in a heartrending tone. Singleton peered downwards with puzzled attention, as though he couldn't find him.—"Damn you!" he said, vaguely, giving it up. He radiated unspeakable wisdom, hard unconcern, the chilling air of resignation. Round him all the listeners felt themselves somehow completely enlightened by their disappointment, and mute, they lolled about with the careless ease of men who can discern perfectly the irremediable aspect of their existence. He, profound and unconscious, waved his arm once, and strode out on deck without another word.

Belfast was lost in a round-eyed meditation. One or two vaulted heavily into upper berths, and, once there, sighed; others dived head first inside lower bunks—swift, and turning round instantly upon themselves, like animals going into lairs. The grating of a knife scraping burnt clay was heard. Knowles grinned no more. Davis said, in a tone of ardent conviction: "Then our skipper's looney." Archie muttered: "My faith! we haven't heard the last of it yet!" Four bells were struck.—"Half our watch below gone!" cried Knowles in alarm, then reflected. "Well, two hours' sleep is something towards a rest," he observed, consolingly. Some already pretended to slumber; and

Charley, sound asleep, suddenly said a few slurred words in an arbitrary, blank voice.—"This blamed boy has worrums!" commented Knowles from under a blanket, in a learned manner. Belfast got up and approached Archie's berth.—"We pulled him out," he whispered, sadly.—"What?" said the other, with sleepy discontent.—"And now we will have to chuck him overboard," went on Belfast, whose lower lip trembled.—"Chuck what? asked Archie.—"Poor Jimmy," breathed out Belfast.—"He be blowed!" said Archie with untruthful brutality, and sat up in his bunk; "It's all through him. If it hadn't been for me, there would have been murder on board this ship!"—" 'Tain't his fault, is it?" argued Belfast, in a murmur; "I've put him to bed . . . an' he ain't no heavier than an empty beef-cask," he added, with tears in his eyes. Archie looked at him steadily, then turned his nose to the ship's side with determination. Belfast wandered about as though he had lost his way in the dim forecastle, and nearly fell over Donkin. He contemplated him from on high for a while. "Ain't ye going to turn in?" he asked. Donkin looked up hopelessly.—"That black'earted Scotch son of a thief kicked me!" he whispered from the floor, in a tone of utter desolation.— "And a good job, too!" said Belfast, still very depressed; "You were as near hanging as damn-it to-night, sonny. Don't you play any of your murthering games around my Jimmy! You haven't pulled him out. You just mind! 'Cos if I start to kick you"—he brightened up a bit—"if I start to kick you, it will be Yankee fashion—to break something!" He tapped lightly with his knuckles the top of the bowed head. "You moind that, my bhoy!" he concluded, cheerily. Donkin let it pass.—"Will they split on me?" he asked, with pained anxiety.—"Who—split?" hissed Belfast, coming back a step. "I would split your nose this minyt if I hadn't Jimmy to look after! Who d'ye think we are?" Donkin rose and watched Belfast's back lurch through the doorway. On all sides invisible men slept, breathing calmly. He seemed to draw courage and fury from the peace around him. Venomous and thin-faced, he glared from the ample misfit of borrowed clothes as if looking for something he could smash.

His heart leaped wildly in his narrow chest. They slept! He wanted to wring necks, gouge eyes, spit on faces. He shook a dirty pair of meagre fists at the smoking lights. "Ye're no men!" he cried, in a deadened tone. No one moved. "Yer 'aven't the pluck of a mouse!" His voice rose to a husky screech. Wamibo darted out a dishevelled head, and looked at him wildly. "Ye're sweepings ov ships! I 'ope you will all rot before you die!" Wamibo blinked, uncomprehending but interested. Donkin sat down heavily; he blew with force through quivering nostrils, he ground and snapped his teeth, and, with the chin pressed hard against the breast, he seemed busy gnawing his way through it, as if to get at the heart within. . . .

In the morning the ship, beginning another day of her wandering life, had an aspect of sumptuous freshness, like the springtime of the earth. The washed decks glistened in a long clear stretch; the oblique sunlight struck the yellow brasses in dazzling splashes, darted over the polished rods in lines of gold, and the single drops of salt water forgotten here and there along the rail were as limpid as drops of dew, and sparkled more than scattered diamonds. The sails slept, hushed by a gentle breeze. The sun, rising lonely and splendid in the blue sky, saw a solitary ship gliding close-hauled on the blue sea.

The men pressed three deep abreast of the mainmast and opposite the cabin-door. They shuffled, pushed, had an irresolute mien and stolid faces. At every slight movement Knowles lurched heavily on his short leg. Donkin glided behind backs, restless and anxious, like a man looking for an ambush. Captain Allistoun came out on the quarter-deck suddenly. He walked to and fro before the front. He was grey, slight, alert, shabby in the sunshine, and as hard as adamant. He had his right hand in the side-pocket of his jacket, and also something heavy in there that made folds all down that side. One of the seamen cleared his throat ominously.—"I haven't till now found fault with you men," said the master, stopping short. He faced them with his worn, steely gaze, that by a universal illusion looked straight into every individual pair of the twenty pairs of eyes before his face. At his back Mr. Baker, gloomy and bull-necked, grunted low; Mr. Creighton, fresh as paint, had rosy cheeks and a ready, resolute bearing. "And I don't now," continued the master; "but I am here to drive this ship and keep every man-jack aboard of her up to the mark. If you knew your work as well as I do mine, there would be no trouble. You've been braying in the dark about 'See to-morrow morning!' Well, you see me now. What do you want?" He waited, stepping quickly to and fro, giving them searching glances. What did they want? They shifted from foot to foot, they balanced their bodies; some, pushing back their caps, scratched their heads. What did they want? Jimmy was forgotten; no one thought of him, alone forward in his cabin, fighting great shadows, clinging to brazen lies, chuckling painfully over his transparent deceptions. No, not Jimmy; he was more forgotten than if he had been dead. They wanted great things. And suddenly all the simple words they knew seemed to be lost for ever in the immensity of their vague and burning desire. They knew what they wanted, but they could not find anything worth saying. They stirred on one spot, swinging, at the end of muscular arms, big tarry hands with crooked fingers. A murmur died out.—"What is it—food?" asked the master, "you know the stores have been spoiled off the Cape."—"We know that, sir," said a bearded shell-back in the front rank.—"Work too hard—eh? Too much for your strength?" he asked again. There was an offended silence.—"We don't want to go shorthanded, sir," began at last Davis in a wavering voice, "and this 'ere black— . . ."—"Enough!" cried the master. He stood scanning them for a moment, then walking a few steps this way and that began to storm at them coldly, in gusts violent and cutting like the gales of those icy seas that had known his youth. —"Tell you what's the matter? Too big for your boots. Think yourselves damn good men. Know half your work. Do half your duty. Think it too much. If you did ten times as much it wouldn't be enough."—"We did our best by her, sir," cried some one with shaky exasperation.—"Your best," stormed on the master; "You hear a lot on shore, don't you? They don't tell you there your best isn't much to boast of. I tell you—your best is no better than bad. You can do no more? No, I know, and say nothing. But you stop your caper or I will stop it for you. I am ready for you! Stop it!" He shook a finger at the crowd. "As to that man," he raised his voice very much; "as to that man, if he puts his nose out on deck without my leave I will clap him in irons. There!" The cook heard him forward, ran out of the galley lifting his arms, horrified, unbelieving, amazed, and ran in again. There was a moment of profound silence during which a bow-legged seaman, stepping aside, expectorated decorously into the scupper. "There is another thing," said the master, calmly. He made a quick stride and with a swing took an iron belaying-pin out of his pocket. "This!" His movement was so unexpected and sudden that the crowd stepped back. He gazed fixedly at their faces, and some at once put on a surprised air as though they had never seen a belaying-pin before. He held it up. "This is my affair. I don't ask you any questions, but you all know it; it has got to go where it came from." His eyes became angry. The crowd stirred uneasily. They looked away from the piece of iron, they appeared shy, they were embarrassed and shocked as though it had been something horrid, scandalous, or indelicate, that in common decency should not have been flourished like this in broad daylight. The master watched them attentively. "Donkin," he called out in a short, sharp tone.

Donkin dodged behind one, then behind another, but they looked over their shoulders and moved aside. The ranks kept on opening before him, closing behind, till at last he appeared alone before the master as though he had come up through the deck. Captain Allistoun moved close to him. They were much of a size, and at short range the master exchanged a deadly glance with the beady eyes. They wavered.—"You know this?" asked the master.—"No, I don't," answered the other, with cheeky trepidation.—"You are a cur. Take it," ordered the master. Donkin's arms seemed glued to his thighs; he stood, eyes front, as if drawn on parade. "Take it," repeated the master, and stepped

closer; they breathed on one another. "Take it," said Captain
Allistoun again, making a menacing gesture. Donkin tore away
one arm from his side.—"Vy are yer down on me?" he mumbled
with effort and as if his mouth had been full of dough.—"If you
don't . . ." began the master. Donkin snatched at the pin as
though his intention had been to run away with it, and remained
stock still holding it like a candle. "Put it back where you took
it from," said Captain Allistoun, looking at him fiercely. Donkin
stepped back opening wide eyes. "Go, you blackguard, or I will
make you," cried the master, driving him slowly backwards by
a menacing advance. He dodged, and with the dangerous iron
tried to guard his head from a threatening fist. Mr. Baker ceased
grunting for a moment.—"Good! By Jove," murmured appre-
ciatively Mr. Creighton in the tone of a connoisseur.—"Don't
tech me," snarled Donkin, backing away.—"Then go. Go faster."
—"Don't yer 'it me. . . . I will pull yer up afore the magistryt. . . .
I'll show yer up." Captain Allistoun made a long stride, and
Donkin, turning his back fairly, ran off a little, then stopped
and over his shoulder showed yellow teeth.—"Further on, fore-
rigging," urged the master, pointing with his arm.—"Are yer
goin' to stand by and see me bullied?" screamed Donkin at the
silent crowd that watched him. Captain Allistoun walked at him
smartly. He started off again with a leap, dashed at the fore-
rigging, rammed the pin into its hole violently. "I'll be even
with yer yet," he screamed at the ship at large and vanished
beyond the foremast. Captain Allistoun spun round and walked
back aft with a composed face, as though he had already forgotten the scene. Men moved out of his way. He looked at no
one.—"That will do, Mr. Baker. Send the watch below," he
said, quietly. "And you men try to walk straight for the future,"
he added in a calm voice. He looked pensively for a while at
the backs of the impressed and retreating crowd. "Breakfast,
steward," he called in a tone of relief through the cabin door.—
"I didn't like to see you—Ough!—give that pin to that chap, sir,"
observed Mr. Baker; "he could have bust—Ough!—bust your
head like an eggshell with it."—"O! he!" muttered the master,

absently. "Queer lot," he went on in a low voice. "I suppose it's all right now. Can never tell tho', nowadays, with such a . . . Years ago; I was a young master then—one China voyage I had a mutiny; real mutiny, Baker. Different men tho'. I knew what they wanted: they wanted to broach the cargo and get at the liquor. Very simple. . . . We knocked them about for two days, and when they had enough—gentle as lambs. Good crew. And a smart trip I made." He glanced aloft at the yards braced sharp up. "Head wind day after day," he exclaimed, bitterly. "Shall we never get a decent slant this passage?"—"Ready, sir," said the steward, appearing before them as if by magic and with stained napkin in his hand.—"Ah! All right. Come along, Mr. Baker —it's late—with all this nonsense."

V

A HEAVY atmosphere of oppressive quietude pervaded the ship. In the afternoon men went about washing clothes and hanging them out to dry in the unprosperous breeze with the meditative languor of disenchanted philosophers. Very little was said. The problem of life seemed too voluminous for the narrow limits of human speech, and by common consent it was abandoned to the great sea that had from the beginning enfolded it in its immense grip; to the sea that knew all, and would in time infallibly unveil to each the wisdom hidden in all the errors, the certitude that lurks in doubts, the realm of safety and peace beyond the frontiers of sorrow and fear. And in the confused current of impotent thoughts that set unceasingly this way and that through bodies of men, Jimmy bobbed up upon the surface, compelling attention, like a black buoy chained to the bottom of a muddy stream. Falsehood triumphed. It triumphed through doubt, through stupidity, through pity, through sentimentalism. We set ourselves to bolster it up, from compassion, from recklessness, from a sense of fun. Jimmy's

steadfastness to his untruthful attitude in the face of the in-
evitable truth had the proportions of a colossal enigma—of a
manifestation grand and incomprehensible that at times inspired
a wondering awe; and there was also, to many, something ex-
quisitely droll in fooling him thus to the top of his bent. The
latent egoism of tenderness to suffering appeared in the develop-
ing anxiety not to see him die. His obstinate non-recognition of
the only certitude whose approach we could watch from day to
day was as disquieting as the failure of some law of nature. He
was so utterly wrong about himself that one could not but
suspect him of having access to some source of supernatural
knowledge. He was absurd to the point of inspiration. He was
unique, and as fascinating as only something inhuman could be;
he seemed to shout his denials already from beyond the awful
border. He was becoming immaterial like an apparition; his
cheekbones rose, the forehead slanted more; the face was all hollows, patches of shade; and the fleshless head resembled a
disinterred black skull, fitted with two restless globes of silver in
the sockets of eyes. He was demoralising. Through him we were
becoming highly humanised, tender, complex, excessively de-
cadent: we understood the subtlety of his fear, sympathised with
all his repulsions, shrinkings, evasions, delusions—as though we
had been over-civilised, and rotten, and without any knowledge
of the meaning of life. We had the air of being initiated in some
infamous mysteries; we had the profound grimaces of conspir-
ators, exchanged meaning glances, significant short words. We
were inexpressibly vile and very much pleased with ourselves.
We lied to him with gravity, with emotion, with unction, as if
performing some moral trick with a view to an eternal reward.
We made a chorus of affirmation to his wildest assertions, as
though he had been a millionaire, a politician, or a reformer—
and we a crowd of ambitious lubbers. When we ventured to
question his statements we did it after the manner of obsequious
sycophants, to the end that his glory should be augmented by the
flattery of our dissent. He influenced the moral tone of our
world as though he had it in his power to distribute honours,

treasures, or pain; and he could give us nothing but his contempt. It was immense; it seemed to grow gradually larger, as his body day by day shrank a little more, while we looked. It was the only thing about him—of him—that gave the impression of durability and vigour. It lived within him with an unquenchable life. It spoke through the eternal pout of his black lips; it looked at us through the impertinent mournfulness of his languid and enormous stare. We watched him intently. He seemed unwilling to move, as if distrustful of his own solidity. The slightest gesture must have disclosed to him (it could not surely be otherwise) his bodily weakness, and caused a pang of mental suffering. He was chary of movements. He lay stretched out, chin on blanket, in a kind of sly, cautious immobility. Only his eyes roamed over faces: his eyes disdainful, penetrating and sad.

It was at that time that Belfast's devotion—and also his pugnacity—secured universal respect. He spent every moment of his spare time in Jimmy's cabin. He tended him, talked to him; was as gentle as a woman, as tenderly gay as an old philanthropist, as sentimentally careful of his nigger as a model slave-owner. But outside he was irritable, explosive as gunpowder, sombre, suspicious, and never more brutal than when most sorrowful. With him it was a tear and a blow: a tear for Jimmy, a blow for any one who did not seem to take a scrupulously orthodox view of Jimmy's case. We talked about nothing else. The two Scandinavians, even, discussed the situation—but it was impossible to know in what spirit, because they quarrelled in their own language. Belfast suspected one of them of irreverence, and in this incertitude thought that there was no option but to fight them both. They became very much terrified by his truculence, and henceforth lived amongst us, dejected, like a pair of mutes. Wamibo never spoke intelligibly, but he was as smileless as an animal—seemed to know much less about it all than the cat—and consequently was safe. Moreover, he had belonged to the chosen band of Jimmy's rescuers, and was above suspicion. Archie was silent generally, but often spent an hour or so talking to Jimmy quietly with an air of proprietorship. At any time of the day and often through the night some man could be seen sitting on Jimmy's box. In the evening, between six and eight, the cabin was crowded, and there was an interested group at the door. Every one stared at the nigger.

He basked in the warmth of our interest. His eyes gleamed ironically, and in a weak voice he reproached us with our cowardice. He would say, "If you fellows had stuck out for me I would be now on deck." We hung our heads. "Yes, but if you think I am going to let them put me in irons just to show you sport. . . . Well, no. . . . It ruins my health, this lying-up, it does. You don't care." We were as abashed as if it had been true. His superb impudence carried all before it. We would not have dared to revolt. We didn't want to, really. We wanted to keep him alive till home—to the end of the voyage.

Singleton as usual held aloof, appearing to scorn the insignificant events of an ended life. Once only he came along, and unexpectedly stopped in the doorway. He peered at Jimmy in profound silence, as if desirous to add that black image to the crowd of Shades that peopled his old memory. We kept very quiet, and for a long time Singleton stood there as though he had come by appointment to call for some one, or to see some important event. James Wait lay perfectly still, and apparently not aware of the gaze scrutinising him with a steadiness full of expectation. There was a sense of a contest in the air. We felt the inward strain of men watching a wrestling bout. At last Jimmy with perceptible apprehension turned his head on the pillow.—"Good evening," he said in a conciliating tone.—"H'm," answered the old seaman, grumpily. For a moment longer he looked at Jimmy with severe fixity, then suddenly went away. It was a long time before any one spoke in the little cabin, though we all breathed more freely as men do after an escape from some dangerous situation. We all knew the old man's ideas about Jimmy, and nobody dared to combat them. They were unsettling, they caused pain; and, what was worse, they might have been true for all we knew. Only once did he condescend to explain them fully, but the impression was lasting. He said that

Jimmy was the cause of head winds. Mortally sick men—he maintained—linger till the first sight of land, and then die; and Jimmy knew that the very first land would draw his life from him. It is so in every ship. Didn't we know it? He asked us with austere contempt: what did we know? What would we doubt next? Jimmy's desire encouraged by us and aided by Wamibo's (he was a Finn—wasn't he? Very well!) by Wamibo's spells delayed the ship in the open sea. Only lubberly fools couldn't see it. Whoever heard of such a run of calms and head winds? It wasn't natural. . . . We could not deny that it was strange. We felt uneasy. The common saying, "More days, more dollars," did not give the usual comfort because the stores were running short. Much had been spoiled off the Cape, and we were on half allowance of biscuit. Peas, sugar and tea had been finished long ago. Salt meat was giving out. We had plenty of coffee but very little water to make it with. We took up another hole in our belts and went on scraping, polishing, painting the ship from morning to night. And soon she looked as though she had come out of a band-box; but hunger lived on board of her. Not dead starvation, but steady, living hunger that stalked about the decks, slept in the forecastle; the tormentor of waking moments, the disturber of dreams. We looked to windward for signs of change. Every few hours of night and day we put her round with the hope that she would come up on that tack at last! She didn't. She seemed to have forgotten the way home; she rushed to and fro, heading northwest, heading east; she ran backwards and forwards, distracted, like a timid creature at the foot of a wall. Sometimes, as if tired to death, she would wallow languidly for a day in the smooth swell of an unruffled sea. All up the swinging masts the sails thrashed furiously through the hot stillness of the calm. We were weary, hungry, thirsty; we commenced to believe Singleton, but with unshaken fidelity dissembled to Jimmy. We spoke to him with jocose allusiveness, like cheerful accomplices in a clever plot; but we looked to the westward over the rail with longing eyes for a sign of hope, for a sign of fair wind; even if its first breath should bring death to our reluctant Jimmy. In

vain! The universe conspired with James Wait. Light airs from
the northward sprang up again; the sky remained clear; and
round our weariness the glittering sea, touched by the breeze,
basked voluptuously in the great sunshine, as though it had forgotten our life and trouble.

Donkin looked out for a fair wind along with the rest. No one
knew the venom of his thoughts now. He was silent, and appeared thinner, as if consumed slowly by an inward rage at the
injustice of men and of fate. He was ignored by all and spoke to
no one, but his hate for every man dwelt in his furtive eyes. He
talked with the cook only, having somehow persuaded the good
man that he—Donkin—was a much calumniated and persecuted
person. Together they bewailed the immorality of the ship's
company. There could be no greater criminals than we, who by
our lies conspired to send the unprepared soul of a poor ignorant
black man to everlasting perdition. Podmore cooked what there
was to cook, remorsefully, and felt all the time that by preparing
the food of such sinners he imperilled his own salvation. As to
the Captain—he had sailed with him for seven years, now, he
said, and would not have believed it possible that such a man . . .
"Well. Well . . . There it was . . . Can't get out of it. Judgment
capsized all in a minute . . . Struck in all his pride . . . More like
a sudden visitation than anything else." Donkin, perched sullenly on the coal-locker, swung his legs and concurred. He paid
in the coin of spurious assent for the privilege to sit in the galley;
he was disheartened and scandalised; he agreed with the cook;
could find no words severe enough to criticise our conduct; and
when in the heat of reprobation he swore at us, Podmore, who
would have liked to swear also if it hadn't been for his principles,
pretended not to hear. So Donkin, unrebuked, cursed enough
for two, cadged for matches, borrowed tobacco, and loafed for
hours, very much at home, before the stove. From there he could
hear us on the other side of the bulkhead, talking to Jimmy.
The cook knocked the saucepans about, slammed the oven door,
muttered prophesies of damnation for all the ship's company;
and Donkin, who did not admit of any hereafter (except for

Conrad in 1914, the year he was nearly trapped on a visit to Poland, the country of his birth, by the outbreak of World War I

purposes of blasphemy) listened, concentrated and angry, gloating fiercely over a called-up image of infinite torment—as men gloat over the accursed images of cruelty and revenge, of greed, and of power. . . .

On clear evenings the silent ship, under the cold sheen of the dead moon, took on a false aspect of passionless repose resembling the winter of the earth. Under her a long band of gold barred the black disc of the sea. Footsteps echoed on her quiet decks. The moonlight clung to her like a frosted mist, and the white sails stood out in dazzling cones as of stainless snow. In the magnificence of the phantom rays the ship appeared pure like a vision of ideal beauty, illusive like a tender dream of serene peace. And nothing in her was real, nothing was distinct and solid but the heavy shadows that filled her decks with their unceasing and noiseless stir: the shadows darker than the night and more restless than the thoughts of men.

Donkin prowled spiteful and alone amongst the shadows, thinking that Jimmy too long delayed to die. That evening land had been reported from aloft, and the master, while adjusting the tubes of the long glass, had observed with quiet bitterness to Mr. Baker that, after fighting our way inch by inch to the Western Islands, there was nothing to expect now but a spell of calm. The sky was clear and the barometer high. The light breeze dropped with the sun, and an enormous stillness, forerunner of a night without wind, descended upon the heated waters of the ocean. As long as daylight lasted, the hands collected on the forecastle-head watched on the eastern sky the island of Flores, that rose above the level expanse of the sea with irregular and broken outlines like a sombre ruin upon a vast and deserted plain. It was the first land seen for nearly four months. Charley was excited, and in the midst of general indulgence took liberties with his betters. Men strangely elated without knowing why, talked in groups, and pointed with bared arms. For the first time that voyage Jimmy's sham existence seemed for a moment forgotten in the face of a solid reality. We had got so far anyhow. Belfast discoursed, quoting imaginary examples of short homeward runs from the Islands. "Them smart fruit schooners do it in five days," he affirmed. "What do you want?—only a good little breeze." Archie maintained that seven days was the record passage, and they disputed amicably with insulting words. Knowles declared he could already smell home from here, and with a heavy list on his short leg laughed fit to split his sides. A group of grizzled sea-dogs looked out for a time in silence and with grim absorbed faces. One said suddenly—" 'Tain't far to London now."—"My first night ashore, blamme if I haven't steak and onions for supper . . . and a pint of bitter," said another.— "A barrel ye mean," shouted someone.—"Ham an' eggs three times a day. That's the way I live!" cried an excited voice. There was a stir, appreciative murmurs; eyes began to shine; jaws champed; short, nervous laughs were heard. Archie smiled with reserve all to himself. Singleton came up, gave a careless glance, and went down again without saying a word, indifferent, like a man who had seen Flores an incalculable number of times. The night travelling from the East blotted out of the limpid sky the purple stain of the high land. "Dead calm," said somebody quietly. The murmur of lively talk suddenly wavered, died out; the clusters broke up; men began to drift away one by one, descending the ladders slowly and with serious faces as if sobered by that reminder of their dependence upon the invisible. And when the big yellow moon ascended gently above the sharp rim of the clear horizon it found the ship wrapped up in a breathless silence; a fearless ship that seemed to sleep profoundly, dream-lessly on the bosom of the sleeping and terrible sea.

Donkin chafed at the peace—at the ship—at the sea that stretch-ing away on all sides merged into the illimitable silence of all creation. He felt himself pulled up sharp by unrecognised griev-ances. He had been physically cowed, but his injured dignity remained indomitable, and nothing could heal his lacerated feelings. Here was land already—home very soon—a bad pay-day—no clothes—more hard work. How offensive all this was. Land. The land that draws away life from sick sailors. That nigger there had money—clothes—easy times; and would not die.

Land draws life away. . . . He felt tempted to go and see whether it did. Perhaps already . . . It would be a bit of luck. There was money in the beggar's chest. He stepped briskly out of the shadows into the moonlight, and, instantly, his craving, hungry face from sallow became livid. He opened the door of the cabin and had a shock. Sure enough, Jimmy was dead! He moved no more than a recumbent figure with clasped hands, carved on the lid of a stone coffin. Donkin glared with avidity. Then Jimmy, without stirring, blinked his eyelids, and Donkin had another shock. Those eyes were rather startling. He shut the door behind his back with gentle care, looking intently the while at James Wait as though he had come in there at a great risk to tell some secret of startling importance. Jimmy did not move but glanced languidly out of the corners of his eyes.—"Calm?" he asked.— "Yuss," said Donkin, very disappointed, and sat down on the box.

Jimmy was used to such visits at all times of night or day. Men succeeded one another. They spoke in clear voices, pronounced cheerful words, repeated old jokes, listened to him; and each, going out, seemed to leave behind a little of his own vitality, surrender some of his own strength, renew the assurance of life—the indestructible thing! He did not like to be alone in his cabin, because, when he was alone, it seemed to him as if he hadn't been there at all. There was nothing. No pain. Not now. Perfectly right—but he couldn't enjoy his healthful repose unless some one was by to see it. This man would do as well as anybody. Donkin watched him stealthily:—"Soon home now," observed Wait.—"Vy d'yer whisper?" asked Donkin with interest, "can't yer speak up?" Jimmy looked annoyed and said nothing for a while; then in a lifeless, unringing voice:—"Why should I shout? You ain't deaf that I know."—"Oh! I can 'ear right enough," answered Donkin in a low tone, and looked down. He was thinking sadly of going out when Jimmy spoke again.— "Time we did get home . . . to get something decent to eat . . . I am always hungry." Donkin felt angry all of a sudden.—"What about me," he hissed, "I am 'ungry too an' got ter work. You, 'ungry!"—"Your work won't kill you," commented Wait, feebly; "there's a couple of biscuits in the lower bunk there—you may have one. I can't eat them." Donkin dived in, groped in the corner and when he came up again his mouth was full. He munched with ardour. Jimmy seemed to doze with open eyes. Donkin finished his hard bread and got up.—"You're not going?" asked Jimmy, staring at the ceiling.—"No," said Donkin, impulsively, and instead of going out leaned his back against the closed door. He looked at James Wait, and saw him long, lean, dried up, as though all his flesh had shrivelled on his bones in the heat of a white furnace; the meagre fingers of one hand moved lightly upon the edge of the bunk playing an endless tune. To look at him was irritating and fatiguing; he could last like this for days; he was outrageous—belonging wholly neither to death nor life, and perfectly invulnerable in his apparent ignorance of both. Donkin felt tempted to enlighten him.—"What are yer thinkin' of?" he asked, surlily. James Wait had a grimacing smile that passed over the death-like impassiveness of his bony face, incredible and frightful as would, in a dream, have been the sudden smile of a corpse.

"There is a girl," whispered Wait. . . . "Canton Street girl.—— She chucked a third engineer of a Rennie boat——for me. Cooks oysters just as I like . . . She says——she would chuck——any toff ——for a coloured gentleman. . . . That's me. I am kind to wimmen," he added, a shade louder.

Donkin could hardly believe his ears. He was scandalised— "Would she? Yer wouldn't be any good to 'er," he said with unrestrained disgust. Wait was not there to hear him. He was swaggering up the East India Dock Road; saying kindly, "Come along for a treat," pushing glass swing-doors, posing with superb assurance in the gaslight above a mahogany counter.—"D'yer think yer will ever get ashore?" asked Donkin, angrily. Wait came back with a start.—"Ten days," he said, promptly, and returned at once to the regions of memory that know nothing of time. He felt untired, calm, and safely withdrawn within himself beyond the reach of every grave incertitude. There was something of the immutable quality of eternity in the slow moments of his complete restfulness. He was very quiet and easy amongst his vivid reminiscences which he mistook joyfully for images of an undoubted future. He cared for no one. Donkin felt this vaguely like a blind man feeling in his darkness the fatal antagonism of all the surrounding existences, that to him shall for ever remain irrealisable, unseen and enviable. He had a desire to assert his importance, to break, crush; to be even with everybody for everything; to tear the veil, unmask, expose, leave no refuge—a perfidious desire of truthfulness! He laughed in a mocking splutter and said:

"Ten days. Strike me blind if I ever! . . . You will be dead by this time to-morrow p'r'aps. Ten days!" He waited for a while. "D'ye 'ear me? Blamme if yer don't look dead already."

Wait must have been collecting his strength, for he said almost aloud—"You're a stinking, cadging liar. Every one knows you." And sitting up, against all probability, startled his visitor horribly. But very soon Donkin recovered himself. He blustered,

"What? What? Who's a liar? You are—the crowd are—the skipper—everybody! I ain't! Putting on airs! Who's yer?" He nearly choked himself with indignation. "Who's yer to put on airs," he repeated, trembling. " 'Ave one—'ave one, says 'ee—an' cawn't eat 'em 'isself. Now I'll 'ave both. By Gawd—I will! Yer nobody!"

He plunged into the lower bunk, rooted in there and brought to light another dusty biscuit. He held it up before Jimmy—then took a bite defiantly.

"What now?" he asked with feverish impudence. "Yer may take one—says yer. Why not giv' me both? No. I'm a mangy dorg. One fur a mangy dorg. I'll tyke both. Can yer stop me? Try. Come on. Try."

Jimmy was clasping his legs and hiding his face on the knees. His shirt clung to him. Every rib was visible. His emaciated back was shaken in repeated jerks by the panting catches of his breath.

"Yer won't? Yer can't! What did I say?" went on Donkin,

fiercely. He swallowed another dry mouthful with a hasty effort. The other's silent helplessness, his weakness, his shrinking attitude exasperated him. "Ye're done!" he cried. "Who's yer to be lied to; to be waited on 'and an' foot like a bloomin' ymperor. Yer nobody. Yer no one at all!" he spluttered with such a strength of unerring conviction that it shook him from head to foot in coming out, and left him vibrating like a released string.

James Wait rallied again. He lifted his head and turned bravely at Donkin, who saw a strange face, an unknown face, a fantastic and grimacing mask of despair and fury. Its lips moved rapidly; and hollow, moaning, whistling sounds filled the cabin with a vague mutter full of menace, complaint and desolation, like the far-off murmur of a rising wind. Wait shook his head; rolled his eyes; he denied, cursed, threatened—and not a word had the strength to pass beyond the sorrowful pout of those black lips. It was incomprehensible and disturbing; a gibberish of emotions, a frantic dumb show of speech pleading for impossible things, promising a shadowy vengeance. It sobered Donkin into a scrutinising watchfulness.

"Yer can't oller. See? What did I tell yer?" he said, slowly, after a moment of attentive examination. The other kept on headlong and unheard, nodding passionately, grinning with grotesque and appalling flashes of big white teeth. Donkin, as if fascinated by the dumb eloquence and anger of that black phantom, approached, stretching his neck out with distrustful curiosity; and it seemed to him suddenly that he was looking only at the shadow of a man crouching high in the bunk on the level with his eyes.—"What? What?" he said. He seemed to catch the shape of some words in the continuous panting hiss. "Yer will tell Belfast! Will yer? Are yer a bloomin' kid?" He trembled with alarm and rage, "Tell yer gran'mother! Yer afeard! Who's yer ter be afeard more'n any one?" His passionate sense of his own importance ran away with a last remnant of caution. "Tell an' be damned! Tell, if yer can!" he cried. "I've been treated worser'n a dorg by your bloomin' back-lickers. They 'as set me on, only to turn aginst me. I am the only man 'ere. They clouted me, kicked me—an' yer laffed—yer black, rotten incumbrance, you! You will pay fur it. They giv' yer their grub, their water— yer will pay fur it to me, by Gawd! Who axed me ter 'ave a drink of water? They put their bloomin' rags on yer that night, an' what did they giv' ter me—a clout on the bloomin' mouth—blast their . . . S'elp me! . . . Yer will pay fur it with yer money. I'm goin' ter 'ave it in a minyte; as soon has ye're dead, yer bloomin' useless fraud. That's the man I am. An' ye're a thing—a bloody thing. Yah—you corpse!"

He flung at Jimmy's head the biscuit he had been all the time clutching hard, but it only grazed, and striking with a loud crack the bulkhead beyond burst like a hand-grenade into flying pieces. James Wait, as if wounded mortally, fell back on the pillow. His lips ceased to move and the rolling eyes became quiet and stared upwards with an intense and steady persistence. Donkin was sur- prised; he sat suddenly on the chest, and looked down, exhausted and gloomy. After a moment, he began to mutter to himself, "Die, you beggar—die. Somebody'll come in . . . I wish I was drunk . . . Ten days . . . oysters . . ." He looked up and spoke louder. "No . . . No more for yer . . . no more bloomin' gals that cook oysters . . . Who's yer? It's my turn now . . . I wish I was drunk; I would soon giv' you a leg up. That's where yer bound to go. Feet fust, through a port . . . Splash! Never see yer any more. Overboard! Good 'nuff fur yer."

Jimmy's head moved slightly and he turned his eyes to Don- kin's face; a gaze unbelieving, desolated and appealing, of a child frightened by the menace of being shut up alone in the dark. Donkin observed him from the chest with hopeful eyes; then, without rising, tried the lid. Locked. "I wish I was drunk," he muttered and getting up listened anxiously to the distant sound of footsteps on the deck. They approached—ceased. Some one yawned interminably just outside the door, and the foot- steps went away shuffling lazily. Donkin's fluttering heart eased its pace, and when he looked towards the bunk again Jimmy was staring as before at the white beam.—" 'Ow d'yer feel now?" he asked.—"Bad," breathed out Jimmy.

Donkin sat down patient and purposeful. Every half-hour the bells spoke to one another ringing along the whole length of the ship. Jimmy's respiration was so rapid that it couldn't be counted, so faint that it couldn't be heard. His eyes were terrified as though he had been looking at unspeakable horrors; and by his face one could see that he was thinking of abominable things. Suddenly with an incredibly strong and heart-breaking voice he sobbed out:

"Overboard! . . . I! . . . My God!"

Donkin writhed a little on the box. He looked unwillingly. James Wait was mute. His two long bony hands smoothed the blanket upwards, as though he had wished to gather it all up under his chin. A tear, a big solitary tear, escaped from the corner of his eye and, without touching the hollow cheek, fell on the pillow. His throat rattled faintly.

And Donkin, watching the end of that hateful nigger, felt the anguishing grasp of a great sorrow on his heart at the thought that he himself, some day, would have to go through it all—just like this—perhaps! His eyes became moist. "Poor beggar," he murmured. The night seemed to go by in a flash; it seemed to him he could hear the irremediable rush of precious minutes. How long would this blooming affair last? Too long surely. No luck. He could not restrain himself. He got up and approached the bunk. Wait did not stir. Only his eyes appeared alive and his hands continued their smoothing movement with a horrible and tireless industry. Donkin bent over.

"Jimmy," he called low. There was no answer, but the rattle stopped. "D'yer see me?" he asked, trembling. Jimmy's chest heaved. Donkin, looking away, bent his ear to Jimmy's lips, and heard a sound like the rustle of a single dry leaf driven along the smooth sand of a beach. It shaped itself.

"Light . . . the lamp . . . and . . . go," breathed out Wait.

Donkin, instinctively, glanced over his shoulder at the brilliant flame; then, still looking away, felt under the pillow for a key. He got it at once and for the next few minutes remained on his knees shakily but swiftly busy inside the box. When he

got up, his face—for the first time in his life—had a pink flush
—perhaps of triumph.

He slipped the key under the pillow again, avoiding to glance
at Jimmy, who had not moved. He turned his back squarely
from the bunk, and started to the door as though he were going
to walk a mile. At his second stride he had his nose against it.
He clutched the handle cautiously, but at that moment he received the irresistible impression of something happening behind his back. He spun round as though he had been tapped on
the shoulder. He was just in time to see Wait's eyes blaze up and
go out at once, like two lamps overturned together by a sweeping blow. Something resembling a scarlet thread hung down
his chin out of the corner of his lips—and he had ceased to
breathe.

Donkin closed the door behind him gently but firmly. Sleeping men, huddled under jackets, made on the lighted deck shapeless dark mounds that had the appearance of neglected graves.
Nothing had been done all through the night and he hadn't
been missed. He stood motionless and perfectly astounded to
find the world outside as he had left it; there was the sea, the
ship—sleeping men; and he wondered absurdly at it, as though
he had expected to find the men dead, familiar things gone for
ever: as though, like a wanderer returning after many years, he
had expected to see bewildering changes. He shuddered a little
in the penetrating freshness of the air, and hugged himself for-
lornly. The declining moon drooped sadly in the western board
as if withered by the cold touch of a pale dawn. The ship slept.
And the immortal sea stretched away, immense and hazy, like
the image of life, with a glittering surface and lightless depths.
Donkin gave it a defiant glance and slunk off noiselessly as if
judged and cast out by the august silence of its might.

Jimmy's death, after all, came as a tremendous surprise. We
did not know till then how much faith we had put in his delusions. We had taken his chances of life so much at his own valua-
tion that his death, like the death of an old belief, shook the

foundations of our society. A common bond was gone; the strong, effective and respectable bond of a sentimental lie. All that day we mooned at our work, with suspicious looks and a disabused air. In our hearts we thought that in the matter of his departure Jimmy had acted in a perverse and unfriendly manner. He didn't back us up, as a shipmate should. In going he took away with himself the gloomy and solemn shadow in which our folly had posed, with humane satisfaction, as a tender arbiter of fate. And now we saw it was no such thing. It was just common foolishness; a silly and ineffectual meddling with issues of majestic import—that is, if Podmore was right. Perhaps he was? Doubt survived Jimmy; and, like a community of banded criminals disintegrated by a touch of grace, we were profoundly scandalised with each other. Men spoke unkindly to their best chums. Others refused to speak at all. Singleton only was not surprised. "Dead—is he? Of course," he said, pointing at the island right abeam: for the calm still held the ship spell-bound within sight of Flores. Dead—of course. *He* wasn't surprised. Here was the land, and there, on the forehatch and waiting for the sailmaster—there was that corpse. Cause and effect. And for the first time that voyage, the old seaman became quite cheery and garrulous, explaining and illustrating from the stores of experience how, in sickness, the sight of an island (even a very small one) is generally more fatal than the view of a continent. But he couldn't explain why.

Jimmy was to be buried at five, and it was a long day till then —a day of mental disquiet and even of physical disturbance. We took no interest in our work and, very properly, were rebuked for it. This, in our constant state of hungry irritation, was exasperating. Donkin worked with his brow bound in a dirty rag, and looked so ghastly that Mr. Baker was touched with compassion at the sight of this plucky suffering.—"Ough! You, Donkin! Put down your work and go lay-up this watch. You look ill."—"I am bad, sir—in my 'ead," he said in a subdued voice, and vanished speedily. This annoyed many, and they thought the mate "bloomin' soft to-day." Captain Allistoun could be

seen on the poop watching the sky to the southwest, and it soon
got to be known about the decks that the barometer had begun
to fall in the night, and that a breeze might be expected before
long. This, by a subtle association of ideas, led to violent quarrelling as to the exact moment of Jimmy's death. Was it before
or after "that 'ere glass started down?" It was impossible to
know, and it caused much contemptuous growling at one another. All of a sudden there was a great tumult forward. Pacific
Knowles and good-tempered Davis had come to blows over it.
The watch below interfered with spirit, and for ten minutes there
was a noisy scrimmage round the hatch, where, in the balancing
shade of the sails, Jimmy's body, wrapped up in a white blanket,
was watched over by the sorrowful Belfast, who, in his desolation, disdained the fray. When the noise had ceased, and the
passions had calmed into surly silence, he stood up at the head
of the swathed body, lifting both arms on high, cried with
pained indignation:—"You ought to be ashamed of yourselves! . . ." We were.

Belfast took his bereavement very hard. He gave proofs of
unextinguishable devotion. It was he, and no other man, who
would help the sailmaker to prepare what was left of Jimmy for
a solemn surrender to the insatiable sea. He arranged the weights
carefully at the feet: two holystones, an old anchor-shackle without its pin, some broken links of a worn-out stream cable. He
arranged them this way, then that. "Bless my soul! you aren't
afraid he will chafe his heel?" said the sailmaker, who hated the
job. He pushed the needle, puffing furiously, with his head in
a cloud of tobacco smoke; he turned the flaps over, pulled at the
stitches, stretched at the canvas.—"Lift his shoulders. . . . Pull to
you a bit. . . . So—o—o. Steady." Belfast obeyed, pulled, lifted,
overcome with sorrow, dropping tears on the tarred twine.—
"Don't you drag the canvas too taut over his poor face, Sails,"
he entreated, tearfully.—"What are you fashing yourself for? He
will be comfortable enough," assured the sailmaker, cutting the
thread after the last stitch, which came about the middle of
Jimmy's forehead. He rolled up the remaining canvas, put

away the needles. "What makes you take on so?" he asked. Belfast looked down at the long package of grey sailcloth.—"I pulled him out," he whispered, "and he did not want to go. If I had sat up with him last night he would have kept alive for me . . . but something made me tired." The sailmaker took vigorous draws at his pipe and mumbled:—"When I . . . West India Station . . . In the *Blanche* frigate . . . Yellow Jack . . . sewed in twenty men a week . . . Portsmouth-Devonport men—townies—knew their fathers, mothers, sisters—the whole boiling of 'em. Thought nothing of it. And these niggers like this one—you don't know where it comes from. Got nobody. No use to nobody. Who will miss him?"—"I do—I pulled him out," mourned Belfast dismally.

On two planks nailed together and apparently resigned and still under the folds of the Union Jack with a white border, James Wait, carried aft by four men, was deposited slowly, with his feet pointing at an open port. A swell had set in from the westward, and following on the roll of the ship, the red ensign, at half-mast, darted out and collapsed again on the grey sky, like a tongue of flickering fire; Charley tolled the bell; and at every swing to starboard the whole vast semicircle of steely waters visible on that side seemed to come up with a rush to the edge of the port, as if impatient to get at our Jimmy. Every one was there but Donkin, who was too ill to come; the Captain and Mr. Creighton stood bareheaded on the break of the poop; Mr. Baker, directed by the master, who had said to him gravely:—"You know more about the prayer book than I do," came out of the cabin door quickly and a little embarrassed. All the caps went off. He began to read in a low tone, and with his usual harmlessly menacing utterance, as though he had been for the last time reproving confidentially that dead seaman at his feet. The men listened in scattered groups; they leaned on the fife rail, gazing on the deck; they held their chins in their hands thoughtfully, or, with crossed arms and one knee slightly bent, hung their heads in an attitude of upright meditation. Wamibo dreamed. Mr. Baker read on, grunting reverently at the turn of every page. The words, missing the unsteady hearts of men, rolled out to wander without a home upon the heartless sea; and James Wait, silenced for ever, lay uncritical and passive under the hoarse murmur of despair and hopes.

Two men made ready and waited for those words that send so many of our brothers to their last plunge. Mr. Baker began the passage. "Stand by," muttered the boatswain. Mr. Baker read out: "To the deep," and paused. The men lifted the inboard end of the planks, the boatswain snatched off the Union Jack, and James Wait did not move.—"Higher," muttered the boatswain angrily. All the heads were raised; every man stirred uneasily, but James Wait gave no sign of going. In death and swathed up for all eternity, he yet seemed to cling to the ship with the grip of an undying fear. "Higher! Lift!" whispered the boatswain, fiercely.—"He won't go," stammered one of the men, shakily, and both appeared ready to drop everything. Mr. Baker waited, burying his face in the book, and shuffling his feet nervously. All the men looked profoundly disturbed; from their midst a faint humming noise spread out—growing louder. . . . "Jimmy!" cried Belfast in a wailing tone, and there was a second of shuddering dismay.

"Jimmy, be a man!" he shrieked, passionately. Every mouth was wide open, not an eyelid winked. He stared wildly, twitching all over; he bent his body forward like a man peering at an horror. "Go!" he shouted, and sprang out of the crowd with his arm extended. "Go, Jimmy!—Jimmy, go! Go!" His fingers touched the head of the body, and the grey package started reluctantly to whizz off the lifted planks all at once, with the suddenness of a flash of lightning. The crowd stepped forward like one man; a deep Ah—h—h! came out vibrating from the broad chests. The ship rolled as if relieved of an unfair burden; the sails flapped. Belfast, supported by Archie, gasped hysterically; and Charley, who anxious to see Jimmy's last dive, leaped headlong on the rail, was too late to see anything but the faint circle of a vanishing ripple.

Mr. Baker, perspiring abundantly, read out the last prayer in a deep rumour of excited men and fluttering sails. "Amen!" he said in an unsteady growl, and closed the book.

"Square the yards!" thundered a voice above his head. All hands gave a jump; one or two dropped their caps; Mr. Baker looked up surprised. The master, standing on the break of the poop, pointed to the westward. "Breeze coming," he said, "Man the weather braces." Mr. Baker crammed the book hurriedly into his pocket. "Forward, there—let go the foretack!" he hailed joyfully, bareheaded and brisk; "Square the foreyard, you port-watch!"—"Fair wind—fair wind," muttered the men going to the braces.—"What did I tell you?" mumbled old Singleton, flinging down coil after coil with hasty energy; "I knowed it —he's gone, and here it comes."

It came with the sound of a lofty and powerful sigh. The sails filled, the ship gathered way, and the waking sea began to murmur sleepily of home to the ears of men.

That night, while the ship rushed foaming to the Northward before a freshening gale, the boatswain unbosomed himself to the petty officers' berth:—"The chap was nothing but trouble," he said, "from the moment he came aboard—d'ye remember— that night in Bombay? Been bullying all that softy crowd— cheeked the old man—we had to go fooling all over a half-drowned ship to save him. Dam' nigh a mutiny all for him— and now the mate abused me like a pickpocket for forgetting to dab a lump of grease on them planks. So I did, but you ought to have known better, too, than to leave a nail sticking up—hey, Chips?"

"And you ought to have known better than to chuck all my tools overboard for 'im, like a skeary greenhorn," retorted the morose carpenter. "Well—he's gone after 'em now," he added in an unforgiving tone.—"On the China Station, I remember once, the Admiral he says to me . . ." began the sailmaker.

A week afterwards the *Narcissus* entered the chops of the Channel.

Under white wings she skimmed low over the blue sea like

a great tired bird speeding to its nest. The clouds raced with her mastheads; they rose astern enormous and white, soared to the zenith, flew past, and falling down the wide curve of the sky, seemed to dash headlong into the sea—the clouds swifter than the ship, more free, but without a home. The coast to welcome her stepped out of space into the sunshine. The lofty headlands trod masterfully into the sea; the wide bays smiled in the light; the shadows of homeless clouds ran along the sunny plains, leaped over valleys, without a check darted up the hills, rolled down the slopes; and the sunshine pursued them with patches of running brightness. On the brows of dark cliffs white lighthouses shone in pillars of light. The Channel glittered like a blue mantle shot with gold and starred by the silver of the capping seas. The *Narcissus* rushed past the headlands and the bays. Outward-bound vessels crossed her track, lying over, and with their masts stripped for a slogging fight with the hard sou'-wester. And, inshore, a string of smoking steamboats waddled, hugging the coast, like migrating and amphibious monsters, distrustful of the restless waves.

At night the headlands retreated, the bays advanced into one unbroken line of gloom. The lights of the earth mingled with the lights of heaven; and above the tossing lanterns of a trawling fleet a great lighthouse shone steadily, like an enormous riding light burning above a vessel of fabulous dimensions. Below its steady glow, the coast, stretching away straight and black, resembled the high side of an indestructible craft riding motionless upon the immortal and unresting sea. The dark land lay alone in the midst of waters, like a mighty ship bestarred with vigilant lights—a ship carrying the burden of millions of lives— a ship freighted with dross and with jewels, with gold and with steel. She towered up immense and strong, guarding priceless traditions and untold suffering, sheltering glorious memories and base forgetfulness, ignoble virtues and splendid transgressions. A great ship! For ages had the ocean battered in vain her enduring sides; she was there when the world was vaster and darker, when the sea was great and mysterious, and ready to surrender the prize of fame to audacious men. A ship mother of fleets and nations! The great flagship of the race; stronger than the storms! and anchored in the open sea.

The *Narcissus*, heeling over to off-shore gusts, rounded the South Foreland, passed through the Downs, and, in tow, entered the river. Shorn of the glory of her white wings, she wound obediently after the tug through the maze of invisible channels. As she passed them the red-painted light-vessels, swung at their moorings, seemed for an instant to sail with great speed in the rush of tide, and the next moment were left hopelessly behind. The big buoys on the tails of banks slipped past her sides very low, and, dropping in her wake, tugged at their chains like fierce watch-dogs. The reach narrowed; from both sides the land approached the ship. She went steadily up the river. On the river-side slopes the houses appeared in groups—seemed to stream down the declivities at a run to see her pass, and, checked by the mud of the foreshore, crowded on the banks. Further on, the tall factory chimneys appeared in insolent bands and watched her go by, like a straggling crowd of slim giants, swaggering and upright under the black plummets of smoke, cavalierly aslant. She swept round the bends; an impure breeze shrieked a welcome between her stripped spars; and the land, closing in, stepped between the ship and the sea.

A low cloud hung before her—a great opalescent and tremulous cloud, that seemed to rise from the steaming brows of millions of men. Long drifts of smoky vapours soiled it with livid trails; it throbbed to the beat of millions of hearts, and from it came an immense and lamentable murmur—the murmur of millions of lips praying, cursing, sighing, jeering—the undying murmur of folly, regret, and hope exhaled by the crowds of the anxious earth. The *Narcissus* entered the cloud; the shadows deepened; on all sides there was the clang of iron, the sound of mighty blows, shrieks, yells. Black barges drifted stealthily on the murky stream. A mad jumble of begrimed walls loomed up vaguely in the smoke, bewildering and mournful, like a vision of disaster. The tugs backed and filled in the stream, to hold the ship steady at the dock-gates; from her bows two lines went through the air whistling, and struck at the land viciously, like a pair of snakes. A bridge broke in two before her, as if by enchantment; big hydraulic capstans began to turn all by themselves, as though animated by a mysterious and unholy spell. She moved through a narrow lane of water between two low walls of granite, and men with check-ropes in their hands kept pace with her, walking on the broad flagstones. A group waited impatiently on each side of the vanished bridge: rough heavy men in caps; sallow-faced men in high hats; two bareheaded women; ragged children, fascinated, and with wide eyes. A cart coming at a jerky trot pulled up sharply. One of the women screamed at the silent ship—"Hallo, Jack!" without looking at any one in particular, and all hands looked at her from the forecastle head. —"Stand clear! Stand clear of that rope!" cried the dockmen, bending over stone posts. The crowd murmured, stamped where they stood.—"Let go your quarter-checks! Let go!" sang out a ruddy-faced old man on the quay. The ropes splashed heavily falling in the water, and the *Narcissus* entered the dock.

The stony shores ran away right and left in straight lines, enclosing a sombre and rectangular pool. Brick walls rose high above the water—soulless walls, staring through hundreds of windows as troubled and dull as the eyes of over-fed brutes. At their base monstrous iron cranes crouched, with chains hanging from their long necks, balancing cruel-looking hooks over the decks of lifeless ships. A noise of wheels rolling over stones, the thump of heavy things falling, the racket of feverish winches, the grinding of strained chains, floated on the air. Between high buildings the dust of all the continents soared in short flights; and a penetrating smell of perfumes and dirt, of spices and hides, of things costly and of things filthy, pervaded the space, made for it an atmosphere precious and disgusting. The *Narcissus* came gently into her berth; the shadows of soulless walls fell upon her, the dust of all the continents leaped upon her deck, and a swarm of strange men, clambering up her sides, took pos-

session of her in the name of the sordid earth. She had ceased to
live.

A toff in a black coat and high hat scrambled with agility,
came up to the second mate, shook hands, and said:—"Hallo,
Herbert." It was his brother. A lady appeared suddenly. A real
lady, in a black dress and with a parasol. She looked extremely
elegant in the midst of us, and as strange as if she had fallen
there from the sky. Mr. Baker touched his cap to her. It was the
master's wife. And very soon the Captain, dressed very smartly
and in a white shirt, went with her over the side. We didn't
recognise him at all till, turning on the quay, he called to Mr.
Baker:—"Don't forget to wind up the chronometers to-morrow
morning." An underhand lot of seedy-looking chaps with shifty
eyes wandered in and out of the forecastle looking for a job—
they said.—"More likely for something to steal," commented
Knowles, cheerfully. Poor beggars. Who cared? Weren't we
home! But Mr. Baker went for one of them who had given him
some cheek, and we were delighted. Everything was delightful.
—"I've finished aft, sir," called out Mr. Creighton.—"No water
in the well, sir," reported for the last time the carpenter, sounding-rod in hand. Mr. Baker glanced along the decks at the expectant group of sailors, glanced aloft at the yards.—"Ough!
That will do, men," he grunted. The group broke up. The
voyage was ended.

Rolled-up beds went flying over the rail; lashed chests went
sliding down the gangway—mighty few of both at that. "The rest
is having a cruise off the Cape," explained Knowles enig-
matically to a dock-loafer with whom he had struck a sudden
friendship. Men ran, calling to one another, hailing utter strangers to "lend a hand with the dunnage," then with sudden
decorum approached the mate to shake hands before going
ashore.—"Good-bye, sir," they repeated in various tones. Mr.
Baker grasped hard palms, grunted in a friendly manner at every
one, his eyes twinkled.—"Take care of your money, Knowles.
Ough! Soon get a nice wife if you do." The lame man was delighted.—"Good-bye, sir," said Belfast, with emotion, wringing

the mate's hand, and looked up with swimming eyes. "I thought I would take 'im ashore with me," he went on, plaintively. Mr. Baker did not understand, but said kindly:—"Take care of yourself, Craik," and the bereaved Belfast went over the rail mourning and alone.

Mr. Baker, in the sudden peace of the ship, moved about solitary and grunting, trying door-handles, peering into dark places, never done—a model chief mate! No one waited for him ashore. Mother dead; father and two brothers, Yarmouth fishermen, drowned together on the Dogger Bank; sister married and unfriendly. Quite a lady. Married to the leading tailor of a little town, and its leading politician, who did not think his sailor brother-in-law quite respectable enough for him. Quite a lady, quite a lady, he thought, sitting down for a moment's rest on the quarter-hatch. Time enough to go ashore and get a bite and sup, and a bed somewhere. He didn't like to part with a ship. No one to think about then. The darkness of a misty evening fell, cold and damp, upon the deserted deck; and Mr. Baker sat smoking, thinking of all the successive ships to whom through many long years he had given the best of a seaman's care. And never a command in sight. Not once!—"I haven't somehow the cut of a skipper about me," he meditated, placidly, while the shipkeeper (who had taken possession of the galley), a wizened old man with bleared eyes, cursed him in whispers for "hanging about so."—"Now, Creighton," he pursued the unenvious train of thought, "quite a gentleman . . . swell friends . . . will get on. Fine young fellow . . . a little more experience." He got up and shook himself. "I'll be back first thing to-morrow morning for the hatches. Don't you let them touch anything before I come, shipkeeper," he called out. Then, at last, he also went ashore—a model chief mate!

The men scattered by the dissolving contact of the land came together once more in the shipping office.—"The *Narcissus* pays off," shouted outside a glazed door a brass-bound old fellow with a crown and the capitals B. T. on his cap. A lot trooped in at once but many were late. The room was large, white-washed, and bare; a counter surmounted by a brass-wire grating fenced off a third of the dusty space, and behind the grating a pasty-faced clerk, with his hair parted in the middle, had the quick, glittering eyes and the vivacious, jerky movements of a caged bird. Poor Captain Allistoun also in there, and sitting before a little table with piles of gold and notes on it, appeared subdued by his captivity. Another Board of Trade bird was perching on a high stool near the door: an old bird that did not mind the chaff of elated sailors. The crew of the *Narcissus*, broken up into knots, pushed in the corners. They had new shore togs, smart jackets that looked as if they had been shaped with an axe, glossy trousers that seemed made of crumpled sheet-iron, collarless flannel shirts, shiny new boots. They tapped on shoulders, button-holed one another, asked:—"Where did you sleep last night?" whispered gaily, slapped their thighs with bursts of subdued laughter. Most had clean, radiant faces; only one or two turned up dishevelled and sad; the two young Norwegians looked tidy, meek, and altogether of a promising material for the kind ladies who patronise the Scandinavian Home. Wamibo, still in his working clothes, dreamed, upright and burly in the middle of the room, and, when Archie came in, woke up for a smile. But the wide-awake clerk called out a name, and the paying-off business began.

One by one they came up to the pay-table to get the wages of their glorious and obscure toil. They swept the money with care into broad palms, rammed it trustfully into trousers' pockets, or, turning their backs on the table, reckoned with difficulty in the hollow of their stiff hands.—"Money right? Sign the release. There—there," repeated the clerk, impatiently. "How stupid those sailors are!" he thought. Singleton came up, venerable—and uncertain as to daylight; brown drops of tobacco juice hung in his white beard; his hands, that never hesitated in the great light of the open sea, could hardly find the small pile of gold in the profound darkness of the shore. "Can't write?" said the clerk, shocked. "Make a mark, then." Singleton painfully sketched in a heavy cross, blotted the page. "What a dis-

gusting old brute," muttered the clerk. Somebody opened the
door for him, and the patriarchal seaman passed through unsteadily, without as much as a glance at any of us.

Archie displayed a pocket-book. He was chaffed. Belfast, who
looked wild, as though he had already luffed up through a
public-house or two, gave signs of emotion and wanted to speak
to the Captain privately. The master was surprised. They spoke
through the wires, and we could hear the Captain saying:—"I've
given it up to the Board of Trade." "I should 've liked to get
something of his," mumbled Belfast. "But you can't, my man.
It's given up, locked and sealed, to the Marine Office," expostulated the master; and Belfast stood back, with drooping
mouth and troubled eyes. In a pause of the business we heard
the master and the clerk talking. We caught: "James Wait—
deceased—found no papers of any kind—no relations—no trace—
the Office must hold his wages then." Donkin entered. He
seemed out of breath, was grave, full of business. He went
straight to the desk, talked with animation to the clerk, who
thought him an intelligent man. They discussed the account,
dropping h's against one another as if for a wager—very friendly.
Captain Allistoun paid. "I give you a bad discharge," he said,
quietly. Donkin raised his voice:—"I don't want your bloomin'
discharge—keep it. I'm goin' ter 'ave a job ashore." He turned
to us. "No more bloomin' sea fur me," he said, aloud. All looked
at him. He had better clothes, had an easy air, appeared more at
home than any of us; he stared with assurance, enjoying the
effect of his declaration. "Yuss. I 'ave friends well off. That's
more'n you got. But I am a man. Yer shipmates for all that.
Who's comin fur a drink?"

No one moved. There was a silence; a silence of blank faces
and stony looks. He waited a moment, smiled bitterly, and went
to the door. There he faced round once more. "You won't? You
bloomin' lot of yrpocrits. No? What 'ave I done to yer? Did I
bully yer? Did I 'urt yer? Did I? . . . You won't drink? . . . No!
. . . Then may ye die of thirst, every mother's son of yer! Not one

of yer 'as the spirrit of a bug. Ye're the scum of the world. Work and starve!"

He went out, and slammed the door with such violence that the old Board of Trade bird nearly fell off his perch.

"He's mad," declared Archie. "No! No! He's drunk," insisted Belfast, lurching about, and in a maudlin tone. Captain Allistoun sat smiling thoughtfully at the cleared pay-table.

Outside, on Tower Hill, they blinked, hesitated clumsily, as if blinded by the strange quality of the hazy light, as if discomposed by the view of so many men; and they who could hear one another in the howl of gales seemed deafened and distracted by the dull roar of the busy earth.—"To the Black Horse! To the Black Horse!" cried some. "Let us have a drink together before we part." They crossed the road, clinging to one another. Only Charley and Belfast wandered off alone. As I came up I saw a red-faced, blowsy woman, in a grey shawl, and with dusty, fluffy hair, fall on Charley's neck. It was his mother. She slobbered over him:—"O, my boy! My boy!"—"Leggo of me," said Charley, "Leggo, mother!" I was passing him at the time, and over the untidy head of the blubbering woman he gave me a humorous smile and a glance ironic, courageous, and profound, that seemed to put all my knowledge of life to shame. I nodded and passed on, but heard him say again, good-naturedly:—"If you leggo of me this minyt—ye shall 'ave a bob for a drink out of my pay." In the next few steps I came upon Belfast. He caught my arm with tremulous enthusiasm.—"I couldn't go wi' 'em," he stammered, indicating by a nod our noisy crowd, that drifted slowly along the other sidewalk. "When I think of Jimmy . . . Poor Jim! When I think of him I have no heart for drink. You were his chum, too . . . but I pulled him out . . . didn't I? Short wool he had. . . . Yes. And I stole the blooming pie. . . . He wouldn't go. . . . He wouldn't go for nobody." He burst into tears. "I never touched him—never—never!" he sobbed. "He went for me like . . . like . . . a lamb."

I disengaged myself gently. Belfast's crying fits generally ended in a fight with some one, and I wasn't anxious to stand the brunt of his inconsolable sorrow. Moreover, two bulky policemen stood near by, looking at us with a disapproving and incorruptible gaze.—"So long!" I said, and went on my way.

But at the corner I stopped to take my last look at the crew of the *Narcissus*. They were swaying irresolute and noisy on the broad flagstones before the Mint. They were bound for the Black Horse, where men, in fur caps with brutal faces and in shirt sleeves, dispense out of varnished barrels the illusions of strength, mirth, happiness; the illusion of splendour and poetry of life, to the paid-off crews of southern-going ships. From afar I saw them discoursing, with jovial eyes and clumsy gestures, while the sea of life thundered into their ears ceaseless and unheeded. And swaying about there on the white stones, surrounded by the hurry and clamour of men, they appeared to be creatures of another kind—lost, alone, forgetful, and doomed; they were like castaways, like reckless and joyous castaways, like mad castaways making merry in the storm and upon an insecure ledge of a treacherous rock. The roar of the town resembled the roar of topping breakers, merciless and strong, with a loud voice and cruel purpose; but overhead the clouds broke; a flood of sunshine streamed down the walls of grimy houses. The dark knot of seamen drifted in sunshine. To the left of them the trees in Tower Gardens sighed, the stones of the Tower gleaming, seemed to stir in the play of light, as if remembering suddenly all the great joys and sorrows of the past, the fighting prototypes of these men; pressgangs; mutinous cries; the wailing of women by the riverside, and the shouts of men welcoming victories. The sunshine of heaven fell like a gift of grace on the mud of the earth, on the remembering and mute stones, on greed, selfishness; on the anxious faces of forgetful men. And to the right of the dark group the stained front of the Mint, cleansed by the flood of light, stood out for a moment dazzling and white like a marble palace in a fairy tale. The crew of the *Narcissus* drifted out of sight.

I never saw them again. The sea took some, the steamers took others, the graveyards of the earth will account for the rest. Singleton has no doubt taken with him the long record of his faithful work into the peaceful depths of an hospitable sea. And Donkin, who never did a decent day's work in his life, no doubt earns his living by discoursing with filthy eloquence upon the right of labour to live. So be it! Let the earth and the sea each have its own.

A gone shipmate, like any other man, is gone for ever; and I never met one of them again. But at times the spring-flood of memory sets with force up the dark River of the Nine Bends. Then on the waters of the forlorn stream drifts a ship—a shadowy ship manned by a crew of Shades. They pass and make a sign, in a shadowy hail. Haven't we, together and upon the immortal sea, wrung out a meaning from our sinful lives? Good-bye, brothers! You were a good crowd. As good a crowd as ever fisted with wild cries the beating canvas of a heavy foresail; or tossing aloft, invisible in the night, gave back yell for yell to a westerly gale.

Youth

A NARRATIVE

THIS could have occurred nowhere but in England, where men and sea interpenetrate, so to speak—the sea entering into the life of most men, and the men knowing something or everything about the sea, in the way of amusement, of travel, or of bread-winning.

We were sitting round a mahogany table that reflected the bottle, the claret-glasses, and our faces as we leaned on our elbows. There was a director of companies, an accountant, a lawyer, Marlow, and myself. The director had been a *Conway* boy, the accountant had served four years at sea, the lawyer—a fine crusted Tory, High Churchman, the best of old fellows, the soul of honor—had been chief officer in the P. & O. service in the good old days when mail-boats were square-rigged at least on two masts, and used to come down the China Sea before a fair monsoon with stun'-sails set alow and aloft. We all began life in the merchant service. Between the five of us there was the strong bond of the sea, and also the fellowship of the craft, which no amount of enthusiasm for yachting, cruising, and so on can give, since one is only the amusement of life and the other is life itself.

Marlow (at least I think that is how he spelt his name) told the story, or rather the chronicle, of a voyage:

"Yes, I have seen a little of the Eastern seas; but what I remember best is my first voyage there. You fellows know there are those voyages that seem ordered for the illustration of life, that might stand for a symbol of existence. You fight, work, sweat, nearly kill yourself, sometimes do kill yourself, trying to accomplish something—and you can't. Not from any fault of yours. You simply can do nothing, neither great nor little—not a thing in the world—not even marry an old maid, or get a wretched 600-ton cargo of coal to its port of destination.

"It was altogether a memorable affair. It was my first voyage
to the East, and my first voyage as second mate; it was also my
skipper's first command. You'll admit it was time. He was sixty
if a day; a little man, with a broad, not very straight back, with
bowed shoulders and one leg more bandy than the other, he
had that queer twisted-about appearance you see so often in men
who work in the fields. He had a nut-cracker face—chin and nose
trying to come together over a sunken mouth—and it was framed
in iron-gray fluffy hair, that looked like a chin strap of cotton-
wool sprinkled with coal-dust. And he had blue eyes in that
old face of his, which were amazingly like a boy's, with that
candid expression some quite common men preserve to the end
of their days by a rare internal gift of simplicity of heart and
rectitude of soul. What induced him to accept me was a wonder.
I had come out of a crack Australian clipper, where I had been
third officer, and he seemed to have a prejudice against crack
clippers as aristocratic and high-toned. He said to me, 'You
know, in this ship you will have to work.' I said I had to work in
every ship I had ever been in. 'Ah, but this is different, and you
gentlemen out of them big ships; . . . but there! I dare say you
will do. Join to-morrow.'

"I joined to-morrow. It was twenty-two years ago; and I was
just twenty. How time passes! It was one of the happiest days of
my life. Fancy! Second mate for the first time—a really responsible officer! I wouldn't have thrown up my new billet for
a fortune. The mate looked me over carefully. He was also an
old chap, but of another stamp. He had a Roman nose, a snow-
white, long beard, and his name was Mahon, but he insisted that
it should be pronounced Mann. He was well connected; yet
there was something wrong with his luck, and he had never
got on.

"As to the captain, he had been for years in coasters, then
in the Mediterranean, and last in the West Indian trade. He had
never been round the Capes. He could just write a kind of
sketchy hand, and didn't care for writing at all. Both were

thorough good seamen of course, and between those two old
chaps I felt like a small boy between two grandfathers.

"The ship also was old. Her name was the *Judea*. Queer name,
isn't it? She belonged to a man Wilmer, Wilcox—some name
like that; but he has been bankrupt and dead these twenty years
or more, and his name don't matter. She had been laid up in
Shadwell basin for ever so long. You can imagine her state. She
was all rust, dust, grime—soot aloft, dirt on deck. To me it was
like coming out of a palace into a ruined cottage. She was about
400 tons, had a primitive windlass, wooden latches on the doors,
not a bit of brass about her, and a big square stern. There was
on it, below her name in big letters, a lot of scroll work, with
the gilt off, and some sort of a coat of arms, with the motto 'Do
or Die' underneath. I remember it took my fancy immensely.
There was a touch of romance in it, something that made me
love the old thing—something that appealed to my youth!

"We left London in ballast—sand ballast—to load a cargo of
coal in a northern port for Bankok. Bankok! I thrilled. I had
been six years at sea, but had only seen Melbourne and Sydney,
very good places, charming places in their way—but Bankok!

"We worked out of the Thames under canvas, with a North
Sea pilot on board. His name was Jermyn, and he dodged all day
long about the galley drying his handkerchief before the stove.
Apparently he never slept. He was a dismal man, with a per-
petual tear sparkling at the end of his nose, who either had been
in trouble, or was in trouble, or expected to be in trouble—
couldn't be happy unless something went wrong. He mistrusted
my youth, my common-sense, and my seamanship, and made a
point of showing it in a hundred little ways. I dare say he was
right. It seems to me I knew very little then, and I know not
much more now; but I cherish a hate for that Jermyn to this day.

"We were a week working up as far as Yarmouth Roads, and
then we got into a gale—the famous October gale of twenty-two
years ago. It was wind, lightning, sleet, snow, and a terrific sea.
We were flying light, and you may imagine how bad it was when
I tell you we had smashed bulwarks and a flooded deck. On the

second night she shifted her ballast into the lee bow, and by
that time we had been blown off somewhere on the Dogger
Bank. There was nothing for it but go below with shovels and
try to right her, and there we were in that vast hold, gloomy
like a cavern, the tallow dips stuck and flickering on the beams,
the gale howling above, the ship tossing about like mad on her
side; there we all were, Jermyn, the captain, everyone, hardly
able to keep our feet, engaged on that gravedigger's work, and
trying to toss shovelfuls of wet sand up to windward. At every
tumble of the ship you could see vaguely in the dim light men
falling down with a great flourish of shovels. One of the ship's
boys (we had two), impressed by the weirdness of the scene, wept
as if his heart would break. We could hear him blubbering
somewhere in the shadows.

"On the third day the gale died out, and by-and-by a north-
country tug picked us up. We took sixteen days in all to get from
London to the Tyne! When we got into dock we had lost our
turn for loading, and they hauled us off to a pier where we remained for a month. Mrs. Beard (the captain's name was Beard)
came from Colchester to see the old man. She lived on board.
The crew of runners had left, and there remained only the
officers, one boy, and the steward, a mulatto who answered to the
name of Abraham. Mrs. Beard was an old woman, with a face
all wrinkled and ruddy like a winter apple, and the figure of
a young girl. She caught sight of me once, sewing on a button,
and insisted on having my shirts to repair. This was something
different from the captains' wives I had known on board crack
clippers. When I brought her the shirts, she said: 'And the socks?
They want mending, I am sure, and John's—Captain Beard's—
things are all in order now. I would be glad of something to do.'
Bless the old woman. She overhauled my outfit for me, and
meantime I read for the first time 'Sartor Resartus' and Burn-
aby's 'Ride to Khiva.' I didn't understand much of the first then;
but I remember I preferred the soldier to the philosopher at the
time; a preference which life has only confirmed. One was a
man, and the other was either more—or less. However, they are

both dead, and Mrs. Beard is dead, and youth, strength, genius, thoughts, achievements, simple hearts—all die . . . . No matter.

"They loaded us at last. We shipped a crew. Eight able sea-men and two boys. We hauled off one evening to the buoys at the dock-gates, ready to go out, and with a fair prospect of be-ginning the voyage next day. Mrs. Beard was to start for home by a late train. When the ship was fast we went to tea. We sat rather silent through the meal—Mahon, the old couple, and I. I finished first, and slipped away for a smoke, my cabin being in a deck-house just against the poop. It was high water, blowing fresh with a drizzle; the double dock-gates were opened, and the steam colliers were going in and out in the darkness with their lights burning bright, a great plashing of propellers, rattling of winches, and a lot of hailing on the pier-heads. I watched the procession of head-lights gliding high and of green lights gliding low in the night, when suddenly a red gleam flashed at me, vanished, came into view again, and remained. The fore-end of a steamer loomed up close. I shouted down the cabin, 'Come up, quick!' and then heard a startled voice saying afar in the dark, 'Stop her, sir.' A bell jingled. Another voice cried warningly, 'We are going right into that bark, sir.' The answer to this was a gruff 'All right,' and the next thing was a heavy crash as the steamer struck a glancing blow with the bluff of her bow about our fore-rigging. There was a moment of confusion, yelling, and running about. Steam roared. Then somebody was heard say-ing, 'All clear, sir.' . . . 'Are you all right?' asked the gruff voice. I had jumped forward to see the damage, and hailed back, 'I think so.' 'Easy astern,' said the gruff voice. A bell jingled. 'What steamer is that?' screamed Mahon. By that time she was no more to us than a bulky shadow maneuvering a little way off. They shouted at us some name—a woman's name, Miranda or Melissa —or some such thing. 'This means another month in this beastly hole,' said Mahon to me, as we peered with lamps about the splintered bulwarks and broken braces. 'But where's the cap-tain?'

"We had not heard or seen anything of him all that time. We

went aft to look. A doleful voice arose hailing somewhere in the middle of the dock, '*Judea* ahoy!' . . . How the devil did he get there? . . . 'Hallo!' we shouted. 'I am adrift in our boat without oars,' he cried. A belated waterman offered his services, and Mahon struck a bargain with him for half-a-crown to tow our skipper alongside; but it was Mrs. Beard that came up the ladder first. They had been floating about the dock in that mizzly cold rain for nearly an hour. I was never so surprised in my life.

"It appears that when he heard my shout 'Come up,' he understood at once what was the matter, caught up his wife, ran on deck, and across, and down into our boat, which was fast to the ladder. Not bad for a sixty-year-old. Just imagine that old fellow saving heroically in his arms that old woman—the woman of his life. He set her down on a thwart, and was ready to climb back on board when the painter came adrift somehow, and away they went together. Of course in the confusion we did not hear him shouting. He looked abashed. She said cheerfully, 'I suppose it does not matter my losing the train now?' 'No, Jenny— you go below and get warm,' he growled. Then to us: 'A sailor has no business with a wife—I say. There I was, out of the ship. Well, no harm done this time. Let's go and look at what that fool of a steamer smashed.'

"It wasn't much, but it delayed us three weeks. At the end of that time, the captain being engaged with his agents, I carried Mrs. Beard's bag to the railway-station and put her all comfy into a third-class carriage. She lowered the window to say, 'You are a good young man. If you see John—Captain Beard—without his muffler at night, just remind him from me to keep his throat well wrapped up.' 'Certainly, Mrs. Beard,' I said. 'You are a good young man; I noticed how attentive you are to John—to Captain——' The train pulled out suddenly; I took my cap off to the old woman: I never saw her again. . . . Pass the bottle.

"We went to sea next day. When we made that start for Bankok we had been already three months out of London. We had expected to be a fortnight or so—at the outside.

"It was January, and the weather was beautiful—the beautiful

Autographed photograph by Malcolm Arbuthnot of Joseph Conrad, aged
sixty-two

sunny winter weather that has more charm than in the summer-time, because it is unexpected, and crisp, and you know it won't, it can't, last long. It's like a windfall, like a godsend, like an unexpected piece of luck.

"It lasted all down the North Sea, all down Channel; and it lasted till we were three hundred miles or so to the westward of the Lizards: then the wind went round to the sou'west and began to pipe up. In two days it blew a gale. The *Judea*, hove to, wallowed on the Atlantic like an old candlebox. It blew day after day: it blew with spite, without interval, without mercy, without rest. The world was nothing but an immensity of great foaming waves rushing at us, under a sky low enough to touch with the hand and dirty like a smoked ceiling. In the stormy space surrounding us there was as much flying spray as air. Day after day and night after night there was nothing round the ship but the howl of the wind, the tumult of the sea, the noise of water pouring over her deck. There was no rest for her and no rest for us. She tossed, she pitched, she stood on her head, she sat on her tail, she rolled, she groaned, and we had to hold on while on deck and cling to our bunks when below, in a constant effort of body and worry of mind.

"One night Mahon spoke through the small window of my berth. It opened right into my very bed, and I way lying there sleepless, in my boots, feeling as though I had not slept for years, and could not if I tried. He said excitedly—

" 'You got the sounding-rod in here, Marlow? I can't get the pumps to suck. By God! it's no child's play.'

"I gave him the sounding-rod and lay down again, trying to think of various things—but I thought only of the pumps. When I came on deck they were still at it, and my watch relieved at the pumps. By the light of the lantern brought on deck to examine the sounding-rod I caught a glimpse of their weary, serious faces. We pumped all the four hours. We pumped all night, all day, all the week,—watch and watch. She was working herself loose, and leaked badly—not enough to drown us at once, but enough to kill us with the work at the pumps. And while we pumped the ship was going from us piecemeal: the bulwarks went, the stanchions were torn out, the ventilators smashed, the cabin-door burst in. There was not a dry spot in the ship. She was being gutted bit by bit. The long-boat changed, as if by magic, into matchwood where she stood in her gripes. I had lashed her myself, and was rather proud of my handiwork, which had withstood so long the malice of the sea. And we pumped. And there was no break in the weather. The sea was white like a sheet of foam, like a caldron of boiling milk; there was not a break in the clouds, no—not the size of a man's hand—no, not for so much as ten seconds. There was for us no sky, there were for us no stars, no sun, no universe—nothing but angry clouds and an infuriated sea. We pumped watch and watch, for dear life; and it seemed to last for months, for years, for all eternity, as though we had been dead and gone to a hell for sailors. We forgot the day of the week, the name of the month, what year it was, and whether we had ever been ashore. The sails blew away, she lay broadside on under a weather-cloth, the ocean poured over her, and we did not care. We turned those handles, and had the eyes of idiots. As soon as we had crawled on deck I used to take a round turn with a rope about the men, the pumps, and the mainmast, and we turned, we turned incessantly, with the water to our waists, to our necks, over our heads. It was all one. We had forgotten how it felt to be dry.

"And there was somewhere in me the thought: By Jove! this is the deuce of an adventure—something you read about; and it is my first voyage as second mate—and I am only twenty—and here I am lasting it out as well as any of these men, and keeping my chaps up to the mark. I was pleased. I would not have given up the experience for worlds. I had moments of exultation. Whenever the old dismantled craft pitched heavily with her counter high in the air, she seemed to me to throw up, like an appeal, like a defiance, like a cry to the clouds without mercy, the words written on her stern: '*Judea*, London. Do or Die.'

"O youth! The strength of it, the faith of it, the imagination of it! To me she was not an old rattle-trap carting about the world a lot of coal for a freight—to me she was the endeavor, the test, the trial of life. I think of her with pleasure, with affection, with regret—as you would think of someone dead you have loved. I shall never forget her. . . . Pass the bottle.

"One night when tied to the mast, as I explained, we were pumping on, deafened with the wind, and without spirit enough in us to wish ourselves dead, a heavy sea crashed aboard and swept clean over us. As soon as I got my breath, I shouted, as in duty bound, 'Keep on, boys!' when suddenly I felt something hard floating on deck strike the calf of my leg. I made a grab at it and missed. It was so dark we could not see each other's faces within a foot—you understand.

"After that thump the ship kept quiet for a while, and the thing, whatever it was, struck my leg again. This time I caught it—and it was a sauce-pan. At first, being stupid with fatigue and thinking of nothing but the pumps, I did not understand what I had in my hand. Suddenly it dawned upon me, and I shouted, 'Boys, the house on deck is gone. Leave this, and let's look for the cook.'

"There was a deck-house forward, which contained the galley, the cook's berth, and the quarters of the crew. As we had expected for days to see it swept away, the hands had been ordered to sleep in the cabin—the only safe place in the ship. The steward, Abraham, however, persisted in clinging to his berth, stupidly, like a mule—from sheer fright I believe, like an animal that won't leave a stable falling in an earthquake. So we went to look for him. It was chancing death, since once out of our lashings we were as exposed as if on a raft. But we went. The house was shattered as if a shell had exploded inside. Most of it had gone overboard—stove, men's quarters, and their property, all was gone; but two posts, holding a portion of the bulkhead to which Abraham's bunk was attached, remained as if by a miracle. We groped in the ruins and came upon this, and there he was, sitting in his bunk, surrounded by foam and wreckage, jabbering cheerfully to himself. He was out of his mind; completely and for ever mad, with this sudden shock coming upon the fag-end of his endurance. We snatched him up, lugged him aft, and pitched him head-first down the cabin companion. You understand there was no time to carry him down with infinite precautions and wait to see how he got on. Those below would pick him up at the bottom of the stairs all right. We were in a hurry to go back to the pumps. That business could not wait. A bad leak is an inhuman thing.

"One would think that the sole purpose of that fiendish gale had been to make a lunatic of that poor devil of a mulatto. It eased before morning, and next day the sky cleared, and as the sea went down the leak took up. When it came to bending a fresh set of sails the crew demanded to put back—and really there was nothing else to do. Boats gone, decks swept clean, cabin gutted, men without a stitch but what they stood in, stores spoiled, ship strained. We put her head for home, and—would you believe it? The wind came east right in our teeth. It blew fresh, it blew continuously. We had to beat up every inch of the way, but she did not leak so badly, the water keeping comparatively smooth. Two hours' pumping in every four is no joke—but it kept her afloat as far as Falmouth.

"The good people there live on casualties of the sea, and no doubt were glad to see us. A hungry crowd of shipwrights sharpened their chisels at the sight of that carcass of a ship. And, by Jove! they had pretty pickings off us before they were done. I fancy the owner was already in a tight place. There were delays. Then it was decided to take part of the cargo out and calk her topsides. This was done, the repairs finished, cargo reshipped; a new crew came on board, and we went out—for Bankok. At the end of a week we were back again. The crew said they weren't going to Bankok—a hundred and fifty days' passage—in a something hooker that wanted pumping eight hours out of the twenty-four; and the nautical papers inserted again the little paragraph: 'Judea. Bark. Tyne to Bankok; coals; put back to Falmouth leaky and with crew refusing duty.'

"There were more delays—more tinkering. The owner came down for a day, and said she was as right as a little fiddle. Poor

old Captain Beard looked like the ghost of a Geordie skipper—
through the worry and humiliation of it. Remember he was
sixty, and it was his first command. Mahon said it was a foolish
business, and would end badly. I loved the ship more than ever,
and wanted awfully to get to Bankok. To Bankok! Magic name,
blessed name. Mesopotamia wasn't a patch on it. Remember I
was twenty, and it was my first second mate's billet, and the East
was waiting for me.

"We went out and anchored in the outer roads with a fresh
crew—the third. She leaked worse than ever. It was as if those
confounded shipwrights had actually made a hole in her. This
time we did not even go outside. The crew simply refused to
man the windlass.

"They towed us back to the inner harbor, and we became a
fixture, a feature, an institution of the place. People pointed us
out to visitors as 'That 'ere bark that's going to Bankok—has
been here six months—put back three times.' On holidays the
small boys pulling about in boats would hail, '*Judea,* ahoy!' and
if a head showed above the rail shouted, 'Where you bound to?—
Bankok?' and jeered. We were only three on board. The poor
old skipper mooned in the cabin. Mahon undertook the cook-
ing, and unexpectedly developed all a Frenchman's genius for
preparing nice little messes. I looked languidly after the rigging.
We became citizens of Falmouth. Every shopkeeper knew us.
At the barber's or tobacconist's they asked familiarly, 'Do you
think you will ever get to Bankok?' Meantime the owner, the
underwriters, and the charterers squabbled amongst themselves
in London, and our pay went on. . . . Pass the bottle.

"It was horrid. Morally it was worse than pumping for life.
It seemed as though we had been forgotten by the world, belonged to nobody, would get nowhere; it seemed that, as if bewitched, we would have to live for ever and ever in that inner
harbor, a derision and a byword to generations of long-shore
loafers and dishonest boatmen. I obtained three months' pay
and a five days' leave, and made a rush for London. It took me a
day to get there and pretty well another to come back—but three

months' pay went all the same. I don't know what I did with it. I went to a music-hall, I believe, lunched, dined, and supped in a swell place in Regent Street, and was back to time, with nothing but a complete set of Byron's works and a new railway rug to show for three months' work. The boatman who pulled me off the ship said: 'Hallo! I thought you had left the old thing. *She* will never get to Bankok.' 'That's all *you* know about it,' I said scornfully—but I didn't like that prophecy at all.

"Suddenly a man, some kind of agent to somebody, appeared with full powers. He had grog blossoms all over his face, an indomitable energy, and was a jolly soul. We leaped into life again. A hulk came alongside, took our cargo, and then we went into dry dock to get our copper stripped. No wonder she leaked. The poor thing, strained beyond endurance by the gale, had, as if in disgust, spat out all the oakum of her lower seams. She was recalked, new coppered, and made as tight as a bottle. We went back to the hulk and reshipped our cargo.

"Then on a fine moonlight night, all the rats left the ship.

"We had been infested with them. They had destroyed our sails, consumed more stores than the crew, affably shared our beds and our dangers, and now, when the ship was made seaworthy, concluded to clear out. I called Mahon to enjoy the spectacle. Rat after rat appeared on our rail, took a last look over his shoulder, and leaped with a hollow thud into the empty hulk. We tried to count them, but soon lost the tale. Mahon said: 'Well, well! don't talk to me about the intelligence of rats. They ought to have left before, when we had that narrow squeak from foundering. There you have the proof how silly is the superstition about them. They leave a good ship for an old rotten hulk, where there is nothing to eat, too, the fools! . . . I don't believe they know what is safe or what is good for them, any more than you or I.'

"And after some more talk we agreed that the wisdom of rats had been grossly overrated, being in fact no greater than that of men.

"The story of the ship was known, by this, all up the Channel

from Land's End to the Forelands, and we could get no crew on
the south coast. They sent us one all complete from Liverpool,
and we left once more—for Bankok.

"We had fair breezes, smooth water right into the tropics,
and the old *Judea* lumbered along in the sunshine. When she
went eight knots everything cracked aloft, and we tied our caps
to our heads; but mostly she strolled on at the rate of three miles
an hour. What could you expect? She was tired—that old ship.
Her youth was where mine is—where yours is—you fellows who
listen to this yarn; and what friend would throw your years and
your weariness in your face? We didn't grumble at her. To us
aft, at least, it seemed as though we had been born in her, reared
in her, had lived in her for ages, had never known any other
ship. I would just as soon have abused the old village church at
home for not being a cathedral.

"And for me there was also my youth to make me patient.
There was all the East before me, and all life, and the thought
that I had been tried in that ship and had come out pretty well.
And I thought of men of old who, centuries ago, went that road
in ships that sailed no better, to the land of palms, and spices,
and yellow sands, and of brown nations ruled by kings more
cruel than Nero the Roman and more splendid than Solomon
the Jew. The old bark lumbered on, heavy with her age and the
burden of her cargo, while I lived the life of youth in ignorance
and hope. She lumbered on through an interminable procession
of days; and the fresh gilding flashed back at the setting sun,
seemed to cry out over the darkening sea the words painted on
her stern, '*Judea,* London. Do or Die.'

"Then we entered the Indian Ocean and steered northerly
for Java Head. The winds were light. Weeks slipped by. She
crawled on, do or die, and people at home began to think of
posting us as overdue.

"One Saturday evening, I being off duty, the men asked me
to give them an extra bucket of water or so—for washing clothes.
As I did not wish to screw on the fresh-water pump so late, I
went forward whistling, and with a key in my hand to unlock

the forepeak scuttle, intending to serve the water out of a spare tank we kept there.

"The smell down below was as unexpected as it was frightful. One would have thought hundreds of paraffin-lamps had been flaring and smoking in that hole for days. I was glad to get out. The man with me coughed and said, 'Funny smell, sir.' I answered negligently, 'It's good for the health, they say,' and walked aft.

"The first thing I did was to put my head down the square of the midship ventilator. As I lifted the lid a visible breath, something like a thin fog, a puff of faint haze, rose from the opening. The ascending air was hot, and had a heavy, sooty, paraffiny smell. I gave one sniff, and put down the lid gently. It was no use choking myself. The cargo was on fire.

"Next day she began to smoke in earnest. You see it was to be expected, for though the coal was of a safe kind, that cargo had been so handled, so broken up with handling, that it looked more like smithy coal than anything else. Then it had been wetted—more than once. It rained all the time we were taking it back from the hulk, and now with this long passage it got heated, and there was another case of spontaneous combustion.

"The captain called us into the cabin. He had a chart spread on the table, and looked unhappy. He said, 'The coast of West Australia is near, but I mean to proceed to our destination. It is the hurricane month too; but we will just keep her head for Bankok, and fight the fire. No more putting back anywhere, if we all get roasted. We will try first to stifle this 'ere damned combustion by want of air.'

"We tried. We battened down everything, and still she smoked. The smoke kept coming out through imperceptible crevices; it forced itself through bulkheads and covers; it oozed here and there and everywhere in slender threads, in an invisible film, in an incomprehensible manner. It made its way into the cabin, into the forecastle; it poisoned the sheltered places on the deck, it could be sniffed as high as the mainyard.

It was clear that if the smoke came out the air came in. This was disheartening. This combustion refused to be stifled.

"We resolved to try water, and took the hatches off. Enormous volumes of smoke, whitish, yellowish, thick, greasy, misty, choking, ascended as high as the trucks. All hands cleared out aft. Then the poisonous cloud blew away, and we went back to work in a smoke that was no thicker now than that of an ordinary factory chimney.

"We rigged the force pump, got the hose along, and by-and-by it burst. Well, it was as old as the ship—a prehistoric hose, and past repair. Then we pumped with the feeble head-pump, drew water with buckets, and in this way managed in time to pour lots of Indian Ocean into the main hatch. The bright stream flashed in sunshine, fell into a layer of white crawling smoke, and vanished on the black surface of coal. Steam ascended mingling with the smoke. We poured salt water as into a barrel without a bottom. It was our fate to pump in that ship, to pump out of her, to pump into her; and after keeping water out of her to save ourselves from being drowned, we frantically poured water into her to save ourselves from being burnt.

"And she crawled on, do or die, in the serene weather. The sky was a mircle of purity, a miracle of azure. The sea was polished, was blue, was pellucid, was sparkling like a precious stone, extending on all sides, all round to the horizon—as if the whole terrestrial globe had been one jewel, one colossal sapphire, a single gem fashioned into a planet. And on the luster of the great calm waters the *Judea* glided imperceptibly, enveloped in languid and unclean vapors, in a lazy cloud that drifted to leeward, light and slow: a pestiferous cloud defiling the splendor of sea and sky.

"All this time of course we saw no fire. The cargo smoldered at the bottom somewhere. Once Mahon, as we were working side by side, said to me with a queer smile: 'Now, if she only would spring a tidy leak—like that time when we first left the Channel—it would put a stopper on this fire. Wouldn't it?' I remarked irrelevantly, 'Do you remember the rats?'

"We fought the fire and sailed the ship too as carefully as though nothing had been the matter. The steward cooked and attended on us. Of the other twelve men, eight worked while four rested. Everyone took his turn, captain included. There was equality, and if not exactly fraternity, then a deal of good feeling. Sometimes a man, as he dashed a bucketful of water down the hatchway, would yell out, 'Hurrah for Bankok!' and the rest laughed. But generally we were taciturn and serious—and thirsty. Oh! how thirsty! And we had to be careful with the water. Strict allowance. The ship smoked, the sun blazed. . . . Pass the bottle.

"We tried everything. We even made an attempt to dig down to the fire. No good, of course. No man could remain more than a minute below. Mahon, who went first, fainted there, and the man who went to fetch him out did likewise. We lugged them out on deck. Then I leaped down to show how easily it could be done. They had learned wisdom by that time, and contented themselves by fishing for me with a chain-hook tied to a broom-handle, I believe. I did not offer to go and fetch up my shovel, which was left down below.

"Things began to look bad. We put the long-boat into the water. The second boat was ready to swing out. We had also another, a fourteen-foot thing, on davits aft, where it was quite safe.

"Then behold, the smoke suddenly decreased. We redoubled our efforts to flood the bottom of the ship. In two days there was no smoke at all. Everybody was on the broad grin. This was on a Friday. On Saturday no work, but sailing the ship of course was done. The men washed their clothes and their faces for the first time in a fortnight, and had a special dinner given them. They spoke of spontaneous combustion with contempt, and implied *they* were the boys to put out combustions. Somehow we all felt as though we each had inherited a large fortune. But a beastly smell of burning hung about the ship. Captain Beard had hollow eyes and sunken cheeks. I had never noticed so much before how twisted and bowed he was. He and Mahon prowled soberly about hatches and ventilators, sniffing. It struck me suddenly poor Mahon was a very, very old chap. As to me, I was as pleased and proud as though I had helped to win a great naval battle. O! Youth!

"The night was fine. In the morning a homeward-bound ship passed us hull down,—the first we had seen for months; but we were nearing the land at last, Java Head being about 190 miles off, and nearly due north.

"Next day it was my watch on deck from eight to twelve. At breakfast the captain observed, 'It's wonderful how that smell hangs about the cabin.' About ten, the mate being on the poop, I stepped down on the main deck for a moment. The carpenter's bench stood abaft the mainmast: I leaned against it sucking at my pipe, and the carpenter, a young chap, came to talk to me. He remarked, 'I think we have done very well, haven't we?' and then I perceived with annoyance the fool was trying to tilt the bench. I said curtly, 'Don't, Chips,' and immediately became aware of a queer sensation, of an absurd delusion,—I seemed somehow to be in the air. I heard all round me like a pent-up breath released—as if a thousand giants simultaneously had said Phoo!—and felt a dull concussion which made my ribs ache suddenly. No doubt about it—I was in the air, and my body was describing a short parabola. But short as it was, I had the time to think several thoughts in, as far as I can remember, the following order: 'This can't be the carpenter—What is it?— Some accident—Submarine volcano?—Coals, gas!—By Jove! we are being blown up—Everybody's dead—I am falling into the after-hatch—I see fire in it.'

"The coal-dust suspended in the air of the hold had glowed dull-red at the moment of the explosion. In the twinkling of an eye, in an infinitesimal fraction of a second since the first tilt of the bench, I was sprawling full length on the cargo. I picked myself up and scrambled out. It was quick like a rebound. The deck was a wilderness of smashed timber, lying crosswise like trees in a wood after a hurricane; an immense curtain of soiled rags waved gently before me—it was the mainsail blown to strips.

I thought, The masts will be toppling over directly; and to get out of the way bolted on all-fours towards the poop-ladder. The first person I saw was Mahon, with eyes like saucers, his mouth open, and the long white hair standing straight on end round his head like a silver halo. He was just about to go down when the sight of the main-deck stirring, heaving up, and changing into splinters before his eyes, petrified him on the top step. I stared at him in unbelief, and he stared at me with a queer kind of shocked curiosity. I did not know that I had no hair, no eyebrows, no eyelashes, that my young mustache was burnt off, that my face was black, one cheek laid open, my nose cut, and my chin bleeding. I had lost my cap, one of my slippers, and my shirt was torn to rags. Of all this I was not aware. I was amazed to see the ship still afloat, the poop-deck whole—and, most of all, to see anybody alive. Also the peace of the sky and the serenity of the sea were distinctly surprising. I suppose I expected to see them convulsed with horror. . . . Pass the bottle.

"There was a voice hailing the ship from somewhere—in the air, in the sky—I couldn't tell. Presently I saw the captain—and he was mad. He asked me eagerly, 'Where's the cabin-table?' and to hear such a question was a frightful shock. I had just been blown up, you understand, and vibrated with that experience,— I wasn't quite sure whether I was alive. Mahon began to stamp with both feet and yelled at him, 'Good God! don't you see the deck's blown out of her?' I found my voice, and stammered out as if conscious of some gross neglect of duty, 'I don't know where the cabin-table is.' It was like an absurd dream.

"Do you know what he wanted next? Well, he wanted to trim the yards. Very placidly, and as if lost in thought, he insisted on having the foreyard squared. 'I don't know if there's anybody alive,' said Mahon, almost tearfully. 'Surely,' he said, gently, 'there will be enough left to square the foreyard.'

"The old chap, it seems, was in his own berth, winding up the chronometers, when the shock sent him spinning. Immediately it occurred to him—as he said afterwards—that the ship had struck something, and he ran out into the cabin. There, he

saw, the cabin-table had vanished somewhere. The deck being
blown up, it had fallen down into the lazarette of course. Where
we had our breakfast that morning he saw only a great hole in
the floor. This appeared to him so awfully mysterious, and impressed him so immensely, that what he saw and heard after he
got on deck were mere trifles in comparison. And, mark, he
noticed directly the wheel deserted and his bark off her course—
and his only thought was to get that miserable, stripped, un-
decked, smoldering shell of a ship back again with her head
pointing at her port of distination. Bankok! That's what he was
after. I tell you this quiet, bowed, bandy-legged, almost de-
formed little man was immense in the singleness of his idea and
in his placid ignorance of our agitation. He motioned us forward with a commanding gesture, and went to take the wheel
himself.

"Yes; that was the first thing we did—trim the yards of that
wreck! No one was killed, or even disabled, but everyone was
more or less hurt. You should have seen them! Some were in
rags, with black faces, like coalheavers, like sweeps, and had
bullet heads that seemed closely cropped, but were in fact
singed to the skin. Others, of the watch below, awakened by
being shot out from their collapsing bunks, shivered incessantly,
and kept on groaning even as we went about our work. But they
all worked. That crew of Liverpool hard cases had in them the
right stuff. It's my experience they always have. It is the sea that
gives it—the vastness, the loneliness surrounding their dark
stolid souls. Ah! Well! we stumbled, we crept, we fell, we barked
our shins on the wreckage, we hauled. The masts stood, but we
did not know how much they might be charred down below. It
was nearly calm, but a long swell ran from the west and made
her roll. They might go at any moment. We looked at them with
apprehension. One could not foresee which way they would fall.

"Then we retreated aft and looked about us. The deck was a
tangle of planks on edge, of planks on end, of splinters, of
ruined woodwork. The masts rose from that chaos like big trees
above a matted undergrowth. The interstices of that mass of

wreckage were full of something whitish, sluggish, stirring—of something that was like a greasy fog. The smoke of the invisible fire was coming up again, was trailing, like a poisonous thick mist in some valley choked with dead wood. Already lazy wisps were beginning to curl upwards amongst the mass of splinters. Here and there a piece of timber, stuck upright, resembled a post. Half of a fife-rail had been shot through the foresail, and the sky made a patch of glorious blue in the ignobly soiled canvas. A portion of several boards holding together had fallen across the rail, and one end protruded overboard, like a gangway leading upon nothing, like a gangway leading over the deep sea, leading to death—as if inviting us to walk the plank at once and be done with our ridiculous troubles. And still the air, the sky—a ghost, something invisible was hailing the ship.

"Someone had the sense to look over, and there was the helmsman, who had impulsively jumped overboard, anxious to come back. He yelled and swam lustily like a merman, keeping up with the ship. We threw him a rope, and presently he stood amongst us streaming with water and very crest-fallen. The captain had surrendered the wheel, and apart, elbow on rail and chin in hand, gazed at the sea wistfully. We asked ourselves, What next? I thought, Now, this is something like. This is great. I wonder what will happen. O youth!

"Suddenly Mahon sighted a steamer far astern. Captain Beard said, 'We may do something with her yet.' We hoisted two flags, which said in the international language of the sea, 'On fire. Want immediate assistance.' The steamer grew bigger rapidly, and by-and-by spoke with two flags on her foremast, 'I am coming to your assistance.'

"In half an hour she was abreast, to windward, within hail, and rolling slightly, with her engines stopped. We lost our composure, and yelled all together with excitement, 'We've been blown up.' A man in a white helmet, on the bridge, cried, 'Yes! All right! all right!' and he nodded his head, and smiled, and made soothing motions with his hand as though at a lot of frightened children. One of the boats dropped in the water, and walked towards us upon the sea with her long oars. Four Calashes pulled a swinging stroke. This was my first sight of Malay seamen. I've known them since, but what struck me then was their unconcern: they came alongside, and even the bowman standing up and holding to our main-chains with the boathook did not deign to lift his head for a glance. I thought people who had been blown up deserved more attention.

"A little man, dry like a chip and agile like a monkey, clambered up. It was the mate of the steamer. He gave one look, and cried, 'O boys—you had better quit.'

"We were silent. He talked apart with the captain for a time, —seemed to argue with him. Then they went away together to the steamer.

"When our skipper came back we learned that the steamer was the *Sommerville,* Captain Nash, from West Australia to Singapore *viâ* Batavia with mails, and that the agreement was she should tow us to Anjer or Batavia, if possible, where we could extinguish the fire by scuttling, and then proceed on our voyage—to Bankok! The old man seemed excited. 'We will do it yet,' he said to Mahon, fiercely. He shook his fist at the sky. Nobody else said a word.

"At noon the steamer began to tow. She went ahead slim and high, and what was left of the *Judea* followed at the end of seventy fathom of tow-rope,—followed her swiftly like a cloud of smoke with mastheads protruding above. We went aloft to furl the sails. We coughed on the yards, and were careful about the bunts. Do you see the lot of us there, putting a neat furl on the sails of that ship doomed to arrive nowhere? There was not a man who didn't think that at any moment the masts would topple over. From aloft we could not see the ship for smoke, and they worked carefully, passing the gaskets with even turns. 'Harbor furl—aloft there!' cried Mahon from below.

"You understand this? I don't think one of those chaps expected to get down in the usual way. When we did I heard them saying to each other, 'Well, I thought we would come down overboard, in a lump—sticks and all—blame me if I didn't.' 'That's what I was thinking to myself,' would answer wearily another battered and bandaged scarecrow. And, mind, these were men without the drilled-in habit of obedience. To an on-looker they would be a lot of profane scallywags without a re-deeming point. What made them do it—what made them obey me when I, thinking consciously how fine it was, made them drop the bunt of the foresail twice to try to do it better? What? They had no professional reputation—no example, no praise. It wasn't a sense of duty; they all knew well enough how to shirk, and laze, and dodge—when they had a mind to it—and mostly they had. Was it the two pounds ten a month that sent them there? They didn't think their pay half good enough. No; it was something in them, something inborn and subtle and everlast-ing. I don't say positively that the crew of a French or German merchantman wouldn't have done it, but I doubt whether it would have been done in the same way. There was a complete-ness in it, something solid like a principle, and masterful like an instinct—a disclosure of something secret—of that hidden some-thing, that gift, of good or evil that makes racial difference, that shapes the fate of nations.

"It was that night at ten that, for the first time since we had been fighting it, we saw the fire. The speed of the towing had fanned the smoldering destruction. A blue gleam appeared for-ward, shining below the wreck of the deck. It wavered in patches, it seemed to stir and creep like the light of a glowworm. I saw it first, and told Mahon. 'Then the game's up,' he said. 'We had better stop this towing, or she will burst out suddenly fore and aft before we can clear out.' We set up a yell; rang bells to attract their attention; they towed on. At last Mahon and I had to crawl forward and cut the rope with an ax. There was no time to cast off the lashings. Red tongues could be seen licking the wilderness of splinters under our feet as we made our way back to the poop.

"Of course they very soon found out in the steamer that the rope was gone. She gave a loud blast of her whistle, her lights

were seen sweeping in a wide circle, she came up ranging close
alongside, and stopped. We were all in a tight group on the poop
looking at her. Every man had saved a little bundle or a bag.
Suddenly a conical flame with a twisted top shot up forward and
threw upon the black sea a circle of light, with the two vessels
side by side and heaving gently in its center. Captain Beard had
been sitting on the gratings still and mute for hours, but now
he rose slowly and advanced in front of us, to the mizzen-
shrouds. Captain Nash hailed: 'Come along! Look sharp. I have
mail-bags on board. I will take you and your boats to Singapore.'

" 'Thank you! No!' said our skipper. 'We must see the last of
the ship.'

" 'I can't stand by any longer,' shouted the other. 'Mails—you
know.'

" 'Ay! ay! We are all right.'

" 'Very well! I'll report you in Singapore. . . . Good-by!'

"He waved his hand. Our men dropped their bundles quietly.
The steamer moved ahead, and passing out of the circle of light,
vanished at once from our sight, dazzled by the fire which
burned fiercely. And then I knew that I would see the East first
as commander of a small boat. I thought it fine; and the fidelity
to the old ship was fine. We should see the last of her. Oh the
glamour of youth! Oh the fire of it, more dazzling than the
flames of the burning ship, throwing a magic light on the wide
earth, leaping audaciously to the sky, presently to be quenched
by time, more cruel, more pitiless, more bitter than the sea—
and like the flames of the burning ship surrounded by an impenetrable night.

.   .   .   .   .

"The old man warned us in his gentle and inflexible way
that it was part of our duty to save for the underwriters as much
as we could of the ship's gear. According we went to work aft,
while she blazed forward to give us plenty of light. We lugged
out a lot of rubbish. What didn't we save? An old barometer

fixed with an absurd quantity of screws nearly cost me my life: a sudden rush of smoke came upon me, and I just got away in time. There were various stores, bolts of canvas, coils of rope; the poop looked like a marine bazaar, and the boats were lumbered to the gunwales. One would have thought the old man wanted to take as much as he could of his first command with him. He was very, very quiet, but off his balance evidently. Would you believe it? He wanted to take a length of old steam-cable and a kedge-anchor with him in the long-boat. We said, 'Ay, ay, sir,' deferentially, and on the quiet let the thing slip overboard. The heavy medicine-chest went that way, two bags of green coffee, tins of paint—fancy, paint!—a whole lot of things. Then I was ordered with two hands into the boats to make a stowage and get them ready against the time it would be proper for us to leave the ship.

"We put everything straight, stepped the long-boat's mast for our skipper, who was to take charge of her, and I was not sorry to sit down for a moment. My face felt raw, every limb ached as if broken, I was aware of all my ribs, and would have sworn to a twist in the backbone. The boats, fast astern, lay in a deep shadow, and all around I could see the circle of the sea lighted by the fire. A gigantic flame arose forward straight and clear. It flared fierce, with noises like the whir of wings, with rumbles as of thunder. There were cracks, detonations, and from the cone of flame the sparks flew upwards, as man is born to trouble, to leaky ships, and to ships that burn.

"What bothered me was that the ship, lying broadside to the swell and to such wind as there was—a mere breath—the boats would not keep astern where they were safe, but persisted, in a pig-headed way boats have, in getting under the counter and then swinging alongside. They were knocking about dangerously and coming near the flame, while the ship rolled on them, and, of course, there was always the danger of the masts going over the side at any moment. I and my two boat-keepers kept them off as best we could with oars and boat-hooks; but to be constantly at it became exasperating, since there was no reason why we should not leave at once. We could not see those on board, nor could we imagine what caused the delay. The boat-keepers were swearing feebly, and I had not only my share of the work, but also had to keep at it two men who showed a constant inclination to lay themselves down and let things slide.

"At last I hailed 'On deck there,' and someone looked over. 'We're ready here,' I said. The head disappeared, and very soon popped up again. 'The captain says, All right, sir, and to keep the boats well clear of the ship.'

"Half an hour passed. Suddenly there was a frightful racket, rattle, clanking of chain, hiss of water, and millions of sparks flew up into the shivering column of smoke that stood leaning slightly above the ship. The catheads had burned away, and the two red-hot anchors had gone to the bottom, tearing out after them two hundred fathom of red-hot chain. The ship trembled, the mass of flame swayed as if ready to collapse, and the fore top-gallant-mast fell. It darted down like an arrow of fire, shot under, and instantly leaping up within an oar's-length of the boats, floated quietly, very black on the luminous sea. I hailed the deck again. After some time a man in an unex-pectedly cheerful but also muffled tone, as though he had been trying to speak with his mouth shut, informed me, 'Coming directly, sir,' and vanished. For a long time I heard nothing but the whir and roar of the fire. There were also whistling sounds. The boats jumped, tugged at the painters, ran at each other playfully, knocked their sides together, or, do what we would, swung in a bunch against the ship's side. I couldn't stand it any longer, and swarming up a rope, clambered aboard over the stern.

"It was as bright as day. Coming up like this, the sheet of fire facing me, was a terrifying sight, and the heat seemed hardly bearable at first. On a settee cushion dragged out of the cabin, Captain Beard, with his legs drawn up and one arm under his head, slept with the light playing on him. Do you know what the rest were busy about? They were sitting on deck right aft, round an open case, eating bread and cheese and drinking bottled stout.

"On the background of flames twisting in fierce tongues above their heads they seemed at home like salamanders, and looked like a band of desperate pirates. The fire sparkled in the whites of their eyes, gleamed on patches of white skin seen through the torn shirts. Each had the marks as of a battle about him— bandaged heads, tied-up arms, a strip of dirty rag round a knee —and each man had a bottle between his legs and a chunk of cheese in his hand. Mahon got up. With his handsome and dis- reputable head, his hooked profile, his long white beard, and with an uncorked bottle in his hand, he resembled one of those reckless sea-robbers of old making merry amidst violence and disaster. 'The last meal on board,' he explained solemnly. 'We had nothing to eat all day, and it was no use leaving all this.' He flourished the bottle and indicated the sleeping skipper. 'He said he couldn't swallow anything, so I got him to lie down,' he went on; and as I stared, 'I don't know whether you are aware, young fellow, the man had no sleep to speak of for days —and there will be dam' little sleep in the boats.' 'There will be no boats by-and-by if you fool about much longer,' I said, indignantly. I walked up to the skipper and shook him by the shoulder. At last he opened his eyes, but did not move. 'Time to leave her, sir,' I said, quietly.

"He got up painfully, looked at the flames, at the sea sparkling round the ship, and black, black as ink farther away; he looked at the stars shining dim through a thin veil of smoke in a sky black, black as Erebus.

" 'Youngest first,' he said.

"And the ordinary seaman, wiping his mouth with the back of his hand, got up, clambered over the taffrail, and vanished. Others followed. One, on the point of going over, stopped short to drain his bottle, and with a great swing of his arm flung it at the fire. 'Take this!' he cried.

"The skipper lingered disconsolately, and we left him to commune alone for awhile with his first command. Then I went up again and brought him away at last. It was time. The iron-work on the poop was hot to the touch.

"Then the painter of the long-boat was cut, and the three boats, tied together, drifted clear of the ship. It was just sixteen hours after the explosion when we abandoned her. Mahon had charge of the second boat, and I had the smallest—the 14-foot thing. The long-boat would have taken the lot of us; but the skipper said we must save as much property as we could—for the underwriters—and so I got my first command. I had two men with me, a bag of biscuits, a few tins of meat, and a breaker of water. I was ordered to keep close to the long-boat, that in case of bad weather we might be taken into her.

"And do you know what I thought? I thought I would part company as soon as I could. I wanted to have my first command all to myself. I wasn't going to sail in a squadron if there were a chance for independent cruising. I would make land by my-self. I would beat the other boats. Youth! All youth! The silly, charming, beautiful youth.

"But we did not make a start at once. We must see the last of the ship. And so the boats drifted about that night, heaving and setting on the swell. The men dozed, waked, sighed, groaned. I looked at the burning ship.

"Between the darkness of earth and heaven she was burning fiercely upon a disc of purple sea shot by the blood-red play of gleams; upon a disc of water glittering and sinister. A high, clear flame, an immense and lonely flame, ascended from the ocean, and from its summit the black smoke poured continuously at the sky. She burned furiously, mournful and imposing like a funeral pile kindled in the night, surrounded by the sea, watched over by the stars. A magnificent death had come like a grace, like a gift, like a reward to that old ship at the end of her laborious days. The surrender of her weary ghost to the keeping of stars and sea was stirring like the sight of a glorious triumph. The masts fell just before daybreak, and for a moment there was a burst and turmoil of sparks that seemed to fill with flying fire the night patient and watchful, the vast night lying silent upon the sea. At daylight she was only a charred shell, floating still under a cloud of smoke and bearing a glowing mass of coal within.

"Then the oars were got out, and the boats forming in a line moved round her remains as if in procession—the long-boat leading. As we pulled across her stern a slim dart of fire shot out viciously at us, and suddenly she went down, head first, in a great hiss of steam. The unconsumed stern was the last to sink; but the paint had gone, had cracked, had peeled off, and there were no letters, there was no word, no stubborn device that was like her soul, to flash at the rising sun her creed and her name.

"We made our way north. A breeze sprang up, and about noon all the boats came together for the last time. I had no mast or sail in mine, but I made a mast out of a spare oar and hoisted a boat-awning for a sail, with a boat-hook for a yard. She was certainly over-masted, but I had the satisfaction of knowing that with the wind aft I could beat the other two. I had to wait for them. Then we all had a look at the captain's chart, and, after a sociable meal of hard bread and water, got our last instructions. These were simple: steer north, and keep together as much as possible. 'Be careful with that jury rig, Marlow,' said the captain; and Mahon, as I sailed proudly past his boat, wrinkled his curved nose and hailed, 'You will sail that ship of yours under water, if you don't look out, young fellow.' He was a malicious old man—and may the deep sea where he sleeps now rock him gently, rock him tenderly to the end of time!

"Before sunset a thick rain-squall passed over the two boats, which were far astern, and that was the last I saw of them for a time. Next day I sat steering my cockle-shell—my first command —with nothing but water and sky around me. I did sight in the afternoon the upper sails of a ship far away, but said nothing, and my men did not notice her. You see I was afraid she might be homeward bound, and I had no mind to turn back from the portals of the East. I was steering for Java—another blessed name—like Bankok, you know. I steered many days.

"I need not tell you what it is to be knocking about in an

open boat. I remember nights and days of calm when we pulled, we pulled, and the boat seemed to stand still, as if bewitched within the circle of the sea horizon. I remember the heat, the deluge of rain-squalls that kept us baling for dear life (but filled our water-cask), and I remember sixteen hours on end with a mouth dry as a cinder and a steering-oar over the stern to keep my first command head on to a breaking sea. I did not know how good a man I was till then. I remember the drawn faces, the dejected figures of my two men, and I remember my youth and the feeling that will never come back any more—the feeling that I could last for ever, outlast the sea, the earth, and all men; the deceitful feeling that lures us on to joys, to perils, to love, to vain effort—to death; the triumphant conviction of strength, the heat of life in the handful of dust, the glow in the heart that with every year grows dim, grows cold, grows small, and expires —and expires, too soon, too soon—before life itself.

"And this is how I see the East. I have seen its secret places and have looked into its very soul; but now I see it always from a small boat, a high outline of mountains, blue and afar in the morning; like faint mist at noon; a jagged wall of purple at sunset. I have the feel of the oar in my hand, the vision of a scorching blue sea in my eyes. And I see a bay, a wide bay, smooth as glass and polished like ice, shimmering in the dark. A red light burns far off upon the gloom of the land, and the night is soft and warm. We drag at the oars with aching arms, and suddenly a puff of wind, a puff faint and tepid and laden with strange odors of blossoms, of aromatic wood, comes out of the still night—the first sigh of the East on my face. That I can never forget. It was impalpable and enslaving, like a charm, like a whispered promise of mysterious delight.

"We had been pulling this finishing spell for eleven hours. Two pulled, and he whose turn it was to rest sat at the tiller. We had made out the red light in that bay and steered for it, guessing it must mark some small coasting port. We passed two vessels, outlandish and high-sterned, sleeping at anchor, and, approaching the light, now very dim, ran the boat's nose against

the end of a jutting wharf. We were blind with fatigue. My
men dropped the oars and fell off the thwarts as if dead. I made
fast to a pile. A current rippled softly. The scented obscurity
of the shore was grouped into vast masses, a density of colossal
clumps of vegetation, probably—mute and fantastic shapes. And
at their foot the semicircle of a beach gleamed faintly, like an
illusion. There was not a light, not a stir, not a sound. The mysterious East faced me, perfumed like a flower, silent like death,
dark like a grave.

"And I sat weary beyond expression, exulting like a con-
queror, sleepless and entranced as if before a profound, a fateful enigma.

"A splashing of oars, a measured dip reverberating on the
level of water, intensified by the silence of the shore into loud
claps, made me jump up. A boat, a European boat, was coming
in. I invoked the name of the dead; I hailed: *Judea* ahoy! A thin
shout answered.

"It was the captain. I had beaten the flagship by three hours,
and I was glad to hear the old man's voice again, tremulous and
tired. 'Is it you, Marlow?' 'Mind the end of that jetty, sir,' I cried.

"He approached cautiously, and brought up with the deep-
sea lead-line which we had saved—for the underwriters. I eased
my painter and fell alongside. He sat, a broken figure at the
stern, wet with dew, his hands clasped in his lap. His men were
asleep already. 'I had a terrible time of it,' he murmured.
'Mahon is behind—not very far.' We conversed in whispers, in
low whispers, as if afraid to wake up the land. Guns, thunder,
earthquakes would not have awakened the men just then.

"Looking around as we talked, I saw away at sea a bright
light traveling in the night. 'There's a steamer passing the bay,'
I said. She was not passing, she was entering, and she even came
close and anchored. 'I wish,' said the old man, 'you would find
out whether she is English. Perhaps they could give us a passage
somewhere.' He seemed nervously anxious. So by dint of punching and kicking I started one of my men into a state of somnam-

bulism, and giving him an oar, took another and pulled towards the lights of the steamer.

"There was a murmur of voices in her, metallic hollow clangs of the engine-room, footsteps on the deck. Her ports shone, round like dilated eyes. Shapes moved about, and there was a shadowy man high up on the bridge. He heard my oars.

"And then, before I could open my lips, the East spoke to me, but it was in a Western voice. A torrent of words was poured into the enigmatical, the fateful silence; outlandish, angry words, mixed with words and even whole sentences of good English, less strange but even more surprising. The voice swore and cursed violently; it riddled the solemn peace of the bay by a volley of abuse. It began by calling me Pig, and from that went crescendo into unmentionable adjectives—in English. The man up there raged aloud in two languages, and with a sincerity in his fury that almost convinced me I had, in some way, sinned against the harmony of the universe. I could hardly see him, but began to think he would work himself into a fit.

"Suddenly he ceased, and I could hear him snorting and blowing like a porpoise. I said—

" 'What steamer is this, pray?'

" 'Eh? What's this? And who are you?'

" 'Castaway crew of an English bark burnt at sea. We came here to-night. I am the second mate. The captain is in the long-boat, and wishes to know if you would give us a passage somewhere.'

" 'Oh, my goodness! I say. . . . This is the *Celestial* from Singapore on her return trip. I'll arrange with your captain in the morning, . . . and, . . . I say, . . . did you hear me just now?'

" 'I should think the whole bay heard you.'

" 'I thought you were a shore-boat. Now, look here—this infernal lazy scoundrel of a caretaker has gone to sleep again—curse him. The light is out, and I nearly ran foul of the end of this damned jetty. This is the third time he plays me this trick. Now, I ask you, can anybody stand this kind of thing? It's enough to drive a man out of his mind. I'll report him. . . .

I'll get the Assistant Resident to give him the sack, by . . . See—there's no light. It's out, isn't it? I take you to witness the light's out. There should be a light, you know. A red light on the——'

" 'There was a light,' I said, mildly.

" 'But it's out, man! What's the use of talking like this? You can see for yourself it's out—don't you? If you had to take a valuable steamer along this God-forsaken coast you would want a light too. I'll kick him from end to end of his miserable wharf. You'll see if I don't. I will——'

" 'So I may tell my captain you'll take us?' I broke in.

" 'Yes, I'll take you. Good night,' he said, brusquely.

"I pulled back, made fast again to the jetty, and then went to sleep at last. I had faced the silence of the East. I had heard some of its languages. But when I opened my eyes again the silence was as complete as though it had never been broken. I was lying in a flood of light, and the sky had never looked so far, so high, before. I opened my eyes and lay without moving.

"And then I saw the men of the East—they were looking at me. The whole length of the jetty was full of people. I saw brown, bronze, yellow faces, the black eyes, the glitter, the color of an Eastern crowd. And all these beings stared without a murmur, without a sigh, without a movement. They stared down at the boats, at the sleeping men who at night had come to them from the sea. Nothing moved. The fronds of palms stood still against the sky. Not a branch stirred along the shore, and the brown roofs of hidden houses peeped through the green foliage, through the big leaves that hung shining and still like leaves forged of heavy metal. This was the East of the ancient navigators, so old, so mysterious, resplendent and somber, living and unchanged, full of danger and promise. And these were the men. I sat up suddenly. A wave of movement passed through the crowd from end to end, passed along the heads, swayed the bodies, ran along the jetty like a ripple on the water, like a breath of wind on a field—and all was still again. I see it now —the wide sweep of the bay, the glittering sands, the wealth of green infinite and varied, the sea blue like the sea of a dream, the crowd of attentive faces, the blaze of vivid color—the water reflecting it all, the curve of the shore, the jetty, the high-sterned outlandish craft floating still, and the three boats with tired men from the West sleeping unconscious of the land and the people and of the violence of sunshine. They slept thrown across the thwarts, curled on bottom-boards, in the careless attitudes of death. The head of the old skipper, leaning back in the stern of the long-boat, had fallen on his breast, and he looked as though he would never wake. Farther out old Mahon's face was upturned to the sky, with the long white beard spread out on his breast, as though he been shot where he sat at the tiller; and a man, all in a heap in the bows of the boat, slept with both arms embracing the stem-head and with his cheek laid on the gunwale. The East looked at them without a sound.

"I have known its fascinations since: I have seen the mysterious shores, the still water, the lands of brown nations, where a stealthy Nemesis lies in wait, pursues, overtakes so many of the conquering race, who are proud of their wisdom, of their knowledge, of their strength. But for me all the East is contained in that vision of my youth. It is all in that moment when I opened my young eyes on it. I came upon it from a tussle with the sea—and I was young—and I saw it looking at me. And this is all that is left of it! Only a moment; a moment of strength, of romance, of glamour—of youth! . . . A flick of sunshine upon a strange shore, the time to remember, the time for a sigh, and —good-by!—Night—Good-by . . . !"

He drank.

"Ah! The good old time—the good old time. Youth and the sea. Glamour and the sea! The good, strong sea, the salt, bitter sea, that could whisper to you and roar at you and knock your breath out of you."

He drank again.

"By all that's wonderful, it is the sea, I believe, the sea itself —or is it youth alone? Who can tell? But you here—you all had something out of life: money, love—whatever one gets on shore —and, tell me, wasn't that the best time, that time when we were young at sea; young and had nothing, on the sea that gives nothing, except hard knocks—and sometimes a chance to feel your strength—that only—what you all regret?"

And we all nodded at him: the man of finance, the man of accounts, the man of law, we all nodded at him over the polished table that like a still sheet of brown water reflected our faces, lined, wrinkled; our faces marked by toil, by deceptions, by success, by love; our weary eyes looking still, looking always, looking anxiously for something out of life, that while it is expected is already gone—has passed unseen, in a sigh, in a flash —together with the youth, with the strength, with the romance of illusions.

Heart of Darkness

I

THE *Nellie,* a cruising yawl, swung to her anchor without a flutter of the sails, and was at rest. The flood had made, the wind was nearly calm, and being bound down the river, the only thing for it was to come to and wait for the turn of the tide.

The sea-reach of the Thames stretched before us like the beginning of an interminable waterway. In the offing the sea and the sky were welded together without a joint, and in the luminous space the tanned sails of the barges drifting up with the tide seemed to stand still in red clusters of canvas sharply peaked, with gleams of varnished sprits. A haze rested on the low shores that ran out to sea in vanishing flatness. The air was dark above Gravesend, and farther back still seemed condensed into a mournful gloom, brooding motionless over the biggest, and the greatest, town on earth.

The director of Companies was our captain and our host. We four affectionately watched his back as he stood in the bows looking to seaward. On the whole river there was nothing that looked half so nautical. He resembled a pilot, which to a seaman is trustworthiness personified. It was difficult to realize his work was not out there in the luminous estuary, but behind him, within the brooding gloom.

Between us there was, as I have already said somewhere, the bond of the sea. Besides holding our hearts together through long periods of separation, it had the effect of making us tolerant of each other's yarns—and even convictions. The Lawyer—the best of old fellows—had, because of his many years and many virtues, the only cushion on deck, and was lying on the only rug. The Accountant had brought out already a box of dominoes, and was toying architecturally with the bones. Marlow sat cross-legged right aft, leaning against the mizzen-mast. He had sunken cheeks, a yellow complexion, a straight back, an ascetic aspect, and, with his arms dropped, the palms of hands outwards, resembled an idol. The Director, satisfied the anchor had good hold, made his way aft and sat down amongst us. We exchanged a few words lazily. Afterwards there was silence on board the yacht. For some reason or other we did not begin that game of dominoes. We felt meditative, and fit for nothing but placid staring. The day was ending in a serenity of still and exquisite brilliance. The water shone pacifically; the sky, without a speck, was a benign immensity of unstained light; the very mist on the Essex marshes was like a gauzy and radiant fabric, hung from the wooded rises inland, and draping the low shores in diaphanous folds. Only the gloom to the west, brooding over the upper reaches, became more somber every minute, as if angered by the approach of the sun.

And at last, in its curved and imperceptible fall, the sun sank low, and from glowing white changed to a dull red without rays and without heat, as if about to go out suddenly, stricken to death by the touch of that gloom brooding over a crowd of men.

Forthwith a change came over the waters, and the serenity became less brilliant but more profound. The old river in its broad reach rested unruffled at the decline of day, after ages of good service done to the race that peopled its banks, spread out in the tranquil dignity of a waterway leading to the uttermost ends of the earth. We looked at the venerable stream not in the vivid flush of a short day that comes and departs for ever, but in the august light of abiding memories. And indeed nothing is easier for a man who has, as the phrase goes, "followed the sea" with reverence and affection, than to evoke the great spirit of the past upon the lower reaches of the Thames. The tidal current runs to and fro in its unceasing service, crowded with memories of men and ships it had borne to the rest of home or to the battles of the sea. It had known and served all the men of whom the nation is proud, from Sir Francis Drake to Sir John

Conrad reading, a portrait by Muirhead Bone

Franklin, knights all, titled and untitled—the great knights-errant of the sea. It had borne all the ships whose names are like jewels flashing in the night of time, from the *Golden Hind* returning with her round flanks full of treasure, to be visited by the Queen's Highness and thus pass out of the gigantic tale, to the *Erebus* and *Terror,* bound on other conquests—and that never returned. It had known the ships and the men. They had sailed from Deptford, from Greenwich, from Erith—the adventurers and the settlers; kings' ships and the ships of men on 'Change; captains, admirals, the dark "interlopers" of the Eastern trade, and the commissioned "generals" of East India fleets. Hunters for gold or pursuers of fame, they all had gone out on that stream, bearing the sword, and often the torch, messengers of the might within the land, bearers of a spark from the sacred fire. What greatness had not floated on the ebb of that river into the mystery of an unknown earth! . . . The dreams of men, the seed of commonwealths, the germs of empires.

The sun set; the dusk fell on the stream, and lights began to appear along the shore. The Chapman lighthouse, a three-legged thing erect on a mud-flat, shone strongly. Lights of ships moved in the fairway—a great stir of lights going up and going down. And farther west on the upper reaches the place of the monstrous town was still marked ominously on the sky, a brooding gloom in sunshine, a lurid glare under the stars.

"And this also," said Marlow suddenly, "has been one of the dark places of the earth."

He was the only man of us who still "followed the sea." The worst that could be said of him was that he did not represent his class. He was a seaman, but he was a wanderer too, while most seamen lead, if one may so express it, a sedentary life. Their minds are of the stay-at-home order, and their home is always with them—the ship; and so is their country—the sea. One ship is very much like another, and the sea is always the same. In the immutability of their surroundings the foreign shores, the foreign faces, the changing immensity of life, glide past, veiled not by a sense of mystery but by a slightly disdainful ignorance;

for there is nothing mysterious to a seaman unless it be the sea itself, which is the mistress of his existence and as inscrutable as Destiny. For the rest, after his hours of work, a casual stroll or a casual spree on shore suffices to unfold for him the secret of a whole continent, and generally he finds the secret not worth knowing. The yarns of seamen have a direct simplicity, the whole meaning of which lies within the shell of a cracked nut. But Marlow was not typical (if his propensity to spin yarns be excepted), and to him the meaning of an episode was not inside like a kernel but outside, enveloping the tale which brought it out only as a glow brings out a haze, in the likeness of one of these misty halos that sometimes are made visible by the spectral illumination of moonshine.

His remark did not seem at all surprising. It was just like Marlow. It was accepted in silence. No one took the trouble to grunt even; and presently he said, very slow—

"I was thinking of very old times, when the Romans first came here, nineteen hundred years ago—the other day. . . . Light came out of this river since—you say Knights? Yes; but it is like a running blaze on a plain, like a flash of lightning in the clouds. We live in the flicker—may it last as long as the old earth keeps rolling! But darkness was here yesterday. Imagine the feelings of a commander of a fine—what d'ye call 'em?— trireme in the Mediterranean, ordered suddenly to the north; run overland across the Gauls in a hurry; put in charge of one of these craft the legionaries,—a wonderful lot of handy men they must have been too—used to build, apparently by the hundred, in a month or two, if we may believe what we read. Imagine him here—the very end of the world, a sea the color of lead, a sky the color of smoke, a kind of ship about as rigid as a concertina— and going up this river with stores, or orders, or what you like. Sandbanks, marshes, forests, savages,—precious little to eat fit for a civilized man, nothing but Thames water to drink. No Falernian wine here, no going ashore. Here and there a military camp lost in a wilderness, like a needle in a bundle of hay—cold, fog, tempests, disease, exile, and death,—death skulking in the

air, in the water, in the bush. They must have been dying like
flies here. Oh yes—he did it. Did it very well, too, no doubt, and
without thinking much about it either, except afterwards to
brag of what he had gone through in his time, perhaps. They
were men enough to face the darkness. And perhaps he was
cheered by keeping his eye on a chance of promotion to the fleet
at Ravenna by-and-by, if he had good friends in Rome and
survived the awful climate. Or think of a decent young citizen
in a toga—perhaps too much dice, you know—coming out here
in the train of some prefect, or tax-gatherer, or trader even, to
mend his fortunes. Land in a swamp, march through the woods,
and in some inland post feel the savagery, the utter savagery, had
closed round him,—all that mysterious life of the wilderness that
stirs in the forest, in the jungles, in the hearts of wild men.
There's no initiation either into such mysteries. He has to live
in the midst of the incomprehensible, which is also detestable.
And it has a fascination, too, that goes to work upon him. The
fascination of the abomination—you know. Imagine the growing
regrets, the longing to escape, the powerless disgust, the surrender, the hate."

He paused.

"Mind," he began again, lifting one arm from the elbow, the
palm of the hand outwards, so that, with his legs folded before
him, he had the pose of a Buddha preaching in European clothes
and without a lotus-flower—"Mind, none of us would feel exactly
like this. What saves us is efficiency—the devotion to efficiency.
But these chaps were not much account, really. They were no
colonists; their administration was merely a squeeze, and nothing more, I suspect. They were conquerors, and for that you
want only brute force—nothing to boast of, when you have it,
since your strength is just an accident arising from the weakness
of others. They grabbed what they could get for the sake of
what was to be got. It was just robbery with violence, aggravated
murder on a great scale, and men going at it blind—as is very
proper for those who tackle a darkness. The conquest of the
earth, which mostly means the taking it away from those who

have a different complexion or slightly flatter noses than ourselves, is not a pretty thing when you look into it too much.
What redeems it is the idea only. An idea at the back of it; not
a sentimental pretense but an idea; and an unselfish belief in
the idea—something you can set up, and bow down before, and
offer a sacrifice to. . . ."

He broke off. Flames glided in the river, small green flames,
red flames, white flames, pursuing, overtaking, joining, crossing
each other—then separating slowly or hastily. The traffic of the
great city went on in the deepening night upon the sleepless
river. We looked on, waiting patiently—there was nothing else
to do till the end of the flood; but it was only after a long silence,
when he said, in a hesitating voice, "I suppose you fellows remember I did once turn fresh-water sailor for a bit," that we
knew we were fated, before the ebb began to run, to hear about
one of Marlow's inconclusive experiences.

"I don't want to bother you much with what happened to
me personally," he began, showing in this remark the weakness
of many tellers of tales who seem so often unaware of what their
audience would best like to hear: "yet to understand the effect
of it on me you ought to know how I got out there, what I saw,
how I went up that river to the place where I first met the poor
chap. It was the farthest point of navigation and the culminating point of my experience. It seemed somehow to throw a kind
of light on everything about me—and into my thoughts. It was
somber enough too—and pitiful—not extraordinary in any way—
not very clear either. No, not very clear. And yet it seemed to
throw a kind of light.

"I had then, as you remember, just returned to London after
a lot of Indian Ocean, Pacific, China Seas—a regular dose of the
East—six years or so, and I was loafing about, hindering you
fellows in your work and invading your homes, just as though
I had got a heavenly mission to civilize you. It was very fine
for a time, but after a bit I did get tired of resting. Then I began
to look for a ship—I should think the hardest work on earth. But

the ships wouldn't even look at me. And I got tired of that game too.

"Now when I was a little chap I had a passion for maps. I would look for hours at South America, or Africa, or Australia, and lose myself in all the glories of exploration. At that time there were many blank spaces on the earth, and when I saw one that looked particularly inviting on a map (but they all look that) I would put my finger on it and say, When I grow up I will go there. The North Pole was one of these places, I remember. Well, I haven't been there yet, and shall not try now. The glamour's off. Other places were scattered about the Equator, and in every sort of latitude all over the two hemispheres. I have been in some of them, and . . . well, we won't talk about that. But there was one yet—the biggest, the most blank, so to speak—that I had a hankering after.

"True, by this time it was not a blank space any more. It had got filled since my boyhood with rivers and lakes and names. It had ceased to be a blank space of delightful mystery—a white patch for a boy to dream gloriously over. It had become a place of darkness. But there was in it one river especially, a mighty big river, that you could see on the map, resembling an immense snake uncoiled, with its head in the sea, its body at rest curving afar over a vast country, and its tail lost in the depths of the land. And as I looked at the map of it in a shop-window, it fascinated me as a snake would a bird—a silly little bird. Then I remembered there was a big concern, a Company for trade on that river. Dash it all! I thought to myself, they can't trade without using some kind of a craft on that lot of fresh water—steamboats! Why shouldn't I try to get charge of one. I went on along Fleet Street, but could not shake off the idea. The snake had charmed me.

"You understand it was a Continental concern, that Trading society; but I have a lot of relations living on the Continent, because it's cheap and not so nasty as it looks, they say.

"I am sorry to own I began to worry them. This was already a fresh departure for me. I was not used to get things that way, you know. I always went my own road and on my own legs where I had a mind to go. I wouldn't have believed it of myself; but, then—you see—I felt somehow I must get there by hook or by crook. So I worried them. The men said 'My dear fellow,' and did nothing. Then—would you believe it?—I tried the women. I, Charlie Marlow, set the women to work—to get a job. Heavens! Well, you see, the notion drove me. I had an aunt, a dear enthusiastic soul. She wrote: 'It will be delightful. I am ready to do anything, anything for you. It is a glorious idea. I know the wife of a very high personage in the Administration, and also a man who has lots of influence with,' &c., &c. She was determined to make no end of fuss to get me appointed skipper of a river steamboat, if such was my fancy.

"I got my appointment—of course; and I got it very quick. It appears the Company had received news that one of their captains had been killed in a scuffle with the natives. This was my chance, and it made me the more anxious to go. It was only months and months afterwards, when I made the attempt to recover what was left of the body, that I heard the original quarrel arose from a misunderstanding about some hens. Yes, two black hens. Fresleven—that was the fellow's name, a Dane—thought himself wronged somehow in the bargain, so he went ashore and started to hammer the chief of the village with a stick. Oh, it didn't surprise me in the least to hear this, and at the same time to be told that Fresleven was the gentlest, quietest creature that ever walked on two legs. No doubt he was; but he had been a couple of years already out there engaged in the noble cause, you know, and he probably felt the need at last of asserting his self-respect in some way. Therefore he whacked the old nigger mercilessly, while a big crowd of his people watched him, thunderstruck, till some man,—I was told the chief's son,—in desperation at hearing the old chap yell, made a tentative jab with a spear at the white man—and of course it went quite easy between the shoulder-blades. Then the whole population cleared into the forest, expecting all kinds of calamities to happen, while, on the other hand, the steamer Fresleven commanded left also in a bad panic, in charge of the engineer, I believe. Afterwards nobody seemed to trouble much about Fresleven's remains, till I got out and stepped into his shoes. I couldn't let it rest, though; but when an opportunity offered at last to meet my predecessor, the grass growing through his ribs was tall enough to hide his bones. They were all there. The supernatural being had not been touched after he fell. And the village was deserted, the huts gaped black, rotting, all askew within the fallen enclosures. A calamity had come to it, sure enough. The people had vanished. Mad terror had scattered them, men, women, and children, through the bush, and they had never returned. What became of the hens I don't know either. I should think the cause of progress got them, anyhow. However, through this glorious affair I got my appointment, before I had fairly begun to hope for it.

"I flew around like mad to get ready, and before forty-eight hours I was crossing the Channel to show myself to my employers, and sign the contract. In a very few hours I arrived in a city that always makes me think of a whited sepulcher. Prejudice no doubt. I had no difficulty in finding the Company's offices. It was the biggest thing in the town, and everybody I met was full of it. They were going to run an over-sea empire, and make no end of coin by trade.

"A narrow and deserted street in deep shadow, high houses, innumerable windows with venetian blinds, a dead silence, grass sprouting between the stones, imposing carriage archways right and left, immense double doors standing ponderously ajar. I slipped through one of these cracks, went up a swept and ungarnished staircase, as arid as a desert, and opened the first door I came to. Two women, one fat and the other slim, sat on straw-bottomed chairs, knitting black wool. The slim one got up and walked straight at me—still knitting with downcast eyes—and only just as I began to think of getting out of her way, as you would for a somnambulist, stood still, and looked up. Her dress was as plain as an umbrella-cover, and she turned round without a word and preceded me into a waiting-room. I gave my name, and looked about. Deal table in the middle, plain chairs all round the walls, on one end a large shining map, marked with all the colors of a rainbow. There was a vast amount of red—good to see at any time, because one knows that some real work is done in there, a deuce of a lot of blue, a little green, smears of orange, and, on the East Coast, a purple patch, to show where the jolly pioneers of progress drink the jolly lager-beer. However, I wasn't going into any of these. I was going into the yellow. Dead in the center. And the river was there—fascinating—deadly—like a snake. Ough! A door opened, a white-haired secretarial head, but wearing a compassionate expression, appeared, and a skinny forefinger beckoned me into the sanctuary. Its light was dim, and a heavy writing-desk squatted in the middle. From behind that structure came out an impression of pale plumpness in a frock-coat. The great man himself. He was five feet six, I should judge, and had his grip on the handle-end of ever so many millions. He shook hands, I fancy, murmured vaguely, was satisfied with my French. *Bon voyage.*

"In about forty-five seconds I found myself again in the waiting-room with the compassionate secretary, who, full of desolation and sympathy, made me sign some document. I believe I undertook amongst other things not to disclose any trade secrets. Well, I am not going to.

"I began to feel slightly uneasy. You know I am not used to such ceremonies, and there was something ominous in the atmosphere. It was just as though I had been let into some conspiracy—I don't know—something not quite right; and I was glad to get out. In the other room the two women knitted black wool feverishly. People were arriving, and the younger one was walking back and forth introducing them. The old one sat on her chair. Her flat cloth slippers were propped up on a foot-warmer, and a cat reposed on her lap. She wore a starched white affair on her head, had a wart on one cheek, and silver-rimmed spectacles hung on the tip of her nose. She glanced at me above the glasses. The swift and indifferent placidity of that look troubled me. Two youths with foolish and cheery countenances were being piloted over, and she threw at them the same quick glance of unconcerned wisdom. She seemed to know all about them and about me too. An eerie feeling came over me. She seemed uncanny and fateful. Often far away there I thought of these two, guarding the door of Darkness, knitting black wool as for a warm pall, one introducing, introducing continuously to the unknown, the other scrutinizing the cheery and foolish faces with unconcerned old eyes. *Ave!* Old knitter of black wool. *Morituri te salutant.* Not many of those she looked at ever saw her again—not half, by a long way.

"There was yet a visit to the doctor. 'A simple formality,' assured me the secretary, with an air of taking an immense part in all my sorrows. Accordingly a young chap wearing his hat over the left eyebrow, some clerk I suppose,—there must have been clerks in the business, though the house was as still as a house in a city of the dead,—came from somewhere up-stairs, and led me forth. He was shabby and careless, with ink-stains on the sleeves of his jacket, and his cravat was large and billowy, under a chin shaped like the toe of an old boot. It was a little too early for the doctor, so I proposed a drink, and thereupon he developed a vein of joviality. As we sat over our vermouths he glorified the Company's business, and by-and-by I expressed casually my surprise at him not going out there. He became very cool and collected all at once. 'I am not such a fool as I look, quoth Plato to his disciples,' he said sententiously, emptied his glass with great resolution, and we rose.

"The old doctor felt my pulse, evidently thinking of something else the while. 'Good, good for there,' he mumbled, and then with a certain eagerness asked me whether I would let him measure my head. Rather surprised, I said Yes, when he produced a thing like calipers and got the dimensions back and front and every way, taking notes carefully. He was an unshaven little man in a threadbare coat like a gaberdine, with his feet in slippers, and I thought him a harmless fool. 'I always ask leave, in the interests of science, to measure the crania of those going

out there,' he said. 'And when they come back too?' I asked.
'Oh, I never see them,' he remarked; 'and, moreover, the changes
take place inside, you know.' He smiled, as if at some quiet joke.
'So you are going out there. Famous. Interesting too.' He gave
me a searching glance, and made another note. 'Ever any madness in your family?' he asked, in a matter-of-fact tone. I felt
very annoyed. 'Is that question in the interests of science too?'
'It would be,' he said, without taking notice of my irritation, 'interesting for science to watch the mental changes of individuals,
on the spot, but . . .' 'Are you an alienist?' I interrupted. 'Every
doctor should be—a little,' answered that original, imperturb-
ably. 'I have a little theory which you Messieurs who go out there
must help me to prove. This is my share in the advantages my
country shall reap from the possession of such a magnificent
dependency. The mere wealth I leave to others. Pardon my
questions, but you are the first Englishman coming under my
observation. . . .' I hastened to assure him I was not in the least
typical. 'If I were,' said I, 'I wouldn't be talking like this with
you.' 'What you say is rather profound, and probably erroneous,'
he said, with a laugh. 'Avoid irritation more than exposure to
the sun. Adieu. How do you English say, eh? Good-by. Ah!
Good-by. Adieu. In the tropics one must before everything
keep calm.' . . . He lifted a warning forefinger. . . . '*Du calme, du
calme. Adieu.*'

"One thing more remained to do—say good-by to my excellent
aunt. I found her triumphant. I had a cup of tea—the last decent
cup of tea for many days—and in a room that most soothingly
looked just as you would expect a lady's drawing-room to look,
we had a long quiet chat by the fireside. In the course of these
confidences it became quite plain to me I had been represented
to the wife of the high dignitary, and goodness knows to how
many more people besides, as an exceptional and gifted creature
—a piece of good fortune for the Company—a man you don't
get hold of every day. Good heavens! and I was going to take
charge of a two-penny-halfpenny river-steamboat with a penny
whistle attached! It appeared, however, I was also one of the

Workers, with a capital—you know. Something like an emissary
of light, something like a lower sort of apostle. There had been
a lot of such rot let loose in print and talk just about that time,
and the excellent woman, living right in the rush of all that
humbug, got carried off her feet. She talked about 'weaning
those ignorant millions from their horrid ways,' till, upon my
word, she made me quite uncomfortable. I ventured to hint
that the Company was run for profit.

" 'You forget, dear Charlie, that the laborer is worthy of his
hire,' she said, brightly. It's queer how out of touch with truth
women are. They live in a world of their own, and there had
never been anything like it, and never can be. It is too beautiful
altogether, and if they were to set it up it would go to pieces
before the first sunset. Some confounded fact we men have been
living contentedly with ever since the day of creation would
start up and knock the whole thing over.

"After this I got embraced, told to wear flannel, be sure to
write often, and so on—and I left. In the street—I don't know
why—a queer feeling came to me that I was an imposter. Odd
thing that I, who used to clear out for any part of the world
at twenty-four hours' notice, with less thought than most men
give to the crossing of a street, had a moment—I won't say of
hesitation, but of startled pause, before this commonplace affair.
The best way I can explain it to you is by saying that, for a
second or two, I felt as though, instead of going to the center of
a continent, I were about to set off for the center of the earth.

"I left in a French steamer, and she called in every blamed
port they have out there, for, as far as I could see, the sole purpose of landing soldiers and custom-house officers. I watched
the coast. Watching a coast as it slips by the ship is like thinking
about an enigma. There it is before you—smiling, frowning,
inviting, grand, mean, insipid, or savage, and always mute with
an air of whispering, Come and find out. This one was almost
featureless, as if still in the making, with an aspect of monotonous grimness. The edge of a colossal jungle, so dark-green as
to be almost black, fringed with white surf, ran straight, like

a ruled line, far, far away along a blue sea whose glitter was blurred by a creeping mist. The sun was fierce, the land seemed to glisten and drip with steam. Here and there grayish-whitish specks showed up, clustered inside the white surf, with a flag flying above them perhaps. Settlements some centuries old, and still no bigger than pin-heads on the untouched expanse of their background. We pounded along, stopped, landed soldiers; went on, landed custom-house clerks to levy toll in what looked like a God-forsaken wilderness, with a tin shed and a flag-pole lost in it; landed more soldiers—to take care of the custom-house clerks, presumably. Some, I heard, got drowned in the surf; but whether they did or not, nobody seemed particularly to care. They were just flung out there, and on we went. Every day the coast looked the same, as though we had not moved; but we passed various places—trading places—with names like Gran' Bassam Little Popo; names that seemed to belong to some sordid farce acted in front of a sinister backcloth. The idleness of a passenger, my isolation amongst all these men with whom I had no point of contact, the oily and languid sea, the uniform somberness of the coast, seemed to keep me away from the truth of things, within the toil of a mournful and senseless delusion. The voice of the surf heard now and then was a positive pleasure, like the speech of a brother. It was something natural, that had its reason, that had a meaning. Now and then a boat from the shore gave one a momentary contact with reality. It was paddled by black fellows. You could see from afar the white of their eyeballs glistening. They shouted, sang; their bodies streamed with perspiration; they had faces like grotesque masks—these chaps; but they had bone, muscle, a wild vitality, an intense energy of movement, that was as natural and true as the surf along their coast. They wanted no excuse for being there. They were a great comfort to look at. For a time I would feel I belonged still to a world of straightforward facts; but the feeling would not last long. Something would turn up to scare it away. Once, I remember, we came upon a man-of-war anchored off the coast. There wasn't even a shed there, and she was shelling the bush. It appears the French had one of their wars going on thereabouts. Her ensign dropped limp like a rag; the muzzles of the long six-inch guns stuck out all over the low hull; the greasy, slimy swell swung her up lazily and let her down, swaying her thin masts. In the empty immensity of earth, sky, and water, there she was, incomprehensible, firing into a continent. Pop, would go one of the six-inch guns; a small flame would dart and vanish, a little white smoke would disappear, a tiny projectile would give a feeble screech—and nothing happened. Nothing could happen. There was a touch of insanity in the proceeding, a sense of lugubrious drollery in the sight; and it was not dissipated by somebody on board assuring me earnestly there was a camp of natives—he called them enemies!—hidden out of sight somewhere.

"We gave her her letters (I heard the men in that lonely ship were dying of fever at the rate of three a day) and went on. We called at some more places with farcical names, where the merry dance of death and trade goes on in a still and earthy atmosphere as of an overheated catacomb; all along the formless coast bordered by dangerous surf, as if Nature herself had tried to ward off intruders; in and out of rivers, streams of death in life, whose banks were rotting into mud, whose waters, thickened into slime, invaded the contorted mangroves, that seemed to writhe at us in the extremity of an impotent despair. Nowhere did we stop long enough to get a particularized impression, but the general sense of vague and oppressive wonder grew upon me. It was like a weary pilgrimage amongst hints for nightmares.

"It was upward of thirty days before I saw the mouth of the big river. We anchored off the seat of the government. But my work would not begin till some two hundred miles farther on. So as soon as I could I made a start for a place thirty miles higher up.

"I had my passage on a little sea-going steamer. Her captain was a Swede, and knowing me for a seaman, invited me on the bridge. He was a young man, lean, fair, and morose, with lanky hair and a shuffling gait. As we left the miserable little wharf, he tossed his head contemptuously at the shore. 'Been living there?' he asked. I said, 'Yes.' 'Fine lot these government chaps— are they not?' he went on, speaking English with great precision and considerable bitterness. 'It is funny what some people will do for a few francs a month. I wonder what becomes of that kind when it goes up country?' I said to him I expected to see that soon. 'So-o-o!' he exclaimed He shuffled athwart, keeping one eye ahead vigilantly. 'Don't be too sure,' he continued. 'The other day I took up a man who hanged himself on the road. He was a Swede, too.' 'Hanged himself! Why, in God's name?' I cried. He kept on looking out watchfully. 'Who knows? The sun too much for him, or the country perhaps.'

At last we opened a reach. A rocky cliff appeared, mounds of turned-up earth by the shore, houses on a hill, others, with iron roofs, amongst a waste of excavations, or hanging to the declivity. A continuous noise of the rapids above hovered over this scene of inhabited devastation. A lot of people, mostly black and naked, moved about like ants. A jetty projected into the river. A blinding sunlight drowned all this at times in a sudden recrudescence of glare. 'There's your Company's station,' said the Swede, pointing to three wooden barrack-like structures on the rocky slope. 'I will send your things up. Four boxes did you say? So. Farewell.'

"I came upon a boiler wallowing in the grass, then found a path leading up the hill. It turned aside for the bowlders, and also for an undersized railway-truck lying there on its back with its wheels in the air. One was off. The thing looked as dead as the carcass of some animal. I came upon more pieces of decaying machinery, a stack of rusty rails. To the left a clump of trees made a shady spot, where dark things seemed to stir feebly. I blinked, the path was steep. A horn tooted to the right, and I saw the black people run. A heavy and dull detonation shook the ground, a puff of smoke came out of the cliff, and that was all. No change appeared on the face of the rock. They were building a railway. The cliff was not in the way or anything; but this objectless blasting was all the work going on.

"A slight clinking behind me made me turn my head. Six black men advanced in a file, toiling up the path. They walked erect and slow, balancing small baskets full of earth on their heads, and the clink kept time with their footsteps. Black rags were wound round their loins, and the short ends behind waggled to and fro like tails. I could see every rib, the joints of their limbs were like knots in a rope; each had an iron collar on his neck, and all were connected together with a chain whose bights swung between them, rhythmically clinking. Another report from the cliff made me think suddenly of that ship of war I had seen firing into a continent. It was the same kind of ominous voice; but these men could by no stretch of imagination be called enemies. They were called criminals, and the outraged law, like the bursting shells, had come to them, an insoluble mystery from the sea. All their meager breasts panted together, the violently dilated nostrils quivered, the eyes stared stonily uphill. They passed me within six inches, without a glance, with that complete, deathlike indifference of unhappy savages. Behind this raw matter one of the reclaimed, the product of the new forces at work, strolled despondently, carrying a rifle by its middle. He had a uniform jacket with one button off, and seeing a white man on the path, hoisted his weapon to his shoulder with alacrity. This was simple prudence, white men being so much alike at a distance that he could not tell who I might be. He was speedily reassured, and with a large, white, rascally grin, and a glance at his charge, seemed to take me into partnership in his exalted trust. After all, I also was a part of the great cause of these high and just proceedings.

"Instead of going up, I turned and descended to the left. My idea was to let that chain-gang get out of sight before I climbed the hill. You know I am not particularly tender; I've had to strike and to fend off. I've had to resist and to attack sometimes —that's only one way of resisting—without counting the exact cost, according to the demands of such sort of life as I had blundered into. I've seen the devil of violence, and the devil of greed, and the devil of hot desire; but, by all the stars! these were strong, lusty, red-eyed devils, that swayed and drove men—men, I tell you. But as I stood on this hillside, I foresaw that in the blinding sunshine of that land I would become acquainted with a flabby, pretending, weak-eyed devil of a rapacious and pitiless folly. How insidious he could be, too, I was only to find out several months later and a thousand miles farther. For a moment I stood appalled, as though by a warning. Finally I descended the hill, obliquely, towards the trees I had seen.

"I avoided a vast artificial hole somebody had been digging on the slope, the purpose of which I found it impossible to divine. It wasn't a quarry or a sandpit, anyhow. It was just a hole. It might have been connected with the philanthropic desire of giving the criminals something to do. I don't know. Then I nearly fell into a very narrow ravine, almost no more than a scar in the hillside. I discovered that a lot of imported drainage-pipes for the settlement had been tumbled in there. There wasn't one that was not broken. It was a wanton smash-up. At last I got under the trees. My purpose was to stroll into the shade for a moment; but no sooner within than it seemed to me I had stepped into a gloomy circle of some Inferno. The rapids were near, and an uninterrupted, uniform, headlong, rushing noise filled the mournful stillness of the grove, where not a breath stirred, not a leaf moved, with a mysterious sound—as though the tearing pace of the launched earth had suddenly become audible.

"Black shapes crouched, lay, sat between the trees, leaning against the trunks, clinging to the earth, half coming out, half effaced within the dim light, in all the attitudes of pain, abandonment, and despair. Another mine on the cliff went off, followed by a slight shudder of the soil under my feet. The work was going on. The work! And this was the place where some of the helpers had withdrawn to die.

"They were dying slowly—it was very clear. They were not enemies, they were not criminals, they were nothing earthly now,—nothing but black shadows of disease and starvation, lying confusedly in the greenish gloom. Brought from all the recesses of the coast in all the legality of time contracts, lost in uncongenial surroundings, fed on unfamiliar food, they sickened, became inefficient, and were then allowed to crawl away and rest. These moribund shapes were free as air—and nearly as thin. I began to distinguish the gleam of the eyes under the trees. Then, glancing down, I saw a face near my hand. The black bones reclined at full length with one shoulder against the tree, and slowly the eyelids rose and the sunken eyes looked up at me, enormous and vacant, a kind of blind, white flicker in the depths of the orbs, which died out slowly. The man seemed young—almost a boy—but you know with them it's hard to tell. I found nothing else to do but to offer him one of my good Swede's ship's biscuits I had in my pocket. The fingers closed slowly on it and held—there was no other movement and no other glance. He had tied a bit of white worsted round his neck—Why? Where did he get it? Was it a badge—an ornament—a charm—a propitiatory act? Was there any idea at all connected with it? It looked startling round his black neck, this bit of white thread from beyond the seas.

"Near the same tree two more bundles of acute angles sat with their legs drawn up. One, with his chin propped on his knees, stared at nothing, in an intolerable and appalling manner: his brother phantom rested its forehead, as if overcome with a great weariness; and all about others were scattered in every pose of contorted collapse, as in some picture of a massacre or a pestilence. While I stood horror-struck, one of these creatures rose to his hands and knees, and went off on all-fours towards the river to drink. He lapped out of his hand, then sat up in the sunlight, crossing his shins in front of him, and after a time let his woolly head fall on his breastbone.

"I didn't want any more loitering in the shade, and I made haste towards the station. When near the buildings I met a white man, in such an unexpected elegance of get-up that in the first moment I took him for a sort of vision. I saw a high starched collar, white cuffs, a light alpaca jacket, snowy trousers, a clean necktie, and varnished boots. No hat. Hair parted, brushed, oiled, under a green-lined parasol held in a big white hand. He was amazing, and had a penholder behind his ear.

"I shook hands with this miracle, and I learned he was the Company's chief accountant, and that all the bookkeeping was done at this station. He had come out for a moment, he said, 'to get a breath of fresh air.' The expression sounded wonderfully odd, with its suggestion of sedentary desk-life. I wouldn't have mentioned the fellow to you at all, only it was from his lips that I first heard the name of the man who is so indissolubly connected with the memories of that time. Moreover, I respected the fellow. Yes; I respected his collars, his vast cuffs, his brushed hair. His appearance was certainly that of a hairdresser's dummy; but in the great demoralization of the land he kept up his appearance. That's backbone. His starched collars and got-up shirtfronts were achievements of character. He had been out nearly three years; and, later on, I could not help asking him how he managed to sport such linen. He had just the faintest blush, and said modestly, 'I've been teaching one of the native women about the station. It was difficult. She had a distaste for the work.' Thus this man had verily accomplished something. And he was devoted to his books, which were in apple-pie order.

"Everything else in the station was in a muddle,—heads, things, buildings. Strings of dusty niggers with splay feet arrived and departed; a stream of manufactured goods, rubbishy cottons, beads, and brass-wire set into the depths of darkness, and in the return came a precious trickle of ivory.

"I had to wait in the station for ten days—an eternity. I lived in a hut in the yard, but to be out of the chaos I would sometimes get into the accountant's office. It was built of horizontal planks, and so badly put together that, as he bent over his desk, he was barred from neck to heels with narrow strips of sunlight. There was no need to open the big shutter to see. It was hot there too; big flies buzzed fiendishly, and did not sting, but stabbed. I sat generally on the floor, while, of faultless appearance (and even slightly scented), perching on a high stool, he wrote, he wrote. Sometimes he stood up for exercise. When a truckle-bed with a sick man (some invalided agent from up-country) was put in there, he exhibited a gentle annoyance. 'The groans of this sick person,' he said, 'distract my attention. And without that it is extremely difficult to guard against clerical errors in this climate.'

"One day he remarked, without lifting his head, 'In the interior you will no doubt meet Mr. Kurtz.' On my asking who Mr. Kurtz was, he said he was a first-class agent; and seeing my disappointment at this information, he added slowly, laying down his pen, 'He is a very remarkable person.' Further questions elicited from him that Mr. Kurtz was at present in charge of a trading post, a very important one, in the true ivory-country, at 'the very bottom of there. Sends in as much ivory as all the others put together. . . .' He began to write again. The sick man was too ill to groan. The flies buzzed in a great peace.

"Suddenly there was a growing murmur of voices and a great tramping of feet. A caravan had come in. A violent babble of uncouth sounds burst out on the other side of the planks. All the carriers were speaking together, and in the midst of the up-roar the lamentable voice of the chief agent was heard 'giving it up' tearfully for the twentieth time that day. . . . He rose slowly. 'What a frightful row,' he said. He crossed the room gently to look at the sick man, and returning, said to me, 'He does not hear.' 'What! Dead?' I asked, startled. 'No, not yet,' he answered, with great composure. Then, alluding with a toss of the head to the tumult in the station-yard, 'When one has got to make correct entries, one comes to hate those savages—hate them to the death.' He remained thoughtful for a moment. 'When you see Mr. Kurtz,' he went on, 'tell him from me that every-thing here'—he glanced at the desk—'is very satisfactory. I don't like to write to him—with those messengers of ours you never know who may get hold of your letter—at that Central Station.' He stared at me for a moment with his mild, bulging eyes. 'Oh, he will go far, very far,' he began again. 'He will be a somebody in the Administration before long. They, above—the Council in Europe, you know—mean him to be.'

"He turned to his work. The noise outside had ceased, and presently in going out I stopped at the door. In the steady buzz of flies the homeward-bound agent was lying flushed and insensible; the other, bent over his books, was making correct entries of perfectly correct transactions; and fifty feet below the doorstep I could see the still tree-tops of the grove of death.

"Next day I left that station at last, with a caravan of sixty men, for a two-hundred-mile tramp.

"No use telling you much about that. Paths, paths, everywhere; a stamped-in network of paths spreading over the empty land, through long grass, through burnt grass, through thickets, down and up chilly ravines, up and down stony hills ablaze with heat; and a solitude, nobody, not a hut. The population had cleared out a long time ago. Well, if a lot of mysterious niggers armed with all kinds of fearful weapons suddenly took to traveling on the road between Deal and Gravesend, catching the yokels right and left to carry heavy loads for them, I fancy every farm and cottage thereabouts would get empty very soon. Only here the dwellings were gone too. Still I passed through several abandoned villages. There's something pathetically childish in the ruins of grass walls. Day after day, with the stamp and shuffle of sixty pair of bare feet behind me, each pair under a 60-lb. load. Camp, cook, sleep, strike camp, march. Now and then a carrier dead in harness, at rest in the long grass near the path, with an empty water-gourd and his long staff lying by his side. A great silence around and above. Perhaps on some quiet night the tremor of far-off drums, sinking, swelling, a tremor vast, faint; a sound weird, appealing, suggestive, and wild—and perhaps with as profound a meaning as the sound of bells in a Christian country. Once a white man in an unbuttoned uniform, camping on the path with an armed escort of lank Zanzibaris, very hospitable and festive—not to say drunk. Was looking after the upkeep of the road, he declared. Can't say I saw any road or any upkeep, unless the body of a middle-aged negro, with a bullet-hole in the forehead, upon which I absolutely stumbled three miles farther on, may be considered as a permanent improvement. I had a white companion too, not a bad chap, but rather too fleshy and with the exasperating habit of fainting on the hot hillsides, miles away from the least bit of shade and water. Annoying, you know, to hold your own coat like a parasol over a man's head while he is coming-to. I couldn't help asking him once what he meant by coming there at all. 'To make money, of course. What do you think?' he said, scornfully. Then he got fever, and had to be carried in a hammock slung under a pole. As he weighed sixteen stone I had no end of rows with the carriers. They jibbed, ran away, sneaked off with their loads in the night—quite a mutiny. So, one evening, I made a speech in English with gestures, not one of which was lost to the sixty pairs of eyes before me, and the next morning I started the hammock off in front all right. An hour afterwards I came upon the whole concern wrecked in a bush—man, hammock, groans, blankets, horrors. The heavy pole had skinned his poor nose. He was very anxious for me to kill somebody, but there wasn't the shadow of a carrier near. I remembered the old doctor,—'It would be interesting for science to watch the mental changes of individuals, on the spot.' I felt I was becoming scientifically interesting. However, all that is to no purpose. On the fifteenth day I came in sight of the big river again, and hobbled into the Central Station. It was on a back water surrounded by scrub and forest, with a pretty border of smelly mud on one side, and on the three others inclosed by a crazy fence of rushes. A neglected gap was all the gate it had, and the first glance at the place was enough to let you see the flabby devil was running that show. White men with long staves in their hands appeared languidly from amongst the buildings, strolling up to take a look at me, and then retired out of sight somewhere. One of them, a stout, excitable chap with black mustaches, informed me with great volubility and many digressions, as soon as I told him who I was, that my steamer was at the bottom of the river. I was thunderstruck. What, how, why? Oh, it was 'all right.' The 'manager himself' was there. All quite correct. 'Everybody had behaved splendidly! splendidly!'—'you must,' he said in agitation, 'go and see the general manager at once. He is waiting!'

"I did not see the real significance of that wreck at once. I fancy I see it now, but I am not sure—not at all. Certainly the affair was too stupid—when I think of it—to be altogether natural. Still. . . . But at the moment it presented itself simply as a confounded nuisance. The steamer was sunk. They had started two days before in a sudden hurry up the river with the manager on board, in charge of some volunteer skipper, and before they had been out three hours they tore the bottom out of her on stones, and she sank near the south bank. I asked myself what I was to do there, now my boat was lost. As a matter of fact, I had plenty to do in fishing my command out of the river. I had to set about it the very next day. That, and the repairs when I brought the pieces to the station, took some months.

"My first interview with the manager was curious. He did not ask me to sit down after my twenty-mile walk that morning. He was commonplace in complexion, in feature, in manners, and in voice. He was of middle size and of ordinary build. His eyes, of the usual blue, were perhaps remarkably cold, and he certainly could make his glance fall on one as trenchant and heavy as an ax. But even at these times the rest of his person seemed to disclaim the intention. Otherwise there was only an indefinable, faint expression of his lips, something stealthy—a smile—not a smile—I remember it, but I can't explain. It was unconscious, this smile was, though just after he had said something it got intensified for an instant. It came at the end of his speeches like a seal applied on the words to make the meaning of the commonest phrase appear absolutely inscrutable. He was a common trader, from his youth up employed in these parts—nothing more. He was obeyed, yet he inspired neither love nor fear, nor even respect. He inspired uneasiness. That was it! Uneasiness. Not a definite mistrust—just uneasiness—nothing more. You have no idea how effective such a . . . a . . . faculty can be.

He had no genius for organizing, for initiative, or for order even. That was evident in such things as the deplorable state of the station. He had no learning, and no intelligence. His position had come to him—why? Perhaps because he was never ill . . . He had served three terms of three years out there . . . Because triumphant health in the general rout of constitutions is a kind of power in itself. When he went home on leave he rioted on a large scale—pompously. Jack ashore—with a difference—in externals only. This one could gather from his casual talk. He originated nothing, he could keep the routine going—that's all. But he was great. He was great by this little thing that it was impossible to tell what could control such a man. He never gave that secret away. Perhaps there was nothing within him. Such a suspicion made one pause—for out there there were no external checks. Once when various tropical diseases had laid low almost every 'agent' in the station, he was heard to say, 'Men who come out here should have no entrails.' He sealed the utterance with that smile of his, as though it had been a door opening into a darkness he had in his keeping. You fancied you had seen things—but the seal was on. When annoyed at meal-times by the constant quarrels of the white men about precedence, he ordered an immense round table to be made, for which a special house had to be built. This was the station's mess-room. Where he sat was the first place—the rest were nowhere. One felt this to be his unalterable conviction. He was neither civil nor uncivil. He was quiet. He allowed his 'boy' —an overfed young negro from the coast—to treat the white men, under his very eyes, with provoking insolence.

"He began to speak as soon as he saw me. I had been very long on the road. He could not wait. Had to start without me. The up-river stations had to be relieved. There had been so many delays already that he did not know who was dead and who was alive, and how they got on—and so on, and so on. He paid no attention to my explanations, and, playing with a stick of sealing-wax, repeated several times that the situation was 'very grave, very grave.' There were rumors that a very important station was in jeopardy, and its chief, Mr. Kurtz, was ill. Hoped it was not true. Mr. Kurtz was . . . I felt weary and irritable. Hang Kurtz, I thought. I interrupted him by saying I had heard of Mr. Kurtz on the coast. 'Ah! So they talk of him down there,' he murmured to himself. Then he began again, assuring me Mr. Kurtz was the best agent he had, an exceptional man, of the greatest importance to the Company; therefore I could understand his anxiety. He was, he said, 'very, very uneasy.' Certainly he fidgeted on his chair a good deal, exclaimed, 'Ah, Mr. Kurtz!' broke the stick of sealing-wax and seemed dumbfounded by the accident. Next thing he wanted to know 'how long it would take to' . . . I interrupted him again. Being hungry, you know, and kept on my feet too, I was getting savage. 'How could I tell,' I said. 'I hadn't even seen the wreck yet—some months, no doubt! All this talk seemed to me so futile. 'Some months,' he said. 'Well, let us say three months before we can make a start. Yes. That ought to do the affair.' I flung out of his hut (he lived all alone in a clay hut with a sort of veranda) muttering to myself my opinion of him. He was a chattering idiot. Afterwards I took it back when it was borne in upon me startlingly with what extreme nicety he had estimated the time requisite for the 'affair.'

"I went to work the next day, turning, so to speak, my back on that station. In that way only it seemed to me I could keep my hold on the redeeming facts of life. Still, one must look about sometimes; and then I saw this station, these men strolling aimlessly about in the sunshine of the yard. I asked myself sometimes what it all meant. They wandered here and there with their absurd long staves in their hands, like a lot of faithless pilgrims bewitched inside a rotten fence. The word 'ivory' rang in the air, was whispered, was sighed. You would think they were praying to it. A taint of imbecile rapacity blew through it all, like a whiff from some corpse. By Jove! I've never seen anything so unreal in my life. And outside, the silent wilderness surrounding this cleared speck on the earth struck me as something great and invincible, like evil or truth, waiting patiently for the passing away of this fantastic invasion.

"Oh, these months! Well, never mind. Various things happened. One evening a grass shed full of calico, cotton prints, beads, and I don't know what else, burst into a blaze so suddenly that you would have thought the earth had opened to let an avenging fire consume all that trash. I was smoking my pipe quietly by my dismantled steamer, and saw them all cutting capers in the light, with their arms lifted high, when the stout man with mustaches came tearing down to the river, a tin pail in his hand, assured me that everybody was 'behaving splendidly, splendidly,' dipped about a quart of water and tore back again. I noticed there was a hole in the bottom of his pail.

"I strolled up. There was no hurry. You see the thing had gone off like a box of matches. It had been hopeless from the very first. The flame had leaped high, driven everybody back, lighted up everything—and collapsed. The shed was already a heap of embers glowing fiercely. A nigger was being beaten near by. They said he had caused the fire in some way; be that as it may, he was screeching most horribly. I saw him, later on, for several days, sitting in a bit of shade looking very sick and trying to recover himself: afterwards he arose and went out—and the wilderness without a sound took him into its bosom again. As I approached the glow from the dark I found myself at the back of two men, talking. I heard the name of Kurtz pronounced, then the words, 'take advantage of this unfortunate accident.' One of the men was the manager. I wished him a good evening. 'Did you ever see anything like it—eh? it is incredible,' he said, and walked off. The other man remained. He was a first-class agent, young, gentlemanly, a bit reserved, with a forked little beard and a hooked nose. He was stand-offish with the other agents, and they on their side said he was the manager's spy upon them. As to me, I had hardly ever spoken to him before. We got into talk, and by-and-by we strolled away from the hissing ruins. Then he asked me to his room, which was in the main building of the station. He struck a match, and I perceived that this young aristocrat had not only a silver-mounted dressing-case but also a whole candle all to himself. Just at that time the manager was the only man supposed to have any right to candles. Native mats covered the clay walls; a collection of spears, assegais, shields, knives was hung up in trophies. The business intrusted to this fellow was the making of bricks—so I had been informed; but there wasn't a fragment of a brick anywhere in the station, and he had been there more than a year—waiting. It seems he could not make bricks without something, I don't know what—straw maybe. Anyways, it could not be found there, and as it was not likely to be sent from Europe, it did not appear clear to me what he was waiting for. An act of special creation perhaps. However, they were all waiting—all the sixteen or twenty pilgrims of them—for something; and upon my word it did not seem an uncongenial occupation, from the way they took it, though the only thing that ever came to them was disease—as far as I could see. They beguiled the time by backbiting and intriguing against each other in a foolish kind of way. There was an air of plotting about that station, but nothing came of it, of course. It was as unreal as everything else—as the philanthropic pretense of the whole concern, as their talk, as their government, as their show of work. The only real feeling was a desire to get appointed to a trading-post where ivory was to be had, so that they could earn percentages. They intrigued and slandered and hated each other only on that account,—but as to effectually lifting a little finger—oh, no. By heavens! there is something after all in the world allowing one man to steal a horse while another must not look at a halter. Steal a horse straight out. Very well. He has done it. Perhaps he can ride. But there is a way of looking at a halter that would provoke the most charitable of saints into a kick.

"I had no idea why he wanted to be sociable, but as we chatted in there it suddenly occurred to me the fellow was trying to get at something—in fact, pumping me. He alluded constantly to Europe, to the people I was supposed to know there—

putting leading questions as to my acquaintances in the sepulchral city, and so on. His little eyes glittered like mica discs—
with curiosity,—though he tried to keep up a bit of supercilious-
ness. At first I was astonished, but very soon I became awfully
curious to see what he would find out from me. I couldn't possibly imagine what I had in me to make it worth his while.
It was very pretty to see how he baffled himself, for in truth my
body was full of chills, and my head had nothing in it but that
wretched steamboat business. It was evident he took me for a
perfectly shameless prevaricator. At last he got angry, and, to
conceal a movement of furious annoyance, he yawned. I rose.
Then I noticed a small sketch in oils, on a panel, representing
a woman, draped and blindfolded, carrying a lighted torch. The
background was somber—almost black. The movement of the
woman was stately, and the effect of the torchlight on the face
was sinister.

"It arrested me, and he stood by civilly, holding an empty
half-pint champagne bottle (medical comforts) with the candle
stuck in it. To my question he said Mr. Kurtz had painted this
—in this very station more than a year ago—while waiting for
means to go to his trading-post. 'Tell me, pray,' said I, 'who is
this Mr. Kurtz?'

" 'The chief of the Inner Station,' he answered in a short tone,
looking away, 'Much obliged,' I said, laughing. 'And you are
the brickmaker of the Central Station. Everyone knows that.'
He was silent for a while. 'He is a prodigy,' he said at last. 'He
is an emissary of pity, and science, and progress, and devil knows
what else. We want,' he began to declaim suddenly, 'for the
guidance of the cause intrusted to us by Europe, so to speak,
higher intelligence, wide sympathies, a singleness of purpose.'
'Who says that?' I asked. 'Lots of them,' he replied. 'Some even
write that; and so *he* comes here, a special being, as you ought
to know.' 'Why ought I to know?' I interrupted, really surprised.
He paid no attention. 'Yes. To-day he is chief of the best
station, next year he will be assistant-manager, two years more
and . . . but I dare say you know what he will be in two years'

time. You are of the new gang—the gang of virtue. The same people who sent him specially also recommended you. Oh, don't say no. I've my own eyes to trust.' Light dawned upon me. My dear aunt's influential acquaintances were producing an unexpected effect upon that young man. I nearly burst into a laugh. 'Do you read the Company's confidential correspondence?' I asked. He hadn't a word to say. It was great fun. 'When Mr. Kurtz,' I continued severely, 'is General Manager, you won't have the opportunity.'

"He blew the candle out suddenly, and we went outside. The moon had risen. Black figures strolled about listlessly, pouring water on the glow, whence proceeded a sound of hissing; steam ascended in the moonlight, the beaten nigger groaned somewhere. 'What a row the brute makes!' said the indefatigable man with the mustaches, appearing near us. 'Serve him right. Transgression—punishment—bang! Pitiless, pitiless. That's the only way. This will prevent all conflagration for the future. I was just telling the manager . . .' He noticed my companion, and became crestfallen all at once. 'Not in bed yet,' he said, with a kind of servile heartiness; 'it's so natural. Ha! Danger-agitation.' He vanished. I went on to the river-side, and the other followed me. I heard a scathing murmur at my ear, 'Heap of muffs—go to.' The pilgrims could be seen in knots gesticulating, discussing. Several had still their staves in their hands. I verily believe they took these sticks to bed with them. Beyond the fence the forest stood up spectrally in the moonlight, and through the dim stir, through the faint sounds of that lamentable courtyard, the silence of the land went home to one's very heart,—its mystery, its greatness, the amazing reality of its concealed life. The hurt nigger moaned feebly somewhere near by, and then fetched a deep sigh that made me mend my pace away from there. I felt a hand introducing itself under my arm. 'My dear sir,' said the fellow, 'I don't want to be misunderstood, and especially by you, who will see Mr. Kurtz long before I can have that pleasure. I wouldn't like him to get a false idea of my disposition. . . .'

"I let him run on, this papier-maché Mephistopheles, and it

seemed to me that if I tried I could poke my forefinger through him, and would find nothing inside but a little loose dirt, maybe. He, don't you see, had been planning to be assistant-manager by-and-by under the present man, and I could see that the coming of that Kurtz had upset them both not a little. He talked precipitately, and I did not try to stop him. I had my shoulders against the wreck of my steamer, hauled up on the slope like a carcass of some big river animal. The smell of mud, of primeval mud, by Jove! was in my nostrils, the high stillness of primeval forest was before my eyes; there were shiny patches on the black creek. The moon had spread over everything a thin layer of silver—over the rank grass, over the mud, upon the wall of matted vegetation standing higher than the wall of a temple, over the great river I could see through a somber gap glittering, glittering, as it flowed broadly by without a murmur. All this was great, expectant, mute, while the man jabbered about himself. I wondered whether the stillness on the face of the immensity looking at us two were meant as an appeal or as a menace. What were we who had strayed in here? Could we handle that dumb thing, or would it handle us? I felt how big, how confoundedly big, was that thing that couldn't talk, and perhaps was deaf as well. What was in there? I could see a little ivory coming out from there, and I had heard Mr. Kurtz was in there. I had heard enough about it too—God knows! Yet somehow it didn't bring any image with it—no more than if I had been told an angel or a fiend was in there. I believed it in the same way one of you might believe there are inhabitants in the planet Mars. I knew once a Scotch sailmaker who was certain, dead sure, there were people in Mars. If you aked him for some idea how they looked and behaved, he would get shy and mutter something about 'walking on all-fours.' If you as much as smiled, he would—though a man of sixty—offer to fight you. I would not have gone so far as to fight for Kurtz, but I went for him near enough to a lie. You know I hate, detest, and can't bear a lie, not because I am straighter than the rest of us, but simply because it appalls me. There is a taint of death, a flavor of mortality in lies,—which is exactly what I hate and detest in the world—what I want to forget. It makes me miserable and sick, like biting something rotten would do. Temperament, I suppose. Well, I went near enough to it by letting the young fool there believe anything he liked to imagine as to my influence in Europe. I became in an instant as much of a pretense as the rest of the bewitched pilgrims. This simply because I had a notion it somehow would be of help to that Kurtz whom at the time I did not see—you understand. He was just a word for me. I did not see the man in the name any more than you do. Do you see him? Do you see the story? Do you see anything? It seems to me I am trying to tell you a dream—making a vain attempt, because no relation of a dream can convey the dream-sensation, that commingling of absurdity, surprise, and bewilderment in a tremor of struggling revolt, that notion of being captured by the incredible which is of the very essence of dreams. . . ."

He was silent for a while.

". . . No, it is impossible; it is impossible to convey the life-sensation of any given epoch of one's existence,—that which makes its truth, its meaning—its subtle and penetrating essence. It is impossible. We live, as we dream—alone. . . ."

He paused again as if reflecting, then added—

"Of course in this you fellows see more than I could then. You see me, whom you know. . . ."

It had become so pitch dark that we listeners could hardly see one another. For a long time already he, sitting apart, had been no more to us than a voice. There was not a word from anybody. The others might have been asleep, but I was awake. I listened, I listened on the watch for the sentence, for the word, that would give me the clew to the faint uneasiness inspired by this narrative that seemed to shape itself without human lips in the heavy night-air of the river.

". . . Yes—I let him run on," Marlow began again, "and think what he pleased about the powers that were behind me. I did! And there was nothing behind me! There was nothing but that wretched, old, mangled steamboat I was leaning against, while he talked fluently about 'the necessity for every man to get on.' 'And when one comes out here, you conceive, it is not to gaze at the moon.' Mr. Kurtz was a 'universal genius,' but even a genius would find it easier to work with 'adequate tools—intelligent men.' He did not make bricks—why, there was a physical impossibility in the way—as I was well aware; and if he did secretarial work for the manager, it was because 'no sensible man rejects wantonly the confidence of his superiors.' Did I see it? I saw it. What more did I want? What I really wanted was rivets, by heaven! Rivets. To get on with the work—to stop the hole. Rivets I wanted. There were cases of them down at the coast—cases—piled up—burst—split! You kicked a loose rivet at every second step in that station yard on the hillside. Rivets had rolled into the grove of death. You could fill your pockets with rivets for the trouble of stooping down—and there wasn't one rivet to be found where it was wanted. We had plates that would do, but nothing to fasten them with. And every week the messenger, a lone negro, letter-bag on shoulder and staff in hand, left our station for the coast. And several times a week a coast caravan came in with trade goods,—ghastly glazed calico that made you shudder only to look at it, glass beads value about a penny a quart, confounded spotted cotton handkerchiefs. And no rivets. Three carriers could have brought all that was wanted to set that steamboat afloat.

"He was becoming confidential now, but I fancy my unresponsive attitude must have exasperated him at last, for he judged it necessary to inform me he feared neither God nor devil, let alone any mere man. I said I could see that very well, but what I wanted was a certain quantity of rivets—and rivets were what really Mr. Kurtz wanted. if he had only known it. Now letters went to the coast every week. . . . 'My dear sir,' he cried, 'I write from dictation.' I demanded rivets. There was a way—for an intelligent man. He changed his manner; became very cold, and suddenly began to talk about a hippopotamus; wondered whether sleeping on board the steamer (I stuck to my salvage night and day) I wasn't disturbed. There was an old hippo that had the bad habit of getting out on the bank and roaming at night over the station grounds. The pilgrims use to turn out in a body and empty every rifle they could lay hands on at him. Some even had sat up o' nights for him. All this energy was wasted, though. 'That animal has a charmed life,' he said; 'but you can say this only of brutes in this country. No man—you apprehend me?—no man here bears a charmed life.' He stood there for a moment in the moonlight with his delicate hooked nose set a little askew, and his mica eyes glittering without a wink, then, with a curt Good night, he strode off. I could see he was disturbed and considerably puzzled, which made me feel more hopeful than I had been for days. It was a great comfort to turn from that chap to my influential friend, the battered, twisted, ruined, tin-pot steamboat. I clambered on board. She rang under my feet like an empty Huntley & Palmer biscuit-tin kicked along a gutter; she was nothing so solid in make, and rather less pretty in shape, but I had expended enough hard work on her to make me love her. No influential friend would have served me better. She had given me a chance to come out a bit—to find out what I could do. No, I don't like work. I had rather laze about and think of all the fine things that can be done. I don't like work—no man does—but I like what is in the work,—the chance to find yourself. Your own reality—for yourself, not for others—what no other man can ever know. They can only see the mere show, and never can tell what it really means.

"I was not surprised to see somebody sitting aft, on the deck, with his legs dangling over the mud. You see I rather chummed with the few mechanics there were in that station, whom the other pilgrims naturally despised—on account of their imperfect manners, I suppose. This was the foreman—a boiler-maker by trade—a good worker. He was a lank, bony, yellow-faced man, with big intense eyes. His aspect was worried, and his head was as bald as the palm of my hand; but his hair in falling seemed to have stuck to his chin, and had prospered in the new locality, for his beard hung down to his waist. He was a widower with

Joseph Conrad on the bridge of the liner *Tuscania*, with his friend
Captain Bone, as they approached New York on his first and only
visit to the United States in 1923, the year before his death

six young children (he had left them in charge of a sister of his
to come out there), and the passion of his life was pigeon-flying.
He was an enthusiast and a connoisseur. He would rave about
pigeons. After work hours he used sometimes to come over from
his hut for a talk about his children and his pigeons; at work,
when he had to crawl in the mud under the bottom of the steamboat, he would tie up that beard of his in a kind of white
serviette he brought for the purpose. It had loops to go over his
ears. In the evening he could be seen squatted on the bank
rinsing that wrapper in the creek with great care, then spreading
it solemnly on a bush to dry.

"I slapped him on the back and shouted 'We shall have rivets!'
He scrambled to his feet exclaiming 'No! Rivets!' as though he
couldn't believe his ears. Then in a low voice, 'You . . . eh?' I
don't know why we behaved like lunatics. I put my finger to the
side of my nose and nodded mysteriously. 'Good for you!' he
cried, snapped his fingers above his head, lifting one foot. I tried
a jig. We capered on the iron deck. A frightful clatter came out
of that hulk, and the virgin forest on the other bank of the
creek sent it back in a thundering roll upon the sleeping station.
It must have made some of the pilgrims sit up in their hovels. A
dark figure obscured the lighted doorway of the manager's hut,
vanished, then, a second or so after, the doorway itself vanished
too. We stopped, and the silence driven away by the stamping
of our feet flowed back again from the recesses of the land. The
great wall of vegetation, an exuberant and entangled mass of
trunks, branches, leaves, boughs, festoons, motionless in the
moonlight, was like a rioting invasion of soundless life, a rolling
wave of plants piled up, crested, ready to topple over the creek,
to sweep every little man of us out of his little existence. And it
moved not. A deadened burst of mighty splashes and snorts
reached us from afar, as though an ichthyosaurus had been
taking a bath of glitter in that great river. 'After all,' said the
boiler-maker in a reasonable tone, 'why shouldn't we get the
rivets?' Why not, indeed! I did not know of any reason why we
shouldn't. 'They'll come in three weeks,' I said, confidently.

"But they didn't. Instead of rivets there came an invasion, an infliction, a visitation. It came in sections during the next three weeks, each section headed by a donkey carrying a white man in new clothes and tan shoes, bowing from that elevation right and left to the impressed pilgrims. A quarrelsome band of footsore sulky niggers trod on the heels of the donkey; a lot of tents, camp-stools, tin boxes, white cases, brown bales would be shot down in the courtyard, and the air of mystery would deepen a little over the muddle of the station. Five such installments came, with their absurd air of disorderly flight with the loot of innumerable outfit shops and provision stores, that, one would think, they were lugging, after a raid, into the wilderness for equitable division. It was an inextricable mess of things decent in themselves but that human folly made look like the spoils of thieving.

"This devoted band called itself the Eldorado Exploring Expedition, and I believe they were sworn to secrecy. Their talk, however, was the talk of sordid buccaneers: it was reckless without hardihood, greedy without audacity, and cruel without courage; there was not an atom of foresight or of serious intention in the whole batch of them, and they did not seem aware these things are wanted for the work of the world. To tear treasure out of the bowels of the land was their desire, with no more moral purpose at the back of it than there is in burglars breaking into a safe. Who paid the expenses of the noble enterprise I don't know; but the uncle of our manager was leader of that lot.

"In exterior he resembled a butcher in a poor neighborhood, and his eyes had a look of sleepy cunning. He carried his fat paunch with ostentation on his short legs, and during the time his gang infested the station spoke to no one but his nephew. You could see these two roaming about all day long with their heads close together in an everlasting confab.

"I had given up worrying myself about the rivets. One's capacity for that kind of folly is more limited than you would suppose. I said Hang!—and let things slide. I had plenty of time for meditation, and now and then I would give some thought to Kurtz. I wasn't very interested in him. No. Still, I was curious to see whether this man, who had come out equipped with moral ideas of some sort, would climb to the top after all, and how he would set about his work when there."

II

"ONE evening as I was lying flat on the deck of my steamboat, I heard voices approaching—and there were the nephew and the uncle strolling along the bank. I laid my head on my arm again, and had nearly lost myself in a doze, when somebody said in my ear, as it were: 'I am as harmless as a little child, but I don't like to be dictated to. Am I the manager—or am I not? I was ordered to send him there. It's incredible.' . . . I became aware that the two were standing on the shore alongside the forepart of the steamboat, just below my head. I did not move; it did not occur to me to move: I was sleepy. 'It *is* unpleasant,' grunted the uncle. 'He has asked the Administration to be sent there,' said the other, 'with the idea of showing what he could do; and I was instructed accordingly. Look at the influence that man must have. Is it not frightful?' They both agreed it was frightful, then made several bizarre remarks: 'Make rain and fine weather—one man—the Council—by the nose'—bits of absurd sentences that got the better of my drowsiness, so that I had pretty near the whole of my wits about me when the uncle said, 'The climate may do away with this difficulty for you. Is he alone there?' 'Yes,' answered the manager; 'he sent his assistant down the river with a note to me in these terms: "Clear this poor devil out of the country, and don't bother sending more of that sort. I had rather be alone than have the kind of men you can dispose of with me." It was more than a year ago. Can you imagine such impudence!' 'Anything since then?' asked the other, hoarsely. 'Ivory,' jerked the nephew; 'lots of it—prime sort—lots—most annoying, from him.' 'And with that?' questioned the heavy rumble. 'Invoice,' was the reply fired out, so to speak. Then silence. They had been talking about Kurtz.

"I was broad awake by this time, but, lying perfectly at ease, remained still, having no inducement to change my position. 'How did that ivory come all this way?' growled the elder man, who seemed very vexed. The other explained that it had come with a fleet of canoes in charge of an English half-caste clerk Kurtz had with him; that Kurtz had apparently intended to return himself, the station being by that time bare of goods and stores, but after coming three hundred miles, had suddenly decided to go back, which he started to do alone in a small dug-out with four paddlers, leaving the half-caste to continue down the river with the ivory. The two fellows there seemed astounded at anybody attempting such a thing. They were at a loss for an adequate motive. As to me, I seemed to see Kurtz for the first time. It was a distinct glimpse: the dug-out, four paddling savages, and the lone white man turning his back suddenly on the headquarters, on relief, on thoughts of home—perhaps; setting his face towards the depths of the wilderness, towards his empty and desolate station. I did not know the motive. Perhaps he was just simply a fine fellow who stuck to his work for its own sake. His name, you understand, had not been pronounced once. He was 'that man.' The half-caste, who, as far as I could see, had conducted a difficult trip with great prudence and pluck, was invariably alluded to as 'that scoundrel.' The 'scoundrel' had reported that the 'man' had been very ill—had recovered imperfectly. . . . The two below me moved away then a few paces, and strolled back and forth at some little distance. I heard: 'Military post—doctor—two hundred miles—quite alone now—unavoidable delays—nine months—no news—strange rumors.' They approached again, just as the manager was saying, 'No one, as far as I know, unless a species of wandering trader—a pestilential fellow, snapping ivory from the natives.' Who was it they were talking about now? I gathered in snatches that this was some man supposed to be in Kurtz's district, and of whom the manager did not approve. 'We will not be free from unfair

competition till one of these fellows is hanged for an example,'
he said. 'Certainly,' grunted the other; 'get him hanged! Why
not? Anything—anything can be done in this country. That's
what I say; nobody here, you understand, *here,* can endanger
your position. And why? You stand the climate—you outlast
them all. The danger is in Europe; but there before I left I
took care to——' They moved off and whispered, then their
voices rose again. 'The extraordinary series of delays is not my
fault. I did my possible.' The fat man sighed, 'Very sad.' 'And
the pestiferous absurdity of his talk,' continued the other; 'he
bothered me enough when he was here. "Each station should
be like a beacon on the road towards better things, a center for
trade of course, but also for humanizing, improving, instruct-
ing." Conceive you—that ass! And he wants to be manager! No,
it's——' Here he got choked by excessive indignation, and I lifted
my head the beast bit. I was surprised to see how near they
were—right under me. I could have spat upon their hats. They
were looking on the ground, absorbed in thought. The manager
was switching his leg with a slender twig: his sagacious relative
lifted his head. 'You have been well since you came out this
time?' he asked. The other gave a start. 'Who? I? Oh! Like a
charm—like a charm. But the rest—oh, my goodness! All sick.
They die so quick, too, that I haven't the time to send them
out of the country—it's incredible!' 'H'm. Just so,' grunted the
uncle. 'Ah! my boy, trust to this—I say, trust to this.' I saw him
extend his short flipper of an arm for a gesture that took in the
forest, the creek, the mud, the river,—seemed to beckon with a
dishonoring flourish before the sunlit face of the land a treacherous appeal to the lurking death, to the hidden evil, to the profound darkness of its heart. It was so startling that I leaped to
my feet and looked back at the edge of the forest, as though I
had expected an answer of some sort to that black display of
confidence. You know the foolish notions that come to one sometimes. The high stillness confronted these two figures with its
ominous patience, waiting for the passing away of a fantastic
invasion.

"They swore aloud together—out of sheer fright, I believe—then pretending not to know anything of my existence, turned back to the station. The sun was low; and leaning forward side by side, they seemed to be tugging painfully uphill their two ridiculous shadows of unequal length, that trailed behind them slowly over the tall grass without bending a single blade.

"In a few days the Eldorado Expedition went into the patient wilderness, that closed upon it as the sea closes over a diver. Long afterwards the news came that all the donkeys were dead. I know nothing as to the fate of the less valuable animals. They, no doubt, like the rest of us, found what they deserved. I did not inquire. I was then rather excited at the prospect of meeting Kurtz very soon. When I say very soon I mean it comparatively. It was just two months from the day we left the creek when we came to the bank below Kurtz's station.

"Going up that river was like traveling back to the earliest beginnings of the world, when vegetation rioted on the earth and the big trees were kings. An empty stream, a great silence, and impenetrable forest. The air was warm, thick, heavy, sluggish. There was no joy in the brilliance of sunshine. The long stretches of the waterway ran on, deserted, into the gloom of over-shadowed distances. On silvery sandbanks hippos and alligators sunned themselves side by side. The broadening waters flowed through a mob of wooded islands; you lost your way on that river as you would in a desert, and butted all day long against shoals, trying to find the channel, till you thought yourself bewitched and cut off for ever from everything you had known once—somewhere—far away—in another existence perhaps. There were moments when one's past came back to one, as it will sometimes when you have not a moment to spare to yourself; but it came in the shape of an unrestful and noisy dream, remembered with wonder amongst the overwhelming realities of this strange world of plants, and water, and silence. And this stillness of life did not in the least resemble a peace. It was the stillness of an implacable force brooding over an inscrutable intention. It looked at you with a vengeful aspect. I got used to it afterwards; I did not see it any more; I had no time. I had to keep guessing at the channel; I had to discern, mostly by inspiration, the signs of hidden banks; I watched for sunken stones; I was learning to clap my teeth smartly before my heart flew out, when I shaved by a fluke some infernal sly old snag that would have ripped the life out of the tin-pot steamboat and drowned all the pilgrims; I had to keep a look-out for the signs of dead wood we could cut up in the night for next day's steaming. When you have to attend to things of that sort, to the mere incidents of the surface, the reality—the reality, I tell you—fades. The inner truth is hidden—luckily, luckily. But I felt it all the same; I felt often its mysterious stillness watching me at my monkey tricks, just as it watches you fellows performing on your respective tight-ropes for—what is it? half-a-crown a tumble——"

"Try to be civil, Marlow," growled a voice, and I knew there was at least one listener awake besides myself.

"I beg your pardon. I forgot the heartache which makes up the rest of the price. And indeed what does the price matter, if the trick be well done? You do your tricks very well. And I didn't do badly either, since I managed not to sink that steamboat on my first trip. It's a wonder to me yet. Imagine a blindfolded man set to drive a van over a bad road. I sweated and shivered over that business considerably, I can tell you. After all, for a seaman, to scrape the bottom of the thing that's supposed to float all the time under his care is the unpardonable sin. No one may know of it, but you never forget the thump—eh? A blow on the very heart. You remember it, you dream of it, you wake up at night and think of it—years after—and go hot and cold all over. I don't pretend to say that steamboat floated all the time. More than once she had to wade for a bit, with twenty cannibals splashing around and pushing. We had enlisted some of these chaps on the way for a crew. Fine fellows—cannibals—in their place. They were men one could work with, and I am grateful to them. And, after all, they did not eat each other before my face: they had brought along a provision of hippo-meat which went rotten, and made the mystery of the wilderness stink in my nostrils. Phoo! I can sniff it now. I had the manager on board and three or four pilgrims with their staves—all complete. Sometimes we came upon a station close by the bank, clinging to the skirts of the unknown, and the white men rushing out of a tumble-down hovel, with great gestures of joy and surprise and welcome, seemed very strange,—had the appearance of being held there captive by a spell. The word ivory would ring in the air for a while—and on we went again into the silence, along empty reaches, round the still bends, between the high walls of our winding way, reverberating in hollow claps the ponderous beat of the stern-wheel. Trees, trees, millions of trees, massive, immense, running up high; and at their foot, hugging the bank against the stream, crept the little begrimed steamboat, like a sluggish beetle crawling on the floor of a lofty portico. It made you feel very small, very lost, and yet it was not altogether depressing that feeling. After all, if you were small, the grimy beetle crawled on—which was just what you wanted it to do. Where the pilgrims imagined it crawled to I don't know. To some place where they expected to get something, I bet! For me it crawled toward Kurtz—exclusively; but when the steam-pipes started leaking we crawled very slow. The reaches opened before us and closed behind, as if the forest had stepped leisurely across the water to bar the way for our return. We penetrated deeper and deeper into the heart of darkness. It was very quiet there. At night sometimes the roll of drums behind the curtain of trees would run up the river and remain sustained faintly, as if hovering in the air high over our heads, till the first break of day. Whether it meant war, peace, or prayer we could not tell. The dawns were heralded by the descent of a chill stillness; the wood-cutters slept, their fires burned low; the snapping of a twig would make you start. We were wanderers on a prehistoric earth, on an earth that wore the aspect of an unknown planet. We could have fancied ourselves the first of men taking possession of an accursed inheritance, to be subdued at the cost of profound anguish and of excessive toil. But suddenly, as we struggled round a bend, there would be a glimpse of rush walls, of peaked grass-roofs, a burst of yells, a whirl of black limbs, a mass of hands clapping, of feet stamping, of bodies swaying, of eyes rolling, under the droop of heavy and motionless foliage. The steamer toiled along slowly on the edge of a black and incomprehensible frenzy. The prehistoric man was cursing us, praying to us, welcoming us—who could tell? We were cut off from the comprehension of our surroundings; we glided past like phantoms, wondering and secretly appalled, as sane men would be before an enthusiastic outbreak in a madhouse. We could not understand, because we were too far and could not remember, because we were traveling in the night of first ages, of those ages that are gone, leaving hardly a sign—and no memories.

"The earth seemed unearthly. We are accustomed to look upon the shackled form of a conquered monster, but there— there you could look at a thing monstrous and free. It was un- earthly, and the men were—— No, they were not inhuman. Well, you know, that was the worst of it—this suspicion of their not being inhuman. It would come slowly to one. They howled, and leaped, and spun, and made horrid faces; but what thrilled you was just the thought of their humanity—like yours—the thought of your remote kinship with this wild and passionate uproar. Ugly. Yes, it was ugly enough; but if you were man enough you would admit to yourself that there was in you just the faintest trace of a response to the terrible frankness of that noise, a dim suspicion of there being a meaning in it which you —you so remote from the night of first ages—could comprehend. And why not? The mind of a man is capable of anything—be- cause everything is in it, all the past as well as all the future. What was there after all? Joy, fear, sorrow, devotion, valor, rage—who can tell?—but truth—truth stripped of its cloak of time. Let the fool gape and shudder—the man knows, and can look on without a wink. But he must at least be as much of a man as these on the shore. He must meet that truth with his own true stuff—with his own inborn strength. Principles? Prin- ciples won't do. Acquisitions, clothes, pretty rags—rags that would fly off at the first good shake. No; you want a deliberate belief. An appeal to me in this fiendish row—is there? Very well; I hear; I admit, but I have a voice too, and for good or evil mine is the speech that cannot be silenced. Of course, a fool, what with sheer fright and fine sentiments, is always safe. Who's that grunting? You wonder I didn't go ashore for a howl and a dance? Well, no—I didn't. Fine sentiments, you say? Fine sentiments, be hanged! I had no time. I had to mess about with white-lead and strips of woolen blanket helping to put bandages on those leaky steam-pipes—I tell you. I had to watch the steering, and circumvent those snags, and get the tin-pot along by hook or by crook. There was surface-truth enough in these things to save a wiser man. And between whiles I had to look after the savage who was fireman. He was an improved specimen; he could fire up a vertical boiler. He was there below me, and, upon my word, to look at him was as edifying as seeing a dog in a parody of breeches and a feather hat, walking on his hind-legs. A few months of training had done for that really fine chap. He squinted at the steam-gauge and at the water-gauge with an evident effort of intrepidity—and he had filed teeth too, the poor devil, and the wool of his pate shaved into queer patterns, and three ornamental scars on each of his cheeks. He ought to have been clapping his hands and stamping his feet on the bank, instead of which he was hard at work, a thrall to strange witch-craft, full of improving knowledge. He was useful because he had been instructed; and what he knew was this—that should the water in that transparent thing disappear, the evil spirit in-side the boiler would get angry through the greatness of his thirst, and take a terrible vengeance. So he sweated and fired up and watched the glass fearfully (with an impromptu charm, made of rags, tied to his arm, and a piece of polished bone, as big as a watch, stuck flatways through his lower lip), while the wooded banks slipped past us slowly, the short noise was left behind, the interminable miles of silence—and we crept on, to-wards Kurtz. But the snags were thick, the water was treacherous and shallow, the boiler seemed indeed to have a sulky devil in it, and thus neither that fireman nor I had any time to peer into our creepy thoughts.

"Some fifty miles below the Inner Station we came upon a hut of reeds, an inclined and melancholy pole, with the un-recognizable tatters of what had been a flag of some sort flying from it, and a neatly stacked wood-pile. This was unexpected. We came to the bank, and on the stack of firewood found a flat piece of board with some faded pencil-writing on it. When desciphered it said: 'Wood for you. Hurry up. Approach cau-tiously.' There was a signature, but it was illegible—not Kurtz —a much longer word. Hurry up. Where? Up the river? 'Ap-proach cautiously.' We had not done so. But the warning could not have been meant for the place where it could be only found after approach. Something was wrong above. But what—and how much? That was the question. We commented adversely upon the imbecility of that telegraphic style. The bush around said nothing, and would not let us look very far, either. A torn curtain of red twill hung in the doorway of the hut, and flapped sadly in our faces. The dwelling was dismantled; but we could see a white man had lived there not very long ago. There re-mained a rude table—a plank on two posts; a heap of rubbish reposed in a dark corner, and by the door I picked up a book. It had lost its covers, and the pages had been thumbed into a state of extremely dirty softness; but the back had been lovingly stitched afresh with white cotton thread, which looked clean yet. It was an extraordinary find. Its title was, 'An Inquiry into some Points of Seamanship,' by a man Tower, Towson—some such name—Master in his Majesty's Navy. The matter looked dreary reading enough, with illustrative diagrams and repulsive tables of figures, and the copy was sixty years old. I handled this amazing antiquity with the greatest possible tenderness, lest it should dissolve in my hands. Within, Towson or Towser was inquiring earnestly into the breaking strain of ships' chains and tackle, and other such matters. Not a very enthralling book; but at the first glance you could see there a singleness of inten-tion, an honest concern for the right way of going to work, which made these humble pages, thought out so many years ago, luminous with another than a professional light. The simple old sailor, with his talk of chains and purchases, made me forget the jungle and the pilgrims in a delicious sensation of having come upon something unmistakably real. Such a book being there was wonderful enough; but still more astounding were the notes penciled in the margin, and plainly referring to the text. I couldn't believe my eyes! They were in cipher! Yes, it looked like cipher. Fancy a man lugging with him a book of that description into this nowhere and studying it—and making notes—in cipher at that! It was an extravagant mystery.

"I had been dimly aware for some time of a worrying noise, and when I lifted my eyes I saw the wood-pile was gone, and the manager, aided by all the pilgrims, was shouting at me from the river-side. I slipped the book into my pocket. I assure you to leave off reading was like tearing myself away from the shelter of an old and solid friendship.

"I started the lame engine ahead. 'It must be this miserable trader—this intruder,' exclaimed the manager, looking back malevolently at the place we had left. 'He must be English,' I said. 'It will not save him from getting into trouble if he is not careful,' muttered the manager darkly. I observed with assumed innocence that no man was safe from trouble in this world.

"The current was more rapid now, the steamer seemed at her last gasp, the stern-wheel flopped languidly, and I caught my-self listening on tiptoe for the next beat of the float, for in sober truth I expected the wretched thing to give up every moment. It was like watching the last flickers of life. But still we crawled. Sometimes I would pick out a tree a little way ahead to measure our progress towards Kurtz by, but I lost it invariably before we got abreast. To keep the eyes so long on one thing was too much for human patience. The manager displayed a beautiful resignation. I fretted and fumed and took to arguing with myself whether or no I would talk openly with Kurtz; but before I could come to any conclusion it occurred to me that my speech or my silence, indeed any action of mine, would be a mere futility. What did it matter what anyone knew or ignored? What did it matter who was manager? One gets sometimes such a flash of insight. The essentials of this affair lay deep under the surface, beyond my reach, and beyond my power of meddling.

"Towards the evening of the second day we judged ourselves about eight miles from Kurtz's station. I wanted to push on; but the manager looked grave, and told me the navigation up there was so dangerous that it would be advisable, the sun being very low already, to wait where we were till next morning. Moreover, he pointed out that if the warning to approach cautiously were to be followed, we must approach in daylight—not at dusk, or in the dark. This was sensible enough. Eight miles meant nearly three hours' steaming for us, and I could also see suspicious ripples at the upper end of the reach. Nevertheless, I was annoyed beyond expression at the delay, and most unreasonably too, since one night more could not matter much after so many months. As we had plenty of wood, and caution was the word, I brought up in the middle of the stream. The reach was narrow, straight, with high sides like a railway cutting. The dusk came gliding into it long before the sun had set. The current ran smooth and swift, but a dumb immobility sat on the banks. The living trees, lashed together by the creepers and every living bush of the undergrowth, might have been changed into stone, even to the slenderest twig, to the lightest leaf. It was not sleep—it seemed unnatural, like a state of trance. Not the faintest sound of any kind could be heard. You looked on amazed, and began to suspect yourself of being deaf—then the night came suddenly, and struck you blind as well. About three in the morning some large fish leaped, and the loud splash made me jump as though a gun had been fired. When the sun rose there was a white fog, very warm and clammy, and more blinding than the night. It did not shift or drive; it was just there, standing all round you like something solid. At eight or nine, perhaps, it lifted as a shutter lifts. We had a glimpse of the towering multitude of trees, of the immense matted jungle, with the blazing little ball of the sun hanging over it—all perfectly still—and then the white shutter came down again, smoothly, as if sliding in greased grooves. I ordered the chain, which we had begun to heave in, to be paid out again. Before it stopped running with a muffled rattle, a cry, a very loud cry, as of infinite desolation, soared slowly in the opaque air. It ceased. A complaining clamor, modulated in savage discords, filled our ears. The sheer unexpectedness of it made my hair stir under my cap. I don't know how it struck the others: to me it seemed as though the mist itself had screamed, so suddenly, and apparently from all sides at once, did this tumultuous and mournful uproar arise. It culminated in a hurried outbreak of almost intolerably excessive shrieking, which stopped short, leaving us stiffened in a variety of silly attitudes, and obstinately listening to the nearly as appalling and excessive silence. 'Good God! What is the meaning——?' stammered at my elbow one of the pilgrims,—a little fat man, with sandy hair and red whiskers, who wore side-spring boots, and pink pyjamas tucked into his socks. Two others remained open-mouthed a whole minute, then dashed into the little cabin, to rush out incontinently and stand darting scared glances, with Winchesters at 'ready' in their hands. What we could see was just the steamer we were on, her outlines blurred as though she had been on the point of dissolving, and a misty strip of water, perhaps two feet broad, around her—and that was all. The rest of the world was nowhere, as far as our eyes and ears were concerned. Just nowhere. Gone, disappeared; swept off without leaving a whisper or a shadow behind.

"I went forward, and ordered the chain to be hauled in short, so as to be ready to trip the anchor and move the steamboat at once if necessary. 'Will they attack?' whispered an awed voice. 'We will be all butchered in this fog,' murmured another. The faces twitched with the strain, the hands trembled slightly, the eyes forgot to wink. It was very curious to see the contrast of expressions of the white men and of the black fellows of our crew, who were as much strangers to that part of the river as we, though their homes were only eight hundred miles away.

The whites, of course greatly discomposed, had besides a curious look of being painfully shocked by such an outrageous row. The others had an alert, naturally interested expression; but their faces were essentially quiet, even those of the one or two who grinned as they hauled at the chain. Several exchanged short, grunting phrases, which seemed to settle the matter to their satisfaction. Their headman, a young, broad-chested black, severely draped in dark-blue fringed cloths, with fierce nostrils and his hair all done up artfully in oily ringlets, stood near me. 'Aha!' I said, just for good fellowship's sake. 'Catch 'im,' he snapped, with a bloodshot widening of his eyes and a flash of sharp teeth—'catch 'im. Give 'im to us.' 'To you, eh?' I asked; 'what would you do with them?' 'Eat 'im!' he said curtly, and, leaning his elbow on the rail, looked out into the fog in a dig- nified and profoundly pensive attitude. I would no doubt have been properly horrified, had it not occurred to me that he and his chaps must be very hungry: that they must have been grow- ing increasingly hungry for at least this month past. They had been engaged for six months (I don't think a single one of them had any clear idea of time, as we at the end of countless ages have. They still belonged to the beginnings of time—had no inherited experience to teach them as it were), and of course, as long as there was a piece of paper written over in accordance with some farcical law or other made down the river, it didn't enter anybody's head to trouble how they would live. Certainly they had brought with them some rotten hippo-meat, which couldn't have lasted very long, anyway, even if the pilgrims hadn't, in the midst of a shocking hullabaloo, thrown a con- siderable quantity of it overboard. It looked like a high-handed proceeding; but it was really a case of legitimate self-defense. You can't breathe dead hippo waking, sleeping, and eating, and at the same time keep your precarious grip on existence. Besides that, they had given them every week three pieces of brass wire, each about nine inches long; and the theory was they were to buy their provisions with that currency in river-side villages. You can see how *that* worked. There were either no villages, or the people were hostile, or the director, who like the rest of us fed out of tins, with an occasional old he-goat thrown in, didn't want to stop the steamer for some more or less recondite reason. So, unless they swallowed the wire itself, or made loops of it to snare the fishes with, I don't see what good their extravagant salary could be to them. I must say it was paid with a regularity worthy of a large and honorable trading company. For the rest, the only thing to eat—though it didn't look eatable in the least—I saw in their possession was a few lumps of some stuff like half-cooked dough, of a dirty lavender color, they kept wrapped in leaves, and now and then swallowed a piece of, but so small that it seemed done more for the looks of the thing than for any serious purpose of sustenance. Why in the name of all the gnawing devils of hunger they didn't go for us—they were thirty to five—and have a good tuck in for once, amazes me now when I think of it. They were big powerful men, with not much capacity to weigh the consequences, with courage, with strength, even yet, though their skins were no longer glossy and their muscles no longer hard. And I saw that something restraining, one of those human secrets that baffle probability, had come into play there. I looked at them with a swift quickening of interest—not because it occurred to me I might be eaten by them before very long, though I own to you that just then I perceived —in a new light, as it were—how unwholesome the pilgrims looked, and I hoped, yes, I positively hoped, that my aspect was not so—what shall I say?—so—unappetizing: a touch of fantastic vanity which fitted well with the dream-sensation that pervaded all my days at that time. Perhaps I had a little fever too. One can't live with one's finger everlastingly on one's pulse. I had often 'a little fever,' or a little touch of other things—the playful paw-strokes of the wilderness, the preliminary trifling before the more serious onslaught which came in due course. Yes; I looked at them as you would on any human being, with a curiosity of their impulses, motives, capacities, weaknesses, when brought to the test of an inexorable physical necessity. Restraint! What possible restraint? Was it superstition, disgust, patience,

fear—or some kind of primitive honor? No fear can stand up
to hunger, no patience can wear it out, disgust simply does not
exist where hunger is; and as to superstition, beliefs, and what
you may call principles, they are less than chaff in a breeze.
Don't you know the devilry of lingering starvation, its exasperating torment, its black thoughts, its somber and brooding ferocity? Well, I do. It takes a man all his inborn strength to fight
hunger properly. It's really easier to face bereavement, dishonor,
and the perdition of one's soul—than this kind of prolonged
hunger. Sad, but true. And these chaps too had no earthly reason
for any kind of scruple. Restraint! I would just as soon have
expected restraint from a hyena prowling amongst the corpses
of a battlefield. But there was the fact facing me—the fact dazzling, to be seen, like the foam on the depths of the sea, like a
ripple on an unfathomable enigma, a mystery greater—when I
thought of it—than the curious, inexplicable note of desperate
grief in this savage clamor that had swept by us on the river-
bank, behind the blind whiteness of the fog.

"Two pilgrims were quarreling in hurried whispers as to
which bank. 'Left.' 'No, no; how can you? Right, right, of
course.' 'It is very serious,' said the manager's voice behind me;
'I would be desolated if anything should happen to Mr. Kurtz
before we came up.' I looked at him, and had not the slightest
doubt he was sincere. He was just the kind of man who would
wish to preserve appearances. That was his restraint. But when
he muttered something about going on at once, I did not even
take the trouble to answer him. I knew, and he knew, that it was
impossible. Were we to let go our hold of the bottom, we would
be absolutely in the air—in space. We wouldn't be able to tell
where we were going to—whether up or down stream, or across
—till we fetched against one bank or the other,—and then we
wouldn't know at first which it was. Of course I made no move.
I had no mind for a smash-up. You couldn't imagine a more
deadly place for a shipwreck. Whether drowned at once or not,
we were sure to perish speedily in one way or another. 'I au-
thorize you to take all the risks,' he said, after a short silence.

'I refuse to take any,' I said shortly; which was just the answer he expected, though its tone might have surprised him. 'Well, I must defer to your judgment. You are captain,' he said, with marked civility. I turned my shoulder to him in sign of my appreciation, and looked into the fog. How long would it last? It was the most hopeless look-out. The approach to this Kurtz grubbing for ivory in the wretched bush was beset by as many dangers as though he had been an enchanted princess sleeping in a fabulous castle. 'Will they attack, do you think?' asked the manager, in a confidential tone.

"I did not think they would attack, for several obvious reasons. The thick fog was one. If they left the bank in their canoes they would get lost in it, as we would be if we attempted to move. Still, I had also judged the jungle of both banks quite impenetrable—and yet eyes were in it, eyes that had seen us. The river-side bushes were certainly very thick; but the undergrowth behind was evidently penetrable. However, during the short lift I had seen no canoes anywhere in the reach—certainly not abreast of the steamer. But what made the idea of attack inconceivable to me was the nature of the noise—of the cries we had heard. They had not the fierce character boding of immediate hostile intention. Unexpected, wild, and violent as they had been, they had given me an irresistible impression of sorrow. The glimpse of the steamboat had for some reason filled those savages with unrestrained grief. The danger, if any, I expounded, was from our proximity to a great human passion let loose. Even extreme grief may ultimately vent itself in violence —but more generally takes the form of apathy. . . .

"You should have seen the pilgrims stare! They had no heart to grin, or even to revile me; but I believe they thought me gone mad—with fright, maybe. I delivered a regular lecture. My dear boys, it was no good bothering. Keep a look-out? Well, you may guess I watched the fog for the signs of lifting as a cat watches a mouse; but for anything else our eyes were of no more use to us than if we had been buried miles deep in a heap of cotton-wool. It felt like it too—choking, warm, stifling. Besides, all I said, though it sounded extravagant, was absolutely true to fact. What we afterwards alluded to as an attack was really an attempt at repulse. The action was very far from being aggressive—it was not even defensive, in the usual sense: it was undertaken under the stress of desperation, and in its essence was purely protective.

"It developed itself, I should say, two hours after the fog lifted, and its commencement was at a spot, roughly speaking, about a mile and a half below Kurtz's station. We had just floundered and flopped round a bend, when I saw an islet, a mere grassy hummock of bright green, in the middle of the stream. It was the only thing of the kind; but as we opened the reach more, I perceived it was the head of a long sandbank, or rather of a chain of shallow patches stretching down the middle of the river. They were discolored, just awash, and the whole lot was seen just under the water, exactly as a man's backbone is seen running down the middle of his back under the skin. Now, as far as I did see, I could go to the right or to the left of this. I didn't know either channel, of course. The banks looked pretty well alike, the depth appeared the same; but as I had been informed the station was on the west side, I naturally headed for the western passage.

"No sooner had we fairly entered it than I became aware it was much narrower than I had supposed. To the left of us there was the long uninterrupted shoal, and to the right a high, steep bank heavily overgrown with bushes. Above the bush the trees stood in serried ranks. The twigs overhung the current thickly, and from distance to distance a large limb of some tree projected rigidly over the stream. It was then well on in the afternoon, the face of the forest was gloomy, and a broad strip of shadow had already fallen on the water. In this shadow we steamed up —very slowly, as you may imagine. I sheered her well inshore— the water being deepest near the bank, as the sounding-pole informed me.

"One of my hungry and forbearing friends was sounding in the bows just below me. This steamboat was exactly like a decked scow. On the deck there were two little teak-wood houses, with doors and windows. The boiler was in the fore-end, and the machinery right astern. Over the whole there was a light roof, supported on stanchions. The funnel projected through that roof, and in front of the funnel a small cabin built of light planks served for a pilot-house. It contained a couch, two camp-stools, a loaded Martini-Henry leaning in one corner, a tiny table, and the steering-wheel. It had a wide door in front and a broad shutter at each side. All these were always thrown open, of course. I spent my days perched up there on the extreme fore-end of that roof, before the door. At night I slept, or tried to, on the couch. An athletic black belonging to some coast tribe, and educated by my poor prodecessor, was the helmsman. He sported a pair of brass earrings, wore a blue cloth wrapper from the waist to the ankles, and thought all the world of him-self. He was the most unstable kind of fool I had ever seen. He steered with no end of a swagger while you were by; but if he lost sight of you, he became instantly the prey of an abject funk, and would let that cripple of a steamboat get the upper hand of him in a minute.

"I was looking down at the sounding-pole, and feeling much annoyed to see at each try a little more of it stick out of that river, when I saw my poleman give up the business suddenly, and stretch himself flat on the deck, without even taking the trouble to haul his pole in. He kept hold on it though, and it trailed in the water. At the same time the fireman, whom I could also see below me, sat down abruptly before his furnace and ducked his head. I was amazed. Then I had to look at the river mighty quick, because there was a snag in the fairway. Sticks, little sticks, were flying about—thick: they were whizzing before my nose, dropping below me, striking behind me against my pilot-house. All this time the river, the shore, the woods, were very quiet—perfectly quiet. I could only hear the heavy splashing thump of the stern-wheel and the patter of these things. We cleared the snag clumsily. Arrows, by Jove! We were being shot at! I stepped in quickly to close the shutter on the land side.

That fool-helmsman, his hands on the spokes, was lifting his knees high, stamping his feet, champing his mouth, like a reined-in horse. Confound him! And we were staggering within ten feet of the bank. I had to lean right out to swing the heavy shutter, and I saw a face amongst the leaves on the level with my own, looking at me very fierce and steady; and then suddenly, as though a veil had been removed from my eyes, I made out, deep in the tangled gloom, naked breasts, arms, legs, glaring eyes,—the bush was swarming with human limbs in movement, glistening, of bronze color. The twigs shook, swayed, and rustled, the arrows flew out of them, and then the shutter came to. 'Steer her straight,' I said to the helmsman. He held his head rigid, face forward; but his eyes rolled, he kept on lifting and setting down his feet gently, his mouth foamed a little. 'Keep quiet!' I said in a fury. I might just as well have ordered a tree not to sway in the wind. I darted out. Below me there was a great scuffle of feet on the iron deck; confused exclamations; a voice screamed, 'Can you turn back?' I caught sight of a V-shaped ripple on the water ahead. What? Another snag! A fusillade burst out under my feet. The pilgrims had opened with their Winchesters, and were simply squirting lead into that bush. A deuce of a lot of smoke came up and drove slowly forward. I swore at it. Now I couldn't see the ripple or the snag either. I stood in the doorway, peering, and the arrows came in swarms. They might have been poisoned, but they looked as though they wouldn't kill a cat. The bush began to howl. Our wood-cutters raised a warlike whoop; the report of a rifle just at my back deafened me. I glanced over my shoulder, and the pilot-house was yet full of noise and smoke when I made a dash at the wheel. The fool-nigger had dropped everything, to throw the shutter open and let off that Martini-Henry. He stood before the wide opening, glaring, and I yelled at him to come back, while I straightened the sudden twist out of that steamboat. There was no room to turn even if I had wanted to, the snag was somewhere very near ahead in that confounded smoke, there was no time to lose, so I just crowded her into the bank—right into the bank, where I knew the water was deep.

"We tore slowly along the overhanging bushes in a whirl of broken twigs and flying leaves. The fusillade below stopped short, as I had foreseen it would when the squirts got empty. I threw my head back to a glinting whizz that traversed the pilot-house, in at one shutter-hole and out at the other. Looking past that mad helmsman, who was shaking the empty rifle and yelling at the shore, I saw vague forms of men running bent double, leaping, gliding, distinct, incomplete, evanescent. Something big appeared in the air before the shutter, the rifle went over-board, and the man stepped back swiftly, looked at me over his shoulder in an extraordinary, profound, familiar manner, and fell upon my feet. The side of his head hit the wheel twice, and the end of what appeared a long cane clattered round and knocked over a little camp-stool. It looked as though after wrenching that thing from somebody ashore he had lost his balance in the effort. The thin smoke had blown away, we were clear of the snag, and looking ahead I could see that in another hundred yards or so I would be free to sheer off, away from the bank; but my feet felt so very warm and wet that I had to look down. The man had rolled on his back and stared straight up at me; both his hands clutched that cane. It was the shaft of a spear that, either thrown or lunged through the opening, had caught him in the side just below the ribs; the blade had gone in out of sight, after making a frightful gash; my shoes were full; a pool of blood lay very still, gleaming dark-red under the wheel; his eyes shone with an amazing luster. The fusillade burst out again. He looked at me anxiously, gripping the spear like something precious, with an air of being afraid I would try to take it away from him. I had to make an effort to free my eyes from his gaze and attend to the steering. With one hand I felt above my head for the line of the steam-whistle, and jerked out screech after screech hurriedly. The tumult of angry and warlike yells was checked instantly, and then from the depths of the woods went out such a tremulous and prolonged wail of mourn-

ful fear and utter despair as may be imagined to follow the
flight of the last hope from the earth. There was a great commotion in the bush; the shower of arrows stopped, a few dropping shots rang out sharply—then silence, in which the languid
beat of the stern-wheel came plainly to my ears. I put the helm
hard a-starboard at the moment when the pilgrim in pink pyjamas, very hot and agitated, appeared in the doorway. 'The manager sends me——' he began in an official tone, and stopped short.
'Good God!' he said, glaring at the wounded man.

"We two whites stood over him, and his lustrous and inquiring glance enveloped us both. I declare it looked as though he
would presently put to us some question in an understandable
language; but he died without uttering a sound, without moving
a limb, without twitching a muscle. Only in the very last moment, as though in response to some sign we could not see, to
some whisper we could not hear, he frowned heavily, and that
frown gave to his black death-mask an inconceivably somber,
brooding, and menacing expression. The luster of inquiring
glance faded swiftly into vacant glassiness. 'Can you steer?' I
asked the agent eagerly. He looked very dubious; but I made
a grab at his arm, and he understood at once I meant him to
steer whether or no. To tell you the truth, I was morbidly anxious to change my shoes and socks. 'He is dead,' murmured the
fellow, immensely impressed. 'No doubt about it,' said I, tugging like mad at the shoe-laces. 'And, by the way, I suppose Mr.
Kurtz is dead as well by this time.'

"For the moment that was the dominant thought. There was
a sense of extreme disappointment, as though I had found out
I had been striving after something altogether without a substance. I couldn't have been more disgusted if I had traveled
all this way for the sole purpose of talking with Mr. Kurtz.
Talking with. . . . I flung one shoe overboard, and became aware
that that was exactly what I had been looking forward to—a
talk with Kurtz. I made the strange discovery that I had never
imagined him as doing, you know, but as discoursing. I didn't
say to myself, 'Now I will never see him,' or 'Now I will never

shake him by the hand,' but, 'Now I will never hear him.' The man presented himself as a voice. Not of course that I did not connect him with some sort of action. Hadn't I been told in all the tones of jealousy and admiration that he had collected, bartered, swindled, or stolen more ivory than all the other agents together? That was not the point. The point was in his being a gifted creature, and that of all his gifts the one that stood out preeminently, that carried with it a sense of real presence, was his ability to talk, his words—the gift of expression, the bewildering, the illuminating, the most exalted and the most contemptible, the pulsating stream of light, or the deceitful flow from the heart of an impenetrable darkness.

"The other shoe went flying unto the devil-god of that river. I thought, By Jove! it's all over. We are too late; he has vanished—the gift has vanished, by means of some spear, arrow, or club. I will never hear that chap speak after all,—and my sorrow had a startling extravagance of emotion, even such as I had noticed in the howling sorrow of these savages in the bush. I couldn't have felt more of lonely desolation somehow, had I been robbed of a belief or had missed my destiny in life. . . . Why do you sigh in this beastly way, somebody? Absurd? Well, absurd. Good Lord! mustn't a man ever—— Here, give me some tobacco."

There was a pause of profound stillness, then a match flared, and Marlow's lean face appeared, worn, hollow, with downward folds and dropped eyelids, with an aspect of concentrated attention; and as he took vigorous draws at his pipe, it seemed to retreat and advance out of the night in the regular flicker of the tiny flame. The match went out.

"Absurd!" he cried. "This is the worst of trying to tell. . . . Here you all are, each moored with two good addresses, like a hulk with two anchors, a butcher round one corner, a policeman round another, excellent appetites, and temperature normal—you hear—normal from year's end to year's end. And you say, Absurd! Absurd be—exploded! Absurd! My dear boys, what can you expect from a man who out of sheer nervousness had just flung overboard a pair of new shoes. Now I think of it, it is amazing I did not shed tears. I am, upon the whole, proud of my fortitude. I was cut to the quick at the idea of having lost the inestimable privilege of listening to the gifted Kurtz. Of course I was wrong. The privilege was waiting for me. Oh yes, I heard more than enough. And I was right, too. A voice. He was very little more than a voice. And I heard—him—it—this voice—other voices—all of them were so little more than voices —and the memory of that time itself lingers around me, impalpable, like a dying vibration of one immense jabber, silly, atrocious, sordid, savage, or simply mean, without any kind of sense. Voices, voices—even the girl herself—now——"

He was silent for a long time.

"I laid the ghost of his gifts at last with a lie," he began suddenly. "Girl! What? Did I mention a girl? Oh, she is out of it— completely. They—the women I mean—are out of it—should be out of it. We must help them to stay in that beautiful world of their own, lest ours gets worse. Oh, she had to be out of it. You should have heard the disinterred body of Mr. Kurtz saying, 'My Intended.' You would have perceived directly then how completely she was out of it. And the lofty frontal bone of Mr. Kurtz! They say the hair goes on growing sometimes, but this— ah—specimen, was impressively bald. The wilderness had patted him on the head, and, behold, it was like a ball—an ivory ball; it had caressed him, and—lo!—he had withered; it had taken him, loved him, embraced him, got into his veins, consumed his flesh, and sealed his soul to its own by the inconceivable ceremonies of some devilish initiation. He was its spoiled and pampered favorite. Ivory? I should think so. Heaps of it, stacks of it. The old mud shanty was bursting with it. You would think there was not a single tusk left either above or below the ground in the whole country. 'Mostly fossil,' the manager had remarked disparagingly. It was no more fossil than I am; but they call it fossil when it is dug up. It appears these niggers do bury the tusks sometimes—but evidently they couldn't bury this parcel deep enough to save the gifted Mr. Kurtz from his fate. We filled the steamboat with it, and had to pile a lot on the deck. Thus he could see and enjoy as long as he could see, because the appreciation of this favor had remained with him to the last. You should have heard him say, 'My ivory.' Oh yes, I heard him. 'My Intended, my ivory, my station, my river, my——' everything belonged to him. It made me hold my breath in expectation of hearing the wilderness burst into a prodigious peal of laughter that would shake the fixed stars in their places. Everything belonged to him—but that was a trifle. The thing was to know what he belonged to, how many powers of darkness claimed him for their own. That was the reflection that made you creepy all over. It was impossible—it was not good for one either—trying to imagine. He had taken a high seat amongst the devils of the land—I mean literally. You can't understand. How could you?—with solid pavement under your feet, surrounded by kind neighbors ready to cheer you or to fall on you, stepping delicately between the butcher and the policeman, in the holy terror of scandal and gallows and lunatic asylums—how can you imagine what particular region of the first ages a man's untrammeled feet may take him into by the way of solitude—utter solitude without a policeman—by the way of silence—utter silence, where no warning voice of a kind neighbor can be heard whispering of public opinion? These little things make all the great difference. When they are gone you must fall back upon your own innate strength, upon your own capacity for faithfulness. Of course you may be too much of a fool to go wrong—too dull even to know you are being assaulted by the powers of darkness. I take it, no fool ever made a bargain for his soul with the devil: the fool is too much of a fool, or the devil too much of a devil—I don't know which. Or you may be such a thunderingly exalted creature as to be altogether deaf and blind to anything but heavenly sights and sounds. Then the earth for you is only a standing place—and whether to be like this is your loss or your gain I won't pretend to say. But most of us are neither one nor the other. The earth for us is a place to live in, where we must put up with sights, with sounds, with smells too, by Jove!—

breathe dead hippo, so to speak, and not be contaminated. And there, don't you see? your strength comes in, the faith in your ability for the digging of unostentatious holes to bury the stuff in—your power of devotion, not to yourself, but to an obscure, back-breaking business. And that's difficult enough. Mind, I am not trying to excuse or even explain—I am trying to account to myself for—for—Mr. Kurtz—for the shade of Mr. Kurtz. This initiated wraith from the back of Nowhere honored me with its amazing confidence before it vanished altogether. This was because it could speak English to me. The original Kurtz had been educated partly in England, and—as he was good enough to say himself—his sympathies were in the right place. His mother was half-English, his father was half-French. All Europe contributed to the making of Kurtz; and by-and-by I learned that, most appropriately, the International Society for the Suppression of Savage Customs had intrusted him with the making of a report, for its future guidance. And he had written it too. I've seen it. I've read it. It was eloquent, vibrating with eloquence, but too high-strung, I think. Seventeen pages of close writing he had found time for! But this must have been before his—let us say—nerves, went wrong, and caused him to preside at certain midnight dances ending with unspeakable rites, which—as far as I reluctantly gathered from what I heard at various times—were offered up to him—do you understand?— to Mr. Kurtz himself. But it was a beautiful piece of writing. The opening paragraph, however, in the light of later information, strikes me now as ominous. He began with the argument that we whites, from the point of development we had arrived at, 'must necessarily appear to them [savages] in the nature of supernatural beings—we approach them with the might as of a deity,' and so on, and so on. 'By the simple exercise of our will we can exert a power for good practically unbounded,' &c., &c. From that point he soared and took me with him. The peroration was magnificent, though difficult to remember, you know. It gave me the notion of an exotic Immensity ruled by an august Benevolence. It made me tingle with enthusiasm. This was the unbounded power of eloquence—of words—of burning noble words. There were no practical hints to interrupt the magic current of phrases, unless a kind of note at the foot of the last page, scrawled evidently much later, in an unsteady hand, may be regarded as the exposition of a method. It was very simple, and at the end of that moving appeal to every altruistic sentiment it blazed at you, luminous and terrifying, like a flash of lightning in a serene sky: 'Exterminate all the brutes!' The curious part was that he had apparently forgotten all about that valuable postscriptum, because, later on, when he in a sense came to himself, he repeatedly entreated me to take good care of 'my pamphlet' (he called it), as it was sure to have in the future a good influence upon his career. I had full information about all these things, and, besides, as it turned out, I was to have the care of his memory. I've done enough for it to give me the indisputable right to lay it, if I choose, for an everlasting rest in the dust-bin of progress, amongst all the sweepings and, figuratively speaking, all the dead cats of civilization. But then, you see, I can't choose. He wouldn't be forgotten. Whatever he was, he was not common. He had the power to charm or frighten rudimentary souls into an aggravated witch-dance in his honor; he could also fill the small souls of the pilgrims with bitter misgivings: he had one devoted friend at least, and he had conquered one soul in the world that was neither rudimentary nor tainted with self-seeking. No; I can't forget him, though I am not prepared to affirm the fellow was exactly worth the life we lost in getting to him. I missed my late helmsman awfully,—I missed him even while his body was still lying in the pilot-house. Perhaps you will think it passing strange this regret for a savage who was no more account than a grain of sand in a black Sahara. Well, don't you see, he had done something, he had steered; for months I had him at my back—a help—an instrument. It was a kind of partnership. He steered for me—I had to look after him, I worried about his deficiencies, and thus a subtle bond had been created, of which I only became aware when it was suddenly broken. And the intimate profundity of that look he gave me

when he received his hurt remains to this day in my memory—
like a claim of distant kinship affirmed in a supreme moment.

"Poor fool! If he had only left that shutter alone. He had no
restraint, no restraint—just like Kurtz—a tree swayed in the
wind. As soon as I had put on a dry pair of slippers, I dragged
him out, after first jerking the spear out of his side, which operation I confess I performed with my eyes shut tight. His heels
leaped together over the little door-step; his shoulders were
pressed to my breast; I hugged him from behind desperately.
Oh! he was heavy, heavy; heavier than any man on earth, I
should imagine. Then without more ado I tipped him overboard. The current snatched him as though he had been a wisp
of grass, and I saw the body roll over twice before I lost sight of
it for ever. All the pilgrims and the manager were then congregated on the awning-deck about the pilot-house, chattering at
each other like a flock of excited magpies, and there was a
scandalized murmur at my heartless promptitude. What they
wanted to keep that body hanging about for I can't guess. Em-
balm it, maybe. But I had also heard another, and a very ominous, murmur on the deck below. My friends the wood-cutters
were likewise scandalized, and with a better show of reason—
though I admit that the reason itself was quite inadmissible. Oh,
quite! I had made up my mind that if my late helmsman was to
be eaten, the fishes alone should have him. He had been a very
second-rate helmsman while alive, but now he was dead he
might have become a first-class temptation, and possibly cause
some startling trouble. Besides, I was anxious to take the wheel,
the man in pink pyjamas showing himself a hopeless duffer at
the business.

"This I did directly the simple funeral was over. We were going half-speed, keeping right in the middle of the stream, and I
listened to the talk about me. They had given up Kurtz, they
had given up the station; Kurtz was dead, and the station had
been burnt—and so on—and so on. The red-haired pilgrim was
beside himself with the thought that at least this poor Kurtz had
been properly revenged. 'Say! We must have made a glorious

slaughter of them in the bush. Eh? What do you think? Say?'
He positively danced, the bloodthirsty little gingery beggar. And
he had nearly fainted when he saw the wounded man! I could
not help saying, 'You made a glorious lot of smoke, anyhow.' I
had seen, from the way the tops of the bushes rustled and flew,
that almost all the shots had gone too high. You can't hit anything unless you take aim and fire from the shoulder; but these
chaps fired from the hip with their eyes shut. The retreat, I
maintained—and I was right—was caused by the screeching of
the steam-whistle. Upon this they forgot Kurtz, and began to
howl at me with indignant protests.

"The manager stood by the wheel murmuring confidentially
about the necessity of getting well away down the river before
dark at all events, when I saw in the distance a clearing on the
river-side and the outlines of some sort of building. 'What's
this?' I asked. He clapped his hands in wonder. 'The station!'
he cried. I edged in at once, still going half-speed.

"Through my glasses I saw the slope of a hill interspersed
with rare trees and perfectly free from undergrowth. A long
decaying building on the summit was half buried in the high
grass; the large holes in the peaked roof gaped back from afar;
the jungle and the woods made a background. There was no
inclosure or fence of any kind; but there had been one apparently, for near the house half-a-dozen slim posts remained in
a row, roughly trimmed, and with their upper ends ornamented
with round curved balls. The rails, or whatever there had been
between, had disappeared. Of course the forest surrounded all
that. The river-bank was clear, and on the water-side I saw a
white man under a hat like a cart-wheel beckoning persistently
with his whole arm. Examining the edge of the forest above and
below, I was almost certain I could see movements—human
forms gliding here and there. I steamed past prudently, then
stopped the engines and let her drift down. The man on the
shore began to shout, urging us to land. 'We have been attacked,' screamed the manager. 'I know—I know. It's all right,'

yelled back the other, as cheerful as you please. 'Come along. It's all right. I am glad.'

"His aspect reminded me of something I had seen—something funny I had seen somewhere. As I maneuvered to get alongside, I was asking myself, 'What does this fellow look like?' Suddenly I got it. He looked like a harlequin. His clothes had been made of some stuff that was brown holland probably, but it was covered with patches all over, with bright patches, blue, red, and yellow,—patches on the back, patches on front, patches on elbows, on knees; colored binding round his jacket, scarlet edging at the bottom of his trousers; and the sunshine made him look extremely gay and wonderfully neat withal, because you could see how beautifully all this patching had been done. A beardless, boyish face, very fair, no features to speak of, nose peeling, little blue eyes, smiles and frowns chasing each other over that open countenance like sunshine and shadow on a wind-swept plain. 'Look out, captain!' he cried; 'there's a snag lodged in here last night.' What! Another snag? I confess I swore shamefully. I had nearly holed my cripple, to finish off that charming trip. The harlequin on the bank turned his little pug nose up to me. 'You English?' he asked, all smiles. 'Are you?' I shouted from the wheel. The smiles vanished, and he shook his head as if sorry for my disappointment. Then he brightened up. 'Never mind!' he cried encouragingly. 'Are we in time?' I asked. 'He is up there,' he replied, with a toss of the head up the hill, and becoming gloomy all of a sudden. His face was like the autumn sky, overcast one moment and bright the next.

"When the manager, escorted by the pilgrims, all of them armed to the teeth, had gone to the house, this chap came on board. 'I say, I don't like this. These natives are in the bush,' I said. He assured me earnestly it was all right. 'They are simple people,' he added; 'well, I am glad you came. It took me all my time to keep them off.' 'But you said it was all right,' I cried. 'Oh, they meant no harm,' he said; and as I stared he corrected himself, 'Not exactly.' Then vivaciously, 'My faith, your pilothouse wants a clean up!' In the next breath he advised me to keep enough steam on the boiler to blow the whistle in case of any trouble. 'One good screech will do more for you than all your rifles. They are simple people,' he repeated. He rattled away at such a rate he quite overwhelmed me. He seemed to be trying to make up for lots of silence, and actually hinted, laughing, that such was the case. 'Don't you talk with Mr. Kurtz?' I said. 'You don't talk with that man—you listen to him,' he exclaimed with severe exaltation. 'But now——' He waved his arm, and in the twinkling of an eye was in the uttermost depths of despondency. In a moment he came up again with a jump, possessed himself of both my hands, shook them continuously, while he gabbled: 'Brother sailor . . . honor . . . pleasure . . . delight . . . introduce myself . . . Russian . . . son of an arch-priest . . . Government of Tambov . . . What? Tobacco! English tobacco; the excellent English tobacco! Now, that's brotherly. Smoke? Where's a sailor that does not smoke?'

"The pipe soothed him, and gradually I made out he had run away from school, had gone to sea in a Russian ship; ran away again; served some time in English ships; was now reconciled with the arch-priest. He made a point of that. 'But when one is young one must see things, gather experience, ideas; enlarge the mind.' 'Here!' I interrupted. 'You can never tell! Here I have met Mr. Kurtz,' he said, youthfully solemn and reproachful. I held my tongue after that. It appears he had persuaded a Dutch trading-house on the coast to fit him out with stores and goods, and had started for the interior with a light heart, and no more idea of what would happen to him than a baby. He had been wandering about that river for nearly two years alone, cut off from everybody and everything. 'I am not so young as I look. I am twenty-five,' he said. 'At first old Van Shuyten would tell me to go to the devil,' he narrated with keen enjoyment; 'but I stuck to him, and talked and talked, till at last he got afraid I would talk the hind-leg off his favorite dog, so he gave me some cheap things and a few guns, and told me he hoped he would never see my face again. Good old Dutchman, Van Shuyten. I've sent him one small lot of ivory a year ago, so that he can't

Oswalds, Bishopsbourne, Kent, where Conrad lived from October, 1919, to his death in 1924, his sixty-seventh year

call me a little thief when I get back. I hope he got it. And for the rest I don't care. I had some wood stacked for you. That was my old house. Did you see?'

"I gave him Towson's book. He made as though he would kiss me, but restrained himself. 'The only book I had left, and I thought I had lost it,' he said, looking at it ecstatically. 'So many accidents happen to a man going about alone, you know. Canoes get upset sometimes—and sometimes you've got to clear out so quick when the people get angry.' He thumbed the pages. 'You made notes in Russian?' I asked. He nodded. 'I thought they were written in cipher,' I said. He laughed, then became serious. 'I had lots of trouble to keep these people off,' he said. 'Did they want to kill you?' I asked. 'Oh no!' he cried, and checked himself. 'Why did they attack us?' I pursued. He hesitated, then said shamefacedly, 'They don't want him to go.' 'Don't they?' I said, curiously. He nodded a nod full of mystery and wisdom. 'I tell you,' he cried, 'this man has enlarged my mind.' He opened his arms wide, staring at me with his little blue eyes that were perfectly round."

III

"I LOOKED at him, lost in astonishment. There he was before me, in motley, as though he had absconded from a troupe of mimes, enthusiastic, fabulous. His very existence was improbable, inexplicable, and altogether bewildering. He was an insoluble problem. It was inconceivable how he had existed, how he had succeeded in getting so far, how he had managed to remain—why he did not instantly disappear. 'I went a little farther,' he said, 'then still a little farther—till I had gone so far that I don't know how I'll ever get back. Never mind. Plenty time. I can manage. You take Kurtz away quick—quick—I tell you.' The glamour of youth enveloped his particolored rags, his destitution, his loneliness, the essential desolation of his futile wanderings. For months—for years—his life hadn't been worth a day's purchase; and there he was gallantly, thoughtlessly alive, to all appearance indestructible solely by the virtue of his few years and of his unreflecting audacity. I was seduced into something like admiration—like envy. Glamour urged him on, glamour kept him unscathed. He surely wanted nothing from the wilderness but space to breathe in and to push on through. His need was to exist, and to move onwards at the greatest possible risk, and with a maximum of privation. If the absolutely pure, uncalculating, unpractical spirit of adventure had ever ruled a human being, it ruled this be-patched youth. I almost envied him the possession of this modest and clear flame. It seemed to have consumed all thought of self so completely, that, even while he was talking to you, you forgot that it was he—the man before your eyes—who had gone through these things. I did not envy him his devotion to Kurtz, though. He had not meditated over it. It came to him, and he accepted it with a sort of eager fatalism. I must say that to me it appeared about the most dangerous thing in every way he had come upon so far.

"They had come together unavoidably, like two ships becalmed near each other, and lay rubbing sides at last. I suppose Kurtz wanted an audience, because on a certain occasion, when encamped in the forest, they had talked all night, or more probably Kurtz had talked. 'We talked of everything,' he said, quite transported at the recollection. 'I forgot there was such a thing as sleep. The night did not seem to last an hour. Everything! Everything! . . . Of love too.' 'Ah, he talked to you of love!' I said, much amused. 'It isn't what you think,' he cried, almost passionately. 'It was in general. He made me see things—things.'

"He threw his arms up. We were on deck at the time, and the headman of my wood-cutters, lounging near by, turned upon him his heavy and glittering eyes. I looked around, and I don't know why, but I assure you that never, never before, did this land, this river, this jungle, the very arch of this blazing sky, appear to me so hopeless and so dark, so impenetrable to human thought, so pitiless to human weakness. 'And, ever since, you have been with him, of course?' I said.

"On the contrary. It appears their intercourse had been very much broken by various causes. He had, as he informed me proudly, managed to nurse Kurtz through two illnesses (he alluded to it as you would to some risky feat), but as a rule Kurtz wandered alone, far in the depths of the forest. 'Very often coming to this station, I had to wait days and days before he would turn up,' he said. 'Ah, it was worth wating for!—sometimes.' 'What was he doing? exploring or what?' I asked. 'Oh yes, of course'; he had discovered lots of villages, a lake too—he did not know exactly in what direction, it was dangerous to inquire too much—but mostly his expeditions had been for ivory. 'But he had no goods to trade with by that time,' I objected. 'There's a good lot of cartridges left even yet,' he answered, looking away. 'To speak plainly, he raided the country,' I said. He nodded. 'Not alone, surely!' He muttered something about the villages round that lake. 'Kurtz got the tribe to follow him, did he?' I suggested. He fidgeted a little. 'They adored him,' he said. The tone of these words was so extraordinary that I looked at him searchingly. It was curious to see his mingled eagerness and reluctance to speak of Kurtz. The man filled his life, occupied his thoughts, swayed his emotions. 'What can you expect?' he burst out; 'he came to them with thunder and lightning, you know—and they had never seen anything like it—and very terrible. He could be very terrible. You can't judge Mr. Kurtz as you would an ordinary man. No, no, no! Now—just to give you an idea—I don't mind telling you, he wanted to shoot me too one day—but I don't judge him.' 'Shoot you!' I cried. 'What for?' 'Well, I had a small lot of ivory the chief of that village near my house gave me. You see I used to shoot game for them. Well, he wanted it, and wouldn't hear reason. He declared he would shoot me unless I gave him the ivory and then cleared out of the country, because he could do so, and had a fancy for it, and there was nothing on earth to prevent him killing whom he jolly well pleased. And it was true too. I gave him the ivory. What did I care! But I didn't clear out. No, no. I couldn't leave him. I had to be careful, of course, till we got friendly again for a time. He had his second illness then. Afterwards I had to keep out of the way; but I don't mind. He was living for the most part in those villages on the lake. When he came down to the river, sometimes he would take me, and sometimes it was better for me to be careful. This man suffered too much. He hated all this, and somehow he couldn't get away. When I had a chance I begged him to try and leave while there was time; I offered to go back with him. And he would say yes, and then he would remain; go off on another ivory hunt; disappear for weeks; forget himself amongst these people—forget himself—you know.' 'Why! he's mad,' I said. He protested indignantly. Mr. Kurtz couldn't be mad. If I had heard him talk, only two days ago, I wouldn't dare hint at such a thing. . . . I had taken up my binoculars while we talked and was looking at the shore, sweeping the limit of the forest at each side and at the back of the house. The consciousness of there being people in that bush, so silent, so quiet—as silent and quiet as the ruined house on the hill—made me uneasy. There was no sign on the face of nature of this amazing tale that was not so much told as suggested to me in desolate exclamations, completed by shrugs, in interrupted phrases, in hints ending in deep sighs. The woods were unmoved, like a mask—heavy, like the closed door of a prison—they looked with their air of hidden knowledge, of patient expectation, of unapproachable silence. The Russian was explaining to me that it was only lately that Mr. Kurtz had come down to the river, bringing along with him all the fighting men of that lake tribe. He had been absent for several months—getting himself adored, I suppose—and had come down unexpectedly, with the intention to all appearance of making a raid either across the river or down stream. Evidently the appetite for more ivory had got the better of the—what shall I say?—less material aspirations. However he had got much worse suddenly. 'I heard he was lying helpless, and so I came up—took my chance,' said the Russian. 'Oh, he is bad, very bad.' I directed my glass to the house. There were no signs of life, but there was the ruined roof, the long mud wall peeping above the grass, with three little square window-holes, no two of the same size; all this brought within reach of my hand, as it were. And then I made a brusque movement, and one of the remaining posts of that vanished fence leaped up in the field of my glass. You remember I told you I had been struck at the distance by certain attempts at ornamentation, rather remarkable in the ruinous aspect of the place. Now I had suddenly a nearer view, and its first result was to make me throw my head back as if before a blow. Then I went carefully from post to post with my glass, and I saw my mistake. These round knobs were not ornamental but symbolic; they were expressive and puzzling, striking and disturbing—food for thought and also for the vultures if there had been any look-ing down from the sky; but at all events for such ants as were industrious enough to ascend the pole. They would have been even more impressive, those heads on the stakes, if their faces had not been turned to the house. Only one, the first I had made out, was facing my way. I was not so shocked as you may think. The start back I had given was really nothing but a movement of surprise. I had expected to see a knob of wood there, you know. I returned deliberately to the first I had seen— and there it was, black, dried, sunken, with closed eyelids,—a head that seemed to sleep at the top of that pole, and, with the shrunken dry lips showing a narrow white line of the teeth, was smiling too, smiling continuously at some endless and jocose dream of that eternal slumber.

"I am not disclosing any trade secrets. In fact the manager said afterwards that Mr. Kurtz's methods had ruined the district. I have no opinion on that point, but I want you clearly to under-stand that there was nothing exactly profitable in these heads being there. They only showed that Mr. Kurtz lacked restraint in the gratification of his various lusts, that there was something wanting in him—some small matter which, when the pressing need arose, could not be found under his magnificent eloquence. Whether he knew of this deficiency himself I can't say. I think the knowledge came to him at last—only at the very last. But the wilderness had found him out early, and had taken on him a terrible vengeance for the fantastic invasion. I think it had whispered to him things about himself which he did not know, things of which he had no conception till he took counsel with this great solitude—and the whisper had proved irresistibly fascinating. It echoed loudly within him because he was hollow at the core. . . . I put down the glass, and the head that had appeared near enough to be spoken to seemed at once to have leaped away from me into inaccessible distance.

"The admirer of Mr. Kurtz was a bit crestfallen. In a hurried, indistinct voice he began to assure me he had not dared to take these—say, symbols—down. He was not afraid of the natives; they would not stir till Mr. Kurtz gave the word. His ascendency was extraordinary. The camps of these people surrounded the place, and the chiefs came every day to see him. They would crawl. . . . 'I don't want to know anything of the ceremonies used when approaching Mr. Kurtz,' I shouted. Curious, this feeling that came over me that such details would be more intolerable than those heads drying on the stakes under Mr. Kurtz's windows. After all, that was only a savage sight, while I seemed at one bound to have been transported into some lightless region of subtle horrors, where pure, uncomplicated savagery was a positive relief, being something that had a right to exist—obviously —in the sunshine. The young man looked at me with surprise. I suppose it did not occur to him that Mr Kurtz was no idol of mine. He forgot I hadn't heard any of these splendid monologues on, what was it? on love, justice, conduct of life—or what not. If it had come to crawling before Mr. Kurtz, he crawled as much as the veriest savage of them all. I had no idea of the conditions, he said: these heads were the heads of rebels. I shocked him excessively by laughing. Rebels! What would be the next definition I was to hear? There had been enemies, criminals, workers—and these were rebels. Those rebellious heads looked very subdued to me on their sticks. 'You don't know how such a life tries a man like Kurtz,' cried Kurtz's last disciple. 'Well, and you?' I said. 'I! I! I am a simple man. I have no great thoughts. I want nothing from anybody. How can you compare me to . . . ?' His feelings were too much for speech, and suddenly he broke down. 'I don't understand,' he groaned. 'I've been doing my best to keep him alive, and that's enough. I had no hand in all this. I have no abilities. There hasn't been a drop of medicine or a mouthful of invalid food for months here. He was shamefully abandoned. A man like this, with such ideas. Shamefully! Shamefully! I—I—haven't slept for the last ten nights. . . .'

"His voice lost itself in the calm of the evening. The long shadows of the forest had slipped down hill while we talked, had gone far beyond the ruined hovel, beyond the symbolic row of stakes. All this was in the gloom, while we down there were yet in the sunshine, and the stretch of the river abreast of the clearing glittered in a still and dazzling splendor, with a murky and over-shadowed bend above and below. Not a living soul was seen on the shore. The bushes did not rustle.

"Suddenly round the corner of the house a group of men appeared, as though they had come up from the ground. They waded waist-deep in the grass, in a compact body, bearing an improvised stretcher in their midst. Instantly, in the emptiness of the landscape, a cry arose whose shrillness pierced the still air like a sharp arrow flying straight to the very heart of the land; and, as if by enchantment, streams of human beings—of naked human beings—with spears in their hands, with bows, with shields, with wild glances and savage movements, were poured into the clearing by the dark-faced and pensive forest. The bushes shook, the grass swayed for a time, and then everything stood still in attentive immobility.

" 'Now, if he does not say the right thing to them we are all done for,' said the Russian at my elbow. The knot of men with the stretcher had stopped too, half-way to the steamer, as if petrified. I saw the man on the stretcher sit up, lank and with an uplifted arm, above the shoulders of the bearers. 'Let us hope that the man who can talk so well of love in general will find some particular reason to spare us this time,' I said. I resented bitterly the absurd danger of our situation, as if to be at the mercy of that atrocious phantom had been a dishonoring necessity. I could not hear a sound, but through my glasses I saw the thin arm extended commandingly, the lower jaw moving, the eyes of that apparition shining darkly far in its bony head that nodded with grotesque jerks. Kurtz—Kurtz—that means short in German—don't it? Well, the name was as true as everything else in his life—and death. He looked at least seven feet long. His covering had fallen off, and his body emerged from it pitiful and appalling as from a winding-sheet. I could see the cage of his ribs all astir, the bones of his arm waving. It was as though an animated image of death carved out of old ivory had been shaking its hand with menaces at a motionless crowd of men made of dark and glittering bronze. I saw him open his mouth wide— it gave him a weirdly voracious aspect, as though he had wanted to swallow all the air, all the earth, all the men before him. A deep voice reached me faintly. He must have been shouting. He fell back suddenly. The stretcher shook as the bearers staggered forward again, and almost at the same time I noticed that the crowd of savages was vanishing without any perceptible movement of retreat, as if the forest that had ejected these beings so suddenly had drawn them in again as the breath is drawn in a long aspiration.

"Some of the pilgrims behind the stretcher carried his arms— two shot-guns, a heavy rifle, and a light revolver-carbine—the thunderbolts of that pitiful Jupiter. The manager bent over him murmuring as he walked beside his head. They laid him down in one of the little cabins—just a room for a bed-place and a camp-stool or two, you know. We had brought his belated correspondence, and a lot of torn envelopes and open letters littered his bed. His hand roamed feebly amongst these papers. I was struck by the fire of his eyes and the composed languor of his expression. It was not so much the exhaustion of disease. He did not seem in pain. This shadow looked satiated and calm, as though for the moment it had had its fill of all the emotions.

"He rustled one of the letters, and looking straight in my face said, 'I am glad.' Somebody had been writing to him about me. These special recommendations were turning up again. The volume of tone he emitted without effort, almost without the trouble of moving his lips, amazed me. A voice! a voice! It was grave, profound, vibrating, while the man did not seem capable of a whisper. However, he had enough strength in him—factitious no doubt—to very nearly make an end of us, as you shall hear directly.

"The manager appeared silently in the doorway; I stepped out at once and he drew the curtain after me. The Russian, eyed curiously by the pilgrims, was staring at the shore. I followed the direction of his glance.

"Dark human shapes could be made out in the distance, flitting indistinctly against the gloomy border of the forest, and near the river two bronze figures, leaning on tall spears, stood in the sunlight under fantastic head-dresses of spotted skins, warlike and still in statuesque repose. And from right to left along the lighted shore moved a wild and gorgeous apparition of a woman.

"She walked with measured steps, draped in striped and fringed cloths, treading the earth proudly, with a slight jingle and flash of barbarous ornaments. She carried her head high; her hair was done in the shape of a helmet; she had brass leggings to the knee, brass wire gauntlets to the elbow, a crimson spot on her tawny cheek, innumerable necklaces of glass beads on her neck; bizarre things, charms, gifts of witch-men, that hung about her, glittered and trembled at every step. She must have had the value of several elephant tusks upon her. She was savage and superb, wild-eyed and magnificent; there was something ominous and stately in her deliberate progress. And in the hush that had fallen suddenly upon the whole sorrowful land, the immense wilderness, the colossal body of the fecund and mysterious life seemed to look at her, pensive, as though it had been looking at the image of its own tenebrous and passionate soul.

"She came abreast of the steamer, stood still, and faced us. Her long shadow fell to the water's edge. Her face had a tragic and fierce aspect of wild sorrow and of dumb pain mingled with the fear of some struggling, half-shaped resolve. She stood looking at us without a stir and like the wilderness itself, with an air of brooding over an inscrutable purpose. A whole minute passed, and then she made a step forward. There was a low jingle, a glint of yellow metal, a sway of fringed draperies, and she stopped as if her heart had failed her. The young fellow by my side growled. The pilgrims murmured at my back. She looked at us all as if her life had depended upon the unswerving steadiness of her glance. Suddenly she opened her bared arms and threw them up rigid above her head, as though in an uncontrollable desire to touch the sky, and at the same time the swift shadows darted out on the earth, swept around on the river, gathering the steamer into a shadowy embrace. A formidable silence hung over the scene.

"She turned away slowly, walked on, following the bank, and passed into the bushes to the left. Once only her eyes gleamed back at us in the dusk of the thickets before she disappeared.

" 'If she had offered to come aboard I really think I would have tried to shoot her,' said the man of patches, nervously. 'I had been risking my life every day for the last fortnight to keep her out of the house. She got in one day and kicked up a row about those miserable rags I picked up in the storeroom to mend my clothes with. I wasn't decent. At least it must have been that, for she talked like a fury to Kurtz for an hour, pointing at me now and then. I don't understand the dialect of this tribe. Luckily for me, I fancy Kurtz felt too ill that day to care, or there would have been mischief. I don't understand. . . . No—it's too much for me. Ah, well, it's all over now.'

"At this moment I heard Kurtz's deep voice behind the curtain, 'Save me!—save the ivory, you mean. Don't tell me. Save *me!* Why, I've had to save you. You are interrupting my plans now. Sick! Sick! Not so sick as you would like to believe. Never mind. I'll carry my ideas out yet—I will return. I'll show you what can be done. You with your little peddling notions—you are interfering with me. I will return. I . . .'

"The manager came out. He did me the honor to take me under the arm and lead me aside. 'He is very low, very low,' he said. He considered it necessary to sigh, but neglected to be consistently sorrowful. 'We have done all we could for him—haven't we? But there is no disguising the fact, Mr. Kurtz has done more harm than good to the Company. He did not see the time was not ripe for vigorous action. Cautiously, cautiously—that's my principle. We must be cautious yet. The district is closed to us for a time. Deplorable! Upon the whole, the trade will suffer. I don't deny there is a remarkable quantity of ivory—mostly fossil. We must save it, at all events—but look how precarious the position is—and why? Because the method is unsound.' 'Do you,' said I, looking at the shore, 'call it "unsound method"?' 'Without doubt,' he exclaimed, hotly. 'Don't you?' . . . 'No method at all,' I murmured after a while. 'Exactly,' he exulted. 'I anticipated this. Shows a complete want of judgment. It is my duty to point it out in the proper quarter.' 'Oh,' said I, 'that fellow—what's his name?—the brickmaker, will make a readable report for you.' He appeared confounded for a moment. It seemed to me I had never breathed an atmosphere so vile, and I turned mentally to Kurtz for relief—positively for relief. 'Nevertheless I think Mr. Kurtz is a remarkable man,' I said with emphasis. He started, dropped on me a cold heavy glance, said very quietly, 'He *was,*' and turned his back on me. My hour of favor was over; I found myself lumped along with Kurtz as a partisan of methods for which the time was not ripe: I was unsound! Ah! but it was something to have at least a choice of nightmares.

"I had turned to the wilderness really, not to Mr. Kurtz, who, I was ready to admit, was as good as buried. And for a moment it seemed to me as if I also were buried in a vast grave full of unspeakable secrets. I felt an intolerable weight oppressing my breast, the smell of the damp earth, the unseen presence of

victorious corruption, the darkness of an impenetrable night. . . .
The Russian tapped me on the shoulder. I heard him mumbling
and stammering something about 'brother seaman—couldn't
conceal—knowledge of matters that would affect Mr. Kurtz's
reputation.' I waited. For him evidently Mr. Kurtz was not in
his grave; I suspect that for him Mr. Kurtz was one of the immortals. 'Well!' said I at last, 'speak out. As it happens, I am
Mr. Kurtz's friend—in a way.'

"He stated with a good deal of formality that had we not been
'of the same profession,' he would have kept the matter to himself without regard to consequences. 'He suspected there was
an active ill-will towards him on the part of these white men
that——' 'You are right,' I said, remembering a certain conversation I had overheard. 'The manager thinks you ought to be
hanged.' He showed a concern at this intelligence which amused
me at first. 'I had better get out of the way quietly,' he said,
earnestly. 'I can do no more for Kurtz now, and they would soon
find some excuse. What's to stop them? There's a military post
three hundred miles from here.' 'Well, upon my word,' said I,
'perhaps you had better go if you have any friends amongst the
savages near by.' 'Plenty,' he said. 'They are simple people—and
I want nothing, you know.' He stood biting his lip, then: 'I
don't want any harm to happen to these whites here, but of
course I was thinking of Mr. Kurtz's reputation—but you are a
brother seaman and——' 'All right,' said I, after a time. 'Mr.
Kurtz's reputation is safe with me.' I did not know how truly I
spoke.

"He informed me, lowering his voice, that it was Kurtz who
had ordered the attack to be made on the steamer. 'He hated
sometimes the idea of being taken away—and then again. . . .
But I don't understand these matters. I am a simple man. He
thought it would scare you away—that you would give it up,
thinking him dead. I could not stop him. Oh, I had an awful
time of it this last month.' 'Very well,' I said. 'He is all right
now.' 'Ye-e-es,' he muttered, not very convinced apparently.
'Thanks,' said I; 'I shall keep my eyes open.' 'But quiet—eh?'

he urged, anxiously. 'It would be awful for his reputation if anybody here——' I promised a complete discretion with great
gravity. 'I have a canoe and three black fellows waiting not very
far. I am off. Could you give me a few Martini-Henry cartridges?'
I could, and did, with proper secrecy. He helped himself, with
a wink at me, to a handful of my tobacco. 'Between sailors—you
know—good English tobacco.' At the door of the pilot-house he
turned round—'I say, haven't you a pair of shoes you could
spare?' He raised one leg. 'Look.' The soles were tied with
knotted strings sandal-wise under his bare feet. I rooted out an
old pair, at which he looked with admiration before tucking it
under his left arm. One of his pockets (bright red) was bulging
with cartridges, from the other (dark blue) peeped 'Towson's
Inquiry,' &c., &c. He seemed to think himself excellently well
equipped for a renewed encounter with the wilderness. 'Ah!
I'll never, never meet such a man again. You ought to have heard
him recite poetry—his own too it was, he told me. Poetry!' He
rolled his eyes at the recollection of these delights. 'Oh, he enlarged my mind!' 'Good-by,' said I. He shook hands and vanished in the night. Sometimes I ask myself whether I had ever
really seen him—whether it was possible to meet such a phenomenon! . . .

"When I woke up shortly after midnight his warning came
to mind with its hint of danger that seemed, in the starred darkness, real enough to make me get up for the purpose of having
a look round. On the hill a big fire burned, illuminating fitfully
a crooked corner of the station-house. One of the agents with a
picket of a few of our blacks, armed for the purpose, was keeping guard over the ivory; but deep within the forest, red gleams
that wavered, that seemed to sink and rise from the ground
amongst confused columnar shapes of intense blackness, showed
the exact position of the camp where Mr. Kurtz's adorers were
keeping their uneasy vigil. The monotonous beating of a big
drum filled the air with muffled shocks and a lingering vibration.
A steady droning sound of many men chanting each to himself
some weird incantation came out from the black, flat wall of

the woods as the humming of bees comes out of a hive, and had a strange narcotic effect upon my half-awake senses. I believe I dozed off leaning over the rail, till an abrupt burst of yells, an overwhelming outbreak of a pent-up and mysterious frenzy, woke me up in a bewildered wonder. It was cut short all at once, and the low droning went on with an effect of audible and soothing silence. I glanced casually into the little cabin. A light was burning within, but Mr. Kurtz was not there.

"I think I would have raised an outcry if I had believed my eyes. But I didn't believe them at first—the thing seemed so impossible. The fact is I was completely unnerved by a sheer blank fright, pure abstract terror, unconnected with any distinct shape of physical danger. What made this emotion so overpowering was—how shall I define it?—the moral shock I received, as if something altogether monstrous, intolerable to thought and odious to the soul, had been thrust upon me unexpectedly. This lasted of course the merest fraction of a second, and then the usual sense of commonplace, deadly danger, the possibility of a sudden onslaught and massacre, or something of the kind, which I saw impending, was positively welcome and composing. It pacified me, in fact, so much, that I did not raise an alarm.

"There was an agent buttoned up inside an ulster and sleeping on a chair on deck within three feet of me. The yells had not awakened him; he snored very slightly; I left him to his slumbers and leaped ashore. I did not betray Mr. Kurtz—it was ordered I should never betray him—it was written I should be loyal to the nightmare of my choice. I was anxious to deal with this shadow by myself alone,—and to this day I don't know why I was so jealous of sharing with anyone the peculiar blackness of that experience.

"As soon as I got on the bank I saw a trail—a broad trail through the grass. I remember the exultation with which I said to myself, 'He can't walk—he is crawling on all-fours—I've got him.' The grass was wet with dew. I strode rapidly with clenched fists. I fancy I had some vague notion of falling upon him and giving him a drubbing. I don't know. I had some imbecile thoughts. The knitting old woman with the cat obtruded herself upon my memory as a most improper person to be sitting at the other end of such an affair. I saw a row of pilgrims squirting lead in the air out of Winchesters held to the hip. I thought I would never get back to the steamer, and imagined myself living alone and unarmed in the woods to an advanced age. Such silly things —you know. And I remember I confounded the beat of the drum with the beating of my heart, and was pleased at its calm regularity.

"I kept to the track though—then stopped to listen. The night was very clear: a dark blue space, sparkling with dew and starlight, in which black things stood very still. I thought I could see a kind of motion ahead of me. I was strangely cocksure of everything that night. I actually left the track and ran in a wide semicircle (I verily believe chuckling to myself) so as to get in front of that stir, of that motion I had seen—if indeed I had seen anything. I was circumventing Kurtz as though it had been a boyish game.

"I came upon him, and, if he had not heard me coming, I would have fallen over him too, but he got up in time. He rose, unsteady, long, pale, indistinct, like a vapor exhaled by the earth, and swayed slightly, misty and silent before me; while at my back the fires loomed between the trees, and the murmur of many voices issued from the forest. I had cut him off cleverly; but when actually confronting him I seemed to come to my senses, I saw the danger in its right proportion. It was by no means over yet. Suppose he began to shout? Though he could hardly stand, there was still plenty of vigor in his voice. 'Go away—hide yourself,' he said, in that profound tone. It was very awful. I glanced back. We were within thirty yards from the nearest fire. A black figure stood up, strode on long black legs, waving long black arms, across the glow. It had horns—antelope horns, I think—on its head. Some sorcerer, some witch-man, no doubt; it looked fiend-like enough. 'Do you know what you are doing?' I whispered. 'Perfectly,' he answered, raising his voice for that single word: it sounded to me far off and yet loud, like a hail through a speaking-trumpet. If he makes a row we are lost, I thought to myself. This clearly was not a case for fisticuffs, even apart from the very natural aversion I had to beat that Shadow—this wandering and tormented thing. 'You will be lost,' I said—'utterly lost.' One gets sometimes such a flash of inspiration, you know. I did say the right thing, though indeed he could not have been more irretrievably lost than he was at this very moment, when the foundations of our intimacy were being laid—to endure—to endure—even to the end—even beyond.

" 'I had immense plans,' he muttered irresolutely. 'Yes,' said I; 'but if you try to shout I'll smash your head with——' there was not a stick or a stone near. 'I will throttle you for good,' I corrected myself. 'I was on the threshold of great things,' he pleaded, in a voice of longing, with a wistfulness of tone that made my blood run cold. 'And now for this stupid scoundrel——' 'Your success in Europe is assured in any case,' I affirmed, steadily. I did not want to have the throttling of him, you understand—and indeed it would have been very little use for any practical purpose. I tried to break the spell—the heavy, mute spell of the wilderness—that seemed to draw him to its pitiless breast by the awakening of forgotten and brutal instincts, by the memory of gratified and monstrous passions. This alone, I was convinced, had driven him out to the edge of the forest, to the bush, towards the gleam of fires, the throb of drums, the drone of weird incantations; this alone had beguiled his unlawful soul beyond the bounds of permitted aspirations. And, don't you see, the terror of the position was not in being knocked on the head —though I had a very lively sense of that danger too—but in this, that I had to deal with a being to whom I could not appeal in the name of anything high or low. I had, even like the niggers, to invoke him—himself—his own exalted and incredible degradation. There was nothing either above or below him, and I knew it. He had kicked himself loose of the earth. Confound the man! he had kicked the very earth to pieces. He was alone, and I before him did not know whether I stood on the ground or floated in the air. I've been telling you what we said—repeating the phrases we pronounced,—but what's the good? They were common everyday words,—the familiar, vague sounds exchanged on every waking day of life. But what of that? They had behind them, to my mind, the terrific suggestiveness of words heard in dreams, of phrases spoken in nightmares. Soul! If anybody had ever struggled with a soul, I am the man. And I wasn't arguing with a lunatic either. Believe me or not, his intelligence was perfectly clear—concentrated, it is true, upon himself with horrible intensity, yet clear; and therein was my only chance—barring, of course, the killing him there and then, which wasn't so good, on account of unavoidable noise. But his soul was mad. Being alone in the wilderness, it had looked within itself, and, by heavens! I tell you, it had gone mad. I had —for my sins, I suppose—to go through the ordeal of looking into it myself. No eloquence could have been so withering to one's belief in mankind as his final burst of sincerity. He struggled with himself, too. I saw it,—I heard it. I saw the inconceivable mystery of a soul that knew no restraint, no faith, and no fear, yet struggling blindly with itself. I kept my head pretty well; but when I had him at last stretched on the couch, I wiped my forehead, while my legs shook under me as though I had carried half a ton on my back down that hill. And yet I had only supported him, his bony arm clasped around my neck—and he was not much heavier than a child.

"When next day we left at noon, the crowd, of whose presence behind the curtain of trees I had been acutely conscious all the time, flowed out of the woods again, filled the clearing, covered the slope with a mass of naked, breathing, quivering, bronze bodies. I steamed up a bit, then swung down-stream, and two thousand eyes followed the evolutions of the splashing, thumping, fierce river-demon beating the water with its terrible tail and breathing black smoke into the air. In front of the first rank, along the river, three men, plastered with bright red earth from head to foot, strutted to and fro restlessly. When we came abreast again, they faced the river, stamped their feet, nodded their horned heads, swayed their scarlet bodies; they shook towards the fierce river-demon a bunch of black feathers, a mangy skin with a pendent tail—something that looked like a dried gourd; they shouted periodically together strings of amazing words that resembled no sounds of human language; and the deep murmurs of the crowd, interrupted suddenly, were like the response of some satanic litany.

"We had carried Kurtz into the pilot-house: there was more air there. Lying on the couch, he stared through the open shutter. There was an eddy in the mass of human bodies, and the woman with helmeted head and tawny cheeks rushed out to the very brink of the stream. She put out her hands, shouted something, and all that wild mob took up the shout in a roaring chorus of articulated, rapid, breathless utterance.

" 'Do you understand this?' I asked.

"He kept on looking out past me with fiery, longing eyes, with a mingled expression of wistfulness and hate. He made no answer, but I saw a smile, a smile of indefinable meaning, appear on his colorless lips that a moment after twitched convulsively. 'Do I not?' he said slowly, gasping, as if the words had been torn out of him by a supernatural power.

"I pulled the string of the whistle, and I did this because I saw the pilgrims on deck getting out their rifles with an air of anticipating a jolly lark. At the sudden screech there was a movement of abject terror through that wedged mass of bodies. 'Don't! don't! you frighten them away,' cried someone on deck disconsolately. I pulled the string time after time. They broke and ran, they leaped, they crouched, they swerved, they dodged the flying terror of the sound. The three red chaps had fallen flat, face down on the shore, as though they had been shot dead. Only the barbarous and superb woman did not so much as flinch, and stretched tragically her bare arms after us over the somber and glittering river.

"And then that imbecile crowd down on the deck started their little fun, and I could see nothing more for smoke.

"The brown current ran swiftly out of the heart of darkness, bearing us down towards the sea with twice the speed of our

upward progress; and Kurtz's life was running swiftly too,
ebbing, ebbing out of his heart into the sea of inexorable time.
The manager was very placid, he had no vital anxieties now,
he took us both in with a comprehensive and satisfied glance: the
'affair' had come off as well as could be wished. I saw the time
approaching when I would be left alone of the party of 'unsound
method.' The pilgrims looked upon me with disfavor. I was, so
to speak, numbered with the dead. It is strange how I accepted
this unforeseen partnership, this choice of nightmares forced
upon me in the tenebrous land invaded by these mean and
greedy phantoms.

"Kurtz discoursed. A voice! a voice! It rang deep to the very
last. It survived his strength to hide in the magnificent folds of
eloquence the barren darkness of his heart. Oh, he struggled!
he struggled! The wastes of his weary brain were haunted by
shadowy images now—images of wealth and fame revolving ob-
sequiously round his unextinguishable gift of noble and lofty
expression. My Intended, my station, my career, my ideas—these
were the subjects for the occasional utterances of elevated sentiments. The shade of the original Kurtz frequented the bedside
of the hollow sham, whose fate it was to be buried presently
in the mold of primeval earth. But both the diabolic love and
the unearthly hate of the mysteries it had penetrated fought for
the possession of that soul satiated with primitive emotions, avid
of lying fame, of sham distinction, of all the appearances of
success and power.

"Sometimes he was contemptibly childish. He desired to have
kings meet him at railway-stations on his return from some
ghastly Nowhere, where he intended to accomplish great things.
'You show them you have in you something that is really profitable, and then there will be no limits to the recognition of your
ability,' he would say. 'Of course you must take care of the motives—right motives—always.' The long reaches that were like
one and the same reach, monotonous bends that were exactly
alike, slipped past the steamer with their multitude of secular
trees looking patiently after this grimy fragment of another

world, the forerunner of change, of conquest, of trade, of massacres, of blessings. I looked ahead—piloting. 'Close the shutter,' said Kurtz suddenly one day; 'I can't bear to look at this.' I did so. There was a silence. 'Oh, but I will wring your heart yet!' he cried at the invisible wilderness.

"We broke down—as I had expected—and had to lie up for repairs at the head of an island. This delay was the first thing that shook Kurtz's confidence. One morning he gave me a packet of papers and a photograph,—the lot tied together with a shoe-string. 'Keep this for me,' he said. 'This noxious fool' (meaning the manager) 'is capable of prying into my boxes when I am not looking.' In the afternoon I saw him. He was lying on his back with closed eyes, and I withdrew quietly, but I heard him mutter, 'Live rightly, die, die . . .' I listened. There was nothing more. Was he rehearsing some speech in his sleep, or was it a fragment of a phrase from some newspaper article? He had been writing for the papers and meant to do so again, 'for the furthering of my ideas. It's a duty.'

"His was an impenetrable darkness. I looked at him as you peer down at a man who is lying at the bottom of a precipice where the sun never shines. But I had not much time to give him, because I was helping the engine-driver to take to pieces the leaky cylinders, to straighten a bent connecting-rod, and in other such matters. I lived in an infernal mess of rust, filings, nuts, bolts, spanners, hammers, ratchet-drills—things I abominate, because I don't get on with them. I tended the little forge we fortunately had aboard; I toiled wearily in a wretched scrap-heap—unless I had the shakes too bad to stand.

"One evening coming in with a candle I was startled to hear him say a little tremulously, 'I am lying here in the dark waiting for death.' The light was within a foot of his eyes. I forced myself to murmur, 'Oh, nonsense!' and stood over him as if transfixed.

"Anything approaching the change that came over his features I have never seen before, and hope never to see again. Oh, I wasn't touched. I was fascinated. It was as though a veil had been rent. I saw on that ivory face the expression of somber pride, of ruthless power, of craven terror—of an intense and hopeless despair. Did he live his life again in every detail of desire, temptation, and surrender during that supreme moment of complete knowledge? He cried in a whisper at some image, at some vision, —he cried out twice, a cry that was no more than a breath—

" 'The horror! The horror!'

"I blew the candle out and left the cabin. The pilgrims were dining in the mess-room, and I took my place opposite the manager, who lifted his eyes to give me a questioning glance, which I successfully ignored. He leaned back, serene, with that peculiar smile of his sealing the unexpressed depths of his meanness. A continuous shower of small flies streamed upon the lamp, upon the cloth, upon our hands and faces. Suddenly the manager's boy put his insolent black head in the doorway, and said in a tone of scathing contempt—

" 'Mistah Kurtz—he dead.'

"All the pilgrims rushed out to see. I remained, and went on with my dinner. I believe I was considered brutally callous. However, I did not eat much. There was a lamp in there—light, don't you know—and outside it was so beastly, beastly dark. I went no more near the remarkable man who had pronounced a judgment upon the adventures of his soul on this earth. The voice was gone. What else had been there? But I am of course aware that next day the pilgrims buried something in a muddy hole.

"And then they very nearly buried me.

"However, as you see, I did not go to join Kurtz there and then. I did not. I remained to dream the nightmare out to the end, and to show my loyalty to Kurtz once more. Destiny. My destiny! Droll thing life is—that mysterious arrangement of merciless logic for a futile purpose. The most you can hope from it is some knowledge of yourself—that comes too late—a crop of unextinguishable regrets. I have wrestled with death. It is the most unexciting contest you can imagine. It takes place in an impalpable grayness, with nothing underfoot, with nothing around, without spectators, without clamor, without glory, without the great desire of victory, without the great fear of defeat, in a sickly atmosphere of tepid skepticism, without much belief in your own right, and still less in that of your adversary. If such is the form of ultimate wisdom, then life is a greater riddle than some of us think it to be. I was within a hair's-breadth of the last opportunity for pronouncement, and I found with humiliation that probably I would have nothing to say. This is the reason why I affirm that Kurtz was a remarkable man. He had something to say. He said it. Since I had peeped over the edge myself, I understand better the meaning of his stare, that could not see the flame of the candle, but was wide enough to embrace the whole universe, piercing enough to penetrate all the hearts that beat in the darkness. He had summed up—he had judged. 'The horror!' He was a remarkable man. After all, this was the expression of some sort of belief; it had candor, it had conviction, it had a vibrating note of revolt in its whisper, it had the appalling face of a glimpsed truth—the strange commingling of desire and hate. And it is not my own extremity I remember best—a vision of grayness without form filled with physical pain, and a careless contempt for the evanescence of all things—even of this pain itself. No! It is his extremity that I seem to have lived through. True, he had made that last stride, he had stepped over the edge, while I had been permitted to draw back my hesitating foot. And perhaps in this is the whole difference; perhaps all the wisdom, and all truth, and all sincerity, are just compressed into that inappreciable moment of time in which we step over the threshold of the invisible. Perhaps! I like to think my summing-up would not have been a word of careless contempt. Better his cry—much better. It was an affirmation, a moral victory paid for by innumerable defeats, by abominable terrors, by abominable satisfactions. But it was a victory! That is why I have remained loyal to Kurtz to the last, and even beyond, when a long time after I heard once more, not his own voice, but the echo of his magnificent eloquence thrown to me from a soul as translucently pure as a cliff of crystal.

"No, they did not bury me, though there is a period of time which I remember mistily, with a shuddering wonder, like a passage through some inconceivable world that had no hope in it and no desire. I found myself back in the sepulchral city resenting the sight of people hurrying through the streets to filch a little money from each other, to devour their infamous cookery, to gulp their unwholesome beer, to dream their insignificant and silly dreams. They trespassed upon my thoughts. They were intruders whose knowledge of life was to me an irritating pretense, because I felt so sure they could not possibly know the things I knew. Their bearing, which was simply the bearing of commonplace individuals going about their business in the assurance of perfect safety, was offensive to me like the outrageous flauntings of folly in the face of a danger it is unable to comprehend. I had no particular desire to enlighten them, but I had some difficulty in restraining myself from laughing in their faces, so full of stupid importance. I dare say I was not very well at that time. I tottered about the streets—there were various affairs to settle—grinning bitterly at perfectly respectable persons. I admit my behavior was inexcusable, but then my temperature was seldom normal in these days. My dear aunt's endeavors to 'nurse up my strength' seemed altogether beside the mark. It was not my strength that wanted nursing, it was my imagination that wanted soothing. I kept the bundle of papers given me by Kurtz, not knowing exactly what to do with it. His mother had died lately, watched over, as I was told, by his Intended. A clean-shaved man, with an official manner and wearing gold-rimmed spectacles, called on me one day and made inquiries, at first circuitous, afterwards suavely pressing, about what he was pleased to denominate certain 'documents.' I was not surprised, because I had had two rows with the manager on the subject out there. I had refused to give up the smallest scrap out of that package, and I took the same attitude with the spectacled man. He became darkly menacing at last, and with much heat argued that the Company had the right to every bit of information about its 'territories.' And, said he, 'Mr. Kurtz's knowledge of unexplored regions must have been necessarily extensive and peculiar—owing to his great abilities and to the deplorable circumstances in which he had been placed: therefore'——I assured him Mr. Kurtz's knowledge, however extensive, did not bear upon the problems of commerce or administration. He invoked then the name of science. 'It would be an incalculable loss if,' &c., &c. I offered him the report on the 'Suppression of Savage Customs,' with the postscriptum torn off. He took it up eagerly, but ended by sniffing at it with an air of contempt. 'This is not what we had a right to expect,' he remarked. 'Expect nothing else,' I said. 'There are only private letters.' He withdrew upon some threat of legal proceedings, and I saw him no more; but another fellow, calling himself Kurtz's cousin, appeared two days later, and was anxious to hear all the details about his dear relative's last moments. Incidentally he gave me to understand that Kurtz had been essentially a great musician. 'There was the making of an immense success,' said the man, who was an organist, I believe, with lank gray hair flowing over a greasy coat-collar. I had no reason to doubt his statement; and to this day I am unable to say what was Kurtz's profession, whether he ever had any—which was the greatest of his talents. I had taken him for a painter who wrote for the papers, or else for a journalist who could paint—but even the cousin (who took snuff during the interview) could not tell me what he had been —exactly. He was a universal genius—on that point I agreed with the old chap, who thereupon blew his nose noisily into a large cotton handkerchief and withdrew in senile agitation, bearing off some family letters and memoranda without importance. Ultimately a journalist anxious to know something of the fate of his 'dear colleague' turned up. This visitor informed me Kurtz's proper sphere ought to have been politics 'on the popular side.' He had furry straight eyebrows, bristly hair cropped short, an eye-glass on a broad ribbon, and, becoming expansive, confessed his opinion that Kurtz really couldn't write a bit—'but heavens! how that man could talk! He electrified large meetings. He had faith—don't **you** see?—he had the faith. He could get himself to believe anything—anything. He would have been a splendid leader of an extreme party.' 'What party?' I asked. 'Any party,' answered the other. 'He was an—an—extremist.' Did I not think so? I assented. Did I know, he asked, with a sudden flash of curiosity, 'what it was that had induced him to go out there?' 'Yes,' said I, and forthwith handed him the famous Report for publication, if he thought fit. He glanced through it hurriedly, mumbling all the time, judged 'it would do,' and took himself off with this plunder.

"Thus I was left at last with a slim packet of letters and the girl's portrait. She struck me as beautiful—I mean she had a beautiful expression. I know that the sunlight can be made to lie too, yet one felt that no manipulation of light and pose could have conveyed the delicate shade of truthfulness upon those features. She seemed ready to listen without mental reservation, without suspicion, without a thought for herself. I concluded I would go and give her back her portrait and those letters myself. Curiosity? Yes; and also some other feeling perhaps. All that had been Kurtz's had passed out of my hands: his soul, his body, his station, his plans, his ivory, his career. There remained only his memory and his Intended—and I wanted to give that up too to the past, in a way,—to surrender personally all that remained of him with me to that oblivion which is the last word of our common fate. I don't defend myself. I had no clear perception of what it was I really wanted. Perhaps it was an impulse of unconscious loyalty, or the fulfillment of one of these ironic necessities that lurk in the facts of human existence. I don't know. I can't tell. But I went.

"I thought his memory was like the other memories of the dead that accumulate in every man's life,—a vague impress on the brain of shadows that had fallen on it in their swift and final passage; but before the high and ponderous door, between the tall houses of a street as still and decorous as a well-kept alley in a cemetery, I had a vision of him on the stretcher, opening his mouth voraciously, as if to devour all the earth with all its mankind. He lived then before me; he lived as much as he had ever lived—a shadow insatiable of splendid appearances, of frightful realities; a shadow darker than the shadow of the night, and draped nobly in the folds of a gorgeous eloquence. The vision seemed to enter the house with me—the stretcher, the phantom-bearers, the wild crowd of obedient worshipers, the gloom of the forests, the glitter of the reach between the murky bends, the beat of the drum, regular and muffled like the beating of a heart—the heart of a conquering darkness. It was a moment of triumph for the wilderness, an invading and vengeful rush which, it seemed to me, I would have to keep back alone for the salvation of another soul. And the memory of what I had heard him say afar there, with the horned shapes stirring at my back, in the glow of fires, within the patient woods, those broken phrases came back to me, were heard again in their ominous and terrifying simplicity. I remembered his abject pleading, his abject threats, the colossal scale of his vile desires, the meanness, the torment, the tempestuous anguish of his soul. And later on I seemed to see his collected languid manner, when he said one day, 'This lot of ivory now is really mine. The Company did not pay for it. I collected it myself at a very great personal risk. I am afraid they will try to claim it as theirs though. H'm. It is a difficult case. What do you think I ought to do—resist? Eh? I want no more than justice.' . . . He wanted no more than justice —no more than justice. I rang the bell before a mahogany door on the first floor, and while I waited he seemed to stare at me out of the glassy panel—stare with that wide and immense stare embracing, condemning, loathing all the universe. I seemed to hear the whispered cry, 'The horror! The horror!'

"The dusk was falling. I had to wait in a lofty drawing-room with three long windows from floor to ceiling that were like three luminous and bedraped columns. The bent gilt legs and backs of the furniture shone in indistinct curves. The tall marble fireplace had a cold and monumental whiteness. A grand piano stood massively in a corner, with dark gleams on the flat surfaces like a somber and polished sarcophagus. A high door opened—closed. I rose.

"She came forward, all in black, with a pale head, floating towards me in the dusk. She was in mourning. It was more than a year since his death, more than a year since the news came; she seemed as though she would remember and mourn for ever. She took both my hands in hers and murmured, 'I had heard you were coming.' I noticed she was not very young—I mean not girlish. She had a mature capacity for fidelity, for belief, for suffering. The room seemed to have grown darker, as if all the sad light of the cloudy evening had taken refuge on her forehead. This fair hair, this pale visage, this pure brow, seemed surrounded by an ashy halo from which the dark eyes looked out at me. Their glance was guileless, profound, confident, and trustful. She carried her sorrowful head as though she were proud of that sorrow, as though she would say, I—I alone know how to mourn for him as he deserves. But while we were still shaking hands, such a look of awful desolation came upon her face that I perceived she was one of those creatures that are not the playthings of Time. For her he had died only yesterday. And, by Jove! The impression was so powerful that for me too he seemed to have died only yesterday—nay, this very minute. I saw her and him in the same instant of time—his death and her sorrow—I saw her sorrow in the very moment of his death. Do you understand? I saw them together—I heard them together. She had said, with a deep catch of the breath, 'I have survived;' while my strained ears seemed to hear distinctly, mingled with her tone of despairing regret, the summing-up whisper of his eternal condemnation. I asked myself what I was doing there, with a sensation of panic in my heart as though I had blundered into a place of cruel and absurd mysteries not fit for a human being to behold. She motioned me to a chair. We sat down. I laid the packet gently on the little table, and she put her hand over it. . . . 'You knew him well,' she murmured, after a moment of mourning silence.

" 'Intimacy grows quick out there,' I said. 'I knew him as well as it is possible for one man to know another.'

" 'And you admired him,' she said. 'It was impossible to know him and not to admire him. Was it?'

" 'He was a remarkable man,' I said, unsteadily. Then before the appealing fixity of her gaze, that seemed to watch for more words on my lips, I went on, 'It was impossible not to——'

" 'Love him,' she finished eagerly, silencing me into an appalled dumbness. 'How true! how true! But when you think that no one knew him so well as I! I had all his noble confidence. I knew him best.'

" 'You knew him best,' I repeated. And perhaps she did. But with every word spoken the room was growing darker, and only her forehead, smooth and white, remained illumined by the unextinguishable light of belief and love.

" 'You were his friend,' she went on. 'His friend,' she repeated, a little louder. 'You must have been, if he had given you this, and sent you to me. I feel I can speak to you—and oh! I must speak. I want you—you who have heard his last words—to know I have been worthy of him. . . . It is not pride. . . . Yes! I am proud to know I understood him better than anyone on earth—he told me so himself. And since his mother died I have had no one—no one—to—to——'

"I listened. The darkness deepened. I was not even sure whether he had given me the right bundle. I rather suspect he wanted me to take care of another batch of his papers which, after his death, I saw the manager examining under the lamp. And the girl talked, easing her pain in the certitude of my sympathy; she talked as thirsty men drink. I had heard that her engagement with Kurtz had been disapproved by her people. He wasn't rich enough or something. And indeed I don't know whether he had not been a pauper all his life. He had given me some reason to infer that it was his impatience of comparative poverty that drove him out there.

" '. . . Who was not his friend who had heard him speak once?' she was saying. 'He drew men towards him by what was best in them.' She looked at me with intensity. 'It is the gift of the great,' she went on, and the sound of her low voice seemed to have the accompaniment of all the other sounds, full of mystery, desolation, and sorrow, I had ever heard—the ripple of the river, the soughing of the trees swayed by the wind, the murmurs of wild crows, the faint ring of incomprehensible words cried from afar, the whisper of a voice speaking from beyond the threshold of an eternal darkness. 'But you have heard him! You know!' she cried.

" 'Yes, I know,' I said with something like despair in my heart, but bowing my head before the faith that was in her, before that great and saving illusion that shone with an unearthly glow in the darkness, in the triumphant darkness from which I could not have defended her—from which I could not even defend myself.

" 'What a loss to me—to us!'—she corrected herself with beautiful generosity; then added in a murmur, 'To the world.' By the last gleams of twilight I could see the glitter of her eyes, full of tears—of tears that would not fall.

" 'I have been very happy—very fortunate—very proud,' she went on. 'Too fortunate. Too happy for a little while. And now I am unhappy for—for life.'

"She stood up; her fair hair seemed to catch all the remaining light in a glimmer of gold. I rose too.

" 'And of all this,' she went on, mournfully, 'of all his promise, and of all his greatness, of his generous mind, of his noble heart, nothing remains—nothing but a memory. You and I——'

" 'We shall always remember him,' I said, hastily.

" 'No!' she cried. 'It is impossible that all this should be lost —that such a life should be sacrificed to leave nothing—but sorrow. You know what vast plans he had. I knew of them too—I could not perhaps understand,—but others knew of them. Something must remain. His words, at least, have not died.'

" 'His words will remain,' I said.

" 'And his example,' she whispered to herself. 'Men looked up to him,—his goodness shone in every act. His example——'

" 'True,' I said; 'his example too. Yes, his example. I forgot that.'

" 'But I do not. I cannot—I cannot believe—not yet. I cannot believe that I shall never see him again, that nobody will see him again, never, never, never.'

"She put out her arms as if after a retreating figure, stretching them back and with clasped pale hands across the fading and narrow sheen of the window. Never see him! I saw him clearly enough then. I shall see this eloquent phantom as long as I live, and I shall see her too, a tragic and familiar Shade, resembling in this gesture another one, tragic also, and bedecked with powerless charms, stretching bare brown arms over the glitter of the infernal stream, the stream of darkness. She said suddenly very low, 'He died as he lived.'

" 'His end,' said I, with dull anger stirring in me, 'was in every way worthy of his life.'

" 'And I was not with him,' she murmured. My anger subsided before a feeling of infinite pity.

" 'Everything that could be done——' I mumbled.

" 'Ah, but I believed in him more than anyone on earth—more than his own mother, more than—himself. He needed me! Me! I would have treasured every sigh, every word, every sign, every glance.'

"I felt like a chill grip on my chest. 'Don't,' I said, in a muffled voice.

" 'Forgive me. I—I—have mourned so long in silence—in silence. . . . You were with him—to the last? I think of his loneliness. Nobody near to understand him as I would have understood. Perhaps no one to hear. . . .'

" 'To the very end,' I said, shakily. 'I heard his very last words. . . .' I stopped in a fright.

" 'Repeat them,' she murmured in a heart-broken tone. 'I want—I want—something—something—to—to live with.'

"I was on the point of crying at her, 'Don't you hear them?' The dusk was repeating them in a persistent whisper all around us, in a whisper that seemed to swell menacingly like the first whisper of a rising wind. 'The horror! the horror!'

" 'His last word—to live with,' she insisted. 'Don't you understand I loved him—I loved him—I loved him!'

"I pulled myself together and spoke slowly.

" 'The last word he pronounced was—your name.'

"I heard a light sigh, and then my heart stood still, stopped dead short by an exulting and terrible cry, by the cry of inconceivable triumph and of unspeakable pain. 'I knew it—I was sure!' . . . She knew. She was sure. I heard her weeping; she had hidden her face in her hands. It seemed to me that the house would collapse before I could escape, that the heavens would fall upon my head. But nothing happened. The heavens do not fall for such a trifle. Would they have fallen, I wonder, if I had rendered Kurtz that justice which was his due? Hadn't he said he wanted only justice? But I couldn't. I could not tell her. It would have been too dark—too dark altogether. . . ."

Marlow ceased, and sat apart, indistinct and silent, in the pose of a meditating Buddha. Nobody moved for a time. "We have lost the first of the ebb," said the Director, suddenly. I raised my head. The offing was barred by a black bank of clouds, and the tranquil waterway leading to the uttermost ends of the earth flowed somber under an overcast sky—seemed to lead into the heart of an immense darkness.

GREAT ILLUSTRATED CLASSICS

Adam Bede—*Eliot*
The Arabian Nights
Around the World in 80 Days—*Verne*
Autobiography of Benjamin Franklin
Ben-Hur—*Wallace*
The Black Arrow—*Stevenson*
Black Beauty—*Sewell*
The Call of the Wild—*London*
Captains Courageous—*Kipling*
Christmas Tales—*Dickens*
The Cloister and the Hearth—*Reade*
A Connecticut Yankee in King Arthur's Court—*Clemens*
The Cruise of the Cachalot—*Bullen*
David Copperfield—*Dickens*
The Deerslayer—*Cooper*
Dr. Jekyll and Mr. Hyde—*Stevenson*
Emma—*Austen*
Famous Tales of Sherlock Holmes—*Doyle*
From the Earth to the Moon—*Verne*
Great Expectations—*Dickens*
Green Mansions—*Hudson*
Gulliver's Travels—*Swift*
Hawthorne's Short Stories—*Hawthorne*
Henry Esmond—*Thackeray*
The House of the 7 Gables—*Hawthorne*
Huckleberry Finn—*Clemens*
The Hunchback of Notre-Dame—*Hugo*
Ivanhoe—*Scott*
Jane Eyre—*Brontë*
A Journey to the Centre of the Earth—*Verne*
Kenilworth—*Scott*
Kidnapped—*Stevenson*
Kim—*Kipling*
King Arthur—*Malory*
Last Days of Pompeii—*Bulwer-Lytton*
The Last of the Mohicans—*Cooper*
Lord Jim—*Conrad*
Lorna Doone—*Blackmore*
The Luck of Roaring Camp—*Harte*
The Man in the Iron Mask—*Dumas*
The Mill on the Floss—*Eliot*
The Moonstone—*Collins*
The Mysterious Island—*Verne*
The Odyssey—*Homer*
The Old Curiosity Shop—*Dickens*

Oliver Twist—*Dickens*
The Oregon Trail—*Parkman*
The Pathfinder—*Cooper*
Père Goriot—*Balzac*
Pickwick Papers—*Dickens*
The Pilot—*Cooper*
The Pioneers—*Cooper*
The Prairie—*Cooper*
Pride and Prejudice—*Austen*
The Prince and the Pauper—*Clemens*
Quentin Durward—*Scott*
Quo Vadis—*Sienkiewicz*
The Red Badge of Courage—*Crane*
The Return of the Native—*Hardy*
The Rise of Silas Lapham—*Howells*
Robinson Crusoe—*Defoe*
The Scarlet Letter—*Hawthorne*
The Scarlet Pimpernel—*Orczy*
Sense and Sensibility—*Austen*
Silas Marner—*Eliot*
The Sketch Book—*Irving*
The Spy—*Cooper*
A Tale of Two Cities—*Dickens*
Tales—*Poe*
The Talisman—*Scott*
Tess of the D'Urbervilles—*Hardy*
The Three Musketeers—*Dumas*
Three Comedies: A Midsummer Night's Dream, The Merchant of Venice, As You Like It—*Shakespeare*
Three Histories: Henry IV, Part I; Henry IV, Part II; Henry V—*Shakespeare*
Three Tragedies: Julius Caesar, Hamlet, Macbeth—*Shakespeare*
Tom Sawyer—*Clemens*
Treasure Island—*Stevenson*
20,000 Leagues Under the Sea—*Verne*
Two Years Before the Mast—*Dana*
Typhoon—*Conrad*
Uncle Tom's Cabin—*Stowe*
Up From Slavery—*Washington*
Vanity Fair—*Thackeray*
Walden—*Thoreau*
The Way of All Flesh—*Butler*
The White Company—*Doyle*
White Fang and Other Stories—*London*
The Wreck of the Grosvenor—*Russell*
Wuthering Heights—*Brontë*

GREAT ILLUSTRATED CLASSICS—TITANS

Afloat and Ashore—*Cooper*
Anna Karenina—*Tolstoy*
Autobiography of Benvenuto Cellini
Barnaby Rudge—*Dickens*
Bleak House—*Dickens*
Crime and Punishment—*Dostoevsky*
Dombey & Son—*Dickens*
Don Quixote—*Cervantes*

Everybody's Plutarch
Little Dorrit—*Dickens*
Martin Chuzzlewit—*Dickens*
Nicholas Nickleby—*Dickens*
Our Mutual Friend—*Dickens*
Short Novels of Henry James—*James*
Twenty Years After—*Dumas*
Westward Ho!—*Kingsley*